A Vintage Year

By Rosie Howard

The Homecoming
A Vintage Year

A Vintage Year

ROSIE HOWARD

Leabharlanna Poiblí Chathair Baile Átha Cliath

Dublin City Public Libraries

Allison & Busby Limited
11 Wardour Mews
London W1F 8AN
allisonandbusby.com

First published in Great Britain by Allison & Busby in 2019.
This paperback edition published by Allison & Busby in 2019.

A CIP catalogue record for this book is available from
the British Library.

10 9 8 7 6 5 4 3 2 1

ISBN 978-0-7490-2237-2

Typeset in 10.5/15.5 pt Sabon LT Pro by
Allison & Busby Ltd.

The paper used for this Allison & Busby publication
has been produced from trees that have been legally sourced
from well-managed and credibly certified forests.

Printed and bound by
CPI Group (UK) Ltd, Croydon, CR0 4YY

For Rosie, my real-life Dolly,
who I miss every day

CHAPTER ONE

There was barely a breeze ruffling the leaves of the trees in the graveyard as Bella drifted serenely up the path on her father's arm. The only sound was the whispering of the heavy duchess satin dress, not pure white, but a more flattering silvery, oyster hue. The simple draped neckline set off her lightly tanned shoulders before narrowing to a sheath of fabric, clinging to her slim body and then pooling into a short, elegant train. She held a hand-tied bouquet of white lilies with trailing jasmine and three fully opened, pale-pink roses, each petal touched with a blush of peach. Her thick, unruly brown hair was behaving immaculately for once, curled and pinned high, with ringlets dropping to emphasise her long neck. Her green eyes danced as she smiled at her father, just like she always had – that sideways, cheeky grin that made him laugh.

The cloudless summer sky was as blue as her lover's eyes and – for a moment – she was struck by the notion that, in the silence, the little church they were approaching was empty. Her heart did a flip of anxiety. But it wasn't, of course. A trickle of organ music drifted to her ears and the languid hum of conversation, like a contented hive of bees, grew louder as they arrived at the church door.

With a nod to the vicar, and a tremulous squeeze of her father's arm, she straightened and waited. The opening strains of the 'Arrival of the Queen of Sheba' rang out and they stepped forward into the church.

Smiling faces either side of her: her best friend Maddy laughing at herself because she was already crying and fumbling for a tissue; her mother, looking appraisingly at the dress, checking the final tiny adjustments she had made earlier, before giving a nod of satisfaction; her Bespoke Consortium friends from the farmhouse artisan collective, all in a group, grinning and giving her the thumbs up; her mother-in-law Caroline, the spitting image of Camilla Parker-Bowles in her jauntily slanted hat and duck-egg blue dress-coat ensemble. And there was her father-in-law giving her a reassuring nod as he wiped the sweat from his upper lip with a silk handkerchief. Handsome, glowering Lord Havenbury – Zach – was there too, with his latest girlfriend in a huge hat and a navy striped dress and coat. Bella couldn't tell whether she had met her before or not. They were all so alike: blonde, slim, accomplished . . . with names like 'The Honourable Arabella something or other . . .' 'Posh totties', Charlie called them. Local GP Simon, his lovely teacher wife Genny, Maddy's partner Ben, Patrick and Helen from the Havenbury Arms. They were all here. All of them. For her and her husband-to-be.

The sun slanted through the stained-glass windows,

throwing coloured shadows onto the cool, stone floor. The musty, damp odour of the church, mingling with all the perfumes, the aftershaves of the guests in a heady, intoxicating mix . . . the organist stumbling slightly over the more difficult bits, making people smirk and duck their heads. The flowers tumbling down from the pew ends . . . more of the billowing pink roses to match the ones in her bouquet, some Petersham ribbon – goodness, the searches to get the right colour and width – tied just so, to create the relaxed effect she had been after. They looked perfect.

Everything was perfect.

Content at last, Bella looked straight ahead and there, broad-shouldered in his morning coat, standing next to his best man Ben, was Charlie. He was a little taller than his friend, his curly black hair contrasting with Ben's light brown. They had both gone to the barber the day before, revealing a touchingly pale stripe of untanned skin at the backs of their necks. He leant towards Ben and said something. Ben laughed and patted his pocket. The ring.

At the exact moment Bella arrived at his side, Charlie turned, smiled and took her hands in his own.

Suddenly, they were alone. She stood, gazing into his eyes steadily. They repeated the words as if in a trance, quietly, intimately, pledging their troth, for richer, for poorer, in sickness and in health, and then a strange litany of words she definitely didn't remember from the rehearsals. '*Carpe diem . . . Modus operandi . . . Caveat emptor . . . Draco Dormiens Nunquam Titillandus . . .*' she repeated obediently into the echoing silence of the empty church, and then – at last – Charlie leant slowly in for a kiss, his sky-blue eyes on hers, his body pressing heavily against her own, crushing her a little. Her eyelids fluttered closed, she leant forward, her head tilted back and then . . . he licked her, starting at her chin and finishing at her forehead, depositing copious, breath-blocking saliva in both of her nostrils en route.

Spluttering, her eyes flew open and she saw not her husband's face, but a pair of deep-brown eyes, surrounded by shiny black hair. They gazed down at her lovingly, as their owner contemplated the potential benefits of further tonguage. Instead, seeing her darling mistress was awake at last, Dolly sneezed with excitement, adding a fine spray of dog snot to Bella's already wet face.

'Thanks,' she spluttered, noticing the space beside her in the bed was already empty.

She dragged her arm out from under the black Labrador's body with difficulty and looked at her watch. It was just past seven o'clock.

'Fair enough,' she sighed, wiping her face. 'You weigh a tonne, by the way.'

Newly optimistic at developments, Dolly jumped off the bed and bounced up and down, a little too close to Ghengis Cat – Ghengis for short – who withdrew to the safety of the window sill with a look of disapproval. He had been hoping for some appreciation of his marauding the previous night, not this careless and disrespectful affront to his person. Still, it was only a matter of time before Bella saw the mangled corpses and realised how clever he had been.

The bare wooden floor was cold and unyielding, but Bella's slippers were nowhere to be seen. She threw an accusing look at Dolly but didn't pursue the matter as she was diverted by the horror of seeing herself in the bedroom mirror.

'Cripes,' she muttered, 'that's bad.'

She hadn't bothered with pyjamas the previous night. It was too cold to get naked, even briefly, so she had just peeled down to her grey thermals and slept in those.

In the cold light of a February morning, it wasn't a good look. She sucked in her tummy and stood sideways. Nope. There was no hiding it. The bathroom scales had been telling her a story and she could see exactly what they meant.

'I'm voluptuous,' she told Dolly, who was now sitting on her plump, black bottom, regarding her mistress anxiously. She was deeply concerned that Bella might have lost the plot again. The plot being breakfast. Obviously. Without further delay.

'You're a bit bleeding voluptuous too, I might add. Skipping breakfast would do you no harm at all.'

Encouraged by hearing the word 'breakfast', Dolly skittered to the top of the stairs and looked behind her expectantly.

In utter frustration, she then watched her mistress disappear in to the bathroom, closing the door firmly in her face.

The shower thundered briefly, and Bella shot out again wrapped in a large towel that was no longer white and distinctly threadbare.

'God, what I wouldn't do for a bit of central heating,' she muttered, as she rifled through her drawers for clothes, shivering in her damp towel. 'Even a heated flipping towel rail would help. Who doesn't have heated towel rails

11

nowadays? It's a basic human right, for heaven's sake.'

She piled a motley selection of layers onto the unmade bed. Pants, bra, more thermals – these ones even more disreputable and unflattering than the ones she had removed. She looked disconsolately at a large hole that had appeared in the leggings around mid-thigh. They had given up under the strain, she thought.

Turning resolutely from the mirror, she piled on a vest, T-shirt, a cosy checked flannel shirt she had liberated from Charlie's wardrobe and topped off the whole lot with jeans, a massive blue jumper and two pairs of socks.

'Mmm, sexy,' she said, taking a last look in the mirror and blowing herself a kiss. Make-up could wait. She had no client meetings today, or even this week, so she probably wouldn't bother at all.

'Bacon sarnie?' asked Charlie, his back to her, as he heard her rattling down the stairs straight into the flag-stoned kitchen.

The low beamed room, with its scrubbed pine table and a deep Butler's sink under the window, was – because of the Rayburn where Charlie was standing – at least reasonably warm.

'Absolutely not,' said Bella. 'My body is a temple. I'm having muesli. Actually, sod it, go on then.'

He added two more rashers to the pan without comment.

'Been up long?' she asked, wrapping her arms around him and resting her head on his back.

'Couldn't sleep. Done two more rows,' he said. 'Back out straight after this.'

'It's such a lot of work for you on your own,' she said.

'At least with your dad there was two of you. Will you get them all done in time?'

'Before they blossom? Hope so. No one else does it right,' said Charlie.

'You could teach me.'

'Yeah, we tried that, remember? But you always cut the wrong shoots off and then you're not strong enough to tie them onto the wires. I'll get through it. I always do.'

'Sorry I was asleep when you got back last night,' she said, giving up on the vines.

'Don't apologise. I was pretty late. Went out for a drink with Steve and caught the last train. Full of drunks . . . including me. It was running behind schedule, as usual.'

'So, how was London?'

'Still there,' said Charlie, turning the bacon and then – with his back still to her – slicing and buttering four doorsteps of a large white loaf. 'Smelly, noisy, exhausting . . .'

'Does Morris want to list the latest vintage?'

For a moment, she thought Charlie hadn't heard her. She waited.

'I saw that Tom bloke off the telly, that you like,' he said. 'Just walking down the street, he was.'

'You didn't? Wow! Seriously? I love him . . .'

'Yeah, coming right at me. Incredibly short in real life. Practically a dwarf.'

'But that's not the point,' she insisted. 'He's got charisma. The man's a giant in my eyes.'

'Well he's definitely got giant ears. You really don't get a sense of the massive ears when you see him on the screen.

I was deeply struck by them. In fact, so much so, I felt compelled to bring the issue up with him.'

'You didn't!' said Bella, half laughing, half horrified.

'Well, no,' admitted Charlie. 'He was on the phone. It would have been rude to interrupt.'

'Yeah, *that* would have been rude. Anyhow, don't change the subject.'

Charlie sighed. 'He doesn't want to list it this year,' he admitted. 'And I wouldn't either. It tastes like cat's piss.'

'I quite like it.'

'Good, because there's twenty thousand bottles of the stuff. So, dipsomaniacal as you are, my love, even you . . .'

'It's saleable.'

He shook his head. 'It's not good enough. We're trying to build a brand here. We can't afford to tarnish our name with second-rate wine. It was a bad year. It happens. We write it down to experience and chuck it down the drain.'

Bella opened her mouth to say something and then shut it again.

They sat at the table to eat their breakfast, Charlie at the end, Bella to his right, just as they had since his father died and vacated the place at the head of the table. Charlie's mother Caroline had made him do it since the very day it all happened, not able to stand looking at the empty chair. She now lived in Dove Cottage, the little brick and flint gingerbread house fifty yards down the rutted track that linked Dovecot Farmhouse to the main road. When Bella and Charlie had first got together, Bella had made it into a cosy love nest for her and Charlie. She missed it dearly, especially on cold days like this.

He slipped his arms around her from behind as she piled yesterday's mugs and plates plates into the sink, putting her hand under the running tap to see if she had left any hot water after her shower. She hadn't.

'Don't worry,' he murmured, nuzzling her neck. 'It'll work out.'

Encouraged, she turned in his arms, planting a kiss onto his mouth, loving the smell of fresh air in his hair, the stubble on his chin where he had gone out without shaving that morning.

'Come back to bed with me,' she said, reaching around to squeeze his bum suggestively. 'We could make a baby.'

He drew away, breaking eye contact.

'I got you Dolly,' he joked. 'And now you want a baby as well?'

The dog was whiffling her nose hopefully at the remains of the bacon sandwiches on the table. Ropes of drool hung from her mouth, and they swung as she turned her head on hearing her name.

'I know your mum thinks dogs are more important than children,' she replied, 'but you do understand that's not normal, don't you?'

'It isn't?'

'Nope.'

'How can you say such a thing? In front of Dolly, too . . .'

CHAPTER TWO

That evening, exhausted from more than twelve hours tending the vines, Charlie pored over his financial spreadsheet but his concentration was shot, his conversation with Bella that morning preying on his mind. It had been three years since the wedding, and the pointed comments from friends and family were getting a little more strident. Mention was made of 'not waiting too long', and 'rattling around in the big house', 'crying out for the patter of tiny feet'. They were right. And Bella was right. His mother, Caroline, kept mentioning grandchildren. She was right too. But none of them could see what he could see; what his father had known before he died of his heart attack – doubtless brought on at least partly by the stress of knowing how close the family was to ruin.

He sighed, the figures blurring before his eyes. Until his father died, even Charlie hadn't known how dire the financial situation was. He did now. With last year's vintage being almost undrinkable, he reckoned they had another six months until the loans were called in and the wheels came comprehensively off once and for all.

On an impulse, he closed down the file with all the lines of figures marked out in red and opened another. This was his big idea, the one he and his father were working on before the wedding. There was even a picture – an artist's impression of the winery, the stainless-steel vats, the huge machinery required for them to be able to process their own grapes, allowing them to choose the perfect moment to pick and press. Few of the Sussex vineyards had their own facilities, relying instead on picking and then transporting the grapes to a shared facility. The trouble was slots were quickly filled and last year – disastrously – Charlie had been forced to pick too late. It was groan-makingly frustrating. With his own winery, he could not only eliminate that risk, he could also make back money on the investment by hiring out the facility to other local vineyards.

Hearing the door open, he quickly toggled the screen, and by the time Bella was far enough into the room to see, it was innocuously showing his Facebook page.

'Hi, lovely,' she said, ruffling his hair. 'Just thinking about going to bed . . . Ooh, is that Maddy posting?'

She leant over his shoulder. 'Oh my God!' she exclaimed, looking at the fuzzy black and white picture in Maddy's post. 'I can't believe it!' She did a little dance around the room and then came back to look again. 'The cow. I only saw her on Monday. She didn't say a word. I thought she was behaving weirdly, though. Weirder than normal, that is . . . look, you can see its little hand and everything. Boy or girl?'

17

'No idea,' said Charlie, peering at the whitish blob. 'Is it even a baby, one asks oneself?' He tilted his head. 'Actually, maybe, if you consider it the other way up. I suppose you're going to get them over to supper,' he added with resignation. 'I'm sure she's dying to fill you in on every aspect of her girlie bits. Me and Ben will have to talk about football or something manly to counteract you both.'

Bella straightened. 'Yeah. Maybe.'

He stood up and embraced her. 'Just a bit longer,' he murmured in her ear. 'Then you can have triplets if you like.'

'No thanks,' she shuddered. 'We'll leave Dolly to the multiple births, I think.'

'Puppies? You think?' asked Charlie in surprise.

'Maybe. It's a thought.'

'Doesn't make it a good idea.'

'Your mother says I should.'

'That definitely doesn't make it a good idea.'

'They'd be beautiful, though, wouldn't they?'

'Depends on the father.'

'I was wondering about asking Zach if Brutus would do it.'

'Really? Well, he's handsome.'

'Glad you fancy him,' joked Bella. 'Probably more important that Dolly thinks so.'

'It'd make you a fair bit of money,' suggested Charlie. 'They sell for quite a whack. Especially if you can say it's Lord Havenbury's dog.'

'I'll ask Dolly,' said Bella. 'Now, how about we go to bed and get some practice in.'

* * *

Bella always found Zach – Lord Havenbury – disturbingly good-looking, and fierce, so when she spied a familiar, broad back in a green Barbour queueing at a coffee stall at Havenbury market the following day, she nearly bottled it, even though he had Brutus with him and she was newly reminded how handsome the dog was.

Like dog, like owner, thought Bella, blushing in preparation for tapping him on the shoulder.

'Bella,' he said gruffly, giving her a peremptory kiss on the cheek. 'Want one of these?'

She nodded.

'A latte and a black double espresso to take away please,' he told the boy behind the stall.

'How are you both?' he continued, handing her a cardboard cup and taking her by the elbow to walk her across the road to the wider bit of pavement by the river.

'I'm fine, but I honestly dunno about Charlie,' she admitted. 'I barely see him. He's out at first light, tending the vines. Comes back at nightfall, eats, does his paperwork, goes to bed.'

'Glad to hear he's grafting,' said Zach. 'He was a lazy bugger before he married you.'

Neither of them mentioned the main reason Charlie's work ethos had changed so dramatically that day. Zach had been the one who had stepped into action first when Charlie's father collapsed. He and Charlie's GP friend Simon had smoothly managed the whole hideous thing, as far as it could have been managed smoothly, that is. Most of the guests were unaware of the ambulance arriving, the paramedics, the awful moment when Simon shook his head and took Caroline to one side.

'Want some of this?' Zach said, sloshing a decent glug of brandy into her coffee from a hip flask before she had a chance to reply.

'Brass monkey weather,' he said, leaning on the stone parapet of the river edge and swigging his coffee, his tough and calloused blacksmith's hands cradling the paper cup. The sky was nearly as dark as the swirling water. 'Everything feels worse at this time of year,' he added, as he narrowed his eyes, and gazed out to the horizon, giving her sudden tears a chance to resolve themselves almost before Bella even noticed them herself.

Damn, she thought, using the tip of her gloved finger in the corners of her eyes. Hopefully he would think it was the cold wind. She blurted her idea about Dolly having pups with Brutus more to change the subject than anything else.

'That would be fantastic,' said Zach, shoving Brutus gently with the toe of his boot, 'wouldn't it, old chap? You know blokes . . . always keen to get their ends away. You realise he's an idiot, obviously?'

'You can't expect beauty and brains can you, my lovely?' said Bella, giving the dog a stroke. 'Anyhow,' she added to Zach, 'Dolly's really clever. That'll help.'

'Course she is. Her mum is Dilys, my grandmother's dog. Sharp as a knife. A real old sweetheart too. Dolly comes from her last litter. She's getting on a bit now.'

'I'd forgotten that!' said Bella, remembering with a smile how astonished and delighted she had been when Charlie turned up with the eight-week-old puppy as a first wedding anniversary present. 'But does that mean—?'

'You're fine,' said Zach, ahead of her. 'There are two

distinct dynasties with the Havenbury Labradors. Brutus and Dilys aren't related at all so you don't need to add in-breeding to the chances of retardation.'

'I think "retarded" is a bit strong,' said Bella, stroking Brutus again, who was entirely unaware of the rude things being said about him and was just pathetically grateful for the attention.

'So Dolly must be – what? – two and a half now?' said Zach. 'That's perfect for her first litter. I've not seen her for a bit . . .'

'She's got a tiny bit fat,' admitted Bella. 'Like me.'

'You look all right to me,' said Zach, his black eyes raking her in the most disturbing manner. 'Do you shoot with her? That'd get the weight off.'

'I'm not really a "shooting things" sort of person, to be honest,' not knowing if he meant her or Dolly. Both, probably.

Zach looked confused. 'Well, I wouldn't mind borrowing her, if she's trained.'

'She isn't,' said Bella, hurriedly. 'She wouldn't know what to do. Also, I'd worry she might get – well – shot.'

He gave her an incredulous look and then shrugged. 'When's she next in season?'

'Soon, I think,' said Bella, blushing for her at the indelicacy.

'Perfect,' he said, draining the last of his coffee and chucking the cup into the rubbish bin. 'Summer pups. Bring her over when you're ready. Give me a call first, to make sure I'm not up at the forge. Got an order book the length of the Dead Sea scrolls at the moment, Maddy's doing such a good job promoting everyone.' He looked back down at Brutus and then at Bella. 'He's a moron, but he's a gent,' he said, seeing her uncertain expression. 'She'll be fine.'

By the evening Bella had googled pretty much everything she needed to know about dog breeding and felt like she had it nailed. It would be hard work for her – and Dolly, obviously – but so lovely to have puppies in the house and, let's be frank, the money was attractive too.

Charlie wandered into the kitchen from his study rubbing his eyes wearily.

'I might have accidentally invited Ben and Maddy to supper tonight,' Bella admitted.

'Oh God,' said Charlie. 'I mean "oh good" . . . did you really?'

'You said we should. To talk about the baby and stuff.'

'I think what I actually said . . . okay, never mind. Fine. What do you need me to do?'

'Lay the table? And could you please do a salad dressing for me?'

As they worked, Bella filled Charlie in on her plans for Dolly.

'We're talking at least three grand,' she told him. 'Probably more like five or six. With Brutus's breeding, and hers too, they'll be really sought after. I reckon Zach would know people who want them. And we could advertise too. There are these websites . . .' She chewed her lip, doubtfully. 'We'd have to find a way to "vet" people somehow . . .'

'Sounds great, darling,' said Charlie distractedly, his mind already on the paperwork he planned to tackle as soon as they'd got rid of Ben and Maddy. He loved seeing them both, Ben particularly, but it was going to make for a late night, catching up on admin after they had gone.

'It'd help, wouldn't it, if we could have another three grand or so to put into the vineyard?'

He gave a shout of mirthless laughter. 'You keep it, darling,' he said, turning to face her. 'You'll have earned it.'

And three grand was going to make not the slightest difference to the slow car crash of the vineyard's finances anyway.

'What will you spend it on?' he said, pouring more wine into her glass.

'Dunno where to start,' she said. 'I'm sure I'd lose weight if I cut the drinking,' she added, regretfully, taking a grateful slurp all the same. 'Wine's terribly calorific, apparently. Three grand might not be enough, but I thought maybe we could do something to the bathroom?'

'Why? It's been done fairly recently,' he said. 'I remember that bath being put in – it was a big deal.'

'It's avocado,' said Bella. 'My guess is you were about eight years old.'

'Um . . . yeah,' he said, grinning sheepishly. 'I might have been, now you mention it. But a bath's a bath, isn't it?'

The two women greeted each other without words. Screams and hugs were all that was required.

'I actually can't believe it,' said Bella, releasing her friend from a tight embrace and reverting to real words at last. 'Is there really a baby in there?'

'Apparently so,' said Maddy with a hint of smugness.

'It's so quick, though, you've only been together for – what? – actually it is a while, isn't it,' acknowledged Bella. 'Since before me and Charlie were married.'

'Only just but – yeah – four years, nearly,' said Ben, as he kissed Bella on both cheeks and handed her a bunch of lilies.

'We decided a while ago, actually,' admitted Maddy. 'It didn't happen straight away.'

'You're telling me!' said Ben. 'Took a lot of practice to get it right,' he added, to Charlie. 'I was relieved when we finally got the two pink lines. I told Maddy, "Does that mean I can just have a beer and watch the telly for a change?"'

'That is *not* what he said when I told him,' said Maddy, smacking him around the back of the head, but smiling in spite of herself. 'I definitely don't remember you complaining at the time.'

'Also,' said Ben, ducking out of arms reach, 'the old girl's getting on a bit, to be honest, didn't want to leave it 'til bits are dropping off.'

'Cheeky old sod,' said Bella. 'Me and Maddy are years younger, I will remind you . . . bits are far more likely to be dropping off you and Charlie than us two.'

'You know what? You've never really said,' began Maddy, when she and Bella were relaxing on the sofa after supper while the men cleared up, 'what gave between Ben and Charlie when I first came back to Havenbury? I'd been here for months with Ben before Charlie popped up on the horizon and yet clearly they're joined at the hip.' She looked at her friend's face anxiously for signs she was treading on dangerous ground. 'You don't mind me asking? It's always felt like one of those subjects you can't bring up.'

Bella took a sip of the fennel tea Maddy had brought with her and grimaced. 'This is rank,' she said. 'How can you bear it?'

'Your tastes change.' Maddy smiled. 'Suddenly I can't get enough of liquorice. Loathed it before . . .' she took another appreciative gulp. 'Ginger is amazing, as well. You should try it. Seriously, you should get off the caffeine . . . Anyway, back to Ben and Charlie? Am I allowed to ask?' She waited expectantly.

'Of course. You never have, that's all, and it's history now. Not relevant any more,' said Bella slowly. 'So, you're right, they've been really close since they were boys. Grew up together, went to the same school, yada, yada. I think Caroline and Peter were really good to Ben when his dad was killed too. He was terribly young when it happened and he went a bit wild for a while. Anyhow, all the time I was a spotty teenager lusting after Charlie from afar, him and Ben were definitely really good mates.'

'And?'

'And . . . God, I'm not even sure I want to say this to you in your interesting condition.'

'What? What on earth are you going to say? You're freaking me out now.'

'Me and Ben had a thing,' Bella blurted. 'Not since you came along, obviously, before that and before me and Charlie. Just a couple of snogs and a cuddle, for goodness' sake – and, basically, when Charlie and I got it on they fell out.'

'Because Ben was upset at you getting together?' said Maddy in a small voice.

'No! Other way around.'

'I don't understand.'

'Nor do I, it was ridiculous. It definitely wasn't Ben – he's a flipping psychologist, for goodness' sake – you won't catch him behaving like a prat over a woman. No, it was all Charlie, weirdly.'

'Go on?'

'As far as I could gather at the time, having Ben around after me and Charlie started our relationship made Charlie feel – I dunno – insecure? Jealous? He got it into his head that me and Ben still had a "thing" and it drove him mad. Ben decided discretion was the better part of valour and distanced himself a bit. Okay, a lot.'

'So that's why . . .' mused Maddy. 'How long did it last?'

'A couple of years . . . basically until I heard from mutual friends that you had arrived on the scene, and it was the real thing,' said Bella, pragmatically. 'We were planning the wedding by then. Ben was absolutely destined to be Charlie's best man and I didn't want them both to miss out because of a stupid stand-off. I also thought that Ben being with you would help Charlie get over himself more easily than if Ben was still single. So I banged their heads together and now here we all are.'

'And the massive bonus prize is you and me,' said Maddy contentedly, nibbling another almond macaroon.

'Absolutely. BFFs, which is really lucky. Can you imagine how hard it is for blokes to maintain friendships where their women don't get on?'

'Wouldn't work at all,' admitted Maddy. 'Feels like I've known you for years.'

'Me too,' said Bella, tucking her arm through Maddy's and sighing with contentment. 'Now, all I have to do is stop Charlie getting jealous of any other passing male I happen to smile at and agree to make me pregnant too. I've got some catching up to do.'

Next morning, as soon as Charlie had driven off to see a wine merchant he thought he might be able to do business with, Bella took a pencil, notepad and measuring tape to the bathroom and appraised it with an interior designer's eye.

'We haven't earned it yet, have we?' she told Dolly, who had wandered in after her to see what she was doing.

It was going to be quite a job. Currently there was shaggy brown carpet on the floor and even, inexplicably, up the side of the built-in bath. The ceiling paint was peeling off in ribbons and the textured tiles, clearly chosen to match the bathroom suite, were a queasy shade of green.

First, Bella measured up. It was a big, square room with a sash window that looked out onto the vineyard. It even had the morning sun, so she knew exactly where she should put the bath.

Also, a walk-in shower was a must. She was desperate to get rid of the horrid, clammy bath curtain that clung like a jellyfish when you got too close to it. There was plenty of room for a free-standing walk-in shower with a static glass screen instead.

She sighed. The avocado suite with corner bath was going to have to go. Even with the ongoing love affair with retro, it wasn't even ironic – just hideous. After the new plain white sanitary ware and taps there would be no money for posh finishes. She looked around, dismissing her ideas for beautiful tiles. Instead, a decent coat of paint and the existing, original wainscot pine cladding could be transformed. She had already peeled back the carpet in the corner. The dust and filth underneath made her shudder with revulsion, but it did reveal some floorboards that would be fine just stripped and varnished or – better – painted perhaps?

The final transformation would be to install a huge heated towel rail. She was planning to have it pretty much take up a whole wall and be on a boiling heat constantly. And she would get some new towels too. It was going to be amazing.

'It'll probably cost one whole puppy to do the towel rail alone,' she told Dolly. 'Don't feel you have to have loads, just for me. Although seven is the average, just so you know.'

Dolly regarded her soulfully. The chatting was lovely, but she would prefer an interaction with her mistress that involved food. Or a walk. Or even a trip to the office where she stood a good chance of seeing Serena's little dog, Tinker. He tended to be nippy and growly at first, but he had some great toys and didn't mind sharing them when he was in a good mood.

Bella took another appraising look around the room. The basin and loo could stay in their current position, which would save money. Where the bath currently was would make a brilliant place for the airing cupboard, right next to the boiler and hot-water tank. The one in the hallway was tiny and drove her round the bend. For a moment, she allowed herself a daydream of standing in her beautiful new bathroom, serenely folding and tidying away tiny baby clothes, perhaps with her baby sitting on a towel on the floor or maybe he or she would be sleeping in the nursery. That was another room that needed an overhaul. The draughty and dust-smelling attic rooms, which had been Charlie's old nursery, were still untouched, but Bella would want her baby closer anyway, and had her eye on the little dressing room right next to hers and Charlie's.

Minutes later, Bella had scribbled a rough layout and shopping list on her designer's notepad. She could draw it up properly on the computer later.

CHAPTER THREE

'Oh wow!' mumbled Maddy, looking over Bella's shoulder at the screen. She had come into the cramped little converted stable, where Bella ran her interior design business, carrying two cups of tea. Her speech was muffled because of the packet of Jammie Dodgers that she was holding in her teeth.

Bella relieved her of the biscuits and one of the mugs.

The tiny room was crammed with books of fabric and wallpaper samples, not only on the shelves lining the walls, but on the floor, the table and the pair of chairs where Bella sat with clients when they came in. Unbidden, Maddy shoved a pile of sample books off one of the chairs and sat down with a 'poof' of relief.

'So . . . amazing bathroom,' she said, waving at the screen. 'New client?'

'Sort of. It's me.'

'That's Dovecot Farmhouse? Of course, it is, I recognise the window, now you mention it. It'll be beautiful!'

'Hope so,' said Bella, looking back at the screen. The

layout was a huge improvement and the double-ended roll-top bath, on its raised platform in the middle of the room so the occupant could enjoy the view of the vineyard, was inspired.

'I completely adore that bath. I'm desperate for a roll-top in our bathroom but I can't see Ben going for it. There isn't really room, it's all a bit compact and bijou in the boathouse, as you know . . . Expensive, though, surely?' she added, waving at the bath in the picture.

'Actually, it's this one,' explained Bella, toggling the screen.

Maddy peered. 'Mm,' she said uncertainly. 'That's an amazing price, but . . . really?'

'It'll be transformed once I've got my hands on it,' Bella assured her. 'Car paint.'

'What? On those horrible, blingy feet?'

'Trust me. The right shade of car paint and then a layer of black wax on the chrome feet, and they'll look like cast bronze. Then I'm going to do eggshell paint in this amazing midnight-blue colour on the exterior.' She handed over the colour card with the shade marked. 'A coat of clear, matt varnish on top and it'll be bombproof. Or cleanable, anyhow.'

'Gorgeous,' said Maddy. 'You are sooo clever. It's just a shame it's not a paying customer. Talking of which, I'm amazed you've persuaded Charlie.'

'Ah, well I haven't exactly "persuaded" him . . . yet,' Bella admitted, 'but he doesn't need to provide any money, which helps a lot because – of course – we don't have any. Except . . .' She quickly explained the Dolly-centred breeding programme.

'Ooh, I'll have one! I want a boy,' said Maddy. 'Can I have first choice? Where is my favourite black Labrador, by the way?'

'Hopefully she's in the house with Serena, she was desperate to play with Tinker, although I'm a bit worried she's mainly after the snacks. She's fat enough as it is.'

'She needs to hurry up and get pregnant,' said Maddy. 'It's a good excuse for porking out. I've already gained a stone and I'm only three months gone.'

'That's nothing,' said Bella gloomily. 'I've put on more than that this winter and I don't have your excuse. Talking of which, will Ben seriously let you have a puppy as well as a baby?'

'God yes, he's letting me have whatever I want,' said Maddy smugly. 'It's hilarious, bless him. I'm thinking of asking for a unicorn.'

'He's too good for you.'

'Yeah, I know.'

'I saw the ultrasound,' said Bella wistfully. 'Amazing how perfect and – well – "baby-like" they look even at twelve weeks.'

Maddy nodded. 'I wish . . .'

'I know.'

'. . . so why not now?' Maddy went on, diplomatically.

'It's just how things are with the vineyard at the moment. Charlie's incredibly busy, overheads are huge, this,' she gestured around her, 'isn't exactly a licence to print money either, and – frankly – it would practically have to be the immaculate conception.'

Maddy nodded understandingly and took another biscuit.

'I'm surprised Ben hasn't got you eating some special, optimal nutrition pregnancy diet,' said Bella, munching on her third Jammie Dodger.

'He has, but it's all right,' said Maddy. 'These are organic.'

'Wow! Are they really?' Bella looked at her half-eaten biscuit in surprise.

'Nope, but I told Ben they were.'

'Mate,' called Ben, seeing his friend propping up the bar and staring despondently into his beer.

'Want one?' said Charlie.

'Don't mind if I do,' he replied, spotting a certain wild swing in the arm as Charlie's hand connected parlously with his glass. 'Is that your first?'

'Absolutely not,' Charlie announced without apology.

'Hallo, darling,' said Helen, starting to pour Ben's usual pint. 'How's my favourite son-in-law? You looking after my daughter all right?'

'I'm cooking her supper later,' Ben reassured her. 'Just a quick one first, to gird my loins. It's a new recipe for mackerel with mustard sauce – tricky but supposed to be very good for brain development . . .'

'Brain development? Maddy's or yours?' asked Charlie.

'God, neither . . . the baby's. I don't need Maddy to get any brighter, I can hardly keep up with her as it is.'

'How far along is she now?' asked Charlie, making a visible effort to engage in polite conversation.

'Twelve and a half weeks,' interjected Helen.

'Speaks the proud grandmother-to-be,' laughed Ben.

'Of course,' said Helen. 'Can't wait. It'll be an August baby, unfortunately. Not ideal for schools.'

Ben looked suitably chastened at his and Maddy's reckless lack of foresight, but Charlie wasn't listening, lost again in contemplation of his drink, the depths of which clearly held the sum total of his troubles.

'How's it going?' asked Ben, when he had his pint in his hand.

Charlie sighed.

'That good, eh?'

'Doesn't it terrify you?'

'What?'

'The whole "bringing a baby into the world" thing? The expense, the responsibility, the impact on your income . . . your energies . . . I mean – ye gods – getting Dolly was bad enough. That bloody dog rules the household.'

Ben laughed. 'I am having a few sleepless nights already but – mate – life will find a way, you know?'

Charlie didn't reply.

'Tell me?' said Ben.

Charlie just shook his head.

Ben waited.

'Okay,' he said at last, shaking his head again, and taking another deep pull of his pint. 'It's all bollocks, basically. Kaput. Buggered. Stuffed.'

'The vineyard?'

'Of course, the bloody vineyard,' exploded Charlie. 'What else? Mind you, you accidentally raise a valid point. What I hadn't appreciated until Dad died, is that if the vineyard goes tits up, the house goes with it. Everything goes and – I've got to tell you mate – we are seriously circling the drain here . . .'

Ben frowned. 'This isn't like you, mate,' he said. 'You're usually the master of positive thinking.' He put a sympathetic hand on Charlie's shoulder. 'Does Bella know?'

'Not really. Well, she suspects, obviously . . . She doesn't know quite how bad the whole situation is. She wants to do up the flipping bathroom, for goodness' sake!' He stared into space gloomily. 'It'll help sell the house, though, I suppose. Although we'll have been repossessed by then so it'll be the mortgage company doing that, not us. Sod 'em, I don't want to make it easy for them.'

'Is it really as bad as that?'

'It's as bad as that.'

'You've not had a lot of luck with the weather. What happened with the harvest in the end?'

'A rubbish year,' said Charlie, adopting a thousand-yard stare. 'Everything except the Chardonnay went over. I had to pick two days late because of the winery delays in taking the harvest. It poured with rain and the whole lot was swollen and split. We got twenty thousand bottles in the end.'

'Isn't that a lot?' asked Ben.

'Not really. A quarter of our usual output, basically,' explained Charlie. 'Plus, the year before was bad as well. We only have the sparkling Chardonnay to offer currently, no Brut, no rosé . . . and then, next year we'll only have rosé . . .'

Ben sighed. 'How's Bella?'

'I hardly know. I think she feels a bit neglected at the moment.'

'What did you do for Valentine's Day?'

'It was Valentine's Day? When?'

'Last week. 14th February is the conventional date for it, I believe.'

35

'Oops. I did notice a bit of grumpiness on the Wednesday now you mention it. Was that it?'

Ben sighed. 'Mate,' he said, looking at his watch. 'Seriously. Talk to your wife. She'll want to know.'

Bella looked at the congealing fish pie. She had given it her all . . . smoked salmon, prawns, double cream . . . but Charlie had always been useless at checking his phone. It was switched off or had a flat battery most of the time and she knew – once he was cosily ensconced at the Havenbury Arms with his drinking pals – nothing would get him back home until Patrick chucked him out at closing time.

Even though she was already uncomfortably full, it did seem an awful pity to waste it. She undid the top button of her jeans, loaded her plate once more and sloshed some more sparkling Chardonnay into her glass. Charlie had been right about it not being their best year but the more you drank, the better you liked it, she was finding. She eyed Dolly who was lying in front of the Rayburn pretending to be asleep whilst remaining alert for dropped food.

'It's just you and me, babe,' she said, raising her glass in salute. 'Just you and me.'

Charlie found the unlocking of the back door surprisingly complicated. After five minutes of fumbling in the dark he discovered the reason; Bella had left it unlocked for him. This was a promising sign, under the circumstances.

He stumbled into the kitchen, blearily registering the remains of supper on the table and the sleepy thumping of Dolly's tail in welcome. He slipped off his shoes before climbing the stairs to their bedroom, although Bella was unlikely to have slept through the noise he had already been making. Feeling his way into the bedroom via a bruising encounter with the door frame, which was not where he had left it, he could see the dark, unmoving lump of her body in the bed, her back turned. Clearly a shag was out of the question, then.

Again.

Which was probably just as well.

'Seriously,' insisted Bella, careful not to raise her voice above a moderate level, given Charlie's sensitivity to noise. 'I could help.'

Charlie raised his eyes from his triple, well-sugared espresso cup and regarded her appraisingly. It was tempting. He still had four acres to go, and spring had well and truly sprung. He was in serious danger of depleting the vines, letting them waste energy-producing buds on branches he was going to cut. Plus, bending to cut the lower branches with this hangover was almost certainly going to make him throw up. Plus, he was acutely aware he had accidentally behaved like an arse and he probably had some making up to do.

'It would be nice to spend a bit of time together,' she wheedled, around a large mouthful of muesli, with Greek yoghurt and banana – her newest attempt at a healthy breakfast. 'Plus, I'm desperate to shift a bit of this,' she added, grabbing a handful of spare tyre with a despairing eye roll.

'Don't you have fancy, interior designy stuff to do?'

'Not really,' she admitted. 'I've got to pop into the office this afternoon. Bespoke Consortium meeting, that's all.'

'Promise to do as you're told?'

'Promise.'

Out in the vineyard, working their way down the rows, with Bella cutting and Charlie hovering over her, selecting the shoots he wanted left intact so he could tie them to the wires, his spirits rose.

The dawn had risen to reveal a sharp and bright spring day, with a brisk breeze that ruffled his hair and filled his lungs with clean, cold optimism.

It had always been his favourite time of year, working alongside his father while they talked, planned and dreamt about the months ahead. Their ambitions were always colossal; each year, the assumption had been that the weather would be perfect, the yield would be huge, sugar levels would be unprecedented and the wine . . . the resulting wine would be superb. Before the vines were even planted his dad would fill his mind and his heart with his stories of the awards they would win, the plaudits, the fame, how Dovecot Estate wine would take its deserved place alongside the Moët Chandon, the Bollinger, the Laurent-Perrier . . .

Charlie looked down. The last few acres to be pruned were the Pinot Noir grapes. He had been avoiding them, leaving them until last, because even now – six months after what would have been the harvest – evidence of last year's dismal failure was all around him. On the vines and on the ground were the spiky, fine twigs of the bunches of grapes, some with shrivelled fruit still attached, most picked bare by the wildlife over the winter. The grapes that should have been picked and pressed, instead were left to rot. All of them. Well, all of the red grapes, anyhow. The Chardonnay ones had been picked and sent off in trucks to the winery safely earlier in that fateful October week, but the rest? Charlie's mouth twisted in bitter recall, remembering how his mate Dennis at the winery had called him. They were overwhelmed, Dennis had admitted. A bigger local vineyard had harvested and they would not be able to press Charlie's grapes for a couple of days at least, even if they worked twenty-four hours a day, which they were doing. 'Could you leave them for just one more night?' his friend had asked. Well, he did, and he watched, in despair, through the ensuing delay as torrential rain swelled the fruit, bursting the perfectly ripe grapes and wiping out the crop. Without his Pinot Noir and his Meunier grapes, which were also ruined, the champagne-style wine the Dovecot Estate was developing a reputation for was impossible. The Chardonnay crop alone was better than nothing – but not much.

'It'll be good this year,' said Bella, gently, breaking into his thoughts.

He looked up and forced a smile. Poor Bella, his bride, pitched into a nightmare starting with a ruined wedding day and a cancelled honeymoon – now this.

'This is our year,' she went on. 'I can feel it. A vintage year.'

'It's impossible not to feel optimistic in the spring, isn't it?' he agreed, wrapping his arm around her waist and standing beside her as they looked down the hill, through the straight rows, down to the valley, where the market town of Havenbury Magna nestled.

'It's why we get involved in this ridiculous game, Dad always said. There's always another year. Another vintage . . .'

He reached out to stroke a fat bud, bursting into leaf, its bright, acid-green foliage unfurling like a butterfly wing.

'I thought I might try that sparkling rosé again. You know? Where I just leave the grapes in the press a little longer. Get some colour into the wine. A bit early to tell but I reckon that last lot's going to be pretty good. That's assuming we actually get some Pinot Noir grapes this year.'

'We will,' insisted Bella. 'Fantastic idea! You totally should. I love rosé,' she added, giving him an encouraging squeeze.

'Charlie's drinking too much,' said Caroline as she plonked two mugs on the table in the cosy little kitchen at Dove Cottage.

'There's a joke, isn't there?' said Bella, pouring the tea from Caroline's fat, heart-covered teapot. 'The definition of heavy drinking is whatever your GP drinks, plus a bit.'

'Well, I don't know about our GP but he's definitely drinking more than me,' said Caroline. 'So – let's face it – that's a lot.'

She couldn't argue. Her mother-in-law was the most robust drinker she had ever met. She generally started with a stiff gin and tonic at midday on the dot and, most days, got through half a bottle of wine just while she was cooking, with another large glass to drink while she was eating it. And then there was the hot toddy before bed most nights in the winter. When Charlie first brought Bella home for Sunday lunch to meet his mother, Bella politely matched her drink for drink and – to Charlie's huge amusement – had to be put to bed to sleep it off before lunch even made it onto the table.

'What you need,' continued Caroline, taking a swig of tea and pushing the carrot cake closer to Bella in invitation, 'is

40

a holiday. God knows, my son owes you a honeymoon, if nothing else. Three years, it's about time . . .'

Bella said nothing. There was no point letting Caroline know that the refund they got on the Caribbean holiday for their cancelled honeymoon had quickly been spent on repairs to the roof of Dovecot Farmhouse.

'You both need to relax. Get away from the blasted vineyard and remind yourselves why you married each other. Eat . . . sleep . . . make a baby, for heaven's sake! Where are my grandchildren?'

Bella blushed. Talking about her love life with her mother-in-law was going to do nothing to restore hers and Charlie's flagging libidos. She cut herself a large piece of carrot cake, although it was barely two hours since breakfast.

'Talking about babies,' she said, by way of redirection, 'Dolly's going to have puppies.'

'Excellent! Give her something to do,' said Caroline. 'I still think you should send her off for gun dog training, but breeding from her is nearly as good. Her bloodline is impeccable. It would be a waste not to, and she's a sweet little bitch, aren't you, Dolly?'

Dolly rolled on her back to show her tummy and grinned engagingly, eyeing the chunk of cake in Caroline's other hand.

'Good temperament,' Caroline went on. 'She'll make a good mother. As will you . . . if you ever get around to it.'

CHAPTER FOUR

'She's a monster,' said Charlie when Bella reported their conversation.

'I do feel broody sometimes, though.'

'Well, have puppies, then. Now, did I mention I'm off to London tomorrow? The Wine Fair. Got to be seen and all that – press the flesh, hand out the business cards . . .'

'Can I come?'

'Do you want to? You can't just get halfway through the day and tell me you're bored. I've got work to do.'

'I won't,' promised Bella. 'I wouldn't mind getting out of here for a day.'

'Fine. Tell you what, I'll book a table somewhere nice for lunch,' said Charlie, 'A late Valentine's Day treat. Not exactly a fortnight in the Caribbean, I'll grant you . . .'

Dressing for a day in London, Bella began to regret her enthusiasm. Nothing fitted or felt right. Her smart, office clothes were too formal and out of style. In any case her boobs had got so big, she was bursting out of all her tops. Her favourite white shirt had gone grey and droopy from too much washing and her prized cashmere jumper was straining across the bust and covered in bobbles – plus she didn't know how hot it was going to be. The weather was depressingly grey and rainy, but she knew too well it was a couple of degrees hotter in London and the conference centre could get stuffy. It was bad enough looking like the chubby country bumpkin without having a bright-red, shiny face as well.

In the end she put on her newest and darkest jeans – the colour minimised her bum and thighs – worn with the highest, spikiest black ankle boots she owned. At least her legs looked reasonably long. With a lace-trimmed camisole and her trusty black jacket over the top she just needed to add a silky scarf to distract the eye from the fact her jacket wouldn't do up and she was done. She was looking in the mirror appraisingly when Charlie came back in from the bathroom in a towel.

'Is that what you're wearing?' he said.

Bella pulled a face at him.

Charlie didn't seem to feel the cold. He wandered comfortably around the bedroom, a towel around his hips, gathering up clothes. Unlike Bella, he hadn't gained any weight since the wedding – as long as you didn't count the bags under his eyes. He needed a haircut, though. A good wife would have noticed before today and booked him an appointment at the barbers. She wasn't a good wife.

'You need some new shirts,' she said, watching him put in cufflinks, his frayed cuffs trailing threads.

'This is one of Dad's,' he said. 'From Jermyn Street. Got years left in it yet.'

'Here,' she said, waving the nail scissors, 'at least let me . . .' She snipped off a couple of threads. 'I'll get you some new ones. For your birthday.'

'No money for that,' said Charlie. 'Not this year.'

On the train he got out his laptop and spent the entire ninety-minute journey to London poring over spreadsheets.

Bella gazed out of the window. The views as they travelled along the coast away from Havenbury always cheered her. She saw a heron on the wetlands and nudged Charlie but by the time he looked up it had flown away, a little fish in its beak.

Daydreaming, as the landscape changed from fields to villages, to the sprawling, ugly, mean streets of outer London, her eyes welled up. Embarrassed and astonished, she leant down and fumbled in her bag before Charlie or the other passengers saw. What on earth was the matter with her? She sniffed and straightened her spine, fishing out a tissue and blowing her nose to disguise the eye-wiping, trying not to smudge her mascara too catastrophically in the process.

Arriving in London, her spirits rose. Charlie linked his arm into hers as they allowed themselves to be swept along in the stream of people walking purposefully, all of them off to do something important, busy and urgent.

Despite straitened finances Charlie steered Bella towards the taxi rank, rather than the Tube entrance.

'Tax deductible,' he said, as he handed her in and gave the taxi driver the destination. 'Let's allow ourselves a bit of a day out, eh?'

In the conference centre, Bella's ears were assaulted by the familiar hubbub. They worked their way down the aisles of stands, some huge and flash, with massive graphics and beautiful girls pouring samples of wine. Scattered amongst them were the earnest, little wine producers like themselves. Couples, often, who had scraped together the money for a tiny stand, in the hope of landing a big deal with a hotel or restaurant chain buyer or – even better – a major retail wine merchant.

For the last couple of years, Charlie and Bella had made the easy choice not to exhibit. Their production was so small, they could sell the lot themselves to local restaurants and event venues with a few cases, here and there, to friendly and affluent people who knew Charlie's father and had a lot of posh parties.

'See if you can find out what the trends are,' Charlie said to Bella, putting his mouth close to her ear, 'I'm guessing there's a lot of new rosé out there . . .'

He and Bella had worked their way around half the stands and Bella's head was throbbing. She had collected fistfuls of leaflets and wine lists, and tasted several new pink wines, most of them unbearably sweet and tasting of burnt sugar.

Charlie was chatting animatedly with a wine merchant who had previously, briefly, stocked Dovecot Estate wine and Charlie was hoping he could persuade him to do it again. There was a coffee stop just yards away and Bella craved a caffeine shot to relieve her headache. She gestured to it with eyebrows raised in query and Charlie gave her a thumbs up.

By the time she returned with two cardboard cups of bitter-tasting latte, he had his back to her and was standing at right angles with a broad-shouldered man in a shirt and tie. The silk tie was the colour of an old gold picture frame and the shirt was white with a broad purple stripe. The unusual combination had clearly been chosen to complement the man's colouring. He had thick, carefully groomed hair, the colour of a drenched fox. Bella found herself studying his Grecian profile as she approached. God, he was handsome. Tall too . . . he turned as she approached and smirked as if acknowledging her admiring gaze. His eyes were a penetrating yellowy-green – just like a fox's too – and his knowing look made her blush.

'Ah,' said Charlie. 'And here she is, my lovely wife Bella.' He slipped his arm proprietorially around Bella's waist. The man held out his hand, simultaneously subjecting her to a frank, appraising stare that met her eye, ran a quick survey from head to toe and then returned to her face, his smile widening.

'Rufus,' he said, laughing as Bella juggled the coffee, trying to hold both hot cups against her chest so she could reach out to him.

'Allow me,' he said, removing the cup in her right hand so he could shake it. His grip was crushing, making Bella let out an involuntary squeak. His eyes widened in – what was it? Pleasure? – before he relented and let go.

'You don't want to drink this crap,' he said to Charlie, handing him the cup. 'Why don't you let me take you both out for some lunch. Get some decent coffee and have a bite to eat while we're at it?'

Charlie looked at Bella questioningly. 'I don't know,' he said, 'what do you think, darling? Rufus here was just talking about a business venture in our neck of the woods, looking for a local hero wine producer to work alongside.'

'Sounds great,' said Bella, with a tight smile. 'Why not?' She signalled her assent to Charlie with her eyes.

Rufus was already on the phone, talking to someone called François. There was an awful lot of matey swearing and breaking into French. He disconnected and turned again to them both.

'Brilliant, that's sorted. No time like the present . . . shall we?' He ushered them out of the conference hall and into a taxi. Bella was desperate to touch up her make-up. She could see the light bouncing off her shiny nose.

She needn't have worried. After his initial searchlight appraisal, he proceeded to ignore her completely in the taxi until they arrived at the little Kensington bistro, not much more than half a mile from the conference centre. The place was barely noticeable from outside, with a tiny, discreet sign over the door, announcing that this was 'La Maison de François'.

Bella excitedly dug her elbow into Charlie's ribs, attempting to communicate, with a single and possibly slightly violent shove, that this was the amazing and tippity-top trendy new place to be seen; home of the Michelin-starred chef and enfant terrible who frequently shocked the restaurant establishment with his audacious flavour combinations and roaring temper tantrums. No one, absolutely no one, was guaranteed a booking at his elite establishment and he was recently in the gossip columns again when Joan Collins complained she was made to wait three months for a table.

Charlie clearly missed the nuances of this highly communicative shove. 'Ouf,' he said. 'Excuse you,' forcing Bella to waggle her eyebrows meaningfully instead. This didn't do it either, though it doubtless made her look quite mad. She sighed and resolved to tell him later.

An astonishingly beautiful waitress, wearing a black Mao-style jacket and wide, flowing black trousers, took their coats and glided them through to a table in a secluded corner.

Bella excused herself immediately and took her bag off to the loos to see how much damage she could reverse.

The loos were austerely modern but luxurious, in fact so much so Bella took out her notebook and phone to take some notes and pictures for her inspiration board. The sinks were grey, granite troughs, appearing – with clever brackets underneath – to float in space. There was an impeccably curated selection of toiletries on offer and a generous pile of little hand towels in a pure white cotton waffle.

The flattering lighting made it difficult to see precisely how much repair work was required, but once she had blotted the shine and applied another layer of mascara she felt more confident.

The men were deep in conversation when she returned and slipped into her seat, the beautiful waitress coming along to open up her absurdly huge white napkin and pop it on her lap for her as if she had lost the use of her arms.

'I hope you don't mind,' said Rufus, running his eyes over her make-up repairs with approval, 'I ordered for you. I know you and Charlie are keen to get back. I'm only grateful you've agreed to take the time for lunch.'

Bella nodded, taken aback. 'Sure,' she said, shortly.

'Charlie tells me you like crab,' Rufus added, charmingly, 'and the lamb with rhubarb confit is a speciality of the house at this time of year.'

'I'm sure it'll all be delicious,' jumped in Charlie appeasingly, just in case Bella didn't. Which annoyed her even more.

Doubly irritatingly, Rufus was right. The food was amazing; light, beautifully balanced, surprising but familiar.

Rufus had ordered a bottle of white wine for the crab and red for the lamb but was barely drinking himself, she noticed. The beautiful waitress was refilling Bella and Charlie's glasses whilst allowing just a puddle of wine in Rufus's. Clearly, they had an understanding.

'So,' Rufus was saying as she finished her lamb, putting together her knife and fork with regret and wondering about pudding, 'it's about creating something extraordinary at the same time as making every detail relaxed and welcoming. I want local people to feel they've been transported somewhere special and at the same time I want visitors from further away to feel like they are at home . . . I am more than aware,' he said, breaking off to drink some water, 'that I have a responsibility to honour the history of The Grange, at the same time as bringing it into the twenty-first century.'

'Hang on,' interrupted Bella, 'you mean you've bought The Grange at Little Havenbury? I'd heard it had changed hands.'

Rufus grinned. 'I certainly did,' he said. 'The sale completed yesterday but we've not hung about. The permissions are all sorted. We're starting work on the essential building repairs next week.'

'You've got your work cut out,' she said. 'I heard it was practically derelict.'

'It's been empty for two years, I'm told,' he said, angling his whole body towards her and – in the process – all but turning his back on Charlie. He engaged her attention with his extraordinary eyes – they were opal, she decided. Mainly green but shot with flashes of yellow and hazel – his gaze dropped to look lingeringly at her mouth. 'And that's where I understand you and I might have a chance to do something amazing.'

Bella blushed and then blushed even deeper as her mind ran riot – not that sort of 'amazing' surely? She had better stop drinking.

'But,' she said, wiping her mouth on her napkin just in case his preoccupation with her lips was down to a blob of stray asparagus butter, 'hang on a minute. Here we are in London and we're talking about how you've bought a failing country hotel within two miles of the vineyard – I mean – what are the chances?'

'No coincidence,' said Rufus, giving her a cunning smile and turning back to Charlie. 'I had my people find out about you. I was hoping you'd be at the Wine Fair, so I could introduce myself. To be honest, I was expecting you to have your own stand. When I realised you didn't, then – yes – I had to track you down, but it's a small world and we have friends in common . . .'

'We would normally have a presence,' said Charlie, apologetically. 'We decided not to this year.'

'Very wise,' agreed Rufus, 'keep it exclusive.'

Charlie demurred, but didn't bother pointing out they could hardly have raised the several thousands of pounds required after such a disastrous harvest and – in any case – they had virtually nothing to sell.

'So,' said Rufus briskly, 'we will talk more about wine when we meet in Havenbury. I'm glad we're in touch. I can't wait for my guided tour, but now,' he stood and held out his hand to Charlie, 'I must go to my next meeting. Please, finish your lunch, take your time, it's all taken care of . . .'

Turning to Bella he raised her hand to his lips and pressed it against them. 'I look forward to seeing considerably more of you soon,' he murmured.

CHAPTER FIVE

'Don't you think you should have punched him on the nose?' asked Bella, when he had gone.

'What, after he's bought us lunch?' said Charlie, pouring the last of the red into Bella's glass. 'Seems a bit ungrateful.' Secretly, though, he had felt a lurch of jealous fear at Rufus's assiduous attention. He stifled it. His ridiculous estrangement from Ben had taught him about his propensity to overreact. He wasn't going to go down that path again.

'He kissed my hand,' she complained.

'Not fair,' joked Charlie. 'He didn't kiss mine! Sorry, Bells, was he a bit sleazy?'

'A bit,' she said, clinging to her outrage like a modesty blanket.

'There might be some work in it for you.'

'He'll be using some flash London team,' she said. 'I won't get a look in, although it would be amazing. The Grange is beautiful. What I wouldn't do to get my hands on it . . .'

'Weirdly familiar-looking, though . . .' mused Charlie. 'Think I might have met him before somewhere.'

'You always think that, though,' teased Bella. 'What about the time you went up to that bloke at Victoria Station because you were sure you'd sold him some wine. Turned out he was the villain in the James Bond film we were watching the night before. So embarrassing.'

'He was pretty nice about it. I should have asked for his autograph. But are you sure? Is that what it is?'

'Totally. I knew who Rufus was as soon as you introduced him, but we've definitely not met. You'll have read about him in the Sunday supplements like I have. He's this really, really cool guy "setting the trends", best mates with all the celebrity elite . . . He's the one who set up Tavistock House. Even you've heard of that, surely?'

'I don't read the supplements,' insisted Charlie, scratching his head. 'You know I don't. And I'm not sure I want Havenbury to get all trendy.'

'Too late now,' said Bella. 'I think it's brilliant. The Grange will be the making of the place and – just think – we'll probably end up with Gwyneth Paltrow drinking our wine. She'll want to come and see you, I expect,' she added slyly. 'To have a tour of the vineyard or . . . something . . .' She ran her fingers teasingly up Charlie's thigh.

'Oh well, that's all right, then,' he said grabbing her wandering hand in his own. 'Let's get home,' he murmured. 'Or we could just hire a room?'

'What? By the hour?' she whispered, looking around her. 'How sleazy.'

'I love a bit of sleaze,' he said, stroking the back of her

hand with his thumb and then transferring his attentions to the back of her knee, under cover of her napkin.

'Hmm,' she breathed. 'You know I can't refuse you when you do that, but you can't be serious?'

'Watch me.'

He got to his feet and swaggered, slightly unsteadily, over to the reception desk.

By the time Bella had put on her jacket and collected her stuff together he was waggling a key with a large slate key fob attached to it.

'After you, Mrs Smith,' he said, waving her to the lift.

'Tell me you didn't sign us in as Mr and Mrs Smith?' she giggled as he took advantage of the privacy of the lift to kiss her neck some more.

'I was protecting your honour,' he said, holding the room door open for her with one arm and ushering her in before hanging the 'Do Not Disturb' sign out and firmly locking the door behind them.

The room was dark and relatively small, but the bed was a king size.

'Now get your kit off,' he joked, 'I've only booked for an hour.'

'You didn't?' This time Bella really was shocked.

'I didn't,' he agreed, pulling her towards him. 'It's going to take longer than an hour to do what I've got in mind, Mrs Wellbeloved. And by the time I've finished you are going to have been extremely wellbeloved indeed.'

Charlie looked down at Bella as she slept, her head tucked into the crook of his arm. It had been a good move, booking a room, he thought to himself. In the face of their rare but very satisfactory physical connection, the slightly queasy feeling of jealousy and threat that Rufus's attention to Bella had caused had faded away. Of course it had. He really needed to get a grip on himself. Rufus was potentially a real business angel – and if he found Bella attractive, then where was the harm in that? He admired the bloke's taste in women.

'Happy Valentine's,' said Bella, stirring and opening her eyes sleepily. 'This is so nice . . . we should do it more often.'

'Not too often,' joked Charlie, 'I'm not sure my heart would stand it. Actually, I'm not sure my wallet would stand it.'

'I know. Baked beans on toast for the next month. You did book for the whole night really, didn't you?'

'I did. Hungry?'

'Starving.'

'Room service?'

'Mm, maybe later,' sighed Bella contentedly as he nuzzled into her neck.

There was little to occupy Bella in her office over the following weeks. She went in anyway, just so she would be there if the phone rang. She put the finishing touches to her plans for the new bathroom, making up a mood board and doing a formal budget as if Dovecot Farmhouse was a proper client's property. She was doing a sitting room for a sweet lady on the other side of Havenbury Magna but – hopelessly – she couldn't get her to decide between several prints, one of which would make up the backbone of the scheme. Until she did, and managed to go twenty-four hours without changing her mind, Bella couldn't progress. Other than that, she was getting some curtains made up and desultorily drawing up the sketches for a new kitchen for a client who was planning in advance of her husband's bonus coming in. Bella was wise to this 'window shopping' though, and – with the client's four children at private school – thought there was a good chance said bonus might end up being swallowed by school fees before butler sinks and radiant hobs became a real thing.

To feel busy – and because she was nosy – Bella had taken to checking out the estate agent's details on The Grange. There were thirty or so photos, gratifyingly enough, and floor plans too. Brooding far too much on the man with the green eyes, she found herself flicking restlessly through the photos. They clearly showed the tired decor and there were even holes in ceilings in evidence here and there, but the sizes and proportions of the rooms were mouth-watering. Despite their conversation over lunch she had heard nothing from him and gradually began to accept the job would not materialise. He had probably just been sucking up to get Charlie onside. Men like that were charming by default. Just in case someone might be useful. It meant nothing.

'Remember that Rufus bloke?' Charlie said, casually, one morning, in late April, as they finished their coffee. 'Got a call from his office to say he wants to drop in.'

'Really? When?' Bella tried to sound insouciant.

'This morning, as it happens,' said Charlie. 'He's coming

here to go around the vineyard and collect a case of wine to take back to his chef for approval.'

'Great! Just thinking . . .' said Bella, experimentally sucking in her stomach. Damn. If only she had stuck at her diet. 'I actually wouldn't mind if you reminded him about my interior design service,' she said. 'For The Grange.'

'I thought you said he'd be getting his cool, trendy London lot down to do it.'

'Yeah, yeah, he probably will, I'm not expecting anything big. But, you know, there might be some bits and pieces . . . Loos, staff areas, even . . . it would just be quite good having The Grange in my portfolio,' she said casually, secretly picturing herself and Rufus leaning over some stunning designs she had rustled up, their arms brushing accidentally, him being blown away by her talent, proclaiming her genius and insisting that she, alone, should be responsible for the entire look of The Grange, which would be held up as the newest and coolest aesthetic of the twenty-first century.

'You're doing that weird thing again,' observed Charlie, breaking into her reverie.

'What weird thing?'

'That strange grimace that newborn babies make when people think they're smiling but actually it's wind.'

'I do not have wind,' said Bella, giving him a shove. 'And I do not have a "strange grimace" on my face. Anyway, what do you know about newborn babies . . .' Dammit, why did everything lead back to the one thing they couldn't talk about. 'I'm off,' she added, changing the subject. 'Tell me tonight.'

* * *

For such a busy and successful businessman, used to glamour and perfection, Rufus seemed flatteringly impressed by the little, ramshackle vineyard, insisting on a full tour and constantly proclaiming his amazement and awe at the work Charlie and his father had done over the years.

'This,' he said sweeping his arm expansively, 'is exactly the story I want to tell at The Grange. Local, good quality, real produce. Who needs French wine when we've got all this? And I'm looking to supply Tavistock House as well. That sparkling Chardonnay you gave me?'

Charlie nodded.

'It's perfect,' Rufus said. 'I want twenty thousand bottles a year. Can you do it?'

Charlie nodded again. Who was he to look a gift horse in the mouth? The clients at Tavistock House would clearly drink any old shit. That was footballers and soap actors for you.

'I really want you to try the Brut, too,' he said. 'That's the one which is closest to champagne, but I can't supply that in quantity until – well – assuming all goes well, we're talking the year after next.'

'For the right stuff I can wait,' said Rufus, 'but I worry about the scale of the operation you're running here. Are you going to be able to deliver?'

'I can deliver,' said Charlie hastily. 'Don't worry, because I've got it all planned out. I just need a bit of finance, is all.'

When Bella drove down the track to the farmhouse that evening the first thing that struck her was how on earth the silver Porsche crouching on the cobbles could possibly have got down the drive with its twin-exhaust intact.

Male voices greeted her as she let herself in through the back door, navigating around Dolly who galumphed under her feet, threatening to trip her at every step.

'Bella!' exclaimed Charlie. 'Look who I've got here.' He waved an arm at Rufus who got up from the kitchen table to greet her.

'I'm so sorry to still be here. I must get out of your way.'

'Not at all,' insisted Charlie. 'Darling, I'm glad you're home. Rufus and I have been starting to think about supper.'

'To the point of starting to cook it?' she enquired. 'Or just "thinking" about it?'

'Aha,' said Charlie, wagging a finger. There was an open bottle of Dovecot Estate wine on the table, and he seemed a little drunk. 'I hear where you're going with this, and you raise a fair point, but you do know – of course, darling – that I'm a rubbish cook, and that's the last thing we want to inflict on poor Rufus here.'

'Really,' Rufus insisted, 'You're incredibly kind but I must be going. Charlie and I have covered a lot of ground and I'm sure I've taken up enough of your time . . .'

'No, no, do stay,' said Bella, trying to give Rufus an encouraging smile at the same time as subjecting Charlie to a death stare, which probably just made her look mad. 'It'll only be pasta, or something . . .'

'Pasta sounds perfect, if you're sure? To be honest I get tired of fancy food. I seem to spend my life testing out menu ideas. I sometimes pine for cheese on toast.'

'I might be able to do a bit better than cheese on toast,' said Bella, putting on her apron.

* * *

'This is amazing,' insisted Rufus, half an hour later, as he reached over to fill Bella's glass. 'You are a woman of many talents. Charlie's been reminding me about your interior design service too. I think we definitely need to talk.'

Bella threw Charlie a grateful look, but he was half asleep now, eating pasta with one hand, his other propping up his head, which was in danger of falling into his plate. Hardly surprising if he had been drinking all afternoon.

Rufus, by contrast, still had the razor-sharp, shrewd appearance of someone entirely on top of his game; 'Ten o'clock tomorrow?' he went on. 'Meet you at The Grange?'

'I won't have prepared anything!'

'Of course not. How could you have? I just want to get your initial thoughts. Your instinct.' He paused, gazing at her mouth. 'I'd be incredibly grateful . . .'

'I'd love to,' said Bella hastily. 'I'll be there.'

'So, tell me more about you and Rufus?' Bella asked Charlie the following morning. She was exhausted and not a little pissed off. He had been monosyllabic after Rufus left and had then snored all night.

'Bloody brilliant,' he said, buttering his toast lavishly and piling on marmalade. He rarely had a hangover. When she first knew him, it was one of the things that most impressed her, but now it just seemed unfair.

'I ended up showing him the winery proposal. Turns out he's looking for investment opportunities – wants to "diversify his portfolio" or some old bollocks – so he says he's up for the entire two mill'.'

'What winery proposal? What two million? We haven't talked about this . . .'

'Granted,' Charlie conceded. He hadn't shared it with Bella – especially in light of their otherwise desperate finances – but Rufus had been so damned positive, and the liquid lunch might just have contributed to his confidence in deciding to put it to him there and then.

'I was going to. It's a real thing,' he said, mulishly. 'If we're serious about producing wine to rival champagne, we damned well need to be able to harvest our grapes and get them pressed when we're ready, not when the winery twenty miles up the road deigns to give us a slot in their schedule. I'm not going through the debacle we had last autumn ever again. We need our own equipment.'

'Yes, but two million pounds!'

'Like I said, he wants to put the whole lot in. We could be up and running by next year's harvest if we crack on.'

'Why the hell would he want to put two million quid into our business?'

'Why the hell wouldn't he?' said Charlie angrily. 'He has faith in what we – I – am trying to achieve here, oddly enough. It would be nice if you did.'

Bella shook her head. 'Fine,' she said. 'Whatever. I need to go and mug up for my meeting with this investment angel myself. Let's see what he dreams up for my little business, shall we? Maybe I'll launch my own range of fabrics and wallpapers. I could take on Farrow & Ball with their paint? I could be turning over a billion a year in a month or two.'

'Well, that would be very nice,' he said acidly. 'I haven't

seen your business exactly bringing in much to keep bread on the table, so it would make a bloody change.'

After Bella left, Charlie felt like a complete shit. He was a bastard for picking on her lack of financial success. She had only been going for eighteen months and her reason for setting up her little business had been more about his own abject failure to provide for her, and the absence of a baby to distract her, than a desire to become the next Nina Campbell.

He cleared away the breakfast things out of guilt – and then he called Dolly to come out with him to the vineyard. At least he could work a bit of fat off the dog. Shame it wouldn't work on Bella. He assured her he hadn't noticed when she asked but, the truth was, there was a lot more of her to love than there had been at their wedding. It couldn't be healthy. Perhaps they could do a shared endeavour where Bella ate less and he drank less. On the other hand, maybe not. He wasn't sure life without booze was practicable at the moment.

CHAPTER SIX

Walking up the wide, stone steps to the front door of The Grange, Bella's palms were sweating, but even her nerves couldn't distract her from her appraisal of the building. The main double doors were at least six feet wide. The paint was peeling and a couple of the glazed panels were broken, but nothing could obscure their beautiful proportions. The elaborate bell pull and the worn brass door furniture were clearly the original early Georgian ones too. It was lucky they had survived and not been nicked when the building was empty. The right-hand door was ajar, so she slipped inside, her heart thumping in her chest.

The hallway was a tragedy. The cupola window, high above her, had clearly been leaking for some time, damaging the plaster and panelling on the walls extensively. The stench of mould and damp filled her nostrils. She could see that the marble floor, through the thick film of dust and dirt, was beautiful, though – a chequerboard of black and white with a Greek key border, leading to a sweeping double staircase.

'Bella!' said Rufus, appearing through a door on her left. 'I'm so glad you're here. This is Sophia, my PA, PR, and all things in between.'

The woman at Rufus's side was one of those stick-thin, patrician blondes with perfect legs and immaculate red lipstick which Zach Havenbury produced an endless stream of and Bella found so daunting.

'Sorry,' she smiled at the young woman. 'I don't mean to interrupt.'

'You're not,' said Rufus before the blonde had a chance to reply. 'Sophia is just here to take notes of our discussions, anyhow. So . . . whaddayathink?' he said, waving her back into the room he had just come out of – a huge salon with soaring high ceilings and a magnificent marble fireplace. The trio of perfectly matched sash windows, with their original shuttering intact, reached from floor to ceiling, giving uninterrupted views over parkland, dissected by the main drive.

'Amazing,' said Bella, looking around her. 'I've never been inside. Wanted to. I began to think it would be allowed to fall down.'

'It's got pretty close to it,' said Rufus. 'What would you do with this room, for example?'

Bella gulped. 'Blimey. Nothing like being put on the spot . . .'

'No pressure, just your gut instinct.'

'Well,' she said, turning slowly around her, 'the architecture is amazing and we need to be able to admire that, but the trick is to induce a sense of comfort and a more human scale too. I'm thinking contemporary but not jarringly so. I obviously wouldn't want to remove any of the original fabric, the panelling, the floor . . . goodness, the floor . . .' she said, noticing it for the first time.

'I know, it's a state.'

'No, it's beautiful, look . . . these floorboards are hand-sawn oak.' She knelt down and swept her hand over one, to clear away a layer of dust, then brushed her hand unselfconsciously on her trousers, leaving a grey swathe. 'They're so wide. They're from the widest part of the trunk; the best of the best. Look, you can see the original saw marks in the surface. All I'd want to do with these,' she said, looking up to Rufus, 'is carefully clean them and wax them. They'll look amazing.'

'The conservation officer will love you,' said Rufus, nodding sharply in satisfaction. 'What else?'

'Right . . .' Bella looked around her again. 'What a shame about this panelling,' she said, examining it closely. It ran around the entire room to shoulder height but was badly split in places and thick with old paint.

'That can be repaired,' said Rufus. 'We're on it already. So . . . colour schemes? Furniture?'

'Yikes . . .' Bella half closed her eyes and thought. 'Okay, low, sleek sofas. Mahogany leather. A pair either side of the fireplace and a pair either side of each window . . . the scale allows for it in this context. Chandeliers of course, with these beautiful high ceilings, but let's look for something by a contemporary artist. Something that comes right down low, like a waterfall of crystal, not just something stuck up at ceiling height . . . Raw silk curtains, I think. Silk dupion. Not fancy. No frills, no tassled tie-backs – just pure, simple luxury, flowing right down and pooling a little on the floor . . . they'll look amazing in the evening, in low light.'

'Colour?'

'Dark grey,' she said, immediately. 'And the walls dark grey too, but not wallpaper, they can be lined in silk too. The same fabric as the curtains. Or fake suede. Yes. Better. With wadding, of course. It'll cover the uneven plaster, and the acoustic effect will be amazing. The echo in here . . . it's not great for that sense of comfort and intimacy we want. With curtains and fabric walling it will feel still, warm and quiet. Now, going back to colour, the panelling . . .' She looked at Rufus and was taken aback to see him standing, legs apart, arms folded, head tilted slightly back with a broad smile on his face.

'What?' she said, smiling too, despite herself.

'You,' he said. 'Now, what were you going to say about the colour of the panelling?'

'I was going to say . . .' she paused, uncertainly, 'that I'd really like to paint it in a deep, aubergine-purple colour, which would be amazing with the grey.'

He wrinkled his nose.

'Or . . .' she said, hastily, 'there's a dark, stormy teal-blue colour, really intense . . . that would work too.'

He smiled again. 'Enough.'

'Really? Sorry, I do go on.'

'I mean, I've heard enough. You're in.'

Bella's mouth dropped open. She realised and slammed it shut.

'You'll want to see my credentials, of course,' she gabbled, scrabbling in her briefcase for a card, which she handed to Sophia, 'but I'm pleased you like these initial impressions. If you could let me have the details, the budget, the timescale, then I'll prepare you a proper pitch. I imagine I'm in contention along with other interior design companies . . .'

Rufus held up a hand to stop her. 'When I say "you're in" I mean "you're in". As in, the job's yours.'

'What? All of it?' whispered Bella.

'The whole rotting, collapsing, crumbling lot,' he confirmed, smiling again at the delight on her face. He turned to Sophia. 'I want you to get Bella together with Paddy tomorrow,' he said. 'Tell him she's got carte blanche. Anything goes, but nothing happens unless it goes through Bella. Okay?'

Sophia nodded calmly, scribbling in her notebook.

'I want you,' he said, turning back to Bella.

They both paused, digesting what he had just said.

'I – want – you,' he said again, quietly, as if Sophia wasn't there.

Seconds passed. He gazed unashamedly at her and she stared back, mesmerised.

'Now,' he said, breaking the mood as crisply as a hand clap, 'how about a coffee? I'm gasping. You?'

'Rufus,' interrupted Sophia delicately, 'just to say, your eleven o'clock is due in ten minutes You have a car waiting outside and I've arranged for you and Sir Kenneth to have coffee over there. After that it's the helicopter back to London for lunch in the City at one o'clock.'

He turned to Bella regretfully. 'My time is not my own,' he said, taking her hand and holding it in his. 'I'm looking forward to seeing a lot more of you.'

Bella felt herself blush. 'And Charlie, of course,' she

said. 'With the winery thing too? Looks like you're going to be seeing a lot more of both of us.'

'Ah yes,' said Rufus, letting go of her hand. 'Both of you.'

'You've got to bring him here,' squeaked Maddy, excitedly.

'I will,' said Bella. 'Of course, I will. This whole Bespoke Consortium thing is perfect for what he's trying to achieve. He already said, when me and Charlie met him for lunch in London, that he prioritises using local artisans.'

'That's us. We're "local artisans". He could really help put us on the map,' said Maddy, clapping her hands excitedly. She was peering over Bella's shoulder where she had googled 'Rufus Delaney, Tavistock House' so Maddy could see. 'Plus, he's lush.'

'Do you think?' said Bella, tilting her head on one side. 'He's ginger.'

'Sure! Ginger is totally sexy. Think Ed Sheeran,' said Maddy.

'Ed Sheeran? You're kidding . . .'

'Yeah . . . no . . . there's definitely something about him . . . Mind you I think everyone and everything's sexy at the moment. Must be my pregnancy hormones. It's awful,' she said, her grin suggesting it was anything but. 'I can't keep my hands off Ben. I keep telling him it takes my mind off feeling sick.'

'Poor man,' deadpanned Bella.

'Yeah, well, it *is* "poor man" having to make love to such a blimp,' said Maddy, pushing out her pregnant tummy, which barely showed. 'We'll have to start doing it with the lights off.'

'I look more pregnant than you do,' argued Bella. 'Anyhow, you look completely gorgeous pregnant. You're glowing. I'm sure Ben thinks he's died and gone to heaven.'

'Mm . . . so, anyhow,' said Maddy, leaning over so she could scroll through the Google images, 'when are you and this hunky man next going to get together?'

'Dunno,' said Bella. 'But,' she added, giving her friend an admonitory nudge, 'when I next see Rufus it'll be with Charlie in tow.' She explained briefly about the possibility of the winery funding.

'Wow,' said Maddy. 'Two million pounds! Will it worry you? Charlie borrowing that much?'

'I suppose he was always going to have to. I know he and his dad had it as a plan to do together – in the future – so, well, I suppose "the future" is here, isn't it?' Her brow furrowed. 'I am worried, though. Is now really the time?'

'What, you mean with you and Charlie having children?'

'There's been no talk of that.'

'About time . . .'

'I'm only twenty-nine.'

'Nearly thirty, though.'

'All right, all right. You're nearly thirty as well, remember,' said Bella.

'You did remember to get tickets to the May Ball, didn't you?' said Maddy, changing the subject tactfully. 'It's going to be brilliant this year, I heard.'

'Brilliant? I don't think we ought to hold out much hope about that . . . cardboard chicken, cheesy disco and cheap wine in a draughty old conference room at Havenbury Manor, surely? Same old, same old . . . I wondered if you'd want to go, being up the duff and all.'

'Of course I do! Wouldn't miss it for the world – after all, it's not as if there's much on the social calendar round here. Plus, it's for the sick kiddies.' She pulled a mock sad face. 'Don't forget the sick kiddies. Anyway, you've got to come. It's more fun as a foursome.'

'. . . said the bishop to the actress. Sure, I'll get onto it. I suppose we wouldn't want to let the boys down. Anyway, you don't fool me with that cynical stuff about the "sick kiddies". You totally care about the children. I've not forgotten you nearly killed yourself doing that half marathon on your dodgy ankle for them just after I met you.'

'Yeah? Well, I hadn't known Ben long at that stage. I was still trying to impress him. Anyway, hurry up and get your tickets or they'll have sold out.'

'And then there's the issue of what we wear,' said Bella, disconsolately. 'I've put on so much weight. Last year's dress definitely won't fit.'

'Buy a new one! And come with me while I find something to fit over this bump. We can have lunch too. You can afford something "designer" seeing as you've just got all this new business from old fox face here.'

Paddy, it turned out, was a grizzled but handsome builder in his fifties, with twinkling blue eyes and a thick Irish accent.

He shook hands with Bella and then offered her his flask of coffee, along with a cleanish plastic cup.

He nodded approvingly when she took it and drank. 'You and me'll get on just fine,' he said.

Together, with high-vis vests and hard hats on, they toured the house, which Paddy referred to constantly as 'the site'. And it was a 'sight' too, thought Bella. It was looking far worse than when she and Rufus had been there just days before. Paddy and his men had been busy stripping out and some areas were now taken right back to a shell of bare brick.

He took her arm solicitously as she picked her way past scaffolding and missing floorboards. 'Steady here,' he said. 'Don't want a broken leg. That'll send the insurance premiums right up.'

Although it was absolutely a building site, it was a long way from chaos. There was no shouting or effing and blinding – not even the ubiquitous blaring radio. His team of men were working quietly and efficiently, greeting Bella politely but without curiosity, listening carefully to the occasional instruction from Paddy which was delivered with authority and humour.

'They all seem to know what they're doing,' commented Bella.

'We have a site meeting first thing in the morning and another at lunchtime,' explained Paddy. 'You're welcome to attend. Then, I suggest you and I have a meeting at the end of the day. Every day if you like. It's up to you.'

'I don't want to get in the way.'

'Get in the way? You're in charge, girl. At least,' he qualified, with a smile of genuine warmth, 'you're in charge of what gets done, I'm in charge of how it gets done.'

'Thank heaven for that. I have to admit,' she shuffled her feet, 'I don't know everything about building. I'm not an architect or anything.'

'Don't worry, my darling,' said Paddy confidingly. 'You just need to tell me how things have to look. I'll be making sure the building doesn't fall down.'

'You're not like the last one,' he observed, once they made it back to the front hall again. 'She was far too snooty for coffee from a flask, that one,' he said, as he offered a refill.

'What happened to her?' she asked as she sipped. The coffee was good. Thick, black and heavily sugared.

'She got above herself,' he said, with a chuckle. 'Didn't like it when he turfed her out of his bed to make room for the next one.'

'Well, he'll not be turfing *me* out of his bed,' Bella said, firmly. 'And that's because, I'm not *in* his bed,' she added, 'not because . . . I *am* in his bed . . . and I don't want him to throw me out . . . or anything.'

'I advise you to keep it that way,' he laughed.

CHAPTER SEVEN

The building schedule for The Grange was terrifying, Bella discovered. It was absurd that Rufus was planning a September opening, less than four months away. Paddy seemed happy enough – clearly, he had been there before – but Bella was finding that half the bespoke furniture and finishes she wanted to propose simply couldn't be done within the timescale, so she was having to exercise a combination of pleading and compromise.

Her head was aching by the time she had finished the mood boards and budgets for the main two reception rooms. One, the grey silk room, was going to be the bar and the other, which was flooded with light, and led to a currently derelict orangery, was going to be the dining room. The final figures horrified her, but Paddy assured her that money was no object and that she could confidently expect Rufus to go with what she proposed. She hoped he was right. Rufus had insisted on meeting her to sign everything off the following morning, with Sophia having rescheduled several of his meetings to make it possible. She carefully placed the mood boards into her portfolio case to put into the car and drove home. It was nearly nine o'clock.

She was greeted, at the farmhouse, with the delicious smell of garlic frying and Dolly, who wrapped herself around Bella's legs, singing with joy at seeing her mistress again as if they had been separated for a year rather than a day.

'She's been whingeing on and off for hours,' said Charlie, giving Bella a peck on the cheek and handing her a large glass of red wine without being asked. 'Honestly. She doesn't give a monkey's about me. It's you or nothing.' They both regarded Dolly who was now lying on her back, wriggling and rolling her eyes so the whites showed. She was still keening soulfully.

Bella rubbed her tummy with her toe. 'Silly dog,' she said, taking a slurp of wine. 'God that's good,' she said, gratefully. 'She might be coming into season. That makes her daft like this.'

'Why not take her with you tomorrow?'

'Can't really,' said Bella. 'Got to see Rufus first thing and then supplier meetings more or less all day. I could leave her with Serena at Home Farm I suppose . . .'

'I wish you would,' he said, giving the pan on the Rayburn a stir. 'And perfect if you're seeing Rufus,' he added. 'We've got the loan agreement here.' He pointed at the table with his wooden spoon. 'Just need to sign it and get it back to him if you would? It'll save us a stamp.'

'Am I signing it too?' said Bella with surprise. 'I should give it a read, then.'

'I wouldn't bother,' said Charlie, hastily. 'It's pretty

much what we talked about. Just a formality for you to have to sign at all.'

'But I never sign something I haven't read,' insisted Bella, sitting down and starting to leaf through the thick wodge of paperwork. It was impenetrable and she found herself skimming quite a bit.

'Two and a half million?' she exclaimed. 'I thought he was lending two million.'

'Yeah, well, there's a lot of dilapidations to take care of.'

'Dilapidations? I thought this was for a new winery?'

'For God's sake,' snapped Charlie. Bella looked up in surprise. 'I'm just . . . there's capacity there . . . for further borrowing to – well – look, just sign the damned thing and eat your supper, will you?'

Charlie banged Bella's plate of pasta down angrily. She winced.

'Sorry,' he said, rubbing his head as if it hurt. 'I'm just a bit stressed at the moment. This loan is good news – excellent news – let's just crack on and take it, shall we?'

Bella bowed her head. This was a Charlie she didn't recognise. 'I just feel we haven't really talked about it,' she said quietly, taking his hand. 'Of course I'll sign. I want us to do well . . .' She reached for the paperwork and the pen, riffling through the pages and signing in three places while Charlie watched her beadily. He had already signed, she noticed, so now it was just Rufus.

Rufus was late arriving at The Grange the following morning. Bella had come in time to have the morning meeting with Paddy and his team, so she had already been there for nearly an hour. She laid out the two mood boards on a trestle table in the main reception room. The budgets for sign-off and the loan agreement were lined up neatly next to them. Sophia kept calling her with almost minute-by-minute updates on his progress, which just made Bella more nervous.

Finally, he was there, apologising and kissing Bella on the cheek. They had gone beyond handshakes it seemed.

'These look fine,' he said, paying scant attention to the two mood boards. 'I like that. That. That,' he pointed at the choices Bella had made. 'That's fine . . .' he said slowly, looking at the picture of the chandeliers she had chosen. '. . . but I don't love them.'

'I know,' said Bella regretfully. 'They're not exactly what I wanted to give you.'

'So, why are they there?' His yellow eyes flashed with something steely, making Bella's heart quicken.

'It's a timescale thing,' she gabbled. 'A September opening? That's not even four months away – not long enough for a bespoke piece on the scale I was wanting for you . . .'

'I was seeing something by Anton Locatelli there,' he said, 'a pair, crystals flowing down like a waterfall, about eight feet long in all . . .'

Bella blinked. 'That's amazing,' she said. 'I wanted Anton Locatelli's work, he'd be perfect. I spoke to his people but the timescale was impossible. I'm surprised . . .' She broke off.

'Surprised I'd heard of him?' smiled Rufus. 'I'm not as Luddite as I look.'

'You don't look . . .' she said, looking him up and down and blushing. Today he was wearing an impeccable grey suit with a flash of purple lining, which emphasised his broad shoulders and gym-honed waist. It looked like an Ozwald Boateng. It probably was.

'When you've finished,' he said, with a smirk, 'I was going to go on to say I know Anton. He's a mate. I'm sure we can get him to do us something in time.'

'You know him?'

'I know. It's amazing, isn't it?' he smiled at her surprise. 'I want you to meet him. I'll get Sophia to set it up and come back to you with the details.'

'Right, so . . .' He swiftly read and signed off the budgets, sums that made Bella gulp, and then turned his attention to the loan paperwork, sitting next to them.

'There's a problem with this,' he said. 'I need to add a condition, I'm afraid,' he said, closing the distance between them in two strides. She could smell his aftershave. It was warm, woody and dark.

'Oh?'

'Yes, it's just not acceptable as it stands.'

'Sounds like you need to talk to Charlie.'

'This is not something I need to discuss with Charlie,' he said quietly, taking her hand and rubbing his thumb slowly and repeatedly across her slim wrist.

'It isn't?'

'No,' he whispered, gazing down at her mouth.

'So,' Bella swallowed loudly. 'What is it? This extra condition?'

'Surely you know,' he murmured, gazing at her lips. 'You want it as much as I do. Admit it. Just one night, I sign off the loan, everyone's a winner . . .'

Bella snatched back her hand and took a step back,

colliding with the trestle table, which shifted across the floor with a screech like a scream of outrage.

'I can't believe you just said that,' she panted, holding onto the hand he had stroked like it was burnt. 'That's the most . . . the most . . . outrageous thing I've ever heard.'

Rufus laughed. 'Why?' he said. 'I love the way your chest heaves when you're angry, by the way.'

Bella crossed her arms firmly. 'I am a married woman,' she said. 'And you can't do that.'

'Then Charlie can't have his loan,' he said, picking up the loan agreement and handing it back to her. 'Go and tell him the deal's off.'

'I will,' she replied, breathless. 'I will. And I strongly suspect he will want to come up here and have it out with you himself.'

'Ah, but you're not going to tell him.' At that, he turned on his heel, picked up his slim briefcase and walked to the door. 'I'll get Sophia to set up that meeting in London with Anton. You can tell me what you've decided then.'

'Pasta again, sorry,' said Charlie when she got home.

'Not at all,' said Bella. 'It's nice to be cooked for.'

'It's by way of apology,' said Charlie, fetching her a glass. 'Damn,' he said, upending the empty bottle. 'I'll get another.'

'Apology for what?' she asked, as he poured her a large glass of red and then topped up his own generously.

'For behaving like an arse last night. Over the loan and all that stuff . . .'

At mention of the loan, Bella's heart started to thump.

'The truth is,' he carried on, sighing, 'we need the cash. A lot. More than I might have said . . .'

Bella sat down. 'You had better tell me,' she said, dully, cradling her wine glass in both hands.

By the time Charlie had got to the end of his explanation, the water in the saucepan, waiting for the pasta to go into it, had nearly boiled dry.

'But the house too? Did you know your father had already borrowed against it?'

He shook his head. 'I've known for a while. Going through the paperwork after he died was a bit of a revelation. Dad didn't tell me, and he hasn't told Ma either, but – the truth is – there is nothing left to sell off and no value left in the business once debts are taken into account. The opposite, in fact.'

'But,' Bella wrung her hands, 'surely lots of businesses run like that, don't they? Vineyards, in particular, we know that . . .'

'And they go bust,' said Charlie. 'Like this one will. Soon. In the next couple of months.'

'Why the hell didn't you say something before?' shouted Bella.

'We were newly married. All our dreams. The worry . . .'

'Yes but "for richer, for poorer" for God's sake.'

'I know, I know . . .'

'And Dove Cottage? Is that under threat?' Bella was casting around desperately for some ground beneath their feet, even if it meant her and Charlie cramming into the little house with Caroline. They could make that

79

work, couldn't they? They could find a way . . .

'There's a mortgage on that too,' he admitted. 'It would go down the tube with all the rest. Ma doesn't know.'

Bella's wine glass flew across the room, smashing with some force as it hit the wall by the back door. She looked at her newly empty hand, puzzled.

'Shit, Bella,' he said, shocked. 'What the hell are you doing?' His voice cut through her confusion like a knife.

'No,' she shouted suddenly, making Dolly leap to her feet in alarm. 'What the hell are *you* doing? How dare you! How dare you announce this . . . this . . . catastrophe, as if it's something that has only recently become relevant to me. I'm your wife, for God's sake.'

Charlie twisted the stem of his wine glass for a moment. 'But we're fine now,' he said, reaching across the table for Bella's hand as she sat back down, her knees buckling. 'We've got a plan. The loan will see us straight. You'll see. With the extra half million to buy us the time we need, the two mill' to build the winery . . . all we need is a vintage year, Bells. A bit of luck and hard work. We'll be there. The future is rosé, trust me . . .' He looked to her for an acknowledgement of his little joke, but she was stony-faced. 'Where is the paperwork by the way? Did you get it signed?'

Bella pulled her hands away. 'Sorry,' she lied. 'I left it in the car. Completely forgot, with all the design stuff in my head . . .'

'For heaven's sake!' Charlie exploded. 'I'll take it to him myself.'

'No need. I'm seeing him tomorrow. In London. I'll do it.'

* * *

The text had come through from Sophia late that night. Very late. Bella had only heard it because she was still lying awake, rigid and tense, next to Charlie who – despite his stressful reveal of their desperate finances – was snoring peacefully beside her. She was to meet Rufus and Anton at the Saatchi Gallery the following afternoon at four o'clock, the text declared. When was Sophia ever not working, wondered Bella? Maybe she slept with Rufus too. Maybe sorting out his diary for the following day was an activity allocated to their pillow-talk sessions after they had sex. Scheduling sex sessions with other employees was probably part of Sophia's job description too. Bella discovered she was entirely unable to cleanse her mind of the thought of what it would be like to have sex with Rufus. She had snuggled up to Charlie once they had finally got to bed that night, desperate for reassurance, looking around her at the bare-floored bedroom, with its saggy-mattressed bed and draughty windows. Uncomfortable though it was, at the thought of its loss, the house seemed suddenly dear. As was usually the case nowadays, Charlie had moved away with an apologetic kiss on her cheek, muttering about being too knackered, which – given the amount of wine he had drunk – was doubtless true. How could Charlie sleep so peacefully with the thought that he might be losing his childhood home? Because, Bella answered herself, Charlie was under the impression he had finance in place to rescue the situation. But he didn't. Not yet.

All night, Bella's mind raced, lurched and swirled around the various agonies that preoccupied her. As dawn broke, her thoughts hardened into relative stillness, like the eerie calm following a storm when – force spent – the full damage was revealed. Fact: The entire life she had bought into when she married Charlie was just about to disappear in a puff of smoke. Fact: Charlie had kept the true horror of their situation from her for three years. Essentially, he had lied. Fact: she hadn't noticed. Not really. This spoke volumes about their connection or lack of it. Fact: She and she alone now held the key to their salvation albeit it was a Faustian pact that – far from saving the day – had the capacity to end their marriage once and for all. And all because of Charlie's deceit.

Fact: she hated him for it.

'You look tired,' said Rufus as Bella slid into the Mess at the Saatchi Gallery a few minutes after four o'clock the following afternoon.

'I've not slept well,' she muttered, not looking at him.

'Oh?'

'I've had a lot on my mind.'

'Mm,' he said. 'I can imagine. Well, we'll have to see what we can do to get you a bit more relaxed later,' he went on, as he draped his arm over her shoulder, making her jump sideways like a startled deer. Laughing at the effect he had on her, he took her portfolio case from her and walked her over to the table where a tall, dark man she recognised stood to greet them.

'*Bella*,' said Anton in a thick Italian accent. Standing up, he wasn't as tall as he had previously looked, but with his thin frame, eyes so dark they were almost black, and long, dark curly hair with multiple piercings in one ear, he looked like a very sexy pirate.

'That's what he calls all the women he meets,' joked Rufus drily.

'Only the pretty ones,' clarified Anton. 'Which this one definitely is.'

'And, for once, you're right, Anton, this one really is called Bella.'

Anton leant over the table and kissed Bella on both cheeks. 'How fa-a-bulous to meet you.'

Despite his charm, Anton was quick to get down to business, glancing at his watch as Bella lifted the mood boards for the club's new lounge out of her portfolio.

'Nice,' he breathed, taking in her scheme for the room, the grey silk, dark furniture and teal-painted panelling. 'Good colour,' he said, pointing at the paint swatch. 'It reminds me of a stormy sea.'

Bella explained quickly what she was wanting, the position and dimensions of the chandeliers, the focal points of the room, particularly at night, when the curtains were closed and guests were no longer able to admire the view.

Anton grabbed a sketchpad and started to scribble. 'You're close to the sea there, aren't you?'

'It's only four miles away,' Bella confirmed.

'I have this vision of a breaking wave,' he muttered as he sketched. 'The foam of the sea, crashing in an arc, the water surging, dark . . . dramatic . . . beautiful . . .' He was silent for a couple of minutes, leaving Rufus and Bella to watch him draw.

'Here,' he said at last, turning the pad so they could see. 'Something like this. My people will send you designs . . .

samples of the materials . . . We can have clear glass drops of course – long droplets, cut to catch the light like sea foam in the sunshine . . . but also this dark glass, it's like your paint,' he said, pointing, 'in shades of turquoise, navy, right through to your really dark, opaque, almost black . . . all in this sweeping shape,' he pointed at the drawing. 'The lowest parts nearly reaching the floor so' – he looked again at Bella's plans, to check the ceiling heights – 'eight feet long? Nine feet? It will look amazing . . .'

Bella realised she had her mouth open. 'Incredible,' she breathed.

'We'll need two of them then, mate,' said Rufus, sounding like an East End barrow boy, 'by end of July. All right?'

Anton puffed out his cheeks. 'You don't want much, do you?' he replied, lapsing into the same estuary English as Rufus. 'This glass, it comes from Murano . . . I'll have to go there myself. Work with them . . . but . . . sure,' he said, slamming his hand down on the table. 'Call my people,' he added to Bella.

'I already did,' she admitted. 'Last week. I'm still waiting for someone to get back to me.'

'That was last week,' said Anton, shrugging in apology. 'This time, you call them, you tell them your name . . . "Be-e-lla" . . . This time,' he kissed his fingers, reverting to his Italian accent, 'it will be different.'

CHAPTER EIGHT

'Are you hungry?'

'A little.'

'Only a little? Let's go work up an appetite, then,' he said.

'And yet,' she replied, waving her arm at the restaurant behind her, 'here is food.'

'I've got a better idea,' he said, as they headed for the bustling King's Road.

He flagged down a taxi and held open the door for her. She was acutely aware of how close he was as they sat, barely two inches between his thigh and hers. She hoped she didn't smell of sweat.

He did not, as she expected, show her into François's restaurant where she and Charlie had lunch with him before. Instead, barely nodding to the concierge who greeted him deferentially by name, he ushered her into the lift and punched in a code on a keypad she had not noticed the last time she was there.

The lift swept nearly silently beyond the levels where

the guest rooms were to the top floor where it opened into a small, black marble-lined lobby. The little windowless room was furnished only with a side table bearing a vase of flowers, a huge, rococo mirror and a single door leading off it. In the apartment, the air was still and quiet. Her eye was immediately drawn to the glass window, which took up all of one wall. Being on the top floor, the view was astonishing. Beyond the giant pots of plants on the roof terrace, was the whole of Kensington, with the Thames visible beyond.

'I didn't say I would,' she breathed.

'But you will,' he said, as a matter of fact.

'I love Charlie.'

'I know,' he said, stepping nearer, so they were almost touching, looking her up and down appraisingly. 'I know you do. And that is why I knew you would agree to my terms.'

'I'm not a prostitute.'

'I think we've established that you are,'

Bella gasped, her eyes flying wide open.

He laughed. 'Okay, okay. Bad joke. Sorry.'

Somehow the laugh helped. She exhaled, shakily. He was right. She knew she was going to do this. What did it matter? It's not as if she married Charlie a virgin. And if it broke their marriage then it broke their marriage. At this rate there would be nothing left to save from their life together, anyway. She had nothing to lose.

'Fine,' she said, defiantly. 'Where do you want me? Here?' She pointed to the leather sofa. 'Or the bed? Where is the bedroom? I'll get my kit off, shall I?' She fumbled with the buttons of her blouse, but her hands were shaking.

Rufus caught her hands in his own, still laughing softly.

'Shush,' he said. 'Let's enjoy it shall we? Business *and* pleasure, no?'

She pulled away and put her hand into her pocket. Where the hell had it gone?

'We'll be using this,' she said, chucking a wrapped condom onto the bed. She had bought them, looking guiltily behind her, from the vending machine in the ladies' loo.

'I hope you've got more than one.'

'That's not the deal . . .'

'I've bought you for the night,' he said. 'Trust me. We're going to need more than one.'

'Well, fine, but no kissing on the mouth,' she added, fiercely.

'Just like an actual prostitute,' he laughed. 'You've done your research. I'm impressed.'

'Doubtless no research was required on your part.'

'I don't generally pay for sex, actually,' he said, his face stormy now. 'I don't find I have to.' He held out a soft, white robe. 'Get into this. I'll meet you on the terrace.'

Putting on the robe, her hands really shaking now, Bella regretted making him angry, but when she hesitantly joined him, he was in the hot tub, naked, a bottle and two glasses beside him, good mood apparently restored.

Quickly, grateful that dusk had fallen, she slipped out of her robe and straight into the water. She exhaled. It was blissfully warm and the bubbles did a pretty good job of hiding her. Surprisingly, given the circumstances, she felt the tension slipping away. He handed her a glass.

'British, I hope,' she said.

'Naturally. One of your competitors, I'm afraid,' he said turning the bottle label towards her.

She sipped. It was one of her favourites. As close to the best French champagne as you could get. Better, in her view. She savoured the tiny bubbles and the biscuity, creamy finish.

'It'll be Dovecot Estate everyone will be drinking in a year or two,' he said. 'I'll help you make it happen.'

'The loan agreement is on the table, by the way,' Bella said, tersely.

He laughed. 'You're tough. I like that.'

He took her glass, placed them both on the tray and then he moved in, pressing his body against hers.

It was transactional sex. He took what he wanted, and he knew exactly what that was. Despite his single-minded focus on his own pleasure, he was so powerful and sure, and so clearly turned on by Bella's body she was ashamed to find herself responding. It must be because Charlie had been refusing her so often in recent months.

Coming back into focus, she realised Rufus was gone. For a moment, she thought she was alone but then heard him clearing his throat in the bathroom next door.

It was a world away from the tender, funny, passionate sex she had with Charlie, she thought, as she sprawled nerveless with exhaustion on the bed, hearing the water thundering, on and on, in the shower.

Coming back in, Rufus dried himself, dressed quickly and went around the room gathering up his keys, wallet and shoes.

'Sleep,' he said, at last meeting her eye as she watched him, the sheets pulled up to her chin. 'You need it.' His expression was impassive. Distant.

'What about you?'

88

He glanced at his watch. 'I've got work to do,' he said. 'There's food in the fridge. Let yourself out tomorrow. No rush.' Then he left, without looking at her again.

After a moment, when she was sure he wasn't coming back, Bella got up and, wearing the sheet as a sarong, she padded around the apartment. It was past midnight. She must have slept without realising it. There were three texts from Charlie, asking her when she was going to come home. The last one, an hour earlier, announced, rather shortly, that he was going to bed. She quickly pinged a text back to him saying she had missed the last train because the meeting ran late but was crashing in Maddy's flat. She then texted Maddy, asking for backup on her lie. She would pay for that, but Maddy could wait for now.

She was ravenous too. After all, they had had no supper and she had been too nervous for lunch. She began to see how people having illicit sex lost weight. It was so nerve-wracking. She had a quick shower and then rummaged in Rufus's wardrobe. It was impeccably tidy. She quickly located boxers, a soft grey hoody, which came down to mid-thigh on her, and a thick pair of cosy gym socks. An exploration of the immaculate kitchen area, all done out in iroko wood and stainless steel, was rewarding. The fridge was packed with antipasti; there was goats cheese, chorizo, stuffed artichokes and olives, and a perfectly ripe Camembert, making Bella moan again, this time with greed. There was also a well-filled fruit bowl on the worktop and, next to it, a slab of oak with a handle had a selection of breads. She recognised the signature walnut bread she and Charlie had been given in François's restaurant downstairs, along with a delicious-looking dried tomato and herb bread, and a classic French baguette. It was all perfectly fresh. Clearly someone had known they were coming.

Eating her fill, along with a large glass of red wine, Bella started to feel sleepy again. Selecting a perfectly ripe pear she wandered around the little apartment and into the foyer. This time, she noticed the table by the lift doors had the two copies of the loan agreement on it. Both were signed. Rufus's signature was as she might have imagined it; big, decisive and powerful. He had used a thick, black ink pen and it leapt off the page, next to hers and Charlie's biro scribbles. It was done. The Dovecot Estate was safe, and Charlie would never, ever know how she had sealed the deal. Wellbeloved family life would continue as it had for generations, with long summer days, bountiful harvests and babies. Lots of them.

She yawned. Leaving one copy on the table, she slipped the second of the two sheaves of paper carefully into her satchel, did up the straps, leant it neatly against the wall by the door and went back to the bed, the bed where she had both betrayed her husband and saved everything that made up their lives together – the farm, the vineyard, their home and Caroline's . . . she had done it, but at what cost?

'I will be wanting a full explanation, and it had better be good, young lady,' came the text from Maddy at six the following morning.

By the time Bella had caught the train home, showered, changed and driven herself to her little office at Home Farm it was lunchtime.

'Well?' said Maddy, elbowing her way into the room with a pair of mugs in one hand and a plate of biscuits in the other.

Bella looked at her friend wordlessly. Her eyes filled with tears and the corners of her mouth jerked downwards against her will.

'Shit! What?' said Maddy, dumping the cups and sloshing some of the contents in the process. 'What on earth happened? I was only joking. You know you're welcome to use the flat whenever you like . . . only you didn't, did you? Because you didn't have the key. Also, there's actually a tenant in there at the moment so they'd have been a bit surprised . . .' Maddy burbled on while Bella pulled herself together.

'It's something really awful,' she warned, wiping her eyes with the back of her hand and sniffing. '*Really* awful. You have to *swear* not to tell.'

'I swear,' said Maddy, deadly serious now. 'Not even Ben. I swear.'

'Shit!' she said again, when Bella explained. 'Does that even happen in real life? It's like a film, or something . . . shit.' She stared into space, munching mindlessly on her third Jammie Dodger. 'Did he sign, though?'

Bella nodded. 'I gave it to Charlie this morning.'

'And, obviously, he doesn't know?'

'He can't ever know.'

'No,' said Maddy. 'He wouldn't take it well. I can't believe you did it.'

'Nor can I.'

'I think you're really brave.'

Bella grunted her thanks and wrapped her arms around herself as if she were cold.

'Lucky he wasn't a fat, smelly old git though, isn't it?' Maddy went on.

Bella looked at her in astonishment. After a moment, she laughed. In seconds, the two of them were slumped helplessly in their chairs, weeping with mirth. Whenever either of them managed to compose themselves a little they caught the other's eye and burst into laughter again.

Eventually, weakly, they both recovered enough to drink their coffee.

'This calls for a therapeutic shopping expedition,' said Maddy at last.

'It does?'

'It does. When is that evil bastard going to pay you for those designs?'

'He already has,' said Bella, who had noticed just the day before that her previously moribund business bank account was now flush with cash, following her first invoice to Rufus's office going in just days before. She didn't have them down as fast payers, being slick and hard-nosed as they all were. Maybe she was the exception. Maybe they knew why. Maybe she wasn't the first.

'I've got money,' she admitted.

'Good,' said Maddy, 'because we have dresses to buy for the May Ball.'

* * *

If Bella thought Maddy might need to be treated gently because of her delicate condition she was wrong.

'I'm in the second trimester,' she explained. 'According to the instruction manual, I am blooming, coursing with growth hormones and bursting with energy.'

'Pity,' muttered Bella, who was still sleep-deprived from the night before and was on her third latte, watching Maddy try on dresses in the little maternity clothes shop she had recently discovered in the Brighton Lanes.

'How about this one?' she asked, twirling for Bella's benefit. She was wearing a cute, blush-coloured, chiffony concoction with a sweetheart neckline and a black ribbon tied in a bow, just beneath the bust. The layers of skirt billowed from directly beneath the bow, meaning they skimmed gracefully over Maddy's growing bump.

'It'll carry on fitting all the way through,' said Maddy, judiciously, smoothing the layers over her tummy. 'Me and Ben have got a couple of events to go to this summer,' she added. 'I think it'll do for those too.'

'And what about yours?' said Maddy a short time later, through a mouthful of coffee and walnut cake.

Bella put down her fork. 'I shouldn't be eating this, that's for sure,' she said, regretfully. 'I could always have worn my black dress – you know the one . . . it's got the white cuffs and collar like a tuxedo. I wore it for the May Ball last year.'

'I love that dress!'

'You wouldn't love the sight of me in it now.'

'Ah,' said Maddy, sympathetically. 'You were well

93

skinny when you got married, though. Everyone puts on a bit of weight when they get hitched It's contentment.'

'It's three stone of blubber, that's what it is.'

'Three stone. Yikes,' said Maddy, with sympathy. 'But those tits,' she added, pointing at them. 'They're amazing, babes. I'd be surprised if Charlie can keep his hands off them.'

'He does a pretty impressive job of it,' said Bella. 'You'd be astonished.' In truth, Charlie hadn't laid hands on them since the hotel room after they had lunch with Rufus.

'And Rufus probably wasn't complaining, either,' Maddy added.

'Good grief, woman,' Bella exclaimed. 'Anyway,' she added, 'we had the lights off.'

'More fool him. Maybe next time.'

'No next time. It was a one-time thing. Business.'

'It had better be,' said Maddy, suddenly serious. 'Do it again, and it's an affair.'

CHAPTER NINE

'This is the one!' exclaimed Maddy, yanking a dark-green dress off the rail and waving it. The material was a heavy crêpe, a body-con design with flattering draping over the tummy and bust.

'Looks a bit Jessica Rabbit.'

'Exactly,' said Maddy, pointing at Bella's boobs again.

'You're obsessed,' she grumbled. 'What size is it?'

'Never mind,' said Maddy, snatching it away. 'It's the right size, that's all you need to know. Now get in that changing room and trust me.'

It was a size eighteen, Bella saw, with horror, when she was finally allowed to have it. Surely that wasn't what she was now?

Keen to cover up a rather grey bra and pants, to say nothing of her lumpy white thighs, she all but jumped into the dress and zipped it as far as she could reach.

'Lemme see!'

'I can't . . .' Bella peeped around the curtain.

'Come here.' Maddy yanked away the curtain and chivvied Bella to turn around so she could finish pulling up the zip. Surprisingly it rose smoothly, encasing Bella in a comfortingly snug, rather than constricting way.

'Look at that!' Maddy breathed, looking over her friend's shoulder into the mirror.

'Mm,' said Bella, unconvinced. But it wasn't bad, she had to admit. The green was dark enough to be flattering, and she had always looked good in green. The draped neckline showed off her creamy white breasts and nipped in at the waist, giving her an impressive shape but flaring forgivingly below, to skim her heavy thighs.

'That,' said Maddy, thoroughly pleased with herself, 'is definitely the one.'

Bella discovered Charlie's dinner jacket hadn't been cleaned since New Year, so she packed it off to the dry-cleaners. Of course, Charlie should be doing it really. That was what Caroline would say. She had brought her son up well. The fault lay with Bella who had been so giddy about having a husband to look after, she took on all these silly little jobs, arguing that, as she was barely working, she was happy to run the house and everything that went with it. Secretly, she had been expecting to have a clutch of children clinging to her skirts within a couple of years to justify being a homebody.

Seeing her new dress hanging there, she stroked it forlornly. Another May Ball, another year gone, and still no baby.

'You'll have babies before I do,' she said to Dolly, who was tailing her in hope of a snack, or a walk, anything really . . . She felt certain if she stuck close enough something exciting would happen. She cocked her ears at being spoken to, but Bella was distracted and nothing interesting resulted.

'I've never had puppies before,' she continued. 'We'll keep one, of course. Maybe two. It'll be fine,' she reassured Dolly, who pricked her ears again at the attention and had never had a serious worry in all her simple, doggy life.

Meeting Rufus again could have been awkward. In the end, he joined her and Paddy at the end of their near daily catch-up meeting, appearing at Bella's elbow so suddenly he made her shriek and leap sideways.

'Steady on,' he smirked. 'You'll give Paddy a fright.'

'I didn't hear you,' she said, composing herself by putting several feet between them.

Paddy briefed him, efficiently, but Rufus waved him away. 'I'm sure it's all fine, Paddy,' he said. 'I trust you. Now piss off.'

'So,' said Rufus, when they were alone, putting his hands either side of Bella's waist, 'what I really want to know is how are you?'

She pulled away and, as a distraction, put her hands up to check her hair hadn't escaped from the tight bun she had put it in that morning. Nervous about seeing Rufus again, she had put on her most severe black suit that morning, making sure her shirt wasn't showing cleavage and doing up her jacket to the top button.

'I love it when you do that,' he said, raising his arm

in emulation. 'You have the most gorgeous graceful neck. It makes me think about where it leads,' he said, looking pointedly at her chest.

'I'm fine,' she said, tightly. 'Now, these designs for the garden room . . .'

'I don't give a damn about the designs for the garden room,' he said taking the portfolio from her and throwing it on the floor. 'Come here.'

'If you think . . .' Bella's chest was heaving. 'Then you are mistaken, I can assure . . .'

'Yeah, yeah . . .' said Rufus, waving away her protestations. 'It was a one-time thing. I know.'

'You're right,' she said, taking a step back. 'it was a one-time thing.'

'Pity,' he said, going back in on the attack, trying to plant a kiss on her neck, exposed by her severe hairstyle. 'Loving this,' he said, running his hands over her hair. 'Makes me want to just . . .'

'Stop!' shouted Bella, stepping back.

His expression hardened. 'Got it,' he spat. 'But, just remember, it's not about whether you're a tart, it's about the amount of money it takes to persuade you. And you've not told him, have you?'

'I'll never tell him.'

'How touching. Let's hope he never finds out then, eh?'

'Thank goodness you're up,' said Charlie the following morning when Bella arrived in the kitchen, still in her pyjamas. 'Your dog is behaving like a total loon.'

Dolly, on hearing her beloved mistress arrive,

unwrapped herself from around the chair where Charlie was sitting at the table and bounded towards Bella, tail tucked between her legs and back rounded in a parody of submission. She was rolling her eyes and squeaking plaintively.

'For heaven's sake, Dolly,' said Bella, crouching down so the dog could bury her head in her lap, which she did like a mole seeking cover from some terrible and nameless threat. 'What on earth . . . ? Although, seeing as you're eating sausages,' she said to Charlie, 'I don't know why you're surprised she's been glued to your side.'

'Funny you should say,' he replied, buttering a bit of bread to make himself a sausage sandwich, 'because – whilst I agree it is fair to say she is a dog almost entirely driven by her own appetite – it's actually not that, amazingly enough. Or at least I assume it isn't because she's not even finished her breakfast.' He waved his sandwich vaguely at her dog bowl in the corner of the room.

Bella shot to her feet, tumbling Dolly back off her lap unceremoniously. 'And you didn't call the-the-the dog ambulance brigade people? The vet? You didn't even wake me?'

Charlie raised his eyebrows with infuriating calm. 'And she keeps doing that, too,' he added, gesturing in Dolly's direction.

'Eeuw, Dolly,' said Bella. 'Must you?'

Dolly looked apologetic but kept licking her backside, anyhow.

'Of course!' Bella exclaimed in relief. 'She's in season,' she said, hitting her forehead with her palm. 'She was like this last time. I'd forgotten, but also I wasn't expecting it so soon.'

'Better get on and put her with that lummox of a dog Zach's got, then,' said Charlie, chewing. 'If that's the cunning plan?'

'It is, but they haven't even met,' wailed Bella. 'I was going to get them together beforehand so they could – you know – get to know each other first.'

'You are hilarious,' said Charlie, coming up behind her and giving her a hug and a peck on the cheek. 'Got to go.'

'No, wait! Talking about matchmaking . . .'

'Which you were, and I wasn't,' clarified Charlie.

'I was thinking,' continued Bella, undaunted, 'that Caroline should come to the May Ball.'

'Not a very good idea, surely? She always went with Dad. I dunno if it's really the right event for people to come on their own . . . what about the table plans?' A horrifying thought suddenly struck him. 'You don't think she should come along and – well – "pull", do you?'

'Get you,' scoffed Bella, amused. 'When have you ever given a monkey's about table plans, and anyway, why shouldn't she "pull" as you so delightfully put it?' She laughed in Charlie's face. 'Anyhow, as it happens, I agree, I think she should come with a partner.'

'How's she going to do that, then?'

'Obviously, we need to find someone for her.'

'Who?'

Bella hadn't thought that far. 'Well,' she said, racking her brain, 'there's that lovely old gentleman who runs the second-hand bookshop in Havenbury Magna – he's about her age.'

'He's eighty if he's a day.'

'He can be her sugar daddy.'

'Yeah, but, all this romantic stuff . . . At her age?'

Bella ignored him. 'Yes,' she said to herself. 'He could be ideal. He's really polite . . . charming . . . tall, which is important because Caroline is too. I've never seen any sign of a partner, wife, or anyone, the only trouble is, I sort of get the impression he's gay.'

Charlie brightened. 'Really? Well that might work.'

'You think so?'

'Yeah, absolutely,' he said. 'I just think Mum needs a – what would you call it? Escort?'

'A "walker"?'

'Yeah, a "walker",' said Charlie, with relief. 'Someone she can go to concerts and stuff with. Someone cultured. Just not – you know – all the other stuff.'

'*You* are the hilarious one,' teased Bella. 'It's like you're happy for Dolly to go shagging her way around Havenbury but you're the biggest prude ever where your mum's involved. She's only in her early seventies, you know. Plenty of time for a grand romance. Or two.'

Charlie shuddered. 'Do you mind?' he complained. 'I've just had my breakfast.'

'I'm not sure,' said Caroline, when Bella dropped by on the way to Zach's house. 'It would feel odd. Peter and I went together as a couple every year for decades. It was our thing.'

Bella considered her mother-in-law with her head on one side.

101

'It's not to try and replace Peter,' she said gently. 'It doesn't even have to be with someone you're . . . well – "with" . . .'

Caroline smiled sadly. 'You're a good friend,' she said. 'I couldn't ask for more from a daughter-in-law, but I'm a tough old bird. I can't say I'm not occasionally lonely . . .'

'This is it, though,' said Bella, persuasively. 'We were thinking – me and Charlie – that it would just be nice for you to have someone handy to do things with. Maybe not a boyfriend or anything.' She explained about her plan to approach the old gentleman in the bookshop.

Caroline had her head down, motionless. Bella was terrified she might have upset her. She waited.

'Do you know what?' said Caroline, looking up, 'Go on, then! Why not?'

Bella then sang the 'matchmaker' song from *Fiddler on the Roof* all the way to The Dower House at Little Havenbury, where Zach lived with his elderly grandmother.

'Now, Dolly,' she was telling her dog as she got her out of the car, 'you don't have to do this if you don't want to. He may be called "Brutus" but he's not. I mean, he's not brutal. He's really nice. But if you don't like him that's fine. "No" means "no". Okay?'

Dolly, who had had her ears pricked throughout this entire monologue, licked her mistress's face and jumped out of the car. She peed on the front lawn and trotted up to the front door expectantly.

The Dower House was one of Bella's favourites. A real brick and flint gem, with a gracious Georgian frontage, an in and out circular drive and an imposing porch. It took its style from the Manor House up the road. Although Zach was – technically – the Lord of the Manor, he had not, as far as Bella knew, ever lived in it. Instead, The Dower House was his home and his grandmother had raised him herself.

'Bella!' he said, opening the door. He was unshaven and barefoot. He gave her a hug, kissed her on both cheeks and showed her through the wide, flag-stoned hallway through to the back of the house. 'Shall we chuck Dolly into the garden? Brutus is already there. We can keep an eye on them through the kitchen window while I get you a coffee.'

'Should we be watching?' Bella asked, resisting the urge to peek through her fingers as the two dogs cavorted delightedly around the lawn.

'I don't entirely trust him to know which end he's supposed to be working on,' admitted Zach. 'Best to be sure he's actually done the deed. Don't want some random neighbourhood bad boy getting in there first. God knows what you'd end up with.'

Bella thought fleetingly of Rufus. Was he the random neighbourhood bad boy? She quelled the thought hastily.

'I've explained to Dolly she doesn't have to do anything she doesn't want to,' she said, turning her attention back to the matter in hand. 'She shouldn't feel she can't say "no".'

'Can't say "no"?' laughed Zach, pointing. 'Have you ever seen a dog trying quite so hard to say "yes"?'

Dolly was standing with her backside inches from Brutus's face. She had her tail pulled to one side and had her head turned towards him with an eye-rolling, tongue-lolling look of invitation.

'Dolly!' said Bella, in shock. 'You brazen hussy . . .'

Brutus was looking bemused.

Zach laughed. 'This is his first cover. I don't think his talents lie in the direction of top stud dog. In fact,' he sighed, 'I'm not sure where his talents lie, to be honest.'

They both watched, Bella barely able to look, as it seemed so intrusive to stare.

'Thank goodness for that,' said Zach, as Brutus, suddenly realising what was expected of him, mounted Dolly and did the business. It didn't take long.

'Is that it?' said Bella.

'Sorry,' said Zach. 'I apologise on my dog's behalf for the indecent haste. Please don't tar me with the same brush.'

'I mean . . . will that do it?'

'Should do,' said Zach. 'Unless you think we should go out and offer them a cigarette? Fingers crossed, we're talking puppies by the beginning of July, give or take.'

Dolly, looking thoroughly pleased with herself, settled happily on the blanket in the boot of Bella's car and yawned.

'You have a rest, cross your legs and think positive thoughts,' instructed Bella. 'Now for Caroline. Goodness, I should make a career of this.'

CHAPTER TEN

Bella had to stoop to get through the door of the bookshop. Inside was a series of low, interconnecting rooms, heavily beamed, with bookshelves lining the walls. There was a comfortingly familiar smell of dust along with a heavy hint of mildew.

'Hello there,' came a gentle voice. Bella spun around to see an old gentleman standing at her elbow. He was wearing a saggy old tweed jacket with leather patches on the sleeves. It looked ancient, but there was a freshly pressed silk handkerchief in the breast pocket and his outfit was further enhanced by a red-spotted bow tie.

'Are you looking for anything in particular?'

'Actually, I'm looking for a man,' said Bella.

'I see,' he replied. 'Well we don't have many of those in stock,' he said, pretending to look around. 'Is it for yourself? Only I can imagine you might be looking for someone younger – than me, I mean.'

'Oh, no,' said Bella quickly. 'Old is fine. I mean, I'm

looking on behalf of a lady who is also – erm – "older", so – you know – you'll do.'

He smiled, his eyes twinkling reassuringly.

'That's assuming you're available, that is,' Bella blundered on, peering at his left ring finger. Nothing.

'I am available,' he admitted, 'but perhaps you could tell me more about this lady's expectations?'

'Oh, nothing horrendous,' Bella assured him. 'Not, well, "that",' she said, an unwelcome image of Brutus and Dolly less than an hour earlier flashing into her mind. 'She's lovely. She's called Caroline, did I say?' The man shook his head, still smiling. 'And she just needs someone to take her to the May Ball on Saturday.'

'"Caroline", you say?'

Bella nodded. 'Sorry, I really haven't done her justice. But do say you will? Her husband died three years ago, and she hasn't come since. To the May Ball, that is. Here, let me give you her details . . .' Bella scribbled hurriedly on the back of her shopping list and handed over the scrap of paper.

He examined it carefully, holding it away from him and peering through the bottoms of his spectacles before folding the paper neatly and stowing it in his breast pocket. 'Do please tell the lady I would be delighted,' he said, 'and that, if she will do me the honour, I will collect her at seven o'clock to escort her to the ball myself. Although I can't promise a pumpkin coach, I'm afraid.'

'Phew,' said Bella. 'Thank you so much – you know, that's the second beautiful relationship I've knocked off this morning. I'm on fire!'

'Indeed you are,' he said, amused. 'And my name is Geoffrey, by the way. You had better let her know that about me, at least. The rest can remain a mystery for now. It will give us both something to talk about.'

Bella – pink from the hottest shower she could wrangle out of the ancient boiler – wriggled into her new green dress and looked at herself appraisingly in the mirror. She could see a bulge of flesh spilling out of the back, above her bra. Surely that hadn't been there when she tried it on in the shop? She wriggled a little more and yanked up her bra strap. Better. Perhaps she should wear a cardigan. Or a shawl. Or a burqa.

'New dress?' said Charlie, peering over her shoulder so he could see in the mirror to do up his bow tie. She could never resist him in a dinner jacket.

'Hmm,' she said vaguely. 'You look hot,' she added, turning and snuggling up, but he side-stepped deftly.

'Running late,' he said. 'Are you nearly ready, mate?'

'I need to do my face.'

'Oh fine, I'll go and start the car, then.'

Bella supposed she ought to be flattered that he thought it would be such a quick job. Refusing to be rushed, she concentrated on getting her make-up just right. That way perhaps people wouldn't notice that there was a little too much of her from the neck down.

A haircut might have been a good idea but Bella had had neither the time nor the money to do anything about it and it was too late now. She used pins and grips to pull it simply and severely away from her face. Rufus had liked it like that. With the heavily made-up eyes and her body-conscious green dress, she looked dramatic. And a little dangerous.

The beeping of the horn was getting more insistent and, by the time she ran out to the car, teetering on her heels, little clutch bag in hand, Charlie was tight-lipped and tapping impatiently on the wheel. He spun his little car across the gravel as he turned and sped out of the gate without a word.

Bella was on the lookout for Caroline and Geoffrey and was relieved when she saw them both at the other side of the reception hall. Caroline was looking glamorous in a full-skirted electric-blue ball gown with her hair blow-dried and with more make-up than Bella had seen her wear for a long time. She was also sporting some major jewellery.

'Are those real?' she whispered to Charlie, pointing at the sapphire necklace and earrings her mother-in-law was wearing. Even from a distance they were stunning.

'Yeah,' said Charlie without interest. 'Passed down from my mother's side of the family, I think. They spend the majority of the time in the safe, needless to say,' he said. 'She should probably have an armed guard.'

'They are amazing,' breathed Bella.

'Glad you like them. They'll be yours one day.'

'We would probably end up selling them, wouldn't we?' she said, with a trace of wistfulness.

'Yeah,' Charlie admitted. 'I'm surprised Dad didn't, actually . . .'

A horrifying thought suddenly occurred to her. 'You don't suppose Geoffrey is a gold-digger, do you?'

'Didn't you check?'

'Is there a test?'

They both looked at him appraisingly. He was several inches taller than Caroline and was hovering at her elbow, stooping to hear what she was saying. His ancient dinner jacket was slightly green and shiny but his hair was impeccably cut and swept back, his face close-shaved.

'He looks very dapper,' she said. 'I think he trims his ear hair. I definitely noticed that when I met him. And his nose.'

'Good,' said Charlie, whose own grooming routine was resolutely minimal. 'Definitely gay, then.'

'Aha,' came a voice, an arm simultaneously thumping down around Charlie's shoulders. 'My newest and shiniest business investment.'

'Rufus! Mate!' said Charlie, stifling a wince. 'How're you doing?'

Bella smiled politely as the two men greeted each other with the series of back and arm slaps that seemed to have replaced the simple handshake nowadays but always left her amazed that men were not permanently bruised. It used to amuse her that Charlie even went a bit cockney during these encounters, in betrayal of his public school past. Now she thought it might be a bit annoying . . .

Seeing Rufus again up close without warning had made her heart pound so hard she realised she was rocking slightly on her feet. It was like the rest of the room had faded away, leaving her in a state of hyper-alert watching the two men together. The opportunity to compare left Bella unable to deny Charlie's poor state. His hair needed cutting, his eyes were puffy from lack of sleep and too much drink, and his ancient dinner jacket was shiny in the unforgiving overhead light. There was no denying Rufus wore a dinner jacket well, though. Money talked. It was impeccably cut, and narrow, emphasising his sleek torso and wide, athletic shoulders. Unlike his daytime suits, the styling was strictly traditional, with three buttons at the cuffs and satin lapels.

'You look nice,' she blurted, when he turned to her.

'You're looking rather edible yourself,' he murmured in her ear, under cover of kissing her formally on both cheeks. 'In fact, I could definitely eat you. Just like I did last time. Remember?'

Her cheeks flamed.

'And you know Sophia, of course,' he went on, without missing a beat, taking Sophia's hand and drawing her to him so he could slip an arm around her waist. 'Charlie? I want you to meet Sophia, she's my right-hand woman. If you ever need anything from me, you give her a call, night and day . . . Sophia, darling, would you?'

Sophia was wearing an austere grey sheath dress, which showed off her slender beauty to perfection. She slipped a matt black business card from her tiny clutch bag and held it out to Charlie with a smile. 'Any time,' she said.

'So,' said Charlie when they found their seats, 'is she sleeping with him do you reckon?'

'I assume so – I mean she's beautiful and she does everything he tells her . . .'

110

'She's a class act,' said Charlie, finding himself relieved to hear Rufus wasn't roaming around looking for a woman. His woman, perhaps.

'Is he the business angel bloke, then?' said Ben, joining them, and shaking out his napkin. 'Hello, darling, by the way,' he added to Bella, but she was already lost in conversation with Maddy and had barely noticed him arrive.

'That's him,' said Charlie. 'The one with my balls in the palm of his hand.'

'Let's hope he's a nice bloke then, eh?' Ben looked thoughtful. 'I feel like I know him.'

'Yeah, I got that feeling too. He's a bit famous, apparently. At least, that's what Bella says. Tells me I should have heard of him.'

'That'll be it, then,' said Ben, taking a slurp of this beer. He had brought Charlie a pint as well, without being asked. 'I never know anyone, but the girls are always right about that sort of thing.'

'They're always right about every sort of thing. How's Maddy?'

'Doing too much. Loving it, though. I don't have the heart to stop her.'

'Bells wants one. A baby.'

'Then give her one,' he said to Charlie, seriously. 'In the best possible way,' he added in Bella's direction, making an apologetic face as – hearing her name – she turned towards them.

The noise levels were rising as they all tucked into their starter, which claimed to be pork liver terrine with red

111

onion chutney, but could have been anything, including Pedigree Chum.

Bella was in conversation with Maddy and Ben had wandered off again so Charlie looked around him as he forked in his food. He didn't much care about what it tasted like. It was fuel, and he had had no time for lunch again. There was that blonde, he noticed. She was the hard-faced events management woman he had met a few months ago. He had approached the hotel company who leased Havenbury Manor about serving Dovecot Estate wines and she had granted him a meeting but then, after turning up late for it, blanked him completely. That was an hour of his life he wouldn't get back again, he remembered sourly. She was clearly much more enamoured with Zach, though. She was simpering beside him in the doorway to the banqueting hall, fluttering her eyelashes and repeatedly putting her hand on his arm to make a point. Zach was being polite enough but, when her attention was diverted, he rolled his eyes at Charlie pleadingly, who just laughed and saluted him with his glass. Zach would do the same if the tables were turned. He could sweat.

Charlie had drained his pint, although Ben had barely touched his. He reached for the wine in the centre of the table and looked at the label. Typical. It was a filthy Chilean white, retailing for pence above what the duty to import it would have cost. He glugged some into his wine glass and gulped down half of it, wincing, before topping up his glass again. Booze was booze at the end of the day. He might be passionate about his own wine, but he was past caring what he put into his own body. The effect was what mattered, just something to dull the constant, gnawing anxiety, to slow the frantic, churning of his brain . . . he glanced at his phone again.

'Must you?' said Bella. 'You can't be expecting a call, surely?'

'There might be frost tonight,' he replied, shortly, holding up the phone to show the local forecast on his screen. The temperature was zero degrees.

'Ah,' said Bella.

'You are so English,' said Maddy. 'Only the British bang on about the weather . . . can't we talk about sex, politics or religion instead? I vote for sex, personally.'

'It's the vines,' explained Bella. 'They're just coming into leaf. A hard frost will kill off the shoots and buds. They won't recover this year and the harvest will be poor to non-existent.'

'Ah,' said Maddy. 'No wonder you look so serious, Charlie. What can you do?'

'Not as much as I would like,' said Charlie. 'There are some desperate measures people take. Whether they work or not . . . if the temperature goes below minus two then the vines near the base of the valley are the ones that will be most badly damaged. The cold air rolls downhill and pools . . .'

'There must be something?'

Charlie shook his head, wearily. 'Another vineyard I know lit night lights in jars every few feet.'

'Can't have done much, surely?' queried Maddy.

'Doesn't have to do much,' said Charlie. 'Just enough to slightly raise the ground temperature and break up the cold air, even by one degree . . .'

113

'Can you do that?'

He shook his head.

Bella put her hand on his arm. 'What about the gas heaters we used in the marquee when we got married,' she said. 'They're still in the barn, aren't they?'

'Think so,' said Charlie. 'What are you plotting?'

'Well, even if you loaded them onto the tractor and blasted them out up and down the rows, wouldn't that help?'

'Mm,' he said, doubtfully. 'Hopefully we won't have to put the theory to the test,' he said, looking at his phone again. Still zero degrees. That was all right, just about . . . the panic came when it dropped to minus two. Providing it hadn't already.

'I wouldn't mind getting back to the farm,' he said, fretfully. 'I could check the thermometer. God knows how accurate these forecasts actually are . . .'

'Stay,' pleaded Bella. 'This is our first night out for months. At least have dinner and have a dance or two?' Her guilt and Rufus's disturbing presence across the room had made her pine for Charlie's reassuring touch. If he just held her in his arms, on the dance floor, she could convince herself they were okay, the two of them . . .

'You know I don't dance,' he said dismissively, turning away as the waitress approached with the main course. It was a morose-looking hump of something swathed in glutinous yellow sauce. Chicken breast, probably.

Charlie tucked straight in as Bella poked the contents of her plate dubiously.

'I don't know how they get away with it,' she said. At least if she passed on the main course she might be able to weigh herself tomorrow morning. That was something she had been avoiding doing recently.

'I'll have yours,' said Charlie. 'Go and see how my mum's getting on with her fancy man.'

'You're a dustbin,' she said, pushing her plate towards him.

'Hallo, darling,' said Caroline, patting the empty seat next to her. 'Come and have a chat with me and Geoffrey. He was just telling me about his national service. D'you know it actually turns out he and Peter might have trained together?'

'I really am that old,' joked Geoffrey, 'although we were pretty much the last to do it. Your mother-in-law is being awfully patient, listening to my boring old tales.'

'And we have so much else in common,' Caroline gushed. 'Geoffrey is a rhododendron lover too . . .'

'. . . so I've managed to persuade Caroline to let me take her to the gardens at Bignor next week. I can't believe she's never managed to see the azaleas there, and of course this is the time of year to go. It's nothing grand, but the cafe does a decent lunch.'

'Talking of things blooming,' remembered Caroline, 'I've not been up to the vineyard this week, what with all the rain. How are they getting on? Is the blossom out?'

'I bet that's quite a show,' said Geoffrey.

'Not really,' explained Caroline. 'The actual flowers on grapevines are tiny. Little spiky blooms you would barely notice. But you must come up and see. It was Peter's greatest joy, the vineyard . . .' She looked momentarily sad, 'and Geoffrey was quite the hero this evening when he came to collect me,' she declared.

'He was?' said Bella.

'I hardly think waving a crowbar around like a navvy gets me an OBE,' he demurred.

'What on earth were you using a crowbar on?'

'He was getting these out for me,' explained Caroline, putting her hand on the jewels around her neck. 'Ridiculously, I couldn't get the safe open. I could have sworn I knew the code but clearly I didn't. It's been ages since I've been in there.'

'I was just saying to Charlie how lovely you looked in them. I don't know why you don't wear them more often,' said Bella.

'I'll make sure I never put the rubbish out again without putting them on,' joked Caroline.

'So anyway,' said Geoffrey ruefully, 'the safe is now not what it was – to put it mildly . . . I must bring you a new one.'

'Absolutely not,' said Caroline, putting her hand on his arm. 'While you were starting the car I had a fiddle and I've managed to lock it with the key. It's just a bit bent but it works fine.'

'Erm . . .' said Bella. 'If you had a key, why didn't you use it when you couldn't remember the code?'

'Ah, well,' admitted Caroline, 'I was keeping it in a very safe place.'

'In the safe?' joked Geoffrey, but then saw Caroline blush. 'Of course, you kept it in the safe,' he added quickly. 'I'd have done the same, but still, all sorted now, eh? May I have this dance?' he added, holding out his arm in invitation.

God I'm good, Bella told herself as she watched them go before looking around the room to see whose life she could transform next – but only once she had had a wee.

Coming out of the loos she jumped as someone grabbed her arm.

'Rufus,' she squeaked.

'Come with me,' he said, powering her through the door into the room they had their drinks reception. Now practically in darkness, it was empty, other than a waitress clearing the last of the glasses at the other end. He glared at her until she scuttled away.

'You look amazing,' he said, spinning her around to face him and looking hungrily up and down her. 'God I love that dress.'

'You've already told me that,' she said, crossing her arms.

'I bet Charlie hasn't, though. He hasn't, has he?'

He laughed mirthlessly when she didn't reply.

'Didn't think so. He doesn't appreciate what he has. Takes his possessions for granted. Always has, always will. It all just falls into his lap – handsome old, happy-go-lucky Charlie Wellbeloved . . .'

He was slurring his words a little. She had never seen him drunk before. She looked nervously at the door and blinked. 'Is there anything I can help you with?' she said.

'Yeah,' he said, pulling her towards him and grabbing her hand. 'You can help me with this.' He placed her hand on his crotch and moved in for a kiss on the mouth, clashing his teeth against hers.

For a moment, shocked, she succumbed. Just as she

began to pull away, the door behind her crashed open.

'Caroline!' she squeaked.

'Just wondering if I left my shawl,' said Caroline, breezing in as if nothing had happened. 'I could have sworn . . . ah yes, here it is,' she said, grabbing it off the top of a stack of chairs where someone had carefully folded and placed it. 'I'll leave you two young people to it,' she said, but her eyes met Bella's and widened, questioningly.

'Shit,' said Rufus, tucking his shirt in and straightening his bow tie. 'Your mother-in-law?'

She nodded, numbly.

'Shit. Look, Bells, I'm sorry. Got a bit carried away.'

'Charlie's the only one who calls me "Bells".'

'Yeah? Well . . . tell him from me, he's a lucky man.'

CHAPTER ELEVEN

Bella retreated to the ladies again and locked herself into the nearest free cubicle.

'Shit,' she muttered, her head in her hands. 'Shit, shit, shit . . .' She needed to find her. To explain. Only that was the problem, wasn't it? How on earth could she explain this? Bad enough that she was kissing a man who wasn't Caroline's dear son, now she had to decide whether it was worse to confess she was a prostitute or an adultress.

She came out of the cubicle and stood at the mirror breathing deeply. Her lipstick was smeared and her mascara had run a little. She tidied up her face, but nothing could disguise the pallor. She ladled on some blusher, but it just made her look like she was running a fever. She rubbed it off again.

'Feeling a bit sick?' said Maddy, looming up behind her. 'Too much to drink? I told you that Prosecco would rot your stomach . . . Me? My body is a temple, obviously. Until the baby's born anyhow.'

'Fine,' said Bella, faintly. 'I'm fine . . .'

Maddy gave her a searching look. 'No, you're not. Tell me.'

'A bomb's just gone off,' Bella said. 'Caroline knows.'

Maddy's face fell. 'You're going to have to tell Charlie.'

'What? The bit about cheating on him or the bit about doing it for money?'

'Everything.'

Bella took a deep breath, steadied herself on the edge of the basin and looked herself in the eye. 'Right,' she said.

Caroline was waiting outside the ladies' loos.

'I need to explain,' said Bella.

'I know,' replied Caroline, 'but not to me, to Charlie.'

'Yeah,' Bella almost smiled. 'I've had that suggestion already. Can't we just . . . ?'

'No,' said Caroline. 'That would be worse. Trust me.'

'It's actually not what it seems,' said Bella, desperately. She hated seeing the older woman's disapproval – worse – her disappointment.

'It never is,' said Caroline with a weary resignation Bella had never seen before. 'But the truth is best, believe me.'

Bella walked back to the ballroom on stiff legs that didn't feel like they belonged to her. She couldn't see Charlie at first. People had finished dinner and were milling around, socialising, drifting towards the dance floor, which was already filling with the more enthusiastic and well-oiled guests.

Then, the crowd cleared. He was sitting at their table, alone, drinking coffee and looking at his phone. As if he heard her approach, he looked up, watching her as she walked towards him.

She tried to smile, but she could feel her mouth was

only curving up on one side. It was as if she was seeing him clearly for the first time in weeks. He had untied his bow tie, which hung loosely around his neck, and his dinner jacket was unbuttoned. There were deep dark circles etched under his eyes and – unlike Bella – he had lost weight since their wedding, leaving him gaunt and drawn. The hard work and the worry had already taken their toll. And now she was going to break the one thing he had left intact. Their marriage.

'I like that dress,' he said, too late, reaching for her hand as she arrived next to him. He was having to shout now the band had started up again.

'Come outside,' she mouthed to him, holding onto his hand and pulling him towards the door.

'What's up?' he asked, as they got outside, the blast of cold evening air making her shudder.

He slipped off his jacket and wrapped it around her shoulders. His sudden body warmth from the jacket made her shudder again, violently.

'Charlie,' she said. It came out a bit too emphatically.

'Bella,' he replied, equally forcefully, but then his smile faded. 'What?'

'I . . .' she faltered. 'I've got something really awful to tell you,' she said, dropping her eyes to stare at his feet.

'Go on?'

'I slept with Rufus,' she blurted to his shoes before dragging her eyes back up to look at him.

His eyes were narrowed, his mouth straightening to a line, either in pain, anger or a mixture of both.

'Did you?'

'Yes. But it was for you.'

'What the—'

'I did it because we needed the money.'

'We needed . . . ?'

Despair and desperation made her bold. 'I did it so he would give us the loan. He said—'

'Sorry, no, hang on,' Charlie held up a hand to silence her. He took a deep breath. 'Okay, start again, what could he possibly have said . . . ?'

'He said,' continued Bella in a small voice, 'that me sleeping with him was a condition of his making the loan to save the farm. "Just one night" he told me. It was supposed to be a secret but now he wants more . . . and your mother saw us. I didn't want you to know. I'm so, so sorry . . . He said I had to—'

Charlie interrupted. 'You are seriously telling me that, barely three years after we took our vows, you decided it would be a good idea to randomly sleep with some bloke because he said you "had to"?'

He reeled away from her, his hands clutched to his head. 'And you didn't think that it might be something you should – I dunno – mention to me in passing?'

'You would have said "no".'

'Damned right I would.'

'And then we wouldn't have had the money.'

'I'm not keeping it.'

'Then I did it for nothing.'

Charlie's phone beeped. He continued staring at her incredulously as he got it out of his pocket, breaking eye contact only to look at the weather forecast on the screen.

'We're going home,' he said, slipping it into his pocket, and grabbing her arm. It wasn't violence, but he was less gentle than he had ever been before with her, and tears sprang to her eyes.

In the Land Rover he stared grimly ahead.

'Is it freezing?' Bella asked, with a quiver in her voice.

Charlie nodded. 'It can't freeze,' he said. It was almost as if she wasn't there. 'We have to stop it.'

'How?'

'The gas heaters in the barn. I'll put them on the tractor.'

'Will it work?'

'I don't know.'

Back at the farm, she watched, shivering, as he grimly hauled the four gas heaters out of the barn. They were covered in dust and cobwebs. He heaved them onto the back of the tractor, arranging them so they were facing outwards.

'Wait,' she whispered, as he strode away from her to get the tractor key.

'Wait,' she said again, louder. She could feel her heart pumping like it would burst. Her pulse was throbbing in her neck. He turned.

'Are we all right?' she said, tears brimming in her eyes. 'Us?'

'*You* wait,' he said. And with that he walked off and left her shivering by the barn, his jacket still around her shoulders, all his body warmth from it now gone. Shuddering with cold and nerves she let herself into the house, grateful for the warmth of the Rayburn in the kitchen. She huddled in front of it and comforted Dolly who, frowsy with sleep, was weaving her fat little body between Bella and the stove in an attempt to get closer to her than was humanly – or caninely – possible.

She slid down to the floor, with her back to the stove, oblivious to the marks that were doubtless now all over her new emerald dress, and persuaded Dolly to curl up in her lap. This she did with much groaning, overflowing onto the floor in both directions with her head tucked into Bella's armpit for security. And then Bella sat, gazing sightlessly at the kitchen clock as it ticked away the hours of the night. One o'clock. Two o'clock. Three o'clock. She waited.

Charlie's dinner shirt was no protection against the penetrating cold. The sky was clear and the stars were exceptionally bright, their white light penetrating the velvet curtain of the night in a dazzling show. He was impervious, his eyes set on the line he must follow, directly between the rows of vines, not deviating an inch to right or left for fear of damaging the delicate buds he was trying so desperately to save. The blossom, not yet pollinated, the young, green shoots, burgeoning from the branches, so tender and delicate, all potentially blacked and destroyed by the evil pall of frost. Going towards the bottom of the valley, where the Meunier grapes were planted, Charlie could see a ghostly cloud of frozen air rolling across the valley floor. He plodded resolutely, his tractor growling its way implacably between the rows, the heaters blasting away the ice, not too hot or they themselves would wither the vines, but just enough to lift the heavy cold blanket of air away from the branches. When dawn came, and the sun reappeared in the clear sky, the danger would be past. In a week's time, the wind would have pollinated the vines and the tender, green leaves would have grown and toughened and the harvest would be safe.

Would he still have a marriage by then? Charlie's mind swirled like the mist amongst the vines. He had thought that he and Bella were a team. Amongst all the other challenges, the debt, the poor harvest, the sheer physical task of keeping the vineyard off its knees, he had relied on his marriage to Bella like a touchstone. But all this time, due to his own neglect and complacency, the bonds between them had been weakening. He saw that now. The world had shifted on its axis. And then – when this bizarre and outrageous proposal had been made – she had accepted it without a word because she had already drifted a million miles away from him. As dawn broke, the way forward became clear.

Bella must have slept because when Charlie came through the kitchen door, she awoke with a start, Dolly scrambling sleepily off her lap as she got to her feet, rubbing her tear-stained face and looking again at the clock. It was nearly half past five.

Charlie's face was expressionless.

Her stomach flipped. He didn't speak, just gazed at her stone-faced.

'What shall we do?' she whispered, her mouth trembling.

'You have to go.'

A tear gathered and spilt over, tumbling down Bella's cheek and dripping off her chin.

'Charlie . . .'

'You need to go,' he went on. 'Now.' At that, he turned away wearily, and she heard him climbing the stairs, going into the bathroom and closing the door. He never closed the door. She even heard the lock snick into place. The finality of that sound told her everything she needed to know.

Clutching his dinner jacket around her shoulders, she rubbed away the most recent tears, took her car keys from the peg and left, pushing Dolly away, persuading the little dog to stay. She couldn't be responsible for her now. She was barely able to be responsible for herself.

It was comforting being in her car. She took some deep breaths and let herself be soothed by the sound of the engine, the familiarity of the actions, the warmth from the heater on full blast.

She drove on autopilot. There was little traffic. She went through the outskirts of Havenbury Magna, passing the narrow mud track that led to Ben and Maddy's house, imagining them fast asleep in each other's arms, up the steep high street, all closed up and blind-eyed, and then back out into the countryside. She slowed as she drove past The Dower House in Little Havenbury – she didn't know Zach well enough to drag him in and, in any case, what if she knocked on his door? She could imagine him coming to answer it, unshaven, bleary with sleep . . . what would she say? Would he welcome her in? Cook her breakfast? She doubted it. Instead she drove on, out of the village and up into the Downs, through farmland with its stunning views over the valley right down to the sea, before finding herself pulling up outside The Grange, spraying gravel as she went. She yanked on the handbrake and slumped forward, turning her head to one side and resting it on the steering wheel, gazing blearily out at the building site. The watery dawn light caught the rippled glass of the Georgian windows making them wink at her invitingly, deceitfully, because the building was empty and devoid of human warmth.

She closed her eyes. A tear leaked out and ran down her chin.

'Bella!'

She started violently, just as the car door was wrenched open, a blast of freezing air waking her more thoroughly than if he had chucked a bucket of cold water over her.

'What the hell . . . ?'

'Rufus,' she croaked.

They looked at each other, Bella seeing her shock echoed in his own face, and then she dropped her eyes. God she must look a state.

'Heavy night?'

'Charlie knows,' she said, still staring at her own lap, at the emerald dress, now crumpled and stained. She hadn't noticed until now how short it was. She pulled it down, ineffectually, over her thighs.

'Of course. Shit. I'm sorry,' he said grimly, holding out his hand.

Obediently she tried to undo her seat belt and get out, but the complexity of the operation eluded her. Seeing her fumbling he leant in and freed her.

She looked up at him and then he grinned. 'So, he knows, does he?'

She nodded.

'And he's thrown you out?'

She nodded again.

'In that case, you had better come back with me.'

CHAPTER TWELVE

Neither of them spoke as he drove, too fast, hugging the road in his low-slung, grey sports car. She stole a glance at his profile. He looked relaxed she noticed with surprise – happy, even, unmoved by her distress other than a mild impatience at her slowness of thought and movement. He was in his jogging clothes, his taut abdomen clearly apparent below a high-tech windproof zip-up top.

'Let's get you cleaned up,' he said, almost as if he was talking to himself, as they pulled suddenly through a gap in the hedge and drew to a halt outside an ultra-modern house that Bella had never noticed before. Sleek and low, like his car, the panes of darkened glass stretched the whole length of the one-storey building, topped with a floating roof clad in zinc or lead, Bella didn't know the difference. But, like everything else in Rufus's life it looked new, uncompromising and expensive.

She got out of the car, straightening her spine slowly like an old lady. She followed Rufus inside the building, noticing there was no front door key, just a pad, which he pressed his thumb onto to gain entry.

'Biometrics,' he said, briefly, over his shoulder. 'I'm thinking of using the same system for members at The Grange.'

'Access all areas,' said Bella, giggling weakly.

He turned and gave her a piercing look. 'I wouldn't mind "accessing all areas" of you,' he said. 'Seeing as Charlie has been silly enough to let you go.'

She blushed and hung her head. After the stress of waiting for Charlie to come back in and pronounce on the fate of their marriage she suspected her breath was sour and she smelt of sweat. 'I've left my bag behind,' she blurted, breathlessly. 'In my car . . .'

'You don't need it. You're here now. Follow me.'

He took her down a narrow, slate-floored corridor and, as she followed him into the room at the back she couldn't help gasping. The room, which ran the width of the house, was entirely glazed on the opposite side, a forty-foot-long span overlooking the most stunning view Bella had ever seen. From the top of the Downs, into the valley with Havenbury Magna nestling at its feet, and across the coastal plain to the silvery expanse of the sea.

'Good, eh?' said Rufus, wrapping his arms around her waist from behind.

'Is it yours?'

'Rented,' he said. 'Do you like it?'

'Of course, I do,' she said, wriggling away but pretending it was to look at a wooden bowl set onto an immense glass coffee table.

'Then I'll buy it,' he said. 'That's by a local artist,' he

added coming to stand beside her. 'I'll introduce you.'

'It's amazing,' she said, trying hard not to open her mouth too much, conscious of her stale breath.

'Time for all this later,' he said, walking her towards a staircase at the far end of the room, which led, not upstairs but down to a lower floor.

'Built into the side of the hill,' he explained over his shoulder as she followed him down. 'Clever architect. Made good design sense to have the bedrooms downstairs.'

Bella closed the bathroom door with relief. After a long, steaming hot shower her aching limbs grew so heavy she could barely raise her arms to wrap the towel around her. Rufus had found her a new toothbrush but all she could do with her face was wash off the remainder of the make-up she had applied so carefully the night before. Was it really only twelve hours ago she and Charlie had been at the ball, laughing and chatting with their friends?

She came shyly out of the bathroom to find he had laid out a grey tracksuit for her, so she put her bra and pants back on and climbed gratefully into it, leaving her now limp and grubby green dress on top of the laundry basket.

Rufus was solicitous but distantly polite. Despite it being Sunday, he was working, his papers spread all over the glass coffee table. He waved Bella towards croissants and coffee, laid out in the kitchen but – she noticed – he ate very little himself, instead drinking endless cups of black coffee. In contrast to his ardour earlier, he seemed in an increasingly black mood.

'The damage to the vines last night,' he asked Bella. 'What does that mean for yields?'

'I don't know,' she admitted. 'Charlie will . . .' she swallowed back sudden tears, '. . . Charlie will be able to assess the damage today and over the next couple of days. The yield will be cut, certainly, but there will be more buds later in the spring. Fewer and not so productive but . . .' She shrugged. 'It's happened before.'

Rufus looked thunderous.

'It happens,' said Bella again, holding out her hands in an attitude of pleading, her heart hammering in her chest. 'It's a side of the business we accept, being in England.' She paused, nervously. 'Will you withdraw your investment?'

She watched him visibly suppress his rage, before turning to her, a forced smile on his face. 'I can't,' he said. His smile broadened but didn't reach his eyes. 'Of course, I won't. I wouldn't do that. Like you said, it happens.' He held out a hand, but it was like a cat seducing a canary. 'Come here,' he said. 'Read the papers and relax.'

Bella curled up in a ball on the opposite end of the sofa and picked up the colour supplement. She flicked the pages, but the words and pictures blurred before her eyes. Defeated, she chucked it back onto the coffee table and laid her head back, wearily.

Rufus threw down the file of papers he was reading and edged nearer to her. 'It wasn't you I intended to . . .' he began and then stopped himself. 'I mean . . . I'm sorry this has happened – you and Charlie . . . You've been caught in the crossfire, I'm afraid. That's business.'

'Sounds more like a war.'

Rufus gave her a sharp look. 'I saw your wedding photo,' he went on, changing the subject. 'It was when Charlie showed me around. The two of you together . . . nice . . . You've got fat since then, though.'

'Wow,' exclaimed Bella, sucking in her stomach self-consciously. 'Say it like it is, won't you?'

Rufus ignored her affront. 'Just saying. Charlie's looking bloody rough too in comparison to back then. He's drinking far too much and you're stuffing your face, for some reason that has nothing to do with physical hunger. You've porked out by about – what? – four stone?'

'Three, actually,' she said, defiantly.

'And the rest . . . what's the matter with you both? You've only been married a few years. You guys had big problems before I came along.'

Bella found her mouth was hanging open and closed it with a conscious effort. He was right, damn him.

'You've no right . . .' she started, her voice trembling. She stopped and tried again. 'You have no right to comment on other people's relationships,' she said, with an attempt at dignity.

'Okay, fine,' said Rufus, unmoved by her distress. 'But I need you to pull yourself together. The Grange needs to be perfect by September because I don't do mediocre. I don't do late and I don't do excuses. You're charging a pretty steep fee for your services and I'm impressed that you asked for it because it shows you've got balls. I'm happy to pay – don't get me wrong – but I need you at the top of your game. Like I said, baby, this is business.'

'You'll get your project done, I promise,' said Bella, sitting a little more upright. 'But my weight? That's personal. And you don't know how hard it is . . .' she muttered, appalled at how pathetic she sounded.

'I don't know how hard it is? Bullshit. I know everything about how hard it is. I know everything about pulling yourself together, getting yourself fit, presenting yourself to the world in a way that shouts "This is me, I'm a player and I'm not going to take any crap." Believe me . . .' he went on more quietly, 'I know.' He was silent for a moment. Bella looked up at him.

'How would you describe me?' he demanded. 'Come on, what do you see? Tell me.'

Bella swallowed. 'Erm, I see a successful businessman . . .' she faltered.

'Go on . . .'

'. . . who's determined, focused, discerning, expensively dressed . . . fit, obviously . . .' she blushed.

He allowed himself a little smirk at that and then relented.

'Okay, so here I am now, worlds away from the scrawny, ginger, whining kid who was always picked last for games, who got punched for being ginger and then punched again for crying because I'd been punched . . .' He stared into the distance, remembering. The sudden vulnerability made Bella want to throw her arms around him, but in a second the moment was gone, and the adult Rufus was back in charge. 'I've remade myself,' he said. 'I've found the best possible version of myself. You can do it too.'

'I can?'

'You will. With my help, if you'll let me?' His voice dropped.

She looked at him uncertainly. His eyes were soft, as he gazed at her, really looking, seeing her in a way Charlie had not seen her in a long time.

133

'Stay with me?' he went on, putting his arm around her and pulling her onto his chest. 'Be with me?'

Bella nodded.

The following morning, Rufus dropped her off and Bella nervously let herself into her car, which was still parked outside the Grange. She was still wearing Rufus's tracksuit and she was keen to get out of there before Paddy turned up, which would lead to too much explaining on her part and – she suspected – smirking on his. She was heading back to the farmhouse to get some stuff . . . get changed . . . she was counting on Charlie being out at the farm suppliers as he usually was on a Monday morning.

Her heart was in her mouth as she turned into the lane running behind the farmhouse to the little courtyard where they parked. His Land Rover was gone. She was barely aware she had been holding her breath but now she sighed shakily.

The kitchen door was unlocked as usual and there was Dolly, singing with relief that her mistress had returned, her tail wagging and her whole body snaking frantically from side to side as she pressed her head hard against Bella's legs. 'I'm so sorry, darling,' she said, crouching down and burying her head in Dolly's black, hairy neck. 'I'm back, it's fine . . . I'm fine . . .' she crooned, wiping away fresh tears on the little dog's fur.

Upstairs, she felt as nervous as a burglar, jumpy at the prospect of Charlie coming back and catching her. She dragged her overnight bag out of the wardrobe and stuffed it randomly – underwear, clothes, make-up from the dressing table . . . she went into the hideous bathroom and grabbed some bottles and her toothbrush. Her plans for renovation would have to wait now. Chances are they would never happen. Her legs felt heavy at the thought, the adrenaline draining out of her body and being replaced with the bleak, cold reality that she and Charlie would no longer be together here at Dovecot Farmhouse. She looked around her, the dreary decor suddenly seemingly exquisitely dear to her. It was home to her. Charlie was home.

Coming back down the stairs, encumbered with her bag and stymied by Dolly's determination to press herself against Bella's legs all the way down, she stood in the kitchen and regarded the dog doubtfully. Rufus had made it clear he was expecting Bella to be back with him tonight, but she hardly thought a dog was part of the bargain.

She opened the boot for the bags, but Dolly jumped in eagerly – clearly relieved not to be left again. Then, Bella had an idea.

Caroline was out in her tiny front garden, which was already verdant with the cottage garden flowers Bella had planted – hollyhocks, tulips, foxgloves and geraniums all jostling for space along with several rose bushes, a couple of which were already blooming.

'So, it's you, is it?' she said without her usual warmth, as Bella pulled up and got out of the car. Caroline took off her gardening gloves and tucked them into the front pocket of her apron. 'I was wondering when I'd get a visit,' she went on.

'Just hoping you might be up for a bit of dog-sitting?' mumbled Bella.

'Of course, I am,' said Caroline, giving Dolly a brief pat on the head as she careered towards her, thoroughly unsettled by all the emotional vibrations. 'No reason why the poor, innocent dog should suffer with all this ridiculous upset. Now,' she said to Dolly who was singing again, 'stop that silly noise and see what Ginger's up to. The both of you can go and have a play in the back garden. Ginger needs to run off a bit of energy too.'

As Ginger was Caroline's bad-tempered and elderly Jack Russell, who wasn't beyond giving Dolly a nip, Bella doubted he would be as keen on the plan as Caroline seemed to be suggesting. It was clear she wasn't going to escape without a conversation, so she allowed Dolly to be corralled into the back garden and then trailed inside the little cottage obediently.

Caroline said nothing as she put the kettle on the stove and pottered around the tiny kitchen, gathering mugs, a milk jug and a tin of her home-made almond macaroons, which Bella usually loved. This morning her stomach was churning too much to eat anything and Caroline's clear anger, so unusual for her, was distinctly unnerving.

'So,' Caroline said at last, handing Bella a mug of tea. 'How are you?'

It wasn't the question she was expecting and tears prickled at her eyes again.

'Not great, but how's Charlie?'

'Not great either.'

'You must be appalled at me,' said Bella, raising her eyes reluctantly, but saw only kindness and pity in the older woman's face.

'I'm angry with you both,' explained Caroline. 'I could bang your heads together . . . Charlie's told me – of course. I actually think you have been extraordinarily brave.'

Bella brightened.

'. . . as well as spectacularly stupid, naturally,' Caroline went on.

Bella slumped a little.

'I only wish . . .' the older woman said, wistfully.

'What?'

'I only wish Peter hadn't put you in this position.'

'How is it his fault?'

'It would hardly have happened if he hadn't left the farm in so much debt,' explained Caroline. 'I just didn't know how bad it had got. No wonder his heart gave out,' she said, sadly.

'Shame Charlie doesn't share your view.'

'His pride is hurt.'

'I betrayed him.'

'There are worse betrayals.'

'There are?'

Caroline gave her daughter-in-law a considering look. 'Sex is sex,' she said. 'Emotional betrayal? That's another thing entirely.'

Bella nodded.

'Charlie needs to get his head around it,' Caroline continued. 'He doesn't know it but mainly he is angry at himself. You did an incredibly loyal thing. At the moment, Charlie is blaming you for something he will eventually blame himself for. When he does, please don't give him reason to think he is too late to redeem the situation.'

'I think it might be already too late.'

'It isn't,' insisted Caroline. 'But you should stay away from Rufus. This is all his fault, remember. Believe me, that man's trouble.'

* * *

137

Maddy's reaction was in a similar vein.

'He's an evil tosser,' she said.

'You fancied him,' Bella reminded her.

'Yeah, but in a "bad boy", "not knowing what's good for you" kind of way.'

'Charlie chucked me out. At least Rufus is prepared to be in the same room as me.'

'Same bed as you, ideally. Come and stay with me and Ben.'

'Hardly . . .' said Bella, as Ben and Maddy lived in a one-bed wooden boathouse.

'We've got the sofa bed.'

'It's fine,' said Bella. 'You need your space.'

'Mum and Patrick would put you up at the pub if I asked.'

'Please don't!' said Bella, horrified. It would be like moving back in with her parents. 'I'll sort it out. Rufus is being really kind.'

'That man does nothing he doesn't want to do.'

'You hardly know him.'

'Neither do you.'

'Yeah, well . . .' Bella groaned with exhaustion. 'I've made my bed . . .'

'Shut up!' said Maddy, enraged. 'This is you and Charlie we're talking about here. The man you've been in love with since you were fifteen. The man you adore. The man you want to have your children with . . .'

'I know. I was there. But he doesn't want me,' said Bella, flatly. 'And anyway, he doesn't want us to have a baby.'

Maddy paused, her face working in dismay and frustration. 'I'm going to talk to Ben,' she said at last. 'He'll sort you both out.'

* * *

138

Rufus was annoyed when Bella told him she was going to Caroline for supper.

'You should have said,' he snapped. 'I've got some backers coming to look at The Grange. It would have been helpful to have your input – a rundown on the interior design aspect.'

'I'm sorry . . .'

He raised his eyes to heaven. 'Fine,' he said. 'I'll see you later.'

'I do really appreciate being able to stay here,' said Bella nervously. 'I should maybe sort something else out.'

'No. I want you here.'

He slipped his arms around her and held her tight. 'You're mine, remember . . .' He shifted his hands up and started sliding her top down over her shoulders, dropping a kiss onto the bare skin.

'I wanted to ask a favour too,' Bella said, keen to capitalise on the moment.

'Mm?'

'Do you think I could possibly have Dolly here?'

Rufus let go and stepped away, blank-faced. 'Sorry, no,' he said at once. 'I don't "do" dogs. Plus, don't forget, this is a rental. It's probably got a "no pets" rule.'

CHAPTER THIRTEEN

'What do you mean he doesn't "do" dogs?' said Caroline incredulously, reaching over to top up Bella's glass with another good couple of inches of white wine. 'I like this man less and less. Sorry . . .'

'I know,' said Bella, 'I sort of see his point, but it does leave me in a bit of a hole.'

'Not at all,' reassured Caroline, 'you know I'll keep her. She's good company for Ginger and also – I must confess – she's been spending quite a bit of time with Charlie. He came and got her last night, brought her back this morning.'

'That's good, I'm glad he's got company,' said Bella, blinking back a sudden and unexpected tear. 'How is he?'

'Not great,' said Caroline, bluntly. 'Now eat up your pie.'

Bella looked down at her plate, piled high with steak pie, mashed potato and peas. 'It's delicious, as always,' she said, spearing a piece of beef with her fork. 'Thank you so much. It's just that I seem not to have room in my tummy for some reason.'

'You're losing weight.'

'Yay, thank goodness for that,' said Bella, with a hollow laugh.

'Not "yay" at all,' admonished Caroline. 'Charlie's not eating, either. Just when I thought I was done with my mothering duties. You're a right pair,' she said. 'And, talking about mothering duties, I'm pretty sure Dolly's in an interesting condition too.'

'Are you?' said Bella, delightedly, reaching down to give Dolly an ear stroke. The dog thumped her tail appreciatively and then got up to bury her head in Bella's lap.

'She's clingy,' observed Caroline. 'That's a sign.'

'I'm glad you think it's that, and not – well – all this stuff with me and Charlie,' said Bella. 'So, puppies at the beginning of July, then. Fab! I just wish . . .'

'Talking of which,' said Caroline, 'I want you to know I am working on a "solution".'

'Go on . . . ?'

'Early days,' said Caroline tapping the side of her nose. 'I'll let you know when I need you to do something.'

Bella's spirits rose and suddenly she felt a bit more hungry.

'Tell me more about the lovely Geoffrey,' she said, with her mouth full. 'What happened when he brought you home from the ball. Did you . . . ?' she joked.

'Certainly not,' said Caroline. 'On a first date? What do you think I am? He was a perfect gentleman, of course. He saw me in and insisted on getting my jewellery back into the safe for me. Mind you, it's very safe indeed at the moment, because the door's jammed shut.'

'Oh dear!'

'It's fine, he's ordering a replacement and coming to fit it when it arrives.'

'So, you're seeing him again?'

'Already have.' Caroline gave a little secret smile at the thought. 'He's lonely,' she said, as if to herself. 'And so am I.'

'Of course.' Bella's eyes flooded with the easy tears that plagued her nowadays. 'I just don't think. It must be so hard without Peter.'

'It's fine,' said Caroline, bracing herself. 'Mostly it's fine. But Geoffrey is a nice, gentle man who makes me laugh. That's enough.'

'So where's he from?'

'Hasn't said.'

'Family?'

'Hasn't said that, either, other than mentioning a couple of grandchildren. Step-grandchildren I think, actually . . .' she admitted. 'I mean, I haven't interrogated him, obviously.'

'Did I do a good thing with my blind date, then?'

'You did,' said Caroline. 'Clever girl. Now eat up. I've got rhubarb fool for pudding.'

No one used the front door at Dovecot Farmhouse so now the self-seeded hollyhocks and foxgloves almost entirely obscured it from view. Ben went around to the back, as usual, but had to knock twice on the kitchen door. Normally he would have walked straight in – it wasn't locked – but this time he wasn't sure of his welcome. Dolly was definitely aware of his presence, though, stuffing her head through the cat flap to see who it was and singing with excitement when Ben bent down to tickle her ears.

'Get your head back in, you silly girl,' he said. 'You'll get it stuck and we'll have to call the fire brigade.'

Long after the second knock, Ben heard a door in the house slam followed by shuffling feet.

'Move, you daft dog,' growled Charlie, pushing her out of the way with his foot so he could open the door.

'Mate,' said Ben, coming in and clapping his old friend on the shoulder. He was shocked at Charlie's appearance. He was rumpled, red-eyed and puffy-faced, although Ben also noticed he had his belt tightened two notches more than before. There was a strong smell of stale sweat and dirty hair emanating from him, making Ben struggle not to recoil as he gave him a hug and a firm backslap – their normal greeting.

'Beer!' Charlie exclaimed, noticing that Ben was swinging a six-pack from his fingers. 'Good man.'

'Coals to Newcastle?' queried Ben, going through into the kitchen where he could see a tribe of beer cans covering most of the surfaces.

'Time for reinforcements, as it happens . . .' said Charlie, picking up a couple of empty cans and lobbing them in the direction of the kitchen bin which stood, lidless, in the corner. He missed but waved his arm dismissively, swaying on his feet as he did so.

'Looks like you've had enough already.'

'Absolutely not, old man,' insisted Charlie, opening two of the new cans and handing one to his friend. 'Not nearly enough yet. Sit.'

It was an order.

Ben drew up a chair at the kitchen table, which was sticky with spills and crumbs. Wondering if Charlie was eating anything at all or just surviving on the calories in beer, he took a look around. There was some evidence of cooking, with a greasy oven tray floating in a pool of grey washing-up water and the remains of some baked beans in a saucepan dumped on the worktop. They had both been there for a while. The smell of neglect was stronger in here – an unhealthy combination of damp, dirt and drink, a transformation from the haven of baking smells and fresh flowers, which had been the norm before.

'So,' said Ben, clearing his throat. 'How've you been?'

'Did Maddy send you?'

'Of course. She's worried about you. We all are.'

'Do you know what she did?'

'What who did? Maddy or Bella?'

'Do you know?' Charlie raised his voice.

Ben nodded.

'What would you do if you were me?' said Charlie. It was clearly a rhetorical question, but Ben considered it carefully. 'I don't know what I would do, but I think I know how I would feel.'

Charlie grunted, but he waited for more, so – encouraged – Ben continued; 'I think, if Maddy slept with another man, I'd be devastated . . .'

Charlie nodded fiercely, tears springing to his eyes, which he brushed away angrily. He made to speak but Ben held up his hand for permission to continue.

'And then,' he said, 'after the devastation and betrayal and the humiliation, I like to think I would want to find out why. In this case, I would discover she did it to help me and that,' he said, looking sympathetically at his friend, 'would make me feel practically every emotion there is . . . gratitude, shame, confusion, anger – I think it would probably make me feel like I was going insane,' he added, quietly.

Seconds passed and Ben took a swig of beer, gazing out of the window to give his friend time to process what he had just heard.

When he looked back, he saw that Charlie was silently crying, tears running off his chin onto the kitchen table as he sat, motionless.

'That's better,' said Ben. 'Better than just drowning it in alcohol, mate. Feel it. Then we can fix it.'

Charlie shook his head in despair. 'How can we fix this? I chucked her out. That was unforgivable . . .'

'Then get her back.'

'Slightly complicated now, mate. I'm too late. She's with that wanker Rufus and – you have to hand it to the man – he's in a better position to provide for her than I am. If I love her – which I know I absolutely do – I should leave her where she is.'

'Don't be a twat,' said Ben. 'I've never heard such a load of old bollocks in my life. Why on earth would you not try to win her back?'

'Not good enough for her,' muttered Charlie. 'She deserves better. Landed on her feet. Kinder to leave her . . .' He took another swig, draining the can, although Ben had barely started his.

Ben sighed. This was going to take a while. 'When did you last eat?' he said, looking around him.

'Dunno,' he said. 'Not got a lot in . . .'

Ben got up and took a look in the larder. Charlie wasn't kidding. The shelves, normally groaning with food, were more or less bare except for Dolly's dog food. The milk in the fridge was separated into yellowish liquid with an off-white solid layer. He didn't sniff it. A bag of carrots and another of broccoli had clearly been there since before Bella left. He took them out, along with the milk, and chucked the lot into the open kitchen bin. Then he ran his hand down the side, found the lid and returned it to its rightful place. That should help the smell a bit.

Pulling his phone out of his pocket he asked, 'What do you fancy? Curry? Chinese? Pizza?'

'You choose,' said Charlie, apathetically. He opened another can and took a long draw from it.

'Curry, then,' said Ben, dialling the local curry house. It had a particularly good reputation for its naan breads. He ordered two – one each to mop up the alcohol – plus a good assortment of vegetable side dishes. He reckoned Charlie hadn't eaten anything resembling a vegetable for a while.

'Should you be drinking that?' said Charlie, waving his can at Ben's. 'If you're driving?'

'They deliver,' said Ben. 'And I'm not planning to go anywhere as long as you don't mind me nabbing a sofa.'

'Won't Maddy mind if you're not back tonight?'

'She's the one who sent me.'

'Ah, so the women are in charge.'

'As always.'

'I miss her.'

'Then get her back.'

'How?'

'Turn this place around. You've got Rufus's money, whether you like it or not. Can you afford to pay it back, by the way? It would be nice. For morale.'

'Only by throwing in the towel here and now,' admitted Charlie. 'I used the first bit to pay off the mortgage backlog. They were just about to take the lot. The house, the cottage, the farm. Everything.'

'Are they happy now?'

'Not really. They still need paying. And then there are the other borrowings against the farm. I'm not even sure they all know about each other. I daren't think whether it was all set up correctly. It's probably fraud, technically. The only way Dad would have been allowed to borrow so much would have been if he had been economical with the truth.'

'What a mess. I knew it was bad, mate, but I just thought that was the norm. I wish you'd told me.'

'Keeping it from Bella was the main thing. Ma knows bits, but even she doesn't have the full story. I didn't want her to think badly of Dad. It was bad enough for her losing him so suddenly.'

'So, what now?'

'The money from Rufus needs to work pretty hard,' said Charlie. 'I'm due to pay it back next year with interest and with the frost damage on the vines and all . . . However,' he paused for emphasis, 'I have,' he went on, pointing not entirely steadily at Ben with his forefinger, 'a cunning plan.'

'You look all glossy,' observed Maddy, perched on a stool in Rufus's hyper-stylish kitchen.

'Be a first,' muttered Bella, but she held out her hand for Maddy to admire. 'Loving these, though, don't you think?' she said, showing off the newest gel colour on her nails, a subtle shade of nude.

'You do know this level of grooming is just rude, given my own current state of unkemptness?' Maddy complained, smoothing her maternity top over her bulging tummy. 'I can't reach my legs to wax them any more. Apparently, hair colour and fake tan are full of chemicals I should avoid and I even had to get Ben to cut my toenails for me the other day. Not cool.'

'You look fine,' Bella reassured her. 'You're glowing and all that crap people talk about.'

'Hope so. It would be some consolation for my expanding arse and lost relationship with my feet. Are you off to the gym or something?' she said, nodding her head at Bella's tight Lycra running shorts and vest.'

'Rufus's personal trainer Kelvin's coming in a bit,' Bella explained. 'He says I should get "out of my head and into my body", apparently.'

'I have literally no idea what you're talking about,' Maddy admitted. 'Get this into your body instead.' She brought a brown paper bag with a couple of sticky buns out of her basket. 'Your favourite.'

'I'm off wheat and dairy. Actually, I'm on a vegetable juice fast at the moment.'

She laughed at Maddy's incredulous look.

'Don't knock it. I've lost ten pounds. Kelvin reckons it would be more if I wasn't building up muscle.'

'Ten pounds is plenty, muscle or not.'

'Mm, Rufus says I could still lose a bit here,' she said, grabbing her shrinking spare tyre ruefully.

'Rufus says quite a bit that makes me not like him very much,' said Maddy crossly. 'I thought you looked beautiful before.'

'It's all about "being the best I can be",' mused Bella. 'To be honest it feels – I dunno – like a good thing . . . with Charlie I had no ambition. Not really.'

'That's because he loved you – loves you – for the way you are.'

Bella shook her head and turned away, not wanting Maddy to see her face. Instead she picked up a cloth and wiped at the granite worktop, sweeping away near invisible marks. 'It stains otherwise,' she fretted. 'Rufus says it has to be clean all the time. I don't want . . .' She trailed off, rinsing the cloth and then folding it neatly before hanging it precisely on the kitchen tap. Her hand was trembling. She made a fist and put her arm quickly back down by her side so Maddy wouldn't see. Too late.

'I'm fine, I'm just trying to—' she muttered, jumping out of her skin as she heard the front door open. 'Rufus!' she hissed straightening and brushing herself down.

'Hello, darling,' Rufus said, loping into the room and coming over to Bella to give her a peck on the cheek. 'Kelvin not here yet?' he added, holding her around the waist in a gesture that was halfway between affectionate and proprietorial.

He glanced over at Maddy whose cheek was bulging with a large bite of sticky bun.

'Have we been introduced?' he said, annoyance flashing across his face.

Bella gulped. 'This is Maddy. Ben's fiancé. I think you met at the ball?'

'I don't recall . . .' he said, without interest.

'I was the fat bird in the pink dress,' Maddy elucidated,

holding out a sticky hand for Rufus to shake. He did so with a moue of distaste.

'Ah yes,' he said. 'Now you mention it . . .'

'He's an arse,' Maddy said later, to Ben, as she perched on the kitchen stool watching him prepare supper.

'Say it like it is, won't you?'

'Well, he is . . . and he called me a "fat bird".'

'What? He literally said the words "you are a fat bird"?'

'Obviously no, not literally, but he failed to disagree when I called myself a "fat bird".'

Ben laughed. 'You girls have to remember that us blokes are simple souls. You make our brains hurt with all this stuff.'

'You've always managed perfectly well.'

'Yes, well, I am rather special. A bit of a catch, you know,' he added, smoothing his hair.

'If you say so yourself. Anyway, the other thing is, Bella's gone all weird.'

'Go on?' said Ben, serious now.

'Well . . . I dunno, she's all obsessive and cleany – not like her at all. Obviously, she's amazing-looking, manicure, hairdo, personal trainer . . .'

'That's okay, isn't it?'

'What, the cleany thing?'

'No, the grooming thing. The other bit's mildly disturbing. Tell me more.'

'Well, she's nervous and . . .' Maddy trailed off, thinking. 'I know what it is!' she exclaimed, making him jump and nearly cut himself.

'What?'

'She's scared of Rufus.'

'You lot aren't scared of anything. Blokes are scared of *you*, generally,' said Ben, with a faraway look on his face. 'You and Bella are holy terrors. No man is safe . . .'

'I know, I know, right?' agreed Maddy. 'But she *is*. She's frightened.'

She fell silent, listening to what she had just said.

'It's more than that "wanting to impress" thing, at the beginning of a relationship,' she went on at last. 'You know the kind of thing . . . it's different.'

Ben chopped peppers thoughtfully for a moment.

'She's chosen him,' he said. 'She's with him of her own free will. At least for now she wants to be with him and not Charlie. You can't interfere.'

'I know, I know . . .' Maddy twisted a bit of string fitfully in her fingers, wrapping it around her index finger and watching the tip go purple. Ben intervened, unwrapping it and chucking the string in the bin.

'Don't do that, you silly girl,' he said mildly. 'And don't go telling Bella that Rufus is an arse. Even' – he held up a palm to Maddy who had gone to interrupt – 'even if he is. And I agree he probably is. You need to maintain your relationship with Bella. If the two of you fall out over her choices, then – if you're right and Rufus hurts her – she won't have you there when she needs you. That's what matters.'

'You're so wise.'

'Yeah, I know.'

'And modest.'

'Yeah, that too.'

'It's actually quite annoying.'

'Sorry,' said Ben, not looking sorry at all.

'Anyhow, you saw Charlie. How is he?'

'Not good. Missing her. Drinking too much.'

'And the vineyard?'

'A helpful distraction. Which brings me onto my next point. He has a cunning plan to repay the money Rufus gave him.'

'And?'

'Charlie and Zach are having a meeting about it tomorrow. He'd like you to be there, but I don't know . . .'

'To discuss what?'

'He wants to hold a music festival on the estate this August.'

'Impossible.'

'I thought you might say that. He seems pretty determined. You're the only one we can think of with event management experience.'

'I wouldn't call it my main thing.'

'You'd be great. I just wonder if'– he indicated her bulging tummy – 'and all the Bespoke Consortium stuff . . .'

'Actually, they're so busy with current orders, they're pretty much begging me not to do any more marketing at the moment.'

'Soooo . . . ?'

'So maybe I could. I'd be doing it to help Bella because my overriding instinct is to bash Charlie over the head with something very hard to bring him to his senses.'

'Try not to. If you can help him make this work you may not need to.'

CHAPTER FOURTEEN

When Bella dropped in on Dove Cottage halfway through a gruelling cross-country run she was pleased to see her purple poppies were in full flower. The honeysuckle and the rose twining around the pretty latticed porch were better than ever this year too. She had been right about the colour combination she had chosen. The blush-pink rose with the creamy-coloured honeysuckle were perfect together. She caught a waft of their familiar scent and blinked back sudden tears, remembering sitting on the doorstep with Charlie one summer's evening, beer bottle in hand, listening to the bees and smelling that same scent. She distracted herself by fiddling with the fitness tracker Rufus had given her. She didn't really know how to use it but Kelvin had at least shown her how to check her heartbeat and footsteps. Amazing how she could see her fitness improving in such a short time. Absorbed, she barely registered the beaten-up beige car nestling alongside Caroline's red Fiat. Bouncing on her trainer-clad toes to keep warm she knocked on the front door using the wrought iron heart-shaped knocker Zach had made himself. He had given it to them both as a house-warming present.

'Goodness, what a lovely surprise,' said Caroline giving Bella a hug. 'Visitors are like buses this morning, I see no one for days and then you all arrive at once.'

'Not Charlie?' hissed Bella urgently.

'Just Geoffrey. Don't worry.'

Kissing Caroline, she whispered, 'I don't want to be a gooseberry, do you want me to go?'

'Not at all! At least stay for a cup of tea,' she said, loudly. 'Maybe go after that, though,' she added more quietly, with a wink.

Geoffrey greeted Bella with warmth.

'My dear,' he said, shyly. 'How nice to see you again. It gives me a chance to thank you properly for the introduction to this charming lady.'

Caroline blushed and dipped her head. Bella had never seen her do that before. The older woman had gone quite pink in the face and was looking at Geoffrey sideways under her fringe à la Lady Diana. Her hair looked blonder too, all the grey roots were covered up and it was tinted a warmer colour that suited her and brought out the blue of her eyes.

'I am so sorry to hear about your trouble with your husband,' he went on, his face flooded with sympathy and concern.

Bella glanced at Caroline who gave her an innocent look.

'No detail,' he added, hastily, 'your secrets are quite safe, I only know you and Charlie aren't together at the moment and I couldn't be more sad for you both. I know how upsetting . . .' he trailed off, looking into the middle distance, before gathering himself together. 'I just need to pop to the car for another screwdriver, my dear.'

'Tea and cake in a minute,' said Caroline. 'We need to keep your strength up, with all this hard work.'

'Is he divorced, do you think?' asked Bella after she heard the door close.

'I don't know,' said Caroline. 'He has no direct contact with family, that I've seen.'

'Isn't that a bid odd?'

'Is it?'

'Well, it is a bit. You don't suppose he's murdered them all, do you?'

'You're the one who introduced us,' laughed Caroline. 'A fat lot of good you are as a matchmaker if you've fixed me up with a mass murderer.' She handed Bella the tray and pointed to the little sitting room.

Bella carried the tray in carefully and put it on the carpet-covered ottoman in front of the fire. The little sitting room was small but charming, with whitewashed walls, a low, oak-beamed ceiling and a wood-burning stove crouching in the fireplace. The only seating there was room for was a pair of small sofas, facing each other and filled with generously stuffed feather cushions. The early summer sun came streaming in. Bella sat on the sofa under the window and Caroline sat opposite, dealing efficiently with the slightly dribbly teapot and cutting generous chunks of marzipan-covered fruit cake.

'Do sit,' she said to Geoffrey as he came diffidently back

into the room waving a large screwdriver. 'Time to sort out the safe afterwards. No one is going to break in wearing a stripy T-shirt and carrying a swag bag in the time you take to have a cup of tea.'

He sat himself down beside Caroline without awkwardness, despite it being snug enough for their thighs to touch, Bella noticed approvingly. It looked like they had sat this way before.

'So, have you lived here long?' enquired Bella pleasantly of Geoffrey, knowing perfectly well he hadn't.

'Under a year,' he replied, equally pleasantly, stirring his tea. 'And I like it very much so far.'

'You live above the shop?'

'I do,' he replied. 'It's small, but it suits me very well and, of course, it's convenient for work. In fact, my commute is excellent.'

'Where were you before?' Bella pressed, despite a warning frown from Caroline. 'Another bookshop, perhaps?'

'Actually, no,' he said. 'I just fancied a change.'

'But you were a bookseller?'

Caroline coughed a warning.

'I was an accountant.' He pulled a face. 'Most boring profession in the world,' he added with an apologetic shrug. 'Coming here was a new start, a fresh challenge, all the usual stuff, I suppose . . .'

'But you don't have family?' Bella persevered.

Caroline was practically having a fit by this point, coughing pointedly and raising her eyebrows so high they were completely hidden by her floppy blonde fringe. She glared at Bella as she rose and grabbed the teapot.

'More tea?' she said, waving the pot at Bella in a threatening manner.

'Lovely!' said Bella, with a disingenuous smile.

Left with no other option, Caroline went into the kitchen. As soon as she was out of earshot, Bella continued, relentlessly.

'You were saying . . . ?'

'Actually, I wasn't,' said Geoffrey. 'I'm not in touch with family, unfortunately. It goes like that sometimes. I wish it were different but it's not.' He looked deeply sad and Bella felt a little ashamed for pushing him so hard.

'That is sad,' she agreed, reproved. 'I would hate to be separated from my family.'

'It's nice to see you have such a good relationship with your mother-in-law,' he observed. 'Bucking the trend, or so I'm led to believe . . .'

'It's me,' said Bella, when Charlie answered the phone, sounding wary.

'What do you want?'

'I was wanting to pop in and see Dolly this evening,' she said, tremulously. 'See both of you, obviously.'

'Not convenient this evening, I'm afraid,' said Charlie. 'I'm busy.'

Bella opened her mouth to reply but then heard a click and was left looking at her phone in disbelief. He had hung up. She put her hand to her chest to feel her heart thumping wildly. She blinked back tears, wiping under her eyes rapidly as she heard Rufus's car swing into the drive, and crunch to a halt on the gravel.

* * *

Charlie put down the phone and then looked at it, lying on the table. He had been unprepared and had nearly not picked up. His stomach churned. He supposed he should have felt triumphant for having made his point. For putting her off. Ending the call. Instead, he just felt sick. It was true, though, he was busy that evening.

He was not in the habit of taking special measures when friends like Maddy and Zach were coming around. It was common for impromptu boozy suppers to arise with Charlie and Bella already in their pyjamas and people turning up uninvited with wine in their hands. It was generally pasta, with Charlie keeping glasses topped up and Bella working wonders with whatever she could find, with plenty of chocolate to follow in lieu of pudding . . . he stopped himself. He wasn't part of 'Charlie and Bella' any more. He was just Charlie. And this wasn't a social event.

A quick tour with a black bin bag had made an immeasurable improvement in the kitchen. He didn't know where Bella kept the cleaning stuff. He found a spray thing and a manky-looking cloth to wipe the kitchen table. There was a strange and disturbing smell which he thought might be some sort of small, dead animal. He looked accusingly at Ghengis who stopped washing and stared him out implacably. He was in the habit of taking his dead prey and stuffing it into small holes about the house. Bella had known where the usual places were. Unfortunately, Charlie didn't.

'Mate,' said Zach, when he arrived, with Maddy in tow because they had met in the lane. 'You spoil us,' he continued, looking doubtfully at the kitchen table.

Charlie had carefully laid out three printed copies of his proposal along with water and glasses, but it was the pile of items in the middle that had caught Zach's eye. There was an open packet of fig rolls, biscuits spilling out onto the table, a packet of pork scratchings and a jar of olives.

'Catering standards have slipped a bit, I'm bound to say . . .'

'Been busy,' admitted Charlie. 'Need to go shopping, actually . . . Bella deals . . . Bella dealt with that sort of thing.'

'Have you seen her?' asked Maddy.

'No,' Charlie said, shooting a look at his phone as if it might ring again right that moment. It didn't.

'Shall we?' he said, gesturing.

Zach and Maddy sat down and looked at Charlie expectantly.

'This could be the new Glastonbury,' Maddy exclaimed when Charlie got to the end of his presentation, closing his copy of the proposal and tossing it down on the table in a gesture of completion.

Zach was still thumbing through his own copy, thoughtfully.

'And you've got this money,' he said, pointing at the bottom of the budget page. 'You can fund what you're proposing?'

'It's in the bank,' said Charlie. 'What's left after paying off the most urgent debts, anyhow. Sitting doing nothing. And it's cost me dear, that money. My marriage, mainly.'

'I thought you were going to fund the winery with it, though,' said Zach.

'No point doing it this year,' explained Charlie. 'We did our best – I did my best – with the heaters that night but there was still damage. With the yield so destroyed by the frosts, I may as well just send the grapes away again, like I usually do.'

'So, you're doing this instead? You could piss away the lot.'

'Double or quits,' said Charlie. 'Why not? If it goes down the toilet then – frankly – I'll lose everything, which is what I'm close to now anyway. If it succeeds I can pay back Rufus and still have the money I need to build the winery next year instead. Or within a couple of years, anyhow,' he added with a note of realism. 'It could become a regular thing. Like Glastonbury.'

'Won't Rufus have something to say about you changing your plans with the money he lent?'

'He doesn't give a damn. I realise that now. He wasn't trying to help, really, he's tied me up in knots with this loan. He wants me to fall foul of the terms so he can destroy me. This is the only way I have a chance of making it out intact.'

Zach shrugged. 'Everything, though,' he said, simply. 'Everything you have.'

There was a silence, broken by Maddy's loud munching. The men looked at her.

'I think I might have developed a whole new pregnancy craving,' she admitted, tipping the now near empty bag of pork scratchings so she could pour the last crumbs into her mouth.

'Classy,' observed Zach.

'That's me,' she admitted cheerfully, riffling through the

pages of her copy of the proposal. 'Interesting date you've chosen. The end of August. That's just before this one's due,' she said patting her swelling tummy.

'Sounds like it's going to be an exciting month all round, then,' said Zach. 'Dolly's puppies will be with us by then. Actually, she's due a month before, so you'll have four-week-old puppies charging around the place. Chaos.'

'A productive few weeks,' said Charlie. 'And obviously, Maddy, I'd love your help with the publicity early on, but I don't expect you to have to be involved right up to the big event.'

'I'll be fine.'

'Yeah, but I won't be,' he said. 'Ben'll kill me.'

'Mm, there is that. Anyway, point is, I need to get this onto social media, get a buzz going, get these tickets sold – until then all the yurts, catering, toilet blocks and parking plans in the world are a bit academic . . .' She shook her head at the enormity of it.

'And . . .' said Charlie.

'And,' continued Maddy, 'I may be a towering genius when it comes to marketing, but I'm not going to get ticket sales out of thin air. There is the small matter of the bands. Who've you got?'

'No one yet.'

'Mm,' she said, putting her finger to her temple. 'So . . . I don't want to panic you, but it's well into May already and we're talking about August, slap bang in the holiday season, so it's kind of critical. People's diaries get booked up years in advance. Who do you know?'

Charlie and Zach looked at each other.

'It's got to be Zane Stringfellow,' said Zach.

Charlie nodded.

'Yeah, right,' said Maddy, 'let's just get "Inspire" then, shall we?' she said. 'Only the biggest selling band to come out of Manchester since Oasis. Like you do . . . Yeah . . . no . . . so, when I said, "Who do you know", I didn't mean "who have you heard of"; I meant "who do you know who is a) famous b) talented c) owes you the most massive favour in the whole wide world . . ."'

Charlie and Zach were nodding patiently at her.

'Yes to all the above,' said Zach, scrolling through the contacts on his phone. 'Yeah, here you go, Zane Stringfellow – the artist formerly known as Christopher Cholmondeley-Smyth – I'll send him a text . . .' he said, tapping for a few seconds and then putting the phone down on the table.

'How do I know you for years and have no clue you personally know Zane Stringfellow?' asked Maddy, incredulous.

'I'd have told you if you'd asked,' said Zach.

'In retrospect, I can't think why it didn't occur to me to do that. Is that his real name, seriously?'

'Yup,' said Charlie. 'Christopher Cholmondeley-Smyth. Ridiculous, isn't it? I flushed his head down the bog for it, obviously.'

'Although not as ridiculous as his current one but quite right too with the toilet thing,' agreed Zach. 'I did the same when he burnt the toast. He was my fag for a time,' he explained to Maddy who was looking appalled.

'And you think he'll actually want to help you now?'

'God, yes,' said Zach. 'The man loves me like a brother for it. Hang on,' he added as his phone pinged.

'Yep, there you go. "Mate,"' he said, reading aloud, '"I'm supposed to be in Ibiza – or Vegas – can't remember, but count me in. Get your people to talk to mine?"' Zach looked at Maddy's face and nodded with satisfaction. 'Then he says, "shall I bring some mates?"'

'Tell him "yes",' said Maddy, faintly.

Zach tapped briefly. 'I'm sending you his contact details too,' he told Maddy. 'You're our "people".'

Her phone clucked extravagantly in response. 'Sorry,' she said when it finally shut up. 'Chicken laying an egg,' she said. 'Ben put it on.'

The men looked incredulous.

'Private joke,' she explained. 'I just can't believe I've got Zane Stringfellow's number on my phone.'

'So,' said Charlie to them both. 'Can we do this? Will it work?'

Zach nodded, folding his arms.

'It's a totally insane timescale,' said Maddy, slowly, 'but . . . I'm beginning to think it might.'

CHAPTER FIFTEEN

Bella was preparing avocado on toast for her and Rufus. She had learnt how he liked it. Avocado perfectly ripe, well mashed but still with some chunks in and a big sprinkling of chilli flakes. The toast was a sourdough loaf from Pandora's Pantry at the bottom of the high street in Havenbury. She didn't realise they did deliveries, but it seemed they did. For people like Rufus they did, anyway.

Rufus, sitting on one of the high chairs at the breakfast counter, was ignoring the stunning view across the Downs and was studying Bella critically instead.

'You're getting a bit more toned,' he conceded.

She blushed.

'Your abs could do with a bit more work, though.'

She blushed deeper and sucked in her tummy. He was right, it really stuck out. It was gross. She was gross.

'I'm trying,' she said.

'Trying isn't good enough. Succeeding is the only thing that counts.'

She stole a look over at him. His jaw was set. She thought frantically of something safe to talk about.

'I hope you don't mind,' she said. 'I'm baking a cake here this afternoon. Maddy's baby shower . . .'

'Don't make a mess. Isn't it a bit early? I thought she wasn't having it for months.'

'True. Not 'til August,' but she's going to be really busy with this first Havenbury Festival thing – so exciting! – so we thought we had better get it done now. Amazing, the whole baby thing,' she rattled on nervously. 'I only wish she and I were doing it together.' She stopped, blushing again.

'I don't like children,' said Rufus.

'No,' Bella's hand flew to her mouth. 'I didn't mean—'

'I'm not going to be having children,' he went on. 'I'm a businessman. It's my only focus, so if that's what you want . . .'

'They'd all be ginger, your children.' She giggled.

'I am not ginger,' he said, stiff-lipped.

No!' said Bella, horrified. 'Of course not.' Her heart was hammering now. 'You're sort of, auburn . . . Your children would be beautiful,' she went on. 'What a shame . . . I just meant, me and Maddy, having children the same age. Would have been nice.'

'Anyhow,' he said. 'I personally think you and Maddy spend a bit too much time together. Like you said, she's going to be busy with this Havenbury Festival thing for the next few months and you, let us not forget, have a major job to do for me with The Grange. I've decided to bring the opening forward to the festival.'

'But that's August!' said Bella, aghast. 'I can't just lop a month off the schedule. It was tight enough as it was. We won't be ready.'

'We will. You will. And to help you with that, I've arranged with Paddy that he will set you up an office in The Grange. The boot room's plastered and wired now. It's fine. He's going to send one of his guys with a van to come to Home Farm to collect all your stuff on Friday.'

'I'll miss you,' said Maddy, sadly. She was sitting on the little sofa in Bella's chaotic studio at Home Farm watching as Bella filled boxes and bin bags.

'I'll miss you too,' said Bella, briskly, 'but it'll help me concentrate, working on-site. Rufus says I'm too easily distracted.'

'"Rufus says, Rufus says",' parroted Maddy crossly, stroking her bump. 'He's got you under his thumb good and proper.'

'I wouldn't say that. It's a good thing. Change is good. And, if nothing else, it's an excellent chance to get rid of some crap. I've been meaning to sort out these fabric remnants for years.'

'Don't throw them away. I'll take them up to Genny at the school. I am sure she'll have a project to use them for. She loves doing all the arts and crafts stuff.'

'Good idea,' said Bella. 'And what about your cake? I'm baking it this afternoon,' she added, keen to get Maddy firmly off the subject of Rufus.

'Yay!' said Maddy.

'What sort of thing do you want? I googled it last night. There are some really bizarre ones out there.'

'I want a bizarre one!' said Maddy immediately. 'In what way "bizarre"?' she added with belated caution.

'There seems to be a big trend for doing women's bits with baby's heads coming out. Lots of pink fondant and raspberry jam.'

'Gross!' said Maddy. 'Not that bizarre, thanks. Although raspberry jam and fondant icing appeals.'

'Something pretty, then,' said Bella. 'And pink. After all, we know it's a girl.'

'Flowers,' agreed Maddy, happier now. 'Rose petals . . . I can't wait! I really miss booze. Cake is my only consolation. You lot can all drink, though. I've got a crate of Prosecco in the fridge.'

'You're looking a bit thin,' said Caroline, bluntly. She had put the kettle on without asking and Bella was glad to sit down, looking wearily around her at the sunshine pouring in through the little cottage window, highlighting a jug of sweet, cinnamon-smelling stocks on the table.

'I'm not thin,' she countered. 'Look at my tummy. Rufus says I need to do more sit-ups.'

'I continue to dislike Rufus.'

'You're bound to say that, though,' said Bella. 'He's not Charlie.'

'True. I don't remember Charlie being anything other than thrilled with how you look.'

'I was wondering if I could borrow your cake-decorating kit,' said Bella, tactfully changing the subject. She had been getting good at that. 'I'm making Maddy's baby shower cake this afternoon. We want fondant flowers on it. I can't do it without those whizzy mould things you've got. And the leaf things too.'

'Of course,' said Caroline. 'Make it here!'

'I'd better not,' said Bella, regretfully. 'I think Rufus is expecting me home. I said I'd be there.'

'Hmph . . . fine, hang on . . .'

As she was rummaging in the pantry cupboard, which Bella had had built into the space under the stairs, she kept talking: 'I'm glad you dropped by, though. I was wanting to talk to you about my plan.' She emerged with a squashed cardboard box filled with bits of plastic.

'Here you go, and some silver edible cake spray too, if you'd like it.'

'I certainly would,' said Bella, gratefully. 'So, what's this plan?'

'I'll show you.' Caroline disappeared into the sitting room and reappeared with a handful of jewellery.

'Your sapphire necklace?'

'Sapphire and diamond,' confirmed Caroline, putting it down on the table between them.

'I want Charlie to be able to pay back the bit of Rufus's money he's already spent,' she said. 'If this is worth what I reckon it is, that'll just about do it. I appreciate I can't afford to fund the winery too, but it's a start. It allows Charlie to pay back the sum lent and not be obligated.'

'You can't.'

'Not your call,' said Caroline. 'Except that one could argue I would be selling off your inheritance.'

'Charlie's inheritance,' corrected Bella. 'Anyhow, although they're beautiful, you know I don't care about that. Not my right to any more, anyhow, now Charlie and I—'

'I'm not prepared to give up on your marriage to my son,' said Caroline sternly. 'And nor should you be.'

Bella, chastened, took a gulp of tea. 'So, you want to sell it?'

'I do, but first I need to get it valued. There's an old contact of mine in Hatton Garden. I've called him, but I don't want to send it up to him. I was wondering if you could take it? You go to London occasionally don't you?'

'I'm going on Friday,' agreed Bella. 'I'd be glad to. If you're sure?'

'Don't mention it to Charlie. I don't want him to know.'

'Hardly likely to,' admitted Bella.

'Are you not even speaking now?'

'His choice, not mine.'

'I could bang your heads together. What about Dolly, for goodness' sake?'

'Is she all right?'

'Getting fat,' said Caroline. 'It's all puppy, though, because she's not eating as much as you might expect. Pining after you, I reckon . . .'

'Oh God!' said Bella, in dismay. 'Poor Dolly . . . really?'

'She's fine,' said Charlie stiffly when Bella called. He had considered not picking up, but his hand had reached for the phone like it had a mind of its own.

'Your mum says she's pining.'

'Didn't say she wasn't missing you,' he muttered. 'She's definitely eating, though. Mum's just being manipulative.'

'Can I see her?'

'Best not.'

'Why?' she said, trying to keep her voice level as the tears sprang from her eyes.

'Well, you're not stopping, are you? Don't want to give the poor dog false hope that you're coming back or anything.'

'Aren't I?' Bella choked out, tears running down her face and dripping from her chin. She crammed her fist into her mouth to quell the noise of the sobs.

She was damned if she was going to let Charlie know how upset she was.

Charlie hung up, unable to answer, before frantically rubbing his fists into his eyes and taking a deep, shuddering breath.

He was damned if he was going to let Bella know how upset he was.

She looked at the phone in her hand, seeing the 'call ended' sign on the screen. Chucking it on the bed, she threw herself after it and allowed herself the luxury of howling into the pillow until she felt utterly spent. Then, picking herself up, holding her aching head, she climbed stiffly into the shower. Rufus was expecting her to come out for supper with him and some business cronies who were putting money into The Grange. He would not be impressed if she wasn't ready on time.

Rufus arrived home, dripping with sweat from his run, and disappeared into the bathroom without a word. Twenty minutes later, he came into the sitting room where Bella was curled up, barefoot, at one end of the sofa. She was wearing a shift dress, her hair up, in a simple style she knew he approved of, her make-up perfect. Her eyes were hopelessly swollen and her whole body ached, like she had the flu, fatigue sweeping through her bones like liquid concrete, pinning her where she sat.

He ran his eyes over her appraisingly. She braced herself. He would comment on her eyes, surely. He did not.

'Watch your drinking tonight,' he said. 'It makes you talk too much.'

Bella unpacked the final boxes under Paddy's anxiously watchful eye. He had refused to let her carry anything, although they weren't heavy. These were the last which his lad had brought from her cosy, familiar little space at Home Farm to the boot room at The Grange. It was freshly painted and although it had a large window, high on the wall – too high to look out of – it felt dank and gloomy, even on a bright summer's day.

'Be all right here, will you?' he said, anxiously. 'His nibs said to get you in as soon as possible. Only put the light fittings in yesterday . . .'

'It's fine,' said Bella, with a wan smile. 'Thanks. It's fine.'

'He wants you under his eye,' Paddy commented.

'It just makes sense,' countered Bella. 'I'm needing to be here all the time anyway, at the moment. Things are moving fast. He must be pleased with you. He must think you're doing a good job?' She made the last a question. Everyone was anxiously, almost neurotically, concerned with whether Rufus felt they were up to scratch. Praise was sparing and criticism was cutting and harsh. They all dreaded it.

'I'm used to him,' said Paddy, his astonishingly blue eyes twinkling. 'Don't let him rattle you, girl.'

'I don't, I don't . . .' insisted Bella, but she noticed the slight tremor in her hands as she stacked her files on the shelf. She tucked her hands into her armpits defensively. 'But I'm a bit worried about finishing in August, aren't you?' she said turning to face him.

'I've had worse,' said Paddy. 'And it's late August, technically.'

'But the bedrooms . . .' she went on, fretfully. 'He wants all the accommodation to be ready too. He plans to house all the celebs coming to the Havenbury Festival. Wants to have his grand opening on the first night.'

'Makes sense,' agreed Paddy, nodding calmly. 'Always got an eye on a good publicity opportunity, that man. It'll come together. You'll see.'

'Will Zane Stringfellow really come and stay at The Grange when he comes for the festival?' Bella asked Rufus in the car.

'Says he will.'

'Do you . . . do you know him?'

Rufus nodded.

'How?' she said watching him anxiously to see if her persistence annoyed him.

'We were at school together.'

Bella waited for further revelations, but there was nothing.

* * *

'Beeeella,' exclaimed Anton, kissing his fingers at the sight of her.

'I know for a fact you say that to all the girls,' she joked, weakly, remembering their first meeting.

'Ah, but with you I mean it,' he insisted. 'So, how is that Rufus? In fact, scrap that, I don't care how that bugger is. How are you?'

She bridled under his scrutiny. 'Okay.'

'You're not okay. He is pushing you too hard. He will take everything from you if you let him.' His deep brown eyes bored into her. 'I'm just warning you.'

'Yeah, I get that a lot,' said Bella, remembering her conversation with Paddy. 'And you'd know,' she added, fiddling with the strings on her portfolio case to get out the chandelier drawings and trying not to show how her hands were trembling. A new wave of nausea swept over her, leaving her sweating slightly.'

'When did you last have something to eat?' he asked, sharply.

Bella shook her head. 'I'm fine,' she said. In truth, she couldn't remember.

'Not what I asked,' said Anton, but he let it go. 'Anyway . . .' he said, 'you can relax about the chandeliers.'

'They'll be done in time?'

'Almost certainly. Look.'

He led her into his vast, airy studio, an old factory unit, where a dozen staff moved quietly and purposefully. Some were at computers, others standing at huge, white tables where construction was clearly taking place.

Bella could see which was her commission by the colours of the glass.

173

'It looks amazing,' she breathed. The long, hand-blown droplets were arranged in groups by colour, the darkest nearly black with just a hint of greeny-blue, graduating to white via intense and beautiful shades of teal and turquoise.

'And here is the frame,' he said, directing her eye to a wire construction, light but clearly strong, the structure that the crystals were already being attached to.

'This is a dress rehearsal,' he explained, resting the hand that had directed her on her waist. She felt the warmth and could feel his breath on her cheek. 'We will construct them entirely on-site. It will take two days. We will need a clean environment. Space to work.'

She nodded. 'That's fine. I'll schedule it in.'

'You're sleeping with him,' he observed.

'You're hardly one to talk. As far as I can tell, you're sleeping with everyone.'

'Not with you, more's the pity. But – fair comment – that's how I know,' he laughed. Then his smile disappeared. 'You're out of your depth, little one. Playing with the big boys now . . .'

The little shop in Hatton Garden had a locked door to discourage frivolous customers and at least the more half-hearted robbers. Bella rang the bell and then stood at the door feeling daft, waiting to be observed and approved of enough to be granted entry. She didn't look like the sort of customer who would be in the position to buy the kind of jewels she had burning a hole in her handbag.

'And how is Mrs Wellbeloved?' said the grey-haired gentleman who had buzzed her in, once she had introduced herself and her mission. His name was Quentin Clarke he had told her.

'I was so very sorry to hear the news that Peter had passed away,' he went on. 'It was always a pleasure to see them both. He had a good eye.'

'Were they regular customers?' asked Bella, in surprise.

'Well, I wouldn't say that,' Quentin acknowledged. 'Our jewellery' – he gestured around with his arm – 'is hardly an everyday purchase, but yes, Mr Wellbeloved bought some modest pieces over the years. An eternity ring, I remember, for an anniversary . . . it was that sort of thing . . .'

'Ah yes,' he said, when Bella got the jewels out of her bag and untangled them from the scarf she had wrapped them in for both disguise and protection. 'I remember this design. Not one of ours. Much older . . . late Regency, I think we decided. An important piece, to be sure.'

He took the necklace in his hand, and Bella saw a flicker of something cross his face. He handled it briefly and then put it carefully down onto a cushion of black velvet, which was resting on the counter. He took out the bracelet and did the same, then he pursed his lips and covered his mouth briefly with his hand.

'I do remember,' he said.

'But you're telling me it's not one of yours?'

'No, no . . . but we don't just make, you know. We repair, we value . . . Mr Wellbeloved wanted a valuation. For insurance. Or so I assumed. Diplomacy forbids, but – obviously – a six-figure sum.'

Bella gulped.

'We joked about the stories these jewels could tell if they

could talk,' he went on. 'Caroline – Mrs Wellbeloved – believed they had come to her via an ancestor who was supposed to have had a rather scandalous alliance with a minor member of the Russian royal family. Certainly, the style of these pieces is evocative of Fabergé.' He looked at her to check she was following. 'You are aware of Fabergé of course?'

'The eggs?'

'That's right. Some of the most exquisite examples of jewellery design in Russia at the height of its pre-revolution excess.'

'Wow,' said Bella, stroking the necklace with awe. 'To think this might have been seen, even owned, by a member of the Russian royal family . . .'

'No,' said the little man apologetically.

'How can you know?' said Bella, reluctant to let go of her daydream.

'Because this is not the jewellery I was asked to value.'

'You just said . . .'

'I didn't.'

Bella blinked, shaking her head.

'These are not the pieces I saw.'

'Then what . . . ?'

'These are fakes.'

CHAPTER SIXTEEN

'I don't understand,' said Bella, when she had closed her mouth again, practically feeling like she was picking her jaw up off the floor.

'This design is definitely the same,' he went on, hastily. 'The original was platinum, set with diamonds and sapphires. Good stones, I might add. The best.'

'And this . . . ?'

'. . . is a copy,' he said, with audible regret.

'A copy?'

'Glass,' he said. 'Silver, coated with a thin layer of platinum, would be my guess.'

'Worthless?'

'Actually, no,' he brightened. 'Not worthless. These pieces are well made, well designed,' he made a gesture with his hand, to acknowledge the irony, 'good work,' he said. 'A piece like this. Paste. Good paste. This would be worth a few thousand pounds to the right buyer.'

'But not a six-figure sum.'

'Absolutely not.'

'So . . .' Bella's eyes raked the little shop, taking in the display cabinets, filled with real jewels, the necklace, the little man standing diffidently before her, clearly distressed to be the bearer of bad tidings.

'It is not unknown,' he proffered, registering her inability to take the conversation forward, 'for our clients to get their jewellery copied like this. To give them something to wear while the original stays safely locked away. Easier on the insurance premiums, don't you know . . . ?' he said, peering at her in hope of understanding.

Bella nodded dumbly.

'Do you think that might be what happened in this case?'

'No,' she said. 'I really don't. These were the ones in the safe. The ones kept under lock and key.'

Quentin nodded sympathetically. His head on one side. 'Which begs the question,' he began, delicately.

'. . . where are the originals?' Bella finished, for him. She shook her head, violently, like Dolly when she had water in her ears. Trying to clear her brain – to think clearly.

'How long, would it take to make a copy like this? Would you need the original for reference?'

'Oh, most decidedly. One would. And, as for a timescale . . . this is no small piece of work,' he said, stroking the necklace admiringly. 'A skilled jeweller would need almost as long as one would need to make one with honest components,' he said. 'At least four weeks, I should have thought. If I had been asked to do it, I would ask for six.'

* * *

178

A feeling of leaden dread settled on Bella as she travelled back home on the train, the jewellery now burning a cold, guilty hole in the bottom of her satchel.

All of her actions over the previous few months had caused distress to those she loved the most. Her Faustian tryst with Rufus, breaking Charlie's heart, her sadness at putting Caroline in the position of having to sell her most precious possessions to save her son's livelihood and marriage and now this: her task was to destroy the last vestiges of hope that the loan might be repaid alongside enlightening Caroline that the most likely cause of her loss was the man who had so recently brought her a little joy in her widowhood.

Unable to face Rufus and even more unable to imagine having the task hanging over her, she hopped into her little car, now huddling almost alone in the corner of the station car park and headed to Dove Cottage to get it over with.

The lights in the little sitting room glowed cosily. The lane the cottage sat on led only to the farmhouse so neither Bella nor Caroline had ever bothered with curtains.

It was late enough, though, that when Bella knocked, she heard Caroline having to wrestle the door open, undoing bolts that had already been shot closed for the night.

'Sorry,' said Bella, coming in and giving the older woman a hug. 'It's so late.'

'Not too late,' said Caroline. 'Brr, you're all damp. Are you cold? Come by the fire. I know it's summer but still chilly, don't you think? The rain!'

The sitting room was sweltering hot and – true to her word – there was a fire glowing in the little stove. The rain was fine but persistent and even the short journey from train to car and then car to cottage had left her thoroughly damp. There was a heavy glass tumbler of Scotch on the oak coffee table, next to Caroline's glasses and a well-thumbed hardback copy of *Jamaica Inn*.

'I adored this,' said Bella, pointing to the book and gratefully accepting the tumbler of Scotch which Caroline had brought her from the kitchen.

'Just a little nip before we call it a night,' said Caroline. 'It helps me sleep.' She sat on the other end of the sofa and raised her glass.

'Chin-chin,' she said. 'And I agree,' she added, waving at the book, 'although if we are talking Daphne du Maurier, and I always want to read something like this on misty nights, my favourite is *Frenchman's Creek*,' she said. 'I'm a sucker for a good romance. Never averse to the idea of being swept off my feet by a pirate, even at my age. One can hope . . .'

'About that,' said Bella, carefully.

'Which bit?'

'The whole "being swept off your feet" thing . . . how is Geoffrey?'

'Geoffrey,' said Caroline with a happy sigh, 'is my Frenchman. I can't thank you enough for introducing us.'

'You might change your mind.'

'Oh?'

Bella took a deep breath, and then breathed out slowly. 'I took the jewels,' she said.

'I know,' said Caroline. 'Can't remember what they were valued at last time. No accounting for markets but hoping they've gone up a bit, obviously. Fine if they haven't.'

'They haven't,' said Bella. 'They're worth about five grand.'

'They. Are. Not,' said Caroline.

When Bella had explained, Caroline sat motionless, staring into her glass for so long Bella started to wonder if the older woman had fallen into some sort of trance.

'So . . .' Bella said, gently, 'I was just wondering . . .'

Caroline turned her head towards her, eyes dull and lifeless, the hope sucked out.

'You were wondering if Geoffrey stole them?'

Bella gave a tiny nod. 'On the night of the ball, Geoffrey got the safe open for you.'

'They were definitely in there then. I was standing right behind him. He got the crowbar in, the door flew open, there they were. No doubt about that.'

'And later? At the end of the night?'

Caroline nodded, dully. 'He kindly put them back for me,' she said. 'I wasn't in the room at the time. I was making us a cup of tea. He shouted through that he had managed to close the safe door again but that it was now jammed. I said it was fine. Better jammed shut than jammed open and the jewels were on the right side of the door too.'

'So, you didn't actually see them go back in?'

'No, but . . . anyway, as far as I was concerned, that was where they were.'

'When did you next see them?'

'When Geoffrey came back to fix it all again. Turned out in the end he couldn't get new bits for the safe, although he tried. The lovely man went out and ordered a whole replacement safe in the end. Came and fitted it for me. Jemmied open the old safe one last time so I could get everything out and took it away for me too. There wasn't much in it. Just the jewels, a few boring bits of paper. The farm deeds, my Will . . . that's about it.'

'Did you watch him jemmy open the safe?'

Caroline shook her head. 'I admit I didn't. He got the stuff out for me and then left the room while I set up the combination for the new safe. No chance anyone knows that but me.'

'How long was it?'

'Couple of hours . . .'

'No, I mean, between jamming the old safe shut and replacing it?'

'A few weeks.'

'Six?'

'I suppose so . . .'

'Did you call the police?' said Maddy, incredulous, when she heard Bella's story. They were both toying with lattes and *pain au chocolat* at the trattoria, sitting at the bench which ran along the window facing the street. It was a favourite spot for people watching.

'Not up to me.'

'Did Caroline call the police, then?'

'I'm sure she hasn't. She doesn't want to believe that Geoffrey could have done it.'

'It looks an awful lot like he did,' said Maddy. 'Look! There he is . . .' she ducked down, watching him surreptitiously sideways on.

182

'That doesn't look conspicuous at all,' said Bella, giving her a nudge. 'Really natural, that is . . .'

Geoffrey, wearing his trademark tweed jacket with the leather patches at the elbows, was pottering outside his shop, on the opposite side of the street. It was nearly opening time.

'He doesn't look much like a criminal mastermind,' admitted Maddy.

'They don't go around with "criminal mastermind" tattooed on their foreheads.'

'Yes, but he also doesn't look like a man who's got a six-figure sum stashed under the mattress either. I can tell his shoes are knackered from here, for goodness' sake. He's not been here long. Where was he before? What was he doing?'

'Dunno. An accountant, he said. Retired now, I gather, just had a yen to run a bookshop.'

'Caroline probably knows more about him though, doesn't she?'

'I'm not sure she does,' admitted Bella. 'I know she thinks she adores him. It's been hard for her, these last few years, being widowed.'

'Your father-in-law,' said Maddy. 'I never met him. What was he like?'

'Lovely! He was a sweet man. Kind to me. Noisy, boisterous, generous . . .' Bella stared into space remembering. 'Much like Charlie, really.'

'Was he happy about the wedding?'

'He seemed thrilled. I was a bit nervous when we broke the news. Obviously, they knew we were together, me and

Charlie. By the time we got engaged Charlie was already living in Dove Cottage to be away from his parents but still there for the farm. It was a typical bachelor pad. Beer cans everywhere, filthy sheets on the bed. I used to refuse to stay unless he cleaned up. It was the only time he ever did.'

'I can hardly believe that,' said Maddy. 'It's just beautiful now. You must miss it.'

'I do.'

'But the farmhouse will be even more amazing,' said Maddy happily, 'when you and Charlie do it up. Oops, sorry.'

'There's just been no money to do anything to it,' said Bella.

'Did you have a really extravagant wedding? Flora was saying it was absolutely beautiful.'

'It was,' said Bella, smiling at the memory, 'but not massively expensive. We had to keep holding Peter back, actually, he wanted it really grand; huge numbers of guests, dining at Havenbury Manor afterwards, the flowers all from this top London florist. Ridiculous. And not what me and Charlie wanted at all. I did the flowers myself. My mum made the dress, we had a marquee at the farmhouse. A barbecue . . . it was lovely. Perfect. Until . . .' She brushed away the thoughts of what happened after Peter's shocking collapse and took another swig of her coffee.

'That's exactly the kind of thing I would want,' said Maddy, wistfully. 'Me and Ben will get hitched one day, we've decided.'

'Wow! Congratulations.'

'Yeah, yeah. I mean it's fine but – for us – it's not, I dunno, that important, I suppose. We're just thinking it

184

makes more sense for the bump,' she said, stroking her rounded tummy tenderly. 'To make us all have the same name. Simpler.'

'Romantic,' joked Bella.

'That's us. Ben is romantic, actually,' said Maddy, 'not in that way. It's just that we're together, we know we're together, what's the big deal about having a piece of paper?'

'Excuse for a party, though.'

'Absolutely. We'll definitely do it. In a year or two. Will you help?'

'Of course I will. How about having the reception at Home Farm? Will Serena and Giles let you? The boathouse will hardly do . . .'

'Too true,' admitted Maddy, acknowledging that the enchanting little wooden house she and Ben lived in, down a track and right on the edge of the Haven river, was an inappropriate venue. 'Home Farm would be perfect. I'm sure Serena and Giles would be totally up for it.'

'You could do the "getting married" bit in the church at Little Havenbury, like I did,' said Bella. 'It's so pretty. And, if not Home Farm then maybe even The Grange. Rufus could give you a special rate, obviously.'

'It would have to be a very special rate. Not soon, though,' said Maddy, 'you'll have to keep going out with Rufus until we're ready,' she joked. 'This one's evidence we've not exactly done things in the right order,' she added patting her tummy. 'Although it's partly why we're waiting too. I don't want to go down the aisle looking like a whale and we want her to be a bridesmaid. Or a pageboy.'

'I thought you knew it was a girl?'

'Don't want to gender-identify her before she's even born,' joked Maddy. 'Anyway, we don't totally, totally know it's a girl. That whole ultrasound thing is a bit of an art, not a science. Good for sorting the date and spotting problems . . . It looked like a girl but it might be – I dunno – just a boy with a very small willy.'

Bella laughed but then noticed Maddy had, entirely unexpectedly, burst into tears.

'What if it's got a really tiny willy . . . ?' she howled, drawing bemused attention from the other customers.

Bella patted her on the shoulder and handed her a napkin to use as a handkerchief. 'I'm sure it's all going to be fine,' she said, perturbed.

'But it might not be fine. How about if it's got a disability or something and me and Ben are rubbish and we can't cope, and we don't look after it properly . . . ? What if,' she said, suddenly sitting up straighter in horrified realisation, 'what if we're just crap parents?'

Bella looked around her, perplexed, and slumped with relief as she saw Ben push through the door. Spotting them and coming over instantly, he gave Bella a reassuring look.

'Oh dear, have we got this again?' he said, wrapping Maddy in a hug and looking down her snotty and tear-stained face. 'Having a hormone-related wobble?'

'Is that what it is?' wailed Maddy.

'We know it is, don't we?'

She nodded, uncertainly. 'I suppose so.'

'I know so,' said Ben. 'And I also know you're definitely going to be needing a nap today, aren't you? Soon, I reckon . . .'

She yawned, unselfconsciously. 'I suppose I might.' She let out a shaky sigh.

'There,' Ben went on. 'Isn't that better?'

'Yes, but what about all the "things"?'

'What are the "things"?' asked Bella, fascinated and touched at Ben's handling of this new, clearly unhinged Maddy. If this was what pregnancy did to you she wouldn't mind giving it a miss.

'All the things that could go wrong,' explained Ben. 'There's a list. We have to go through it sometimes, think of reasons why it might be just a tiny bit unreasonable. It's a bit of a theme at the moment.' He was still holding Maddy tightly, shifting her into the crook of his arm and settling himself so their chairs were touching.

'So, what have you girlies been gossiping about?' he said, looking meaningfully at Bella, signalling for her to provide a distraction. She briefly explained their concerns about Geoffrey.

'What do you think?' she asked as she finished.

'I don't know him well . . .' said Ben.

'Nobody does,' said Maddy, interested enough to wipe her nose and contribute to the conversation. 'That's the point. Everyone knows everyone in Havenbury. But no one really knows him.'

'But he seems a nice enough chap,' Ben went on. They all gazed out of the window towards the little second-hand bookshop, 'Antiquarian Books of Havenbury,' said the faded gold sign above the window.

As they watched, a dowdily dressed middle-aged woman came along and hovered outside. She peered through the dusty window and raised a hand in a tiny wave, clearly acknowledging someone. The door opened just halfway, they saw Geoffrey usher the woman in, she looked up and down the street, as if checking to see if anyone was watching and then slipped through the door, which shut immediately behind her.

Ben, Maddy and Bella stared at the door, transfixed. As they did so, a green tweed-clad arm reached out and flipped the sign on the door from 'open' to 'closed'.

'Well,' said Maddy in triumph, all tears forgotten. 'What do we make of that?'

Chapter Seventeen

'I'm sorry, Ma,' said Charlie.

'Yes, but we don't know . . .'

'We should involve the police, then. Get them to find out.'

'How are they supposed to do that? They won't. And putting the poor man through it all. I won't do it.'

'He's not a "poor man",' said Charlie. 'Actually, if he's done what we think he's done he's a rather well-off man.'

'We just don't know that,' said Caroline again, less certainly this time.

'Who else could it possibly be?'

She was silent. Her lips formed a thin, straight line and she looked at her son, determined not to speak. Her poor boy. The laughter lines around his eyes, so entrenched they usually showed up white on a face tanned by hours in the vineyard, were barely visible. Instead, there was a deep furrow between his eyes and lines of bitterness and sorrow were establishing themselves from his nose to chin. No. There was no way she was going to add to his distress.

'And there's the other matter,' said Charlie, squaring his shoulders, 'which is how you are going to manage without the money you've lost.'

Now she did speak out. 'I don't need it, you silly boy,' she said. 'I was only trying to get it so I could pay off this ridiculous loan. Sever the link between you and this ghastly Rufus person.'

'He has my wife,' said Charlie sourly. 'And she went willingly. Any amount of money isn't going to resolve that issue.'

'You didn't give her much choice,' she retorted. 'It's your ridiculous pride. You're just like your father.'

They glared at each other.

She picked up her phone which had started to buzz across the table. Staring at the screen, she lifted it, saw who was calling, put it down and then picked it up again, pressing the button to answer and holding it to her ear like it was a hand grenade.

'Geoffrey,' she said, staring straight at Charlie, daring him – with furiously flashing eyes – to make a sound.

'How lovely,' she went on, politely, in answer to something he said, 'but I'm afraid I'm not available this Tuesday.'

She paused. 'I can't do Thursday either, I'm so sorry. In fact,' she said, taking a deep breath, 'I'm generally rather busy at the moment, I wonder if . . .' she listened, her head drooping sadly as he spoke, 'yes, that's so understanding of you. Absolutely. If you're sure? I think that would be best, thank you.'

She ended the call and then, with infinite care, she put the phone back down on the table.

'And that,' she said, her voice husky with sadness she tried hard to disguise, 'is very probably that.'

'The girls have decided it's his secret wife,' said Ben to Charlie over their regular Thursday evening pint in the Havenbury Arms.

'I can't imagine why his wife would be prepared to sneak around pretending she's not his wife, so he can mess around with other women,' reasoned Charlie. 'She's more likely a fence. He's hardly going to go and stick hundreds of grands' worth of jewellery on eBay himself, is he?'

'I've no idea,' admitted Ben. 'He just doesn't seem the type, though. I suppose he had us all fooled.'

They both contemplated their beer in silence.

'And she won't involve the police?' queried Ben.

'Nope. Dunno what that's all about,' said Charlie. 'I can't force her. Not my property. Also, she's been distressed enough . . . a tough few years. I can't say the money wouldn't have come in handy, though. Not that getting the police in would get it back, anyhow. Poor Ma. It would be a tonne of publicity about how she's been done over, probably give other sleazeballs the impression she's worth turning over again, which she isn't. I wouldn't want her to start feeling insecure, being at Dove Cottage on her own . . .' He gazed into his beer with a look of desolation that broke Ben's heart.

'Nah . . .' he went on. 'Those jewels could be anywhere by now. Probably broken up and melted down. And I bet you ten quid this Geoffrey bloke disappears as quickly as he appeared. Off to sucker some other poor lonely widow into a similar scam.'

* * *

191

Charlie did a double-take when he looked at the kitchen clock. Surely that was ten in the morning and not ten to twelve but no, on closer examination, it really was close to midday. Well, never mind. That was the consequence of meeting up with Ben the previous night. That said, he vaguely remembered his friend dissuading him from buying another round with shots at about half past nine, which was pretty early for one of their Thursday night catch-ups. Ben had been keen to get back home, to make sure that Maddy was going to bed at a sensible time. Also, of course, Patrick, Ben's nearly father-in-law, was bound to dob him in if it turned into a bender. Just as well he, Charlie, wasn't facing parenthood now. That was the last complication he wanted to have to deal with on top of everything else. Still, Ben seemed keen on the idea, which was nice.

Also, being dropped back at the farmhouse mid-evening just gave him a chance to hit the whisky bottle with no one nagging him to stop. He had meant to get stuck into his tax return, which he had promised the accountant he would get on top of early this year. Trouble was, none of last year's figures were good news – a fact he was happy to shelve for now. Instead he had thought he might go through the minutes of his last meeting with Zach and Maddy. There were things he was supposed to be dealing with. Like calling the Portaloo guy. He kept remembering it in the early hours of the morning, which was not particularly helpful.

Whisky bottle in one hand and glass in the other, he wandered into the sitting room. It was chilly, despite being late June, and the bulb in the light above the sofa seemed to have blown, so he turned on the overhead light and settled himself in the chair by the unlit stove. Funny how the house just didn't feel homely without Bella in it. After a moment, he reached for the bookshelf. The first thing he laid his hands on was the photo album Bella had made after their wedding. She had refused to have a formal photographer, tasking all their friends to take loads of pictures and pool them on Dropbox instead. She had waited more than a year afterwards to collate the album. Neither of them had felt able to look at any of the photos of the day until then, but one rainy Sunday afternoon – he remembered – she had set to it, printing off and painstakingly recreating a timeline of the day. The shots of her dressing, beautiful, softly lit photos of her and Maddy, the tiny buttons on the back of the dress being fastened, buckling her cream, satin shoes, pinning up her hair. Then, Charlie and Ben messing around in the garden, playing rugby in their morning coats. Who had taken those photos, Charlie wondered now? Who had been there? Zach, he supposed . . . Next, the guests, all walking up the blazingly sunlit path to the church, like a procession of the cast from a play, in bright colours, fancy hats, the men already wilting in their morning coats and stiff collars. Some surreptitious shots of the two of them taking their vows – the vicar had forbidden cameras in church – so the angles were interesting, mostly taken with phones held at waist height. And then, bursting back into the sunshine again, relaxed, giddy, hilarious photos, filled with relief and mild hysteria at what they had done . . . Charlie making a fuss of spitting out rose petals thrown as confetti. A tender shot of him removing a petal from Bella's hair as she gazed up at him in a wonder he couldn't remember having seen in her eyes for a while. Her waist was slender then, her breasts swelling enticingly out of the top of that fabulous gown, classy, luxurious but so God-damned sexy; he remembered when he turned and saw her walking up the aisle to join him. Of course, she still had amazing tits but she was funny about them now. Self-conscious about her tummy, not that he gave a damn. More of her to love, he said, but that hadn't been the right thing to say either, it seemed . . . She had looked amazing, though. He smiled despite himself and took another swig. Damn, empty glass. Oh well, it had only been a small one. Another wouldn't hurt.

There were some great shots of people standing around on the lawn, drinking champagne – not champagne, naturally, but Dovecot Estate wine of course. Then, as the afternoon wore on, the wedding breakfast in the tent. The photos in the marquee were bathed in the golden light of the sunshine glowing through canvas, the tumbling, informal flower arrangements on the tables – mostly daisies – no, not daisies, marguerites, Bella had told him. He gave himself a mental pat on the back for remembering. He knew this stuff. The things that were important to women, to Bella, like the names of flowers and all that fancy stuff. He *was* a good husband, he told himself. He had been . . .

Bella had been meticulous about the timeline of photos, and, turning the pages, Charlie could see, feel everything. He could darned nearly smell the straw-like reek of the sisal matting on the floor of the marquee as it heated up. By this time, it was early evening. Hats were on backs of chairs, shoes had come off, the tables were covered in empty, lipstick-marked glasses and dirty coffee cups, the serving girls in crumpled, grubby aprons now, their faces shiny, hair coming down in wisps. They were still smiling – glad to be earning and surrounded by happy customers. He felt like he was watching a horror film where only he could hear the ominous music, the impending disaster, so inevitable, he saw now. Hindsight, eh? What a bugger it was.

They were all so happy, relaxed, exhilarated. Here they both were, sitting at the top table, a stolen shot of them smiling at each other, he with his dark hair flopping over his eyes, her sweet goofy smile, which she saved just for him – neither of them able to hide their glee, their exhilaration at what they had dared to do, at the golden future they saw rolling out in front of them like the Sussex Downs when they were bathed in sunshine.

He closed the book and leant heavily on it. But it was too late. Like a train that had gathered too much momentum to stop, the show reel continued in his head anyhow. The speeches next. His father was up first. Not his normal ebullient self, they all said afterwards. Like they knew. The measured, slight breathlessness, the curtailed speech . . . Charlie had thought at the time the omissions were to make back time for an event that was running late . . . the tremble in the hand as he raised his glass to the bride and groom. His father had sat down, wiped his forehead and smiled reassuringly at Charlie as he rose. Then, the round of applause and the cheers when he uttered the phrase 'my wife and I', the tunnel vision, trying so hard not to forget anyone in the thank yous, the jokes, the lists of names, the gallop to the finish and then, done, over to Ben for the best man's speech.

Barely had Ben got to his feet, to a round of applause

just for standing up because the audience were so nicely warmed up, that the atmosphere changed.

There was a rumble from the crowd, a noise Charlie played back in his mind endlessly, a mixture of confusion, concern and even nervous laughter. Sitting at the top table near him, his father could be seen more clearly by the other guests than he could be by Charlie or Ben, so when he slid under the table taking the cloth, plates and several glasses with him some of the guests thought it was a joke.

Ben was the quickest to realise. In the split second of silence when the smashing of glass and crockery stopped and before the consternation began, Ben was by Peter's side. Charlie thought, in retrospect, that his ex-army pal might have vaulted right over the table. He must have done. By the time Charlie pushed his way past the others to get around the front himself, Ben had Peter on his back, undoing his tie, unbuttoning his shirt. He barked into the crowd for help, his shout cutting through the rising hubbub like a scimitar. Zach was there too. It was Zach that made the phone call for the ambulance. 'One casualty, unconscious,' he had said, pausing to look gravely at Ben for further information. Ben, by this time, had his ear to Peter's mouth, his head turned to watch the man's chest for signs of respiration. 'Not breathing,' he had added.

Charlie had Bella clinging to him from one side and his mother on the other, his arm resting over Caroline's shoulder. Caroline stood silent, not taking her eyes off her husband's face, not even for a moment, but not making a sound, making sure not to distract any attention from the efforts to save her husband's life. A defibrillator had been brought, breathlessly, by one of the other guests, who had gone to Havenbury Green village hall and wrenched it off the wall, driving it frantically back, taking wing mirrors off four other cars on his return up the lane, it later transpired. By then, Ben and Zach, playing tag team on the chest compressions, even with their muscles and rugby-honed fitness, were beginning to flag.

A murmur of hope ran around the room like the flicker of flame on the edge of a newspaper lit by a match when the defibrillator delivered a shock and then counselled waiting until help arrived. Peter did not regain consciousness during this time, still lying on the floor, grey-faced, but Charlie's constant eye on the screen that monitored his father's barely there life continued to reward him with a reading.

Try as he might, Charlie could never remember the bit between this and being in the hospital. People told him about being driven there. About the police helping to clear the narrow lane so the ambulance could get up close, but it was gone. It was like a cut in a film, the intervening scenes left on the cutting room floor.

Instead, his next clear memory was of bringing his mother in to see his father, grey-skinned and still on a narrow bed in a brightly lit cubicle. There was an oxygen mask, and tubes, and a screen recording figures that meant little to him. He half expected his father to sit up and rip away the equipment, hopping off the bed and clapping them both on the shoulder in the way that he had, ever the dramatist, the bon viveur, suggesting another drink, something to eat, some new, mad adventure . . . but he didn't.

He did do something dramatic, though.

He died.

Blue-cotton-shift-clad staff ran in, pushing past them both to get to the bed, barking orders with military curtness, unravelling wires, twiddling valves on the tubes that ran into both of his arms, preparing to shock him again, to shove a breathing tube down his throat but Charlie became aware of Caroline standing beside him, patting his arm, shaking her head, pleading with her eyes for him to intervene. To make them stop.

'He's gone,' she whispered, through tight white lips. 'He's gone, darling. He wouldn't want this.'

The glass, dropping from his fingers and smashing on the slate floor was what woke him. He started up from the chair, head swimming and pounding with the precursor to a hangover he well deserved. He thought about leaving the broken shards until later but, remembering Dolly's bare paws he staggered, cursing, into the kitchen to find the dustpan.

Broken glass dispensed with, he reached for the Scotch bottle, which was empty, to his surprise. He took this reluctantly as a sign he should probably go to bed. Dolly was already there, licking him sleepily as he shuffled in beside her, not noticing the greyish sheets or the dog paw prints on the duvet cover. Bella would have a fit if she saw.

And now, here he was, in tolerable order, granted it was nearly lunchtime, but June was a funny time of year for the vineyard, with less to do other than hover over the ripening grapes like an anxious parent. Rubbing his hands over his face and scalp, which itched because he needed a shower, he decided to delay breakfast for now. He was feeling queasy anyhow. In fact, even the coffee could wait. Instead, he followed his father's morning ritual of testing the grape sugars. He walked slowly along the rows, taking samples as he went. As he walked, the throbbing in his head eased, although he was grateful for his sunglasses. The sun was directly overhead now, with a stiff breeze and a thin veil of streaky cloud scudding rapidly across the sky. As he went, he checked carefully under leaves and around the swelling bunches of fruit for any sign of mildew or pests. The Meunier was further along than in previous years. The vines for the Pinot were doing well, as they should be – they were on the slope that caught the most sun. He remembered planning it out with his father, marking the ends of the rows with stakes, shading their eyes as they imagined the sight. It was a five-figure sum to plan the additional few acres, bringing up the total to sixty. For anyone standing at the back door of the farmhouse, the vines stretched as far as the eye could see.

The Pinot Noir and Chardonnay were planted furthest away. He was trying to ignore his throbbing head as he went on, with Dolly trotting anxiously at his heels. She knew the routine well, though, and with her swelling stomach and the midday heat against her black fur she slumped to the ground for a rest at intervals, watching obsessively as he moved slowly down the rows. Things had gone smoothly since that night of frosts, but it was still another six weeks at least until harvest, more likely eight or ten. Plenty of time for things to go wrong. That easy-going nature he used to have took a body blow when his father died. When Bella left – well – that was the death knell. Now he expected the worst and was rarely disappointed.

He should have worn a hat. By the time he got back to the kitchen with his grape samples, he was feeling nauseous again and his headache had settled in for the duration as a constant pain behind his right eye and a thumping ache across the back of his head. Nearly one o'clock and no breakfast, let alone lunch. Maybe he should eat. He found some cereal of dubious provenance in the cupboard but the milk in the fridge had turned to yoghurt and the bread had broken out in a rash of green, mouldy spots. He chucked both in the bin and cracked open a beer. Might as well carry on where he left off.

'Hair of the dog,' he told Dolly.

Apparently in response, Dolly exploded into a flurry of barking, stationing herself by the back door and weaving between it and Charlie in her desperation to be let out. Just to stop the noise he threw open the door and she scampered out, the barking quickly being interspersed by delighted singing as Charlie heard the back gate open.

'Hello, old thing,' came a voice. 'You're getting fat.'

'Ben, mate,' said Charlie, swinging his can between finger and thumb, 'can you make the dog shut up do you think? Bit of a sore head.'

'You look rough,' said Ben. 'Had a big night?' he said. 'Didn't think we did . . .'

'Might have had a couple after I got back,' admitted Charlie.

CHAPTER EIGHTEEN

'Mate,' said Ben, when he followed his friend into the kitchen, 'this is a bit of a mess!' He had to be careful not to trip over Dolly who continued to sing and snake around him. She was clearly unable to see herself as the barrel-shape she now was, her tummy hanging heavy with her puppies, and it meant she kept getting herself jammed into narrow gaps.

'Not long now,' said Ben, fondling her ears. 'You're going to be a great mum, I reckon.'

'God, that too,' said Charlie wearily, slumping into a chair and plonking his tin on the table. 'Don't mind telling you, I'm knackered, what with all this and the festival. Not looking forward to being up with puppies half the night.

'The booze can't help,' said Ben.

Charlie gave him a pained look. 'Just a beer,' he said. 'It's past midday.'

'Is it breakfast?'

'Might be . . .'

'Thought so. Plus, can you think why I'm here?'

Charlie shook his head.

'Meeting with Zach and Maddy at midday?'

Charlie sat bolt upright. 'Shit! Sorry . . . completely forgot.' And he still hadn't phoned the Portaloo guy, he remembered guiltily. 'Shall I go now?'

'Too late, mate,' said Ben. 'Zach had to go off and do some trustee stuff for the estate. He said he was fine to reschedule to six tonight and Maddy's okay for that too.' That wasn't exactly how Zach had put it, but Charlie didn't need to know that. It had been Maddy who insisted that Ben go and check things out. She was obsessed with the idea that Charlie might have had a horrible accident and became increasingly anxious until Ben told her, just to make her relax, that he would go and check.

'This bin stinks,' said Ben, who had gathered up a few empty beer cans – they were scattered over most of the kitchen surfaces – and chucked them in. Two of them bounced out again. The bin was full. He could see the takeaway cartons from the other night still not gone. No wonder it stank.

'Think I've missed the rubbish collection,' muttered Charlie, rinsing out a cloth at the sink and using it to wipe, ineffectually, at some dried-on beer, spilt on the table.

'Tell you what,' said Ben. 'It's not just the bin that stinks. You pong a bit too. How about you go clean yourself up. I'll sort this mess while you do it.'

Charlie blinked. 'Nothing like being direct,' he complained. 'It's not that bad. Been a bit busy, that's all . . .'

'You're a mess,' said Ben, meeting Charlie's eyes and holding his gaze. 'You're a bloody mess. I get that you feel

202

sorry for yourself. If Maddy left me I'd . . .' He shook his head. 'And you've dealt with a lot, now there's your mother and this dodgy bloke . . . I get it, I really do. But this,' he said, waving his arm. 'What are you thinking? Are you somehow imagining that Bella will come in here, see you need her, dump her new life and move back in? Do you even want her back?'

'Yeah,' said Charlie. 'Course I bloody want her back. I'd have her back tomorrow, despite what she's done . . .'

'What *she's* done? Get over yourself mate. Frankly I struggle to understand – to believe – the situation you've managed to find yourselves in. It does, in fact, beggar belief.' Ben stared briefly into space, recollecting the story Maddy had told him, making him promise not to tell anyone he knew, of course, but he was pretty sure Charlie didn't count. 'Honestly, mate, you couldn't make it up . . . but you got into it together. You're a team. A bloody good team, have been for years . . . You've got to earn her.'

'How can I compete?' interrupted Charlie, despairing, 'she's with a multimillionaire. All I've got to offer is a filthy farmhouse that's falling down and a bankrupt business that's mortgaged to the hilt and standing to make minimal money this year.'

'Bella doesn't want money,' said Ben with conspicuous patience. 'She wants you. And anyway, what about the cunning plan? You're forking out five-figure sums on a daily basis for this rock festival, you've got your mates working their arses off to make it work and you can't even be bothered to turn up to the meetings . . .'

'All right, all right, you've made your point,' said Charlie.

* * *

203

Half an hour later Charlie reappeared in the kitchen smelling much better. He had shaved and was wearing a clean, albeit crumpled, shirt. His arms were full of washing. Ben had transformed the kitchen and was even wiping down the Rayburn top when Charlie walked in.

'Right,' he said. 'I'll pick you up at quarter to six.'

'I can get myself to Zach's house.'

'Of course you can, but this way I know you will,' replied Ben. 'And anyhow, I need to bring you some supplies. You've got nothing in the fridge. Apart from beer. I'm taking that with me, by the way. You're on the wagon.'

'Oo, you're all film-starry,' declared Flora, when Bella got out of her car at Home Farm. It was only Bella's trusty old Fiat – she had eventually, reluctantly, agreed to Rufus buying her a new Mini Cooper and was waiting for it to arrive – but in the meantime she had come back to the house after a run the day before to find Rufus's driver just finishing off a major car valet job on it. Even the interior was spick and span, which was embarrassing, given the mountains of rubbish he would have had to shovel out.

'It's been waxed and everything,' admitted Bella, closing the car door.

'Not your car – I mean you, silly,' insisted Flora, walking around her and examining her from all angles with forensic thoroughness. 'Straight, shiny hair,' she murmured, ticking off a list, 'orangey-brown legs, no fuzz . . .' she went on, 'and what have you done to your eyebrows? They look all funny.'

'Yeah, well, I've been waxed too, now you mention it,' Bella muttered. 'I'm just a bit more manicured, that's all.'

She didn't tell Flora that she had been ordered to the beauty salon by Rufus a couple of days previously where she had submitted to a head-to-toe overhaul, which included brutal forms of hair removal in places Bella hadn't even known she had, plus a meticulous eyebrow tidy and individual eyelashes glued into place – which, she was informed, would last weeks if she was careful. To finish off, there was a dramatic haircut and colour, which Bella discovered Rufus had pre-briefed the stylist on, leaving her with very little input it seemed, although she had been pleased with the result, which was a collarbone-length curtain of ultra-glossy brown hair with rich copper highlights, making the green of her eyes even more intense. She looked stunning. Rufus had thought so too, taking her straight to bed for a prolonged and athletic sex session wherein he explored and exploited her hairless and fake-tanned body as if he had paid for her services. Which he had, in a way, she thought.

'Bella's gone all shiny,' announced Flora to Maddy who had come out of the Home Farm kitchen to greet her.

'Hello, stranger,' she said, enveloping Bella in a hug, although her huge tummy got in the way rather. 'You *are* all shiny and posh,' she said, standing back to admire. 'And thin,' she added, giving her friend a searching look.

'Strong not skinny, I hope,' said Bella. 'I've not lost that much weight, but that's because Kelvin says I've gained muscle.'

'Kelvin?'

'My personal trainer. Well, Rufus's personal trainer . . .'

'What's yours is his.'

'Yeah, well . . . like I said, not much weight off. Only about a stone, but two inches off each thigh and three inches off my hips,' she announced, not mentioning how disappointed she and Kelvin had been to discover she had not managed to reduce her waist size. He had promised to review her abdominals programme, which had dismayed her. It was pretty tough already.

'You didn't need to lose weight. And you didn't have big thighs,' said Serena, joining them. A glamorous blonde woman in her fifties, she dressed like a teenage hippy with friendship bracelets all up her arm and had absolutely no airs and graces, so no one ever realised it was her and her husband Giles who owned Home Farm with all its artisans working in the converted stable block. 'Anyway, to what do we owe the pleasure?'

'I've got some more work for Judy,' said Bella. 'The curtains and blinds for the bedrooms at The Grange. It's so cool that she's here. Well done for finding her,' she added, to Maddy, 'She's been doing a fantastic job. I don't know how I would be coping without her.'

'I've let her expand into your old offices,' admitted Serena. 'I hope that's all right? With her big work tables in there she barely had room for the fabrics, so she's using your space for storage. I'm sure you could have it back whenever you like.'

'That's a nice thought,' said Bella, and it truly was, she missed her old friends at Home Farm, 'but Rufus is talking about me expanding. He says I'll need to be taking on staff soon and perhaps moving my operation up to London as his next couple of development projects are up there. It's a block of luxury flats in Kensington. I'm doing the show flat there as soon as The Grange is up and running,' she said, proudly.

'London?' said Maddy with dismay. 'We thought you'd be moving back here when The Grange was complete. Why do you have to go to London? Even if your project is up there, you've always said, you could work anywhere . . .'

'I can,' said Bella. 'It's just that . . . well . . . London is where the big projects are. I've always wanted to grow and develop the business . . . it's really exciting the opportunities I'm getting now, the people I'm meeting. Also . . .' she paused, 'Rufus lives up there. He wants me to move in with him. I mean, into his London apartment, not here.'

There was a silence.

'But you're with Charlie,' blurted Flora, near tears. 'It's not right. You married him. I was there . . .' Flora's chin wobbled, her face a picture of confusion.

Maddy put her arm around Flora and gave Bella a look. 'It's all right Flora, Bella's not going anywhere yet. Not for ages. Possibly not at all, are you Bella?'

'No, no . . .' she agreed. 'Not definitely. Just a thought.'

'Have you seen Charlie at all?' Serena asked, gently.

'No, has anyone?'

'I'm seeing him tonight,' admitted Maddy. 'About the festival planning. We're getting together quite a bit obviously, mainly him, me and Zach . . .'

'How is he?' said Bella, her voice filled with yearning.

'Not great, frankly. Shall I pass on a message at all?'

'Give him my love,' blurted Bella. 'Yeah,' she said, reflecting. 'Give him my love. And tell him to look after Dolly. And himself.'

'I want one of Dolly's puppies,' said Flora, brightening.

'It's a big commitment,' warned Serena.

'I know, I know, but I really want one. Can I have one, Bella? Can I?'

'Yes,' said Bella. 'I need to find good homes for them all,' she said. 'That's another thing . . . you must tell Charlie, even if he doesn't want to see me he must let me see Dolly. I need to see her. Tell him?'

'I will,' said Maddy. 'But I dearly want you to tell him yourself. You need to talk to each other.'

'It's something like this I'm after,' said Bella, showing Judy a picture of some curtains on her phone.

'Got it,' said Judy, nodding. 'That's a hand-sewn heading, see? No tape, just the hooks sewn straight on. Gives it a really nice, soft informal look, doesn't it?'

'That's exactly what I'm after, you are a star . . . sounds like hard work, though, sewing everything by hand?'

'It takes a while,' said Judy. 'But I'll give you a good price, don't worry.'

'Budget sensitivity isn't so much of a thing,' admitted Bella. 'It's more about whether you'll have time to get it all done. We've only got four weeks now and there's eight bedrooms with two big windows each, and – like we discussed – all these curtains are lined and interlined. The headings may be simple and informal but there are no flipping corners cut with the curtains themselves.'

'You wouldn't want to, with these amazing fabrics,' said Judy, stroking the nearest one, which was an ultra-soft fake suede finish in a deep, aubergine colour. 'These rooms are going to be so luxurious . . . talking of fabrics, the silk dupion for the main reception room has arrived. D'you want to see?'

There were six rolls of the grey silk stacked next to each other in Bella's old office. Even in the dim light, the iridescence of the fabric was compelling, the subtle variations in colour like a stormy sky shot with silver.

'They are going to look amazing,' said Bella, imagining the floor-length curtains with their ten-foot drop framing the huge Georgian sash windows in the main reception room, which was going to become the piano bar.

'The dye lots are about as close as you can get,' said Judy. 'I've checked them pretty thoroughly. Obviously, I'll make sure to check again before I join the widths. I'm very glad there's no pattern to match up. The size of them is about the maximum I can manage.'

'Sure,' said Bella. 'Did we put a fitting date in the diary? We should. I need to get you in either before or after the chandeliers go in. That's assuming we are working to schedule.'

'Oo, after if you can. I'm dying to see these chandeliers, they sound amazing.'

'They look amazing, but you'll see them at the opening party.'

'What? Will I be invited?'

'Of course you will. And so will all the performers at the festival. I've heard Zane Stringfellow is going to be the lead act that night, and he'll be staying at The Grange hopefully.'

'Oh my God, Inspire are going to perform? I love them! Zane Stringfellow is my idol.'

CHAPTER NINETEEN

Maddy, on the other hand, was less impressed with Zane Stringfellow and his management team. By the time she had joined Zach and Charlie for their progress meeting that evening she was feeling distinctly frazzled.

'I've been nagging his office to send the contract over for days,' she complained to the two men, 'and then – when it finally arrives – it's full of the most bizarre riders I've ever seen.'

'Smarties with the blue ones taken out?' hazarded Zach. 'A basket of puppies, Heinz tomato soup and broccoli already cut up so it's easier to throw away?'

'I wish,' said Maddy, wearily. 'Try a fifteen-foot python and a large tube of KY Jelly with a stipulation that if, on arrival, the python is an inch short of the required length, the artist will exercise his contractual right to refuse to perform.'

Charlie and Zach both snorted with laughter. 'Same old Chris. Sounds like he's having you on.'

'Yeah, so, it turns out you're right, the real contract came through about half an hour ago, but only after I'd spent all afternoon calling up zoos. It turns out they don't hire out fifteen-foot pythons – or any other length, come to that.'

'Thank goodness,' said Zach in mock horror. 'I dread to think . . .'

'Yeah well, laugh it up,' said Maddy sourly, 'because what I need you to do next is work out how we're going to deal with the sewage and rubbish that three thousand visitors are going to produce over three days.'

'Ah yes, sewage,' interjected Charlie. 'I know this one. Now, in my extensive conversations with the Portaloo guru of the UK, I have come up with our requirements for seven separate latrine stations along with a plan for delivery routes and collection schedules,' he said, handing out photocopies of the document he had drawn up, 'along with provision of soap, hand towels and loo paper,' he added, 'which is extra.'

'Welcome back,' said Zach.

'Yeah, okay,' Charlie conceded. 'I hear you. Ben said. I'm on the wagon until the final night of the festival. I promise. Might have a small, dry sherry at The Grange's opening party, though.'

'You'll have earned it by then. Let's just hope you won't be crying into it.'

'Let's,' said Charlie, who had also handed over the money for the Portaloo contract that afternoon too. And it was a lot.

'Is it really three thousand visitors, though?' said Zach, sounding slightly alarmed. 'The logistics don't allow for that.'

'Sorry,' said Maddy, 'Not three thousand at one time . . . I'm thinking ticket sales. We're limiting it to one thousand a day like we agreed – obviously tiny by music festival standards – but, being a three-day event, we are giving people the option to come for a day or the whole weekend. Most people so far want to come for the whole lot and camp, hence the poo calculations, well done Charlie for sorting that.'

'How are ticket sales?' said Charlie.

'Amazingly good, actually,' said Maddy. 'Here's my report,' she added, handing out her paperwork. 'Flora's doing wonders with social media. The website is getting a good lot of hits now, and we're getting fantastic radio publicity. There's a lot of interest in these boutique, family events. Obviously, having Zane Stringfellow headlining is helping enormously,' she added, sounding a bit more forgiving. 'I thought we would be chasing around for other acts to fill the schedule but we've got people calling us, including – I might add – "Three Old Blokes and a Dodgy Amp".'

'What? Patrick's band? Isn't he too busy running the pub?' asked Charlie, clutching at straws.

'Sadly not,' said Maddy, 'not since my mum got him to take on extra staff so they could have more quality time together. You can't say "no", he's my dad.'

'Can't I?' said Charlie, faintly. 'Three Old Blokes . . .' was locally famous for being a band with more enthusiasm than talent. 'Are you sure?'

'Sure,' said Maddy, firmly. 'Anyway, the whole authentic, local talent bit's a definite "thing" with the boutique festivals nowadays. People expect it. They like it.'

'"They like it"?' queried Charlie without conviction. 'I'm not at all sure the wider world is ready for "Three Old Blokes . . ."' he muttered, but he let it go. For now.

'Yeah, so the smaller bands are in the Yellow Zone, like we said last time,' Maddy went on. 'Red Zone's the main stage, obviously, and I think it works that we decided the zones get quieter as we go through the rainbow. The Blue Zone, for the older kids, is coming on really well but I'm a bit worried about the drainage in the Violet field – is it not going to be a bit wet for tents and stuff?'

'Ah, forgot to say,' jumped in Zach. 'I've managed to get Serena and Giles to allocate their outer two paddocks for Indigo and Violet so we don't need to use the lower field at all now. I've told them it's going to be the quieter stuff near their house, but I don't think they care, they're totally up for a party. I doubt they'll go to bed for the whole three days.'

'Excellent,' said Maddy, 'and – to go back to the Blue Zone – I went ahead and spoke to the Bespoke Consortium members about craft activities and they're all on board, so we've got face painting, parachute games, spinning and weaving, suncatcher workshops, loads of other crafts, it's going to be brill. I think the parents are totally going to want to do this stuff too.'

'Good to get as many local people involved as possible,' said Zach. 'It helps with public relations. There's been a bit of grumbling from the community, I'm hearing.'

'Why?' said Charlie, instantly annoyed. 'What on earth have people got to complain about? Potentially the Rainbow Festival is really going to put Havenbury on the map. Don't people want that?'

'A lot of them don't,' said Zach, smiling in spite of himself. 'Look, don't worry, I've been running the estate for years. You get this stuff. Mainly people just want to be reassured. They want to know what's going on. It's just stuff about traffic, parking, crime . . . logistics. By the way, I've got a meeting with the police tomorrow, so I'll know more about our traffic management plans then. Should be okay . . .'

'Sure, sorry Zach,' said Charlie, mollified. 'I forget you've done stuff like this with the estate before . . .'

'Not as big as this,' Zach admitted, 'but – yeah – I've done events. It's seriously important for us to be looking for ways to make the community economically sustainable,' he went on. 'People don't appreciate how vital it is for old estates like this to find ways to survive. We're not the landed gentry any more.'

'You sort of are the landed gentry, mate,' teased Charlie. 'Or should I say "my lord"?'

'You'd better bloody not,' said Zach. 'I'm just saying, we have to duck and dive. Things have to work differently. This is great. It's a grand idea. I hope it becomes a regular event. Not sure the locals will go for it becoming the next Glastonbury, but I'm seriously impressed at you for coming up with the idea.'

'And funding it,' added Maddy.

'Yeah, that,' said Charlie. 'That's thanks to Rufus, actually, not that he's too fussed as long as I get it paid back in time . . .' He paused to inwardly acknowledge the twist of fear in his gut at the payment terms he had agreed. 'Anyhow,' he went on, 'so far so good, but we do need to keep an eye on costs. At least the ticket sales are starting to come in, that's a relief. And we need to be looking for sponsors and concessions.'

'On it,' said Maddy. 'I've got T-shirt and memorabilia

companies, let's see who bids highest, plus a whole load of food producers, burgers, ice creams, curry, falafel, there's vegetarian, vegan, Thai food—'

'Fab,' said Charlie, cutting her short. 'I don't say it enough, but thank you both – so much . . . I may have come up with the idea and the cash, but your expertise – both of you – is essential.'

'Yeah, mate, you don't say it enough,' agreed Zach, but then he softened. 'It's for you and Bella,' he added. 'I want to see you guys sort it out.'

'Have you seen her?' Charlie asked Maddy.

'Just this afternoon.'

'How is she?'

Maddy paused, lost for words. 'She looks healthy,' she admitted at last. 'But not happy.'

He slumped in this chair.

'And she's desperate to see Dolly,' she added, conniving, hoping to engineer a meeting. Zach nodded approvingly at her strategy.

'Tell her she can,' said Charlie. 'I drop her at Ma's tomorrow. Bella can see her there.'

Bella grabbed her phone eagerly, heart thumping when she saw it was from Charlie. The text was brief, just telling her she could see Dolly at Caroline's house that morning if she wanted. 'If she wanted'! Of course she did. After carefully analysing the little text for tone and hidden nuances she rapidly made the arrangements required to clear her diary. Everything else could wait.

* * *

215

She ran from Rufus's house to Dove Cottage so she had nailed her daily cardiac workout too. Dressing to go out, she was reasonably satisfied with her neater hips but searched out a baggy shirt to hide her thick waist. Even when she was heavy she had been proud of her little waist in her little nipped-in fifties dresses. She was sinewy now. Fake-tanned and muscular. They would look terrible on her.

She could hear Dolly singing before she even lifted the catch on the little wooden gate. Coming up the path, jogging on the spot to let her tired muscles cool slowly – she had run at her fastest pace all the way – she didn't even need to use the knocker as Caroline was already there.

'Bella,' she said, holding out her arms for a hug. She looked weary but resigned. 'Come here. You're too thin.'

'You always say that.'

'I didn't used to. Not when you weren't too thin. Now let me give you a hug before that silly dog barges in, she's been desperate for you to arrive. I've been telling her.'

Dolly was already there in the narrow doorway, threatening to knock them both over as she squirmed desperately between the two women, trying to get through gaps her expanded tummy would no longer allow. She was singing and moaning with delight.

Bella took her into the kitchen and crouched down on the floor so Dolly could have her fill. Eventually, with hands and face thoroughly covered in lick, and Dolly less desperately excited, she stood up and looked properly at Caroline who was bustling around filling Bella's favourite teapot. It was the one with the roses and a branch twining around to make the handle. It had a matching knitted tea cosy with knitted roses on the top. Rufus would vehemently disapprove. Bella, on the other hand, adored the cosy cottage aesthetic – quite wrong for The Grange, of course – but the familiar and consoling atmosphere made the tears prick at her eyes for reasons she couldn't have told anyone if they asked.

'I'm so sorry about the jewels,' she said to Caroline.

'Oh, well,' said Caroline, waving her hand to shoo away the thought.

'And Geoffrey,' Bella added.

This time the older woman just nodded. 'So am I,' she said. The words resonated with a deep sadness that made Bella's eyes threaten to spill again.

'Of course, we don't know . . .' said Bella.

'True, but Charlie makes a fair point that he might have done and – in light of the evidence – I have to agree I'm afraid,' she said, lifting her chin in resignation.

'Circumstantial, at best . . .'

'Granted, but if not Geoffrey, then . . . well, who?' Caroline sighed. 'I've never been the best judge of men. Not for myself, anyhow . . . Now, carrot cake,' said Caroline, coming out of the larder with a freshly iced loaf cake. 'Your favourite.'

Bella groaned. 'Is that cream-cheese icing?'

'Of course. Now sit down and pass me your plate.'

'I can't,' she said, regretfully but with determination. 'I'm off carbs.'

'This isn't carbs,' said Caroline, with misplaced authority. 'It's got carrots in it. It's practically a health food.'

'I've got to stick to my regime. Kelvin will kill me.' Slight exaggeration, admitted Bella to herself. Kelvin wasn't paid to kill his clients, although sometimes it felt like he might accidentally do that. She was convinced he was capable of reporting back to Rufus, though. And that was worse.

'She's ready to drop, more or less,' said Caroline changing the subject and fondling Dolly's ears. Dolly looked up at her devotedly.

'I thought I'd be around. I'm so sorry . . .'

'Nothing to be sorry about. It's tough going for the first few weeks, though. A bit like having a newborn baby. I've been clearing out the back porch. It's warm and dry. She can have a bed in there and the pups can be contained when they start moving around.'

'Would you really?'

'Yes, but I'd like one of the pups in payment.'

'Of course! You can have first pick!' said Bella. 'Second pick,' she corrected, remembering her promise to Zach in return for borrowing Brutus to do the deed. 'Third pick,' she added, remembering Maddy's request. 'Flora wants one too, she says.'

'Goodness, I hope she has a big litter. Is that child capable of being responsible for a dog?'

'She's my age, believe it or not.'

'Mm, but Flora's an unusual girl,' mused Caroline. 'An old soul, but an innocent . . . Has she found a boyfriend?'

'I think she's found lots.'

'I don't mean sexual partners, she's always had plenty of those, and well done her,' said Caroline without judgement. 'But that's just entertainment. I'd like to see her settle down with someone. She needs stability, that girl. Goodness knows who, though. She's a funny old stick.'

'She's always walked to the beat of her own drum' said Bella. 'When we were at school she was off in a dream world of her own most of the time. I remember education specialist people coming in and making her do tests. They thought she might be autistic.'

'Is she?'

'I don't know. Possibly. I just think she does things her way. She's really bright, but impossibly dreamy. And she does work her way through boyfriends, but there's nothing sordid about it. She's a child of nature. She exists in the "now". Follows her instincts. I think we could all afford to be a bit more like that, actually. But I worry about her too,' agreed Bella. 'She needs someone very special who "gets" her. It needs to be a guy who can teach her to be a bit more worldly, if I'm honest . . . In fact, I'm thinking about setting her up with someone.'

'Because your last attempt at matchmaking went so well,' commented Caroline, dryly. 'Talking of boyfriends, how are you getting on with the ginger nut?'

'Rufus? Don't let him hear you call him that. He's "auburn", apparently.' Bella looked around her nervously, as if he might appear.

'I don't like him.'

'No, well, you're bound not to.'

'You and Charlie need to talk.'

'Mm. What did you mean just now, when you talked about not being good at choosing men?' asked Bella, sipping her tea.

'Just that.'

'But I thought – well, I'm sure Charlie told me – Peter was your first boyfriend.'

'That's what he liked to think,' admitted Caroline. 'And it's nearly true. I was only twenty-two. Young, but not fantastically young for those days. It was a different generation, after all.'

'But you and Peter were married for – what? – thirty-five years?'

'Thirty-three by the time he died. We made a go of it – for Charlie, and for appearances, and anyway,' Caroline gave herself a little shake, 'we were happy in many ways, of course we were . . .'

'But Peter seemed so lovely, he was kind, funny, generous . . .'

'Oh yes, he was generous all right, with largely my family's money.'

'Ouch.'

'I know, I know . . . he was a lovely man in many ways,' said Caroline. 'I don't want you to think any differently of him. And,' she said suddenly fiercely, 'I don't want you to relay this conversation to Charlie. He deserves to have his memories of his father preserved.'

'Not likely to be talking to him anytime soon,' said Bella, 'but do please tell me . . .'

'Oh,' Caroline sighed, 'don't get me wrong, he was a kind man, Peter, I wouldn't have stayed with him otherwise. I would hardly have exposed Charlie to any sort of abuse, naturally, but he was hopeless with money. That was the thing. So grandiose, so generous, such grand plans . . . but hopeless. I used to joke he had a hole in his wallet, but it wasn't funny really. My own father was furious with him.'

'I don't remember him.'

'No, of course you don't,' said Caroline, smiling fondly at the memory. 'He was a very straightforward man. Called a spade a spade. Not a traditionalist, in the sense that I was allowed to inherit. Primogeniture was a concept adopted only recently by the old farming families.'

'You're kidding!'

Caroline smiled. 'Of course it helped that I was the only child too,' she admitted.

'And Charlie is an only child,' said Bella.

'He comes from a long line of small families,' Caroline acknowledged. 'We would have wanted more, of course, but it wasn't to be . . . and Charlie was – is – so sunny, beautiful, clever. We couldn't be sad. He was everything Peter and I could ever have wanted. He was born on a Sunday, and I always remember the rhyme – do you know it? – the child who is born on the Sabbath day is bonny and blithe, good and gay.'

'Definitely not "gay",' said Bella. 'Although I remember him and Ben pretending to be,' she recalled. 'At least, the girls sometimes thought they were together because they were such close friends.'

'And they encouraged it because it made the girls let their guard down,' said Caroline. 'It used to help them get into their pants.'

'You knew that?'

'I know more than you think,' said Caroline, but she was smiling at the memory. 'Anyway, the point is, my father was looking for me to settle down with someone who would help me run the farm, continue the family tradition, and he reckoned Peter was a good choice. He didn't have the land, but we did. He went off and got a degree at agricultural college, so he knew his stuff. My father thought he was an excellent choice and encouraged the match.'

'It's all very *Pride and Prejudice*,' said Bella. 'I had no idea.'

'It wasn't really. I chose Peter. He was the noisiest, the most charming, the most fun of all the young men in my social circle.'

Bella thought. 'And then you chose Geoffrey.'

'Indeed.'

'He's a bit more of a worse choice than someone who isn't great with money.'

'Possibly.'

'But he's a thief.'

'Possibly.'

'If you're not sure he took the jewels, then surely you should find out?'

'I don't need to. I won't get them back anyway. They weren't insured. Peter always said it was better to roll with the punches than fill underwriters' pockets with fat insurance premiums. All I will do is either accuse an innocent man, which would be unforgivable, or expose myself and Charlie to public attention in a way that will be at best embarrassing and at worst give ne'er-do-wells the impression that Dove Cottage and the farmhouse might be worth targeting for any other valuables we might have. I prefer to stay below the radar.'

'"Ne'er-do-wells"?' Bella teased, gently. 'Who says that . . . ?'

'It's a good expression,' Caroline said. 'The English language is all the poorer for it having fallen out of fashion.'

'So if you're only "not sure", then why are you writing him off?'

'I realised – in retrospect – that there was something more amiss with Geoffrey. Even if there hadn't been the mysterious missing jewellery, then alarm bells ought to have been ringing.'

'Go on?' said Bella, intrigued. She hadn't told Caroline about the mysterious woman outside Geoffrey's shop that day.

'As you were beginning to suspect yourself,' Caroline went on, 'he's a man with secrets. Not just secrets . . . tragedies. Loss. He's deeply, deeply sad . . .'

Bella was shocked and moved to see tears in the older woman's eyes. She had hardly ever seen Caroline cry. She had even been stalwart and dry-eyed throughout most of the time following Peter's death. For her to tear up in pure empathy was a big deal.

'Sad about what?'

'Dunno,' said Caroline briskly, gathering up the dirty crockery and crashing it unnecessarily loudly into the sink. 'Silly old me. Should have known better. Still, the sex was good.'

'Yikes, too much information,' yelped Bella. 'Did you?' she asked, despite herself.

'I certainly did. Old people have sex too, you know.'

'Yeah, but, you brazen hussy. You only knew him for five minutes. Mind you,' she added, remembering, 'coming from me . . .'

Caroline stopped and turned to face Bella. 'Listen,' she said. 'I don't approve. I think you're an idiot, and I think you were wrong, but what you did . . . to get that money for Charlie, that was' – she paused, choosing her words carefully – 'that was brave. It was courageous, and it was a level of loyalty and devotion that Charlie had no right to expect. What *you* did, is not, in isolation, the action that broke your marriage. My son – I am not afraid to say it – is a proud, pig-headed, stubborn fool. Just like his father. I desperately wish he would come to his senses.'

'Do you think he will?' said Bella, hope stirring inside her. Or at least there was definitely something stirring inside her, she was glad she had said no to cake.

'It's going to take something huge,' mused Caroline. 'A big shock. That's what it'll take for my idiotic son to fight for his marriage like he should. I just hope he does it. Before it's too late. Tell me it's not too late.'

Bella blushed. 'To be honest, I was so devastated, a few weeks ago I would have said "no". Now, my life is changing so fast. Rufus is – he's exciting, demanding – I can see my life taking off. I'm fitter, working harder, my business is growing. He's talking about us moving to London together. It makes me question whether my life at the farmhouse was the life I truly wanted. I did think it was . . . perhaps if I'd had a baby straight away . . . but the farm, the vineyard, it's just such hard work and for so little gain. It's not what I thought it would be, maybe . . .' Bella trailed off apologetically.

'You are brave,' said Caroline. 'You are braver than I was. I stayed with Peter – we had Charlie – and perhaps I shouldn't have done. Maybe you are doing the right thing. You don't have ties . . . not if you don't want my son.'

'I have Dolly,' said Bella, stroking the little dog who had planted her head firmly on Bella's feet so that if she fell asleep her mistress couldn't leave without her knowing. 'We have Dolly, me and Charlie. There's no going back on that.'

It was a sixth sense that woke Caroline just two hours after she had gone to sleep. She padded downstairs to find Dolly pacing up and down the hallway anxiously. She was pleased to see Caroline, thumping her tail and licking her hand when it was offered but she was preoccupied, her fretting of earlier that day settling into something more urgent and all-consuming. Once Caroline had got her settled in the porch with her bed, deep with towels, and encouraged her to have a drink she stopped pacing and fretting and got down to the matter in hand. In the darkest hours of the night – the safest time for the vulnerability of giving birth – the first pup popped out, followed within the hour by a second and third.

'Good girl,' crooned Caroline, sitting on a cushion in a corner with a mug of tea. Dolly hadn't needed anything from her other than company and encouragement, but she was there just in case. At one point, Caroline lifted a puppy to check it and place it closer to a nipple but the closest Dolly got to anxiety or protectiveness was to watch Caroline's every move with keen, unblinking interest. Once the puppy was safely back in position she laid her head back down and licked Caroline's hand in a lazy slurp of thanks.

Time passed. Caroline left her at one point to grab a sandwich but was never far from hand. The hours passing had a surreal quality, the two of them alone, cocooned in their little world, creating new life.

At dawn Caroline was making herself the umpteenth cup of tea, confident the whelping was over and nearly ready to turn in and get some sleep at last. When she returned, Dolly was licking a new and unexpected arrival. It was much smaller than the others, its protective sack clinging despite Dolly's tired endeavours.

'Let me, darling,' crooned Caroline, picking the soft, velvety little scrap up in a towel 'let me help.' She wiped the tiny face with a corner of the towel but there was no answering twitch or gasp. She grabbed a handful of towel and rubbed the little ribcage gently. Nothing. Summoning up all the scraps of knowledge she could think of she carried the little dog through to the kitchen where there was more room and swung it gently around, head outermost, using centrifugal force to clear its airways and encourage it to breathe. The minutes passed as she alternated swinging with gentle rubbing. She watched the clock as she worked.

'Cooeee,' came a voice, making her jump and then, two seconds later, jump again as Bella came into the kitchen, jogging on the spot, and wiping the sweat from her brow.

'Beautiful morning,' she panted, 'saw the light on . . . hoped you'd be . . . what's this?'

Caroline quickly explained.

'Dolly?'

'She's fine. In the back porch. This one, I'm afraid, isn't so good.'

Bella craned to see the little face peeking out of the towel.

'Poor little thing,' she whispered. 'May I?' She took the pathetic bundle from Caroline and held it in her hands. 'Should we not keep going?'

'I don't think so,' said Caroline sadly. 'I've tried long enough, to keep going is futile, even unkind, really. I honestly think it must have been born beyond help. These things happen.'

'Poor Dolly!' she said, her breath catching on a sob. 'She'll be heartbroken.'

'She's got six healthy ones to care for,' said Caroline robustly. 'Come through.'

Bella padded after her as she gently popped the little body down in front of Dolly's nose. 'She needs to know what happened,' said Caroline.

After nudging the silky little corpse with her nose and sniffing it, Dolly turned away from it, all interest lost, simply settling herself more comfortably in the bed with her six live pups lined up on her teats like a row of velvety sausages.

Caroline lifted the little dead pup and wrapped it carefully in the towel. 'Sit with her,' she said to Bella. 'I'll bring you a cup of tea.'

When she came back in, minutes later, with a steaming mug of tea along with a slice of toast and Marmite, Bella's favourite breakfast, she found her lying, hunched over Dolly, sobbing helplessly into the dog's fur. Her sobs racked her entire body and, as Caroline rubbed her back in an attempt to comfort her, she was amazed to feel how much weight Bella had lost, her plump curves now entirely gone, replaced with toned muscle.

CHAPTER TWENTY

Charlie had kept to his word on no alcohol until after the festival. The kitchen at the farmhouse had become the Rainbow Festival headquarters, particularly the large kitchen table, which was the hub of the organisation. Both Charlie's and Maddy's laptops were permanently on it and plugged in, trailing wires that constantly threatened to trip everyone up. Zach was there a lot too, striding around with his mobile phone clamped to his ear, making plans and decisions with military authority. He had not been keen on the Rainbow theme, preferring the Havenbury Festival as a title, but he was now happily talking about access and exit roads to the 'Red Zone' and 'Green Zone', whilst baulking at taking responsibility for the children's themed activities like the Unicorn Marquee, which he and Charlie had left, with dubious confidence, to Flora to organise.

Flora and Maddy were giddy that morning, thrilled to hear that Dolly's pups had arrived and could barely be persuaded to get on with their work. They were desperately wanting to invite themselves to Dove Cottage and see them. Even Zach cracked a smile of pleasure and expressed an interest. There was so much to do, though, all were quickly absorbed by what needed sorting.

Flora was in her element, having blagged industrial quantities of face paint and fake tattoos on the promise to take donations for the local children's hospice. Zach had congratulated her and then gently pointed out that Charlie's huge loan from Rufus was actually the 'good cause' she was supposed to be raising funds for and she had promised to make sure all other revenue streams went to the Dovecot Estate.

Maddy had the hat with the antlers on, signifying she was not to be disturbed as she was intensely working to get all the promotional materials, including the T-shirts, off to the printer before it was too late.

'Oo, they're so cool,' breathed Flora, peeking at the designs over Maddy's shoulder while Zach – who was having a nightmare with Highways – barked something about traffic priorities on High Green Lane being 'tantamount to apocalyptic' if Highways insisted on getting their way.

'I never knew there was so much involved,' admitted Charlie repeatedly to anyone who would listen. He was bunging the kettle back on the stove and trying to see if anyone wanted another cup of tea. The kettle had boiled dry twice because he kept being distracted by important emails coming in, or one of the various phones ringing.

'Look, guys, I need to go into the vineyard and do a check before nightfall,' he said, to thin air, with all his friends fully occupied and oblivious.

'Bella would be in her element, wouldn't she?' he said to himself as he mooched slowly down the hill to the first field. He missed having Dolly by his side. She would have loved basking in the July heat, which was withering the poor, neglected sweet peas in the pots either side of the bench. Charlie had bought it as a birthday present for Bella. He had it specially made and put it at the top of the hill with the best view of the vineyard and beyond. They had a habit of coming out in their pyjamas to sit and drink their morning coffee.

There wasn't much to do in the vineyard. He had checked all the sugars that morning. All he could do, over the next few weeks, was watch, worry and wait as the grapes not killed by the frost swelled and ripened. He sat down at the high end of the rows sloping away from him and contemplated the view.

'I'm an idiot,' he said aloud. 'I've taken the farm, I've taken my marriage, and I've ruined it all but – do you know what? – I'm bloody determined to find out what happened to those jewels. And if I can get them back, I'm going to make damn sure they don't get dragged in to pay off debts. If Ma has the money from them she can buy a little cottage somewhere in the village, maybe one of the little almshouses near the pond, and at least – when the farm goes bankrupt – she'll be happy and safe.'

'So you're going to the police after all?' said Ben.

'Nope. Too public, too out of our control.'

'What's the matter with that?'

'Ma doesn't want it. She just doesn't want this Geoffrey

bloke to know we're looking into anything he might be involved in.'

'You mean he doesn't know he's suspected?'

'He doesn't even know the jewels are missing.'

'He does if he flipping nicked them. Anyway, if he didn't steal them, isn't he wondering why Caroline isn't wanting to see him any more? I gather they had quite a thing.'

'Cold feet, second thoughts, woman's prerogative, dunno . . .' said Charlie. 'Anyhow, where do we start?'

'I wouldn't mind finding out who that mysterious woman was. Plus, it's odd, don't you think, that he just popped up in Havenbury out of nowhere?'

'Fair point – so, say we check electoral records, Companies House – is this bookshop a limited company? – google him, at least . . . do we know his full name?

'Funnily enough, we know his middle name is Peter.'

'Your dad's name? Weird coincidence.'

'If it's true. Otherwise it's just a corny trick deliberately designed to get my ma to relate to him.'

'So, first name, middle name and surname. Good. Do we have an age? Date of birth?'

'Not yet, but we will.'

In the end, Bella was kindly but firmly escorted to the door by Paddy who charmingly told her to take herself and her 'to do' lists and find somewhere else to put them.

'But I just need to make sure the tiler understands the mother-of-pearl splashback needs to go in *before* the mixer tap . . . and the plumber – Mike?' – Paddy nodded, patiently – 'needs to know the bath can only go a foot from the wall, because the pipes are on that side, mind you the fall from the plughole is barely enough, I was thinking we should put the whole bath on a plinth, what do you reckon?'

'I reckon,' said Paddy, his blue eyes, which reminded her painfully of Charlie's, 'if I don't get you off-site sharpish my contractors – who all fancy you, by the way, please wear a longer skirt next time – are all going to go home in a huff.'

'But we've only got another couple of weeks,' said Bella, tugging at her skirt self-consciously, Rufus had bought it for her and she daren't refuse to wear it.

'It's all fine,' Paddy said, patting her on the shoulder reassuringly. 'I've worked to tighter deadlines than this. I know it looks a state but once the paint goes on and the soft furnishings go in, you'll see . . . I promise.'

'Yikes, soft furnishings! I wonder if I should go to Home Farm and see how Judy is getting on with the curtains and blinds?'

'I think you should definitely do that,' said Paddy, seizing on the plan with enthusiasm. 'Cracking idea. Off you go.'

At Home Farm Bella had a warm welcome from Serena who was looking for an excuse for a pot of tea and a natter around the kitchen table. Giles was doing some mysterious business deal in London and her precious boys were away at boarding school, so she was feeling bereft. Turning down banana cake, to Serena's astonishment – it used to be her favourite – she had a cup of black tea because Rufus was doing some weird 'no dairy' thing. Over tea she caught up with the news of the Bespoke Consortium.

'It's all down to Maddy's hard work,' said Serena. 'The team are better at coping on their own now than they were, and obviously I'm doing a lot of the logistics, but Maddy is still going all guns firing on the marketing. She has too much on her plate with the festival too, and the baby coming. I'm worried for her.'

Judy was polite when Bella showed up but was obviously not keen to encourage client interference. 'It's all going fine,' she told Bella, and she could see the silk dupion grey curtains for the piano bar were laid out on the long tables, looking amazing, trailing on the floor, despite the length of the tables.

'I'll be up next week to fit them, providing you have the room clean, decorated and ready for me.'

'I will. It has to be. The chandeliers are going in then too.'

After having more or less been chucked out of Judy's workshop too, Bella – feeling guilty at not having seen her since the baby shower – called Maddy.

'Are you at the farmhouse?'

'I am. Up to my neck in festival stuff but come and have lunch with me. I'm starving.'

Bella hesitated.

'Charlie's not here,' Maddy reassured her. 'He's in London all day schmoozing potential sponsors.'

'Yum,' said Maddy. 'I don't know how I got through life until now without pineapple on my pizza.'

'It's gross,' complained Bella, who had got herself a Four

Seasons. 'Pregnancy has turned you into a food monster stroke dustbin-like person.'

'It's turned me into an eating machine,' complained Maddy. 'I'm never not hungry. This baby has me possessed. She's going to come out with a slice of pineapple and ham pizza in her gob.'

'Tell her not to come out just yet. How long have you got?'

'She's due in late August. Just in time for the festival, but she'll be late. Simon says first babies usually are.'

'But what if she comes on time? Or early?'

'It's fine,' said Maddy, with her mouth full. 'In a few days, I'll do some massive "handover" notes just in case. I'd do it now, but – frankly – I'm barely on top of all this myself. It's eye-of-the-storm time.' She made a sweeping gesture with her arm at all the papers, laptops, printers and boxes of merchandise that occupied every surface including the floor. 'Everything's all in my head, though,' she went on. 'I just need to not be hit by a bus or anything for a few more days.'

'I feel the same about The Grange. We're right in the thick of the final stage. It's going to be amazing, but I've got so much going on about colours, fabrics, finishes, doorknobs . . . almost all of it is custom-made . . . I feel like my head's going to explode.'

'Biggest, coolest project yet, though, eh?' prompted Maddy with a wicked, irrepressible grin.

'Yeah,' said Bella, grinning back.

'We're at the height of our powers, girl. We're on fire.'

'Will you do this again?' said Bella.

234

'Damned right I will. This festival is going to be the mutt's nuts. It's going to be heaven on earth. It's going to be the best damned boutique festival in the summer calendar. It'll put Havenbury on the map, that's for sure. And it's us! Who knew?'

Bella sighed with contentment. Her fists loosening just a little. Maddy was right. They were both achieving amazing things and maybe Rufus was right, that she should uproot and follow her interior decorating star in London. With The Grange under her belt and a success, she would be picking and choosing her next projects. She could get an assistant. Maybe a couple of them to help with sourcing and administration. It was what she wanted for her little company. It was why she had set it up, despite Charlie's lack of faith in her. Wasn't it?

Maddy was grimacing and clutching the edge of the table.

'What?' said Bella, alarmed.

'Nothing, nothing,' she said, her voice tight and tense, 'just a bit of a stomach protest at the pineapple pizza . . .'

'Seriously? Looks worse than a bit of heartburn.'

'Okay, maybe plus one of those practice contraction thingies . . . Braxton Hicks?'

'Aren't they supposed to be painless?'

'Not when they're combined with indigestion. I tell you, girl, this pregnancy lark isn't for sissies.'

Bella looked on anxiously as Maddy continued to grip the table and stare at her plate with intense concentration. After a few breaths she visibly relaxed.

'There,' she said. 'Fine now . . . where were we?'

'I think you were telling me the baby wasn't due for

weeks, that only you knew what was currently going on but that you were probably going to jot down a few handover notes when you could be bothered,' said Bella with an innocent expression on her face.

'I'm fine,' said Maddy, with emphasis. 'Did you see these amazing T-shirts? There's this incredible local artist who did the logo, Fergus Bettany?'

'Oh my God, I'm sure I was at school with him. Beaky-looking, thick glasses?'

'No glasses, but, yeah, about our age, quite fanciable I thought . . .'

'Can't be the Fergus I remember, then. These are beautiful,' breathed Bella, picking up a T-shirt that was printed across the front, including the sleeves, with daubs of vibrant colour, running almost imperceptibly through all the hues of the rainbow with whited-out letters twining their way through the middle. Only at a distance could you make out the word 'Havenbury', with the initial impression being of some sort of twining plant or sea creature. 'It's really buff, so natural and, sort of, ethereal, isn't it?'

'That's what we wanted,' said Maddy, clapping her hands excitedly. 'Flora's amazing, she's developing all these wild ideas . . . there's a hot tub in the middle of the woods, a huge willow canopy leading into the sleep section, we're having these luxury yurts with Turkish carpets and lanterns . . . it's going to be really magical. As well as all the music of course, check out the line-up it's . . .' Maddy started walking over to a pile of brochures on the table but then stopped, bent over and clutched her stomach.

'Grrrrrr,' came the noise from deep within her, followed by some quick, shallow panting.

'Mads? What the hell?'

'Gaaaaaaaah,' wailed Maddy, staring at Bella with horror, her eyes wide with fright.

'Maddy . . . ?' Bella stood helplessly rubbing her friend's back. After what seemed an age, she straightened slightly and let out a sigh of relief. 'What the . . . ?' she said, in awe. 'That was . . . like . . .'

'A contraction?' finished Bella, grimly.

'Nooooo, can't be . . .'

'And yet . . .'

'But I've got weeks!'

'Or not. Where's Ben?'

'In the States,' wailed Maddy. 'I made him go. It's a conference about PTSD. They love him over there with all his military PTSD knowledge. The fee was huge, we thought it would come in handy, what with the baby and everything.'

'Okay, so,' said Bella, leading Maddy to a chair and making her sit down. 'We need a plan. Where is your midwife?'

'Good idea,' said Maddy, grabbing her phone. 'I'll send her a text. She'll know what to do.' She tapped out a message rapidly and then put the phone back down on the table, staring at it as if it was a rattlesnake.

'How long will she take to get back?'

'Dunno. Couple of hours?'

'Brilliant. Not. Plan B?'

'Not sure I've got a Plan B.'

'Hospital?'

'No! Don't want to go without Ben. Also, we're supposed to have a home birth. Also, it might not be real . . . argh!' Maddy stared into space again, gripping Bella's hand fiercely.

Time stood still while Maddy battled with her internal demons, rocking and moaning as the pain tore through her.

'So,' said Bella, when Maddy relaxed again. 'Looks a bit real to me.' Then she had a thought.

'Simon,' she said. 'Come on. And for God's sake text Ben on the way.'

CHAPTER TWENTY-ONE

Glancing at her watch, Bella was acutely aware that their GP, Simon, would not necessarily be at the surgery. That said, his practice was a one-man band and he was such a hard worker he generally was. The main challenge was getting past his scary receptionist who generally required copious amounts of blood or deep coma to consider her exalted boss worthy of interruption.

They were in luck. As Bella was trying to manhandle Maddy out of her little car with a contraction kicking in midway, Simon came out of the surgery carrying his bag. Weighing up the situation, he ran over to help, adding an aura of calm to the rapidly increasing stress of the situation.

'Exciting times,' he said to Maddy, encouragingly.

She gave him an incredulous look and then ignored him.

'How long and how often?' he asked Bella.

'Dunno,' she said, helplessly. 'Sorry . . . but, definitely long and often. And getting worse.'

'Can you please explain to Mrs Hollins that I am delayed but will get to her as soon as I can,' said Simon as they went in the door in a huddle of arms and legs.

'Shall I call an ambulance, Doctor?' said the frosty, helmet-haired woman behind the desk. 'Surely this is a case for the maternity ward?'

'Possibly, Mrs Jackson,' he smiled. 'But it's us this patient has come to needing help, so I think we will take a little look, don't you?'

'Don't let her in,' said Maddy, loudly, to Simon's amusement, although he tactfully turned his head away, so Mrs Jackson couldn't see him laughing.

'You're quite safe,' he said, closing the door behind them both and leading Maddy to the examination couch. 'At least, I take it you meant Mrs Jackson and not Bella. Now, I hate to ask, but could you bear it if I quickly examined you?'

Maddy, meantime, was showing no sign of having heard but was yanking off her trousers and clambering inelegantly onto the couch, where she crouched on all fours, rocking and moaning her way through another contraction.

'I'll take that as a "yes",' he said to Bella, with a confidence-inspiring smile.

'Right,' he said, pulling off the latex gloves and washing his hands. 'You're definitely in labour so there's no going back now. That said, don't panic, you've got a few hours to go yet.'

'Hours?' complained Maddy. 'I can't do that. Will it get worse?'

'Yes, you can, and yes it will. That said, you'll feel an awful lot better when we get you somewhere a bit more comfortable. How many weeks, remind me?' he said, tapping at his screen, to bring up her records.

'Ah yes, not due quite yet but thirty-six weeks is far from a disaster. Home birth, I see . . . mmm . . . not sure about that, with a first child and with this slight prematurity. The staff at the new birthing unit are brilliant, though. Home from home and the full medical works right next door if you need it, which I'm sure you won't. I'm going to give them a call, if you don't mind?'

Maddy had her eyes closed, but – to show she heard – she nodded briefly.

'Where's Ben?' he went on.

Bella explained.

'Oh. Genius. Well, I wouldn't want to be in his shoes when he gets here.'

'Has he got back to you?' asked Bella.

In reply Maddy dumbly handed over her phone.

'"On my way to the airport now. Will be with you by morning. Cross your legs",' she read aloud. Maddy growled alarmingly. 'And then he says, "love you, kiss, kiss, kiss",' she added, at which Maddy growled again with marginally less aggression.

'Don't leave me,' she said to Bella, grasping her friend's hand with terrifying strength. It was all Bella could do not to squeak as she nodded her assent.

'It's not completely odd that he's not on the Internet,' argued Zach, swigging the last of his double espresso whilst keeping a beady eye on the bookshop opposite. He had been astonished to hear Charlie's sorry tale of the missing jewels, on top of all the other issues he was facing, and had been keen to help his friend, although he should really have been in his forge, tackling his backlog of orders.

They planted themselves in the trattoria. It was Wednesday, which was the same day of the week as the sighting of the mystery woman previously; they hoped for further intrigue if not enlightenment.

'It is a bit odd not to have any presence online at all,' said Charlie. 'Not even on Facebook? Who isn't on Facebook nowadays? That's odd, for a start.'

'I'm not on Facebook.'

'Yeah, but you're definitely odd. I rest my case.'

'Fair enough,' said Zach, without rancour. 'He's not on the electoral roll for Havenbury either, which is strange, though.'

'That is, because you sort of have to be, don't you? Legally?' said Charlie. 'What does it mean?'

'Nothing specific, it just fails to disprove that he is not who he says he is.'

'So . . . erm . . . triple negative . . .' Charlie scratched his head while he worked it out. 'So, basically . . . we still don't know who he is?'

'We don't.'

'Aha! Mystery woman at three o'clock,' said Charlie excitedly, pointing out of the window.

'That's her! Got to be. Ben said she was a dark-haired woman in a green coat.'

'Doesn't mean much . . .' started Zach but, just like

before, the woman looked up and down the street, and then – as she approached the door of the bookshop – it opened and then closed behind her, the sign saying 'open' immediately being switched to 'closed'.

'Right, let's go and see what's going on,' said Charlie, starting to his feet.

'Hold on, Tonto,' said Zach, putting a hand on his arm. 'Just hold your horses for a minute. Now, you've met Geoffrey, haven't you? I mean, he knows who you are?'

'Yeah?'

'Well, don't you think it might attract his attention if he spots his ex-girlfriend's son gawping through the window at him?'

'I could be buying a book.'

'Stay here,' said Zach. 'I'll go and hang around in an inconspicuous manner.'

'You could be pretending to make a phone call,' offered Charlie.

'Or I could actually make a phone call,' said Zach, slipping out of the door of the trattoria, looking up Charlie's number on his phone as he went.

'Right, so, just having a little look around,' he said, chatting cheerfully as if the person he was calling wasn't just sitting yards away from him, staring fixedly at the shop he was lounging nonchalantly outside. He was leaning on the window pillar and idly looking through the shop window as he spoke, just as if he was looking for something vaguely interesting to engage his eyes while he had a nice little relaxed chat to a mate about nothing in particular.

'He's inside with the mystery woman,' he announced, breezily. 'They're sitting at the table. Talking.'

'Definitely not shagging?'

'Definitely not shagging,' Zach confirmed. 'No snogging, no heavy petting, no sexual activity of any kind.'

'Well what, then? Are there jewels? Any sort of material that you might categorise as swag?'

'Shut up, Charlie, you're an idiot. No. They're talking. She's holding his hand now.'

'Ha! Thought as much, they'll be at it like bunnies in a minute . . . hang on . . . mate . . . why're you coming back? Stick to your post, man.'

As Zach crossed the road back to the cafe he disconnected the call, silencing Charlie's protestations.

'Why are you here?' asked Charlie as Zach slipped back into the chair next to him.

'There are some things you can't watch,' he said.

'Euw, were they . . . ?' Charlie made an obscene gesture.

'He was crying,' said Zach.

'Crying?'

'He was weeping,' elaborated Zach. 'He was reading a letter. I think she gave it to him. He had a handkerchief out and he was wiping his eyes as he read. She was just sitting there. She had her hand on his arm. That was it. You can't just stand there and watch that.' Clearly to Zach this was an intrusion worse than watching a man having sex.

'What the heck do we make of that?' asked Charlie.

'No idea, but . . .' Zach thought. 'I do wonder if we aren't just making two people very unhappy with all this. Your ma is sad, isn't she? Clearly this Geoffrey is too, although, in his case, we don't know why.' He scratched his head and sighed. 'Let's just run through this again. What's with this jewellery?'

Charlie looked perplexed. 'Okay, so, there was jewellery.'

'How long have you known about it?'

'Me? Not sure. Probably since I was a boy.'

'Well, did they have it then or not?'

'I was a boy. I wasn't terribly interested in jewellery,' Charlie said in his defence. 'It's not like Ma was wearing it to do the washing-up but – yeah – I'm pretty sure I saw it once or twice.'

'Okay, and the fake stuff, when did that get spotted?'

'Just the other day, when Bella took it up to London to get it revalued, I gather. Ben told me.'

'So, we know it had been switched by then, and what do we know about this Geoffrey's knowledge of and access to it?'

Charlie thought. 'So, exactly when he knew it existed not sure, but certainly by the Ball because Ma was wearing it. That was when Geoffrey had to prise open the safe with a crowbar so – actually – although he might have known about it before then, presumably he wouldn't have been able to see it or get his hands on it.'

'Presumably not – okay, what next?'

'After that he put it back in the safe and wedged the door shut again.'

'Or not,' interjected Zach.

'Yeah, so, a few weeks later . . .'

'How many weeks?' Zach interrupted.

'About five.'

'Long enough to have produced the fakes?'

'Yeah, just about, that's what I gather.'

'Sorry, go on, "a few weeks later"?'

'. . . a few weeks later he prised the safe door open again, showed Ma the jewels – certainly giving her the impression they had been in the safe all along – and then she locked them in the new safe, which he fitted for her. And she set the code herself without him present,' Charlie added as an afterthought.

'So, he had the opportunity to get the originals, jam the safe, keep them for several weeks, get the fakes made, make the switch back again . . .'

'Stands to reason. It must have been him.'

'And the jewels you saw at the Ball, they were the real thing?'

'Yeah.'

'How do you know?'

Charlie thought. 'I see your point,' he admitted. 'What you're saying is, the jewels were definitely real originally, we know that with a fair degree of confidence because Dad got them valued a few years ago. We also know they were gone by the time Bells took them up to be valued again last week, but what we don't know is how long ago they were switched for fakes.'

'Exactly.'

Bella was seeing a whole new side to Maddy. She was keeping well away from the business end – there were some sights that couldn't be unseen – but the animal noises she was making were novel, varied and endlessly surprising. The midwife Tina was being hugely encouraging, more or less telling Maddy that her quick progress and regular contractions imbued her with some sort of moral superiority of which she should be immensely proud. Maddy was also disposed to like Tina because she was happy to be scathing about absent fathers. In fact, she seemed to be finding criticism of Ben a helpful distraction. Bella didn't like to remind her that Ben's attending the conference had been Maddy's idea. Some things were better left unsaid.

Maddy did keep watching the clock and asking Bella to get updates on Ben's progress. The requests were so frequent and the information – given that Ben was in the air and his phone was in flight mode – was so thin on the ground that she basically started making things up.

'Just three hours 'til he gets here,' she guessed merrily, at one point.

'Three hours?' Maddy roared. 'It might as well be three days.'

'Did I say three hours?' Bella immediately corrected. 'I meant two. One and a half even. Probably.' She looked desperately at Tina, who gave her a grin.

'I'm not keeping this baby in for three bloody hours,' Maddy ranted.

Tina nodded her agreement approvingly. 'No more you aren't, my lovely,' she agreed. 'You're so nearly there . . . doing really well. You're just going to have to tell that Ben all about it. Serves him right. You've got us now, haven't you darling?'

'You won't go, will you?' said Maddy, clutching Tina's hand. 'You've been here for ages. You're not going to just go off shift, are you? I've read about that.'

'I'm not going anywhere, my lovely,' said Tina, looking at the clock. 'Babies don't care about shifts and clocking in do they? More's the pity,' she added wearily, too low for Maddy to hear, giving Bella a complicit grin.

In the end, Maddy gave birth nearly two hours after Tina's shift had ended, but even then, she stayed to help Maddy get settled back into bed, with the little one cradled in her arm.

'You did so well, my lovely,' were her final words before she left. 'That husband of yours doesn't know what he's missed. You make sure he does all the nappies for the next couple of years. That's his punishment.'

Bella had held the baby, too awestruck to move, while Maddy had a bath. She was reluctant to hand her back over.

'She's beautiful,' she said, tearfully. 'You and Ben are going to be such amazing parents.'

Ben still hadn't arrived, but luckily Maddy and the new baby were happy to have a snooze, after the rigours of the day. Bella stayed with them both, watching the tiny baby in Maddy's arms, scared that – if she went anywhere – Maddy might somehow drop her in her sleep. Time passed, and Bella felt her own eyelids drooping. Where on earth was Ben? It was nearly dawn, it had been an incredibly tough night, and she wasn't going to be able to stay awake for much longer.

Just then, Ben came rushing in, sweaty and dishevelled.

He skidded to a halt at Maddy's bedside and stopped dead, drinking in the scene.

'You are so clever,' he whispered, as Maddy opened her eyes. 'My darling girls . . .'

Bella stole quietly away.

CHAPTER TWENTY-TWO

Charlie was cock-a-hoop on the train back to Havenbury that night. All his meetings had gone well. The presentation Maddy had prepared for him went down a treat with his various potential food suppliers and with both the posh, organic food chains vying for exclusive presence in the Blue Zone. This was where the main range of different food concessions were going to be. Both were clearly keen to make an offer over and above what Charlie had asked for. This was because – despite their fluffy, philosophical brand values – they were each desperately keen to do the other out of the deal. He had decided to let them both sweat for a bit. The timing was bloody tight, though. Maddy was going to do her nut as the deal wasn't tied up yet.

Letting himself into the kitchen he tutted to see the laptops and lights still on, although naturally no one was there working, which was a shame. He would have loved to share his news with Zach or Maddy. He considered reaching for a beer but then slid the kettle onto the hob instead. He was feeling clearer and lighter for ditching the booze. He even had his appetite back and was regaining some of the weight that had dropped off him in the days and weeks after Bella first went.

Feeling optimistic he checked the emails and answerphone, slightly annoyed to see so many. What on earth had Maddy been doing all day? It wasn't like her to let things build up. He also needed to break it to her that – with new late participants wanting their logos on things – it looked like those T-shirts would have to be reprinted. She'd be fine, though. It was just a few T-shirts and the money from the sponsorship would more than absorb the extra cost.

Holding his steaming mug, he grabbed a pencil and paper to scribble down the phone messages. There was one from Highways for Zach, a couple from the yurt people for Maddy and then another one from them, increasingly urgently needing her to get back to them by the end of the day. He checked his watch. Too late to call them now. He couldn't tell them what they needed to know anyhow. And then, Ben's voice:

'Mate! I'm back from the States. It's all kicked off and she's here . . . Six pounds ten, beautiful, just like her mother . . . don't know about names yet. It's all – just – amazing . . . got to get back to them both. Catch up tomorrow, yeah?'

Charlie sat back, stunned. Amazing news, but yikes! What about the festival? He took a deep breath. First things first. He'd pop over and see Ben tomorrow. Congratulate him. Hopefully he could hold everyone off for a couple of days – maybe even the yurt people – and then he could probably get Maddy to sort a few things, or at least point

251

him in the right direction. How long did people take to get over these things? It was only a baby, wasn't it? It would be really small, so it couldn't take up that much time or space, surely? She could maybe bring it in with her. Stick it in the corner of the kitchen. He looked hopefully at her section of the kitchen table. It all looked a bit of a mess. He imagined it made perfect sense to her.

'She looks exactly like Ben,' Bella gushed, when she got back to Rufus with her exciting news, but he was not in the mood to share her joy.

'I don't see the appeal myself. And I definitely don't think they have the capacity to look like either of their parents. They barely even look like human beings, for heaven's sake . . . Now, I'm glad you're back at last, we need to go and look at a couple of apartments in London tomorrow. You and me. And one of them is really close to the office I thought you might use. The local area's great. All restaurants and boutique shopping.' He looked at Bella's face. 'Come on, we'll be opening The Grange in a few days. You're done here. Onwards and upwards.'

'Sure,' said Bella, forcing a smile. 'I know. Exciting times.'

'They are,' he said more gently, pressing himself against her back and reaching around to put his hand on her breast.

'You don't talk about your family,' said Bella later, when they were lying in bed, next to each other.

'I don't,' he said, repressively but Bella – feeling reckless – carried on.

'Are your parents from around here?'

'No.'

'Where do they live?'

'My father lives somewhere or other in Bermuda. I haven't seen him for years and I don't intend to. Last time he contacted me it was to congratulate me on my success after he saw an article about me and Tavistock House in the *Sunday Times*. He likes success. He's not interested in anything else. He's not interested in me.'

'And your mother?'

'She died.'

'I'm so sorry,' said Bella, propping herself up on her elbow to look at him. She went to drop a kiss on his cheek, but he turned his head away.

'Don't be. It was centuries ago.'

'Centuries?'

'I was nine.'

'Bloody hell, I can't imagine . . . how absolutely awful! Was your father still around?'

'Not really. He had another woman by then. There have been a few since . . . when my mother died I was dumped on them, naturally, but the woman he was with at the time didn't like me, so my father sent me away to boarding school.'

'At nine?'

'Yeah.'

'That must have been awful.'

'It wasn't great.'

'Were they not kind to you?'

'Not particularly. My fault, though. I cried a lot. It wasn't considered acceptable behaviour.'

'Crying when your mother has died, and your father has rejected you sounds reasonable enough to me.'

'The staff were okay,' Rufus conceded. 'But the other boys . . . I do see their point. I was small, ginger and prone to tears. All pretty tedious stuff for the average privileged nine-year-old from a nice family with ponies and ski holidays and country houses and parents who turn up for sports days and all that crap.'

Rufus's face was stony.

'I'm sorry,' said Bella softly. She curved her body into his unyielding one and held him in her arms.

Laden with flowers, food and a rare, celebratory bottle of Dovecot Estate sparkling, Bella negotiated the rutted track down to Ben and Maddy's boathouse with trepidation. Rufus would be livid if she ripped the exhaust off the new Mini Cooper he had given her. Her trepidation increased when she arrived and saw Charlie's clapped-out old estate car already parked on the muddy lay-by near the house. It was too late to turn back. The sound of her engine would have alerted them all. In any case she wasn't sure if she had the space to turn with Charlie's car in the way.

Heart pounding, she gathered up the presents and knocked quietly.

'Bella!' said Ben, giving her a kiss on both cheeks and taking the stuff off her. 'Yay! More soft cheese . . .'

'Oo, so I thought, now she's not pregnant – she said she was really missing Brie.'

'She said it to a lot of people I gather,' said Ben popping it into the fridge where Bella could already see an array extensive enough to open a cheese shop.

'And some fresh pasta so she can eat with one hand while she's feeding.'

'Fab, thanks – sorry about making you bump into Charlie,' Ben hissed in her ear, steering her towards the lounge area. The entire boathouse was open to the rafters, with a kitchen at one end, living space at the other and a whole wall of glass, overlooking the river. Charlie was sitting awkwardly on the far end of the sofa to Maddy who looked entirely serene and in charge, feeding the baby with a muslin cloth draped expertly over her shoulder so most of her boob was hidden from view.

As soon as she saw Bella she burst noisily into tears.

'What . . .' said Bella, looking at her aghast.

Charlie shifted himself awkwardly and patted Maddy on the shoulder that didn't have baby on it.

'Don't worry, everyone,' said Ben. 'Hormones raging, aren't they, my love?'

Maddy sniffed, giving him a watery smile through her tears. 'Sorry, everyone,' she sobbed. 'It's just seeing you and Charlie and—' She wailed again, fresh tears spurting. 'Sorry, sorry . . .'

Ben grabbed the muslin cloth and wiped her eyes for her. 'Shall I take her?' he said.

'No, just let me . . .' She sniffed noisily. Ben held the cloth to her nose so she could blow it.

'Greater love hath no man,' said Charlie, slightly horrified. 'Not sure I could ever do that for you,' he said to Bella, standing to greet her awkwardly.

They kissed formally on both cheeks. Getting a whiff of

Charlie's familiar aftershave, Bella nearly started howling herself, but Charlie seemed together enough, and she was blowed if she was going to make a tit of herself by being the one to break down.

'How are you?' she said stiffly as they sat down again. Ben was busy with the aftermath of Maddy's tears and the baby who had started to grizzle at the interruption in service.

'Fine,' said Charlie, equally formally. 'You look really well,' he said, trying to tear his eyes from Bella's toned, tanned legs, which were on almost complete display in her brief, suede dress and strappy sandals. She looked smooth, polished, thin and entirely unattainable.

'So do you,' she replied.

'I'm off the booze,' he blurted, for something to say more than anything.

'That's . . . erm – good?' she hazarded. 'Why?'

'Just until the festival. Need to keep a clear head,' he said, wishing Ben and Maddy would chip in.

'We've got something to say to you both,' announced Maddy, who had now relinquished the baby to Ben. He held her expertly, despite – as far as Bella knew – never having done it before.

Bella and Charlie both turned to her with relief.

'We decided a few months ago that we would like you both to be godparents,' Maddy went on. 'Obviously at the time, you were together, being sensible, acting like normal human beings and setting an excellent example to us all.'

Bella braced herself for what was coming next.

'Now,' Maddy went on, 'you're both behaving like a couple of complete idiots, I'm hugely frustrated with you both and I want to bang your heads together. However,' she took a deep breath, while they both picked themselves back up after the onslaught, 'I have every hope you will – eventually – get over yourselves, sort your relationship out, make the farmhouse into a proper family home and fill it with your own children, like you're supposed to be doing. This' – she gestured to them both – 'is a blip. Treat it as such. By the christening I want you side by side pledging to help us bring up this child in Havenbury like she should be. She's called Erica, by the way.'

Bella wiped away a tear before Charlie saw it. 'Lovely name,' she said, bravely. 'I love it. Hello, little Erica. I promise you I will do my best. That's all I can promise, really, I hope that's enough.'

'Sorry about that,' said Ben as he ushered them both to the door so Maddy and the baby could have a nap. 'She's a bit forthright at the moment but . . .' he paused, 'I second everything she says.'

Smarting, the two found themselves in the narrow lane as the door closed behind them.

'After you,' said Bella, gesturing to Charlie's car.

'No, no, after you,' said Charlie, smirking.

'You know perfectly well I would prefer you to go first so I have more room to turn,' said Bella, stiffly.

'Ah yes, I remember it well . . .' he sniped. 'Needing a space the size of a small African country, just to park and turn. I used to find it endearing. Nice car, by the way, present from the boyfriend, was it?'

'Yes actually, what of it?'

257

'Lovely to have found someone prepared to give you a shiny new car, clearly he doesn't know your propensity to finding your way into parking spaces by means of your bumpers rather than your eyes.'

'Clearly, he isn't so precious he gives a damn about a stupid car,' she snapped back.

'On the contrary, I think he's deluded. On the other hand, I feel I demonstrated considerable patience and understanding of your poor record on parking.'

'Shame your patience and understanding didn't extend to the decisions I made to save our home and business.'

'Oh yes, *those* decisions . . . you left me.'

'You chucked me out.'

'Shame *you* seem to have forgotten you cheated on your marriage vows with barely a backward glance.

'I think I have rather more to forgive than you.'

'Well, that's interesting, because I think I have rather more to forgive than you.'

'Really? Well that's your opinion.'

'Yes, it is.'

'Fine.'

'Fine,' snapped Bella, and then – because neither of them could think of anything else to say now the conversation had deteriorated to such a childish level – she got into her car, started it up and slammed it into gear. Her fury made her reckless and she quickly negotiated an eight-point turn under his gaze, managing to avoid hitting his car, but catching the bumper on the gatepost on the final reverse manoeuvre before she accelerated away. She saw Charlie laugh and nod his head in an irritating display of 'I told you so' as she drove off.

'Horrible man,' she chuntered aloud as she drove. How could Maddy and Ben conceivably want him to be a godparent? If they seriously expected her to present a united front with that impossible man at the christening, or at any other time, they could dream on.

Charlie's satisfaction at having the last laugh in his meeting with Bella didn't last long. It was a hollow victory, anyway. Coming back into the farmhouse was dismal. Dolly was at Dove Cottage with her pups and Charlie was amazed to discover how much he missed her. There was a post-it note from Zach saying he was out supervising the road signage for the festival and putting the diversion plan into place. He was pretty tired and wasn't sure what sleep he was going to be getting over the next few days – especially firefighting for all Maddy's stuff – talking of which, he should probably dive in. He yawned, settling himself at the table.

The next hour and a half was responding to phone calls and emails. He picked and chose who he told about Maddy being out of the picture. No need to panic people, but it was a shame he had let her deal with so much on her own. He had been too busy to be looking over her shoulder and, in any case, she was more than capable. Messy, though. Her paperwork was in a complete state. Charlie looked at the clock. It was already past lunchtime and he had had no breakfast either, but no time for that now. He decided to clear a bit of space on the table by sweeping up Maddy's paperwork and taking it into the study. Dumping it on the filing cabinet he started going through it, using the desk to sort it into categories, the merchandise, the musicians, the yurts, the permission stuff, which looked really impenetrable; there were performance permits, a whole load of stuff about licensing for booze and food . . . he didn't have time to look but just dumped it into a pile he mentally labelled as 'admin'. He was just grabbing another slithering handful of papers when a whole section of it slid out from the middle and disappeared down the back of the filing cabinet. Damn. He momentarily wondered about leaving it there. Chances are it wouldn't be needed. Unfortunately, he had spotted a couple of invoices in there, which he was pretty sure hadn't been paid. Probably best not to overlook them. He didn't want people to suddenly bail on him at the last moment and pull out. That could be disastrous.

With a deep sigh, he grabbed hold of the top of the cabinet and, with a dint of sliding and rocking, managed to lever it away from the wall and reach down behind it. The cobwebs barred his way in a sticky, clinging mass. Steeling himself he reached further and managed to grab the corners of a few of the papers and drag them back up. Reaching further, the remaining few sheets were just out of his grasp. Grabbing the desk lamp and plonking it on top so he could see what he was doing, he levered the cabinet out another few inches and tried again. This time he could see the accumulated dust and dirt clinging to the back of the cabinet and the wall. Just as he was grabbing the last few papers at the farthest reach of his fingertips and drawing them gingerly back up, he noticed a paler oblong patch on the back of the cabinet. Depositing the papers on the desk safely he picked up the lamp and angled it down a little further into the gap for a closer look. Feeling it with his fingers he realised it was not metal but paper – an envelope, which had been carefully and thoroughly sellotaped to the back of the filing cabinet, a foot or two down from the top where it would never be spotted in the normal order of things.

Grabbing a paperknife he scraped at the edge of the Sellotape until he could hold the end and peel it away, detaching the envelope without damaging it.

Sliding down to the floor, with his back leaning against the cabinet he looked.

'Caroline' was the single word written on the front of the envelope. It was in his father's hand.

It wasn't addressed to him. Charlie imagined it was intended to be found after Peter's death but he wondered if his dad could possibly have known it would be three years later. Being planted where it was, there had been a good chance it would never be discovered. Whatever it contained, Charlie reasoned, he felt he should know. That decided, he also felt that whatever news it contained should be broken to his mother gently and he was therefore the best person for the job.

Realising he was still holding the paperknife, he used it to carefully slit the envelope open. There were two pieces of paper inside, folded together. One was a brief letter:

Darling, it said.
If you are reading this, then something has happened to me and the chances are I am dead.

I am sorry to have been the first to go, leaving you on your own. If I could have, I would have chosen the other way, for your sake.

261

You probably already know I am a flawed and disappointing husband. I want to take this chance to thank you again for your support and your misplaced loyalty and to say that I am afraid I have a final sin to confess. In my egotistical drive to build the vineyard – a fool's endeavour by any reckoning – I have taken a step I simply cannot explain, justify or apologise for enough.

I have used your family jewels to repay my debts and to pay for my next stage of investment. Because I am ashamed to be in this position, and because you are – to your credit – not a vain woman and never have been – I have taken the opportunity to sell them and hide my actions by replacing them with fakes. I enclose the bill of sale. I do this to ensure no innocent party is ever accused of wrongdoing. It was me and I am more sorry than I can say.

Thank you for being my wife. I was lucky to have you. Luckier than I deserve.

Your loving husband, Peter. X

Chapter Twenty-Three

Charlie sat motionless, reading and rereading. For a time, he wondered about destroying the letter and the sales receipt. Why bother Ma with this devastating betrayal? It wasn't as if anything could be salvaged from the situation. His mother would simply be hurt by the actions of a husband now dead three years when he – Charlie – had the opportunity to spare her. On the other hand, as his father had said in the letter, the declaration was insurance against any innocent party getting the blame for the disappearance of the jewels because, of course, he knew his deception would be revealed in the end. Hadn't exactly that happened with poor Geoffrey?

Whatever secrets the man was hiding, theft – it was clear now – wasn't one of them. As he walked into the kitchen the phone started ringing and Zach came through the back door.

A woman on the phone started wittering before Charlie had even got it to his ear. It was something about payment for electric generators – a bill had not been settled and the contract had been breached . . . there was an entirely unveiled threat that the generators would not be delivered despite being due on-site later that day. Charlie barely heard, passing the phone to Zach as he passed him.

'Going to see Ma,' he said.

The walk down the lane to his mother's house felt other-worldly. He was vaguely aware of the sun beating onto his back, the breeze tugging at the old man's beard in the hedgerow. He could see the blackberries, still hard and green, but plentiful, promising a bountiful autumn and a tempting diversion for the grape pickers who often wandered over to the hedgerow for a snack when they were working their way down the rows of grapes in the short autumn days.

A pigeon cooed on the chimney stack as he approached the little cottage, which was swathed in climbing roses and honeysuckle. He suddenly had a vivid memory of him and Bella lying in the bedroom, the rose wallpaper echoing the flowers nodding at the edge of the low cottage window, which was open in the warm breeze. The bedroom was always pleasantly cool in the summertime, with its thick thatched roof and the vaulted ceiling opening right up to the eaves, after Bella had worked her interior design magic.

They had been lying lazily in each other's arms, listening to the pigeon cooing just feet away, when its mate had toppled down the chimney. Charlie, entirely naked, had had to reach into the fireplace and hoick it out, feathers ruffled, at which point it wriggled free and crashed around the room with Charlie in hot pursuit. Eventually he cornered it and gently cradled it in both hands, bunging it out of the window before it panicked itself into a heart attack. Bella lay in bed watching and laughing until tears ran down her face.

As he drew near he saw Caroline was in the garden, deadheading the roses and yanking up spent poppies, discarding the stems and leaves but breaking off their seed pods to burst open in the beds and hopefully produce another crop next year.

'Darling,' she said, first in pleasure and then, seeing his face, 'whatever is the matter?'

When he had told her, and showed her the letter, both of them sat gazing at the unlit stove in the little sitting room.

'I knew,' she said at last.

'About the jewels? But Geoffrey . . .'

'Not specifically about the jewels, but Peter – your father – he was . . .' she searched for the right words. 'He wasn't good with money,' she said, in the end.

'You mean he . . . what? Lost money? Gambled . . . ?'

'He wasn't a gambler. Well, not in the poker and roulette sense,' said Caroline. 'Your father,' she said with emphasis, making sure she met her son's eye, 'was a lovely, funny, generous, kindly man. You are like him. You are the best of your father and – for what it's worth – you're the best of me. But Peter, although he tried, money just seemed to slip through his fingers.'

'I didn't realise.'

'Why would you?'

'Even when Dad and I were running the farm together . . .'

'I did ask him not to involve you. I didn't want you to have to have the responsibility. Not yet. Of course, he died before any of us expected. And I was so sorry that you have had to sort out the mess he left.'

Charlie waved his hand. 'It's always like this with winemaking. Vineyards take up money. The margins are small. Running a vineyard, they say it's like standing on a hillside setting fire to twenty-pound notes, don't they?' he raised a ghost of a smile.

'I didn't want you to see your father in a bad light.'

'I never will.'

'Good. But now is the time for you to know, he was flawed in that he was poor with money. This' – she indicated the letter – 'is not how I remember him. It's not how I want you to remember him. I accept this as one of the things that made him human and I loved him. End of.'

'And Geoffrey?'

'Well . . . I don't know. Poor Geoffrey. I don't think I ever believed he could have done it.'

'There's something odd, though,' said Charlie, explaining what he and Zach had discovered. What they saw.

'It doesn't surprise me that he is deeply sad,' she said. 'I felt it in him and him in me. That's maybe what drew us to each other. Perhaps we can heal each other's sadness. One day.'

Charlie hung his head.

'And now,' said Caroline briskly, 'I do believe we have another relationship crisis that needs to be resolved.' Charlie groaned, remembering his last conversation with

Bella. Not the kind of sensible, constructive conversation his mother would approve of, he suspected.

'You've got a marriage to save,' she said, 'and a dog to look after. A dog – I might add – who is being a fantastic mum but being driven quite mad by her puppies. You might have deprived me of a grandchild thus far' – she gave him a naughty look – 'although I live in hope, but you have gone far too far down the road of accepting joint responsibility for several vulnerable beings to chuck your own relationship so casually aside.'

'They're puppies,' complained Charlie. 'They don't need us to have marriage counselling. They need Dolly to feed them and lick their bums for a few weeks and then they'll be gone. You're not loading that one on me.'

'You're more involved than you think.'

'How? I'm definitely not licking their bums, I can tell you . . .'

'You and Bella need to find good homes for them all. Together. You need to grow up and take responsibility for that, at least. You're going to have to talk.'

Charlie was just struggling to think of a crushing reply and his phone vibrated in his pocket.

'Saved by the bell,' said Caroline, dryly.

By the time Charlie got it to his ear it had gone through to answerphone. 'It's Zach,' he said. 'Something to do with the festival, probably. We've got to be all set up by tomorrow, which isn't great with Maddy suddenly being out of the picture. I hope you're coming to the party on Saturday night? At The Grange? It's the grand opening but also the after party for the performers on the first night of the festival. Two in one.'

'Wouldn't miss it for the world,' said Caroline. 'Now go and run your festival. In your father's honour. Make me proud.'

Bella was exhausted. She had been up at The Grange since five o'clock that morning. Paddy and his team had got so fed up with her micromanaging and fretting she had taken to checking out their previous day's work earlier and earlier, trying to quell the constant gnawing anxiety that threatened to burgeon into full-blown panic by checking off jobs on her 'to do' list before they arrived on-site. She would then make a list of the most urgent jobs for that day to negotiate with Paddy when he came in.

Paddy, by contrast, was irritatingly calm, patting her on the shoulder, leading her away from the contractors in mid-sentence at times when her agitation threatened to distract them too much from the job in hand. Far from offering her coffee from his flask, as he had done in the beginning, he now had her on a caffeine-free regime, boiling up hot water in the men's rest room kettle and fanning a selection of fruit and herb teas enticingly for her to choose from instead. He refused to listen to her pleas for coffee, something she felt she desperately needed to combat the crushing fatigue that alternated with the agitation.

'You need to rest more,' said Paddy implacably, holding his coffee flask effortlessly out of reach of her attempts to grab it from him because he was so tall. 'And,' he added, 'you need to eat, for heaven's sake. I suppose that Rufus has got you on a food-free exclusion diet, has he? That man's a menace.'

'Not keen on him? Not the impression you give when he comes on-site,' sulked Bella.

'I know what side my bread's buttered,' said Paddy. 'Working for a monster like Rufus is not for everyone.'

'He's not a monster,' said Bella. Since Rufus had confided some of the awful details of his childhood, she felt almost maternal towards him. His cold rages, his ambition, drive, lack of compromise, were more understandable now. Maybe Paddy was right. She might not be the one to handle him. To heal him. But he wasn't a monster. Not now she could see the sad, frightened little boy that dwelt within him.

'You're doing an amazing job,' said Paddy, acceding to her pleas to tour the building with her, pointing out the snagging that still needed to be done with just forty-eight hours to go until the opening, until the rooms were full and the first night after-party started for the privileged few.

'This all looks incredible,' he told her, letting her lead him into the piano bar. It was all now in place, apart from the final clean, and then the installation of the furniture. The wide oak boards on the floor gleamed with multiple layers of beeswax polish, the silk dupion curtains flowed like water, emphasising the grace and the height of the tall windows overlooking the park. The walls, carefully colour-matched to the curtains were in slate-coloured false suede, with a thick layer of wadding behind, soaking up the noise and adding a layer of close luxury and warmth to the atmosphere. Below them, from chest height was wooden panelling painted in the teal colour Rufus had approved of. Although he had rejected the aubergine Bella had hankered after for the paintwork she had managed to get it into the room through the silk cushions scattered on the dark, polished leather furniture, which toned with the gleaming floor.

As the *pièce de résistance*, the chandeliers were a triumph, sweeping down from the high ceilings like breaking waves, the colours graduating from navy to crystal-clear. Their stark modernity, allied with the classical proportions of the room, was breathtaking.

Upstairs, the cleaners were finally able to tackle the rooms set aside for their celebrity guests, including Zane Stringfellow, who Bella was nervous and excited about meeting. He had played an inextricable part in her teenage years, his songs providing the soundtrack to her sixteen-year-old angst and confusion. She even thought it might have been one of his hits that she and Charlie danced to the night they had their first kiss. But she didn't want to think about that.

'Talk about lastminute.com,' she said to Paddy as he nodded approvingly at the painter touching up the final bits and pieces around the room.

'Mind my curtains!' she squeaked as he went to run a final line of colour under the window sill, even though the curtains were already hung.

'Got to make sure it all looks perfect even for people who are lying on the floor,' smiled the man, one of the endlessly cheerful team of Irish workers Paddy preferred to use.

'Who's going to be lying on the floor looking at the underneath of the window sill?' she complained. But actually, if Zane Stringfellow's reputation was anything to go by, someone probably would be in – gosh – twenty-four hours or so.

Bella was just on her way out of the door, satisfied for now, when her phone rang.

'Darling, just to check you're still coming to see Dolly and the pups tonight,' Caroline said, when she answered. 'You said you might.'

'I was hoping to, but I may not have time. I've still got a few more bits to check before the opening. Rufus wants everything to be perfect. Actually, so do I obviously.'

'I would really like it if you did,' said Caroline. 'She's been a bit fretty . . .'

Charlie was using his motorbike to travel between the various zones. Teams of people with high-vis jackets were helping visitors find their way. There was limited car parking, already nearly full, and still people were flooding in. Maddy had made sure to encourage festival-goers to use public transport and many, with their backpacks, had done that. Somehow, she had managed to find a vintage double-decker bus, which was ferrying people from the train station at the bottom of town. Charlie was pleased to see so many families with young children. It was that sort of festival, they had decided at an early stage.

Young couples, too, not bothered by hardship, were setting up their two-man tents in the Violet Zone, where there were showers, power points and food kiosks selling everything from Jamaican fried chicken to falafel.

The main stage was thrumming already. The technical team was all over the rig, setting up the backdrop to the stage and taping down yards of wiring. The amps were huge, but Zach had promised the environmental health officers from the local council that decibels would be kept to a reasonable maximum in deference to local houses. That said, Charlie was pleased to see plenty of the festival-goers were locals. Certainly, all the town's teenagers and students from the college, who had come back early from their summer break, were in evidence, swigging beer and water from bottles and hugging each other extravagantly whenever they met, even though their absence from each other might only have been the length of time it took to go for a wee.

Each of the rainbow zones had its own theme and, on that sunny Saturday afternoon, the jazz area was attracting a relaxed crowd of happy guests, lying around on the grass or on rugs, eating and taking in the atmosphere.

Charlie felt redundant, with the team now slipping so smoothly into action all around him. He had a walkie-talkie but could make no real sense of the messages burbling out of it and certainly had nothing useful to contribute to conversations on parking, power outages and the delivery of hospitality to the green room which was, confusingly, a white tent in the Red Zone. The green room was behind barriers, so the performance artists could be kept away from the crowds before their acts. Zane Stringfellow was, he gathered, due to arrive by helicopter shortly, in time for his slot as the main attraction that evening. Charlie wandered around the tent, checking out the food table, which was laden with huge baskets of fruit, every sort of sandwich and cold snack and a range of drinks covering the gamut from Coke to sparkling mineral water. The coffee was decaffeinated and there was a staggering array of fruit teas.

'Not exactly rock and roll,' he commented to the sweet-faced waitress who was giddy at the fact there was a minor rap star sitting in the corner with his mini-entourage on the long, white sofas provided.

'I know, sick innit? Choc Ice only wanted a fennel tea,' she whispered. 'I were terrified we wouldn't have one, but we did, thank goodness . . . I kept the wrapper,' she added, giving Charlie a peek into her pocket where the tea bag packaging was safely stowed. 'I were going to ask him to sign it, but we're not allowed to talk to the performers unless we're spoken to,' she said. 'Not cool.'

'Is this the coolest job you've ever done?' said Charlie, smiling.

'Totally!' she said. 'And Zane Stringfellow!' she said. 'He's my idol . . . even though he's really old.'

Charlie was just about to impress her by informing her Zane was an old schoolmate, but decided not to mention it, after all.

Just then they both heard the unmistakeable sound of a chopper overhead.

'That's him!' she squeaked. 'Be cool, be cool . . .' she counselled herself, then threw a smile at Charlie and rushed off, straightening her apron and tidying her hair.

CHAPTER TWENTY-FOUR

A ripple of excitement ran through the crowd when the helicopter appeared, landing in the field behind the main stage, which had been marked with a large cross for just this, so the performers could go straight to their hospitality tent. There was a similar set up at The Grange, even though it was less than a mile away, so they could be transported by chopper to the first night after party and grand opening.

The on-site radio station chattered excitedly about this latest development too, promising an exclusive interview with the artist later that day.

Charlie waited and, within a few minutes, his old school friend slipped into the tent, almost unnoticed. An unremarkable girl in jeans and a vest top slipped in after him. She had a mobile phone and a clipboard and he briefly looked back to her for instruction before lazily surveying the scene.

'Charlie, my old mate,' he drawled, arms outstretched. 'What the bloody hell are you doing here?'

'I could ask you the same question,' said Charlie, slapping him on the back. 'We're old – how the hell did that happen?'

'Speak for yourself . . . I'm in my prime, mate,' said Zane, running his hands through his long, luxuriant hair, which swept back from a handsome, faintly lined and suntanned face. His quietly expensive white silk shirt was open just one button more than you might expect, and his faded black jeans were tighter than the average man in his thirties might wear. 'And you're looking pretty reasonable, for an ugly sod.'

'Same to you.'

'Takes money and effort,' he said. 'Best if my fans don't see me up too close. I've cultivated an air of unapproachability and mystique, so they don't see the wrinkles. How long have we got?' he asked the girl with the clipboard.

'Loads of time. Relax,' she said. 'Get some food. An hour until sound checks, then that interview you promised Bryony Knight for *The Observer*. The boys are here at eight. Onstage at nine.'

'She runs my life,' said Zane to Charlie.

'Someone has to,' she said, but she smiled as she said it. 'Tiffany,' she said, holding out her hand to Charlie. 'His PA, for my sins.'

'She is bloody amazing,' said Zane sinking into one of the white sofas and gesturing for Charlie to join him.

'I thought you'd have a crowd of people,' said Charlie. 'Make-up artists, pedicurist, horoscope consultants, all that bollocks.'

'God no,' said Zane. 'Call me Chris, by the way.'

'I was going to.'

'Better than shithead,' said Chris, referring to his old nickname.

'We thought we were so witty, didn't we?'

'You did.'

'Can't believe we haven't seen each other since – when? – not for bloody nearly ten years. There was that wedding . . . and you were at that party in London? God, I can't have been a day over twenty-six . . . it was nearly ten years ago.'

'That's life, mate,' said Chris. 'Gets in the way. And anyway, you might have been twenty-six then, but I'm younger than you, remember?'

'Fame, though, eh? Who knew?'

'It took fifteen years to become an overnight success,' said Chris. 'The trick is keeping it real, I've learnt – thanks Tiff,' he added, taking the mug she offered.

'And don't forget to eat,' she said, putting a fork and napkin on the table next to him along with a plate piled high with a selection from the buffet.

He saluted, and then raised his eyebrows at Charlie. 'Will do, ma'am.'

'Tiff,' he called as she walked away. 'Can't we put this Bryony woman off? I'd rather talk to my mate here.'

'Sorry,' she said, firmly. 'We've rescheduled her several times already. Don't wanting her discovering you're a spoilt brat.'

'Fair enough,' he conceded. 'God, I love that woman,' Chris said, turning back to Charlie. 'I can't tell you how hard it is to get a PA who isn't so giddy they say yes to everything. I don't know what I'll do if she ever wants to move on. I might have to marry her.'

'You could do worse,' said Charlie eyeing her tight little backside as she walked away.

'How about you? Got a good woman?'

'Had one, lost her, working out how to get her back,' he said.

'Getting her back? Good.'

'Don't think I'm allowed her back, though. I've been a bit of an arse.'

Chris nodded. 'Taken me years to work out how not to be an arse,' he admitted. 'Still a bit of a work in progress. I just need to do all this nonsense for another year to eighteen months, then my people tell me I'll be set for life.'

'Then what will you do?'

'Disappear. Come and live somewhere like this,' he said. 'I always remembered this neck of the woods from school. It's God's own country around here – well, I hardly need to tell you that . . . I'll find a nice house, settle in, go under the radar. Have kids. Do all the usual stuff. I might even start a vineyard, if you fancy giving me some advice?'

'Sounds good,' said Charlie.

'It will be, mate. It will be.'

Zach and Bryony Knight the journalist arrived simultaneously and Chris, who was still sitting, sprawled on the sofa chatting to Charlie got up to slap him on the back.

'I forgive you,' he said in greeting.

'Yeah, fair enough,' responded Zach immediately. 'You

were a rubbish fag, but I might have been a bit of a prat. You've grown, by the way.'

'So have you. Can you believe we haven't seen each other since?'

'I've seen you,' said Zach. 'Getting all famous. I do remember you pratting around with that guitar of yours even then. Who knew, though, eh?'

Chris bowed his head self-deprecatingly. 'Talking of getting taller, what the hell does Rufus look like now? He was a skinny little runt at school. I gather he's done quite well for himself too. When I got the invitation to stay at The Grange I felt like I couldn't refuse. I hope he's got a good PR team making the most of it, I'm sure he has . . .' Chris rattled on, not noticing the other two were looking puzzled, staring at each other.

'That Rufus?' Zach asked Charlie. 'What? You mean he's Copper Knob?'

'Dunno,' said Charlie, in disbelief. 'I don't think I ever knew his real name, we just called him Copper Knob. Or Duracell . . . seriously, what parent calls their carrot-haired son Rufus? They'd have to have it in for them, surely.'

'Did you guys not twig?' said Chris. 'Seriously? I don't believe it.'

'Yeah, but he was in your year,' said Zach. 'Not ours.'

'He looks bloody different now,' said Charlie. 'All fit and built and bloody rich too. I wouldn't take him on.'

There was an uncomfortable silence.

'I might not have behaved that well with Copper— sorry – Rufus,' said Charlie quietly.

'Me neither,' said Zach.

'Guys, guys . . . don't worry about it,' said Chris, also remembering. 'You were bastards to me too. It was expected. It was the making of me,' but he failed to convince.

'I wonder if that's why he . . .' said Charlie, voicing what Zach was thinking.

'You think?'

'What, guys . . .' complained Chris.

Charlie briefly explained the last few months, leaving out the bit about Bella sleeping with Rufus as a condition of the loan – not everyone knew that bit – but saying how the festival would hopefully pay back the money as he didn't exactly want to be indebted to the man who stole his wife.

'And your wife is the "good woman"?'

Charlie nodded.

'Oh dear,' said Chris. 'I think apologies might be in order, don't you?'

Just then, Zach's walkie-talkie crackled into life. He spoke into it, moving away from them both, and returned a minute later looking grey.

'What on earth?' said Charlie.

'Bit of a balls-up on the admin front,' he said.

'I doubt it,' said Charlie. 'That's Maddy's department. The woman's got a mind like a steel trap. Petrifying, actually . . . I'm glad I'm not Ben.'

'Okay, well, I hope that's true. Because I've got a man out here asking for our public liability insurance and it looks to me like we haven't got any.'

'Yikes. What happens if that's true?'

'The festival closes down, and everyone has to leave. Now.'

Charlie went pale. 'There must be some mistake,' he said, through stiff lips. 'I'm sure Maddy won't have overlooked it. There's a file. In the office.'

'Then go find it. And take this bloke with you.'

'Hang on,' said Charlie, increasingly desperately, 'I'll just have another go through.' In his haste, half of the admin pile he had gathered up after Maddy left slithered onto the floor.

'I'm thinking it's not there, Mr Wellbeloved,' said the little grey man with no discernible sympathy. 'The full policy document will be a substantial number of pages and the certificate itself is not easy to overlook. I'm afraid we have to conclude—'

'Coo-eee,' came a voice from the kitchen. 'I saw your car,' said Caroline coming through into the study. 'I thought you'd be up at the festival.'

Charlie explained.

'Well can't someone call someone?' said Caroline doughtily. 'These things aren't rocket science, after all. Also, has someone actually asked Maddy?'

'You meet all the best people in the trattoria,' said Bella, trailing wearily in for a double shot of caffeine and seeing Ben apparently on the same task.

'Maddy fancied a caramel latte,' he said, watching the trattoria's newest summer staff member, a spotty, skinny youth of about sixteen, frothing the milk gingerly.

'How is she?'

'A bit wobbly, actually,' admitted Ben. 'Baby blues. Weepy. Irrational . . . actually not irrational,' he added hastily. 'On the contrary, everything she insists is completely true in every way, especially the really weird, random stuff.'

Bella smiled in sympathy. 'Dolly's the same,' she said. 'Up one minute, down the next. But she's a wonderful mum and I know Maddy is too.'

'Ah yes, the puppies,' said Ben. 'Congratulations! Are they all accounted for, by the way? Apparently, we're having one if there's a pup looking for a home.'

'There is,' said Bella, delighted. 'I've got two not homed, a boy and a girl. I'm just off to see them now, in fact. They're all doing really well.'

'Perfect, I'll bring Maddy one day soon—hang on, that's my phone. It's probably her wondering where her latte is. Oh, actually it's Charlie . . .'

The call was brief. Bella watched and listened with growing concern.

'Okay – so, mate, I'm really sorry but I just don't think it's fair to ask her at the moment,' Ben was saying. 'She's not in a good place. If it's been overlooked – and I'm not saying it has, but it does look like it – she'll be devastated, and you'll be no better off. I just can't see how something like that can be fixed at the click of a finger on a bank holiday weekend. I'm really, really sorry.'

'She does seem a bit not herself,' agreed Bella when she got to Dove Cottage. Dolly got up to say hello, ignoring puppies who were in the middle of using her as a climbing frame, but immediately flopped to the floor at Bella's feet and lay, on her side, eyes half closed as if she was exhausted.

'I'm just not sure about leaving her tonight,' said Caroline. 'I'm thinking I'll stay here, just in case.'

'And miss the after-show-festival-stroke-Grange-launch party?' said Bella. 'No! I'll stay . . .'

'You definitely don't want to miss the party,' said Caroline, 'it's your finest hour, everyone admiring your beautiful interiors, all the world's lifestyle press, hopefully paying attention to this hot new interiors talent.'

Bella gave a wan smile. 'That's exactly why I don't want to be there. If I'm going to be judged, I'd rather just find out afterwards. Anyhow, it's people that count, not achievements. Dolly is one of the most important people in my life and I've not been there for her. She needs someone with her. I'd like it to be me.'

'You don't want to meet all those pop stars?'

'I really, really don't,' Bella reassured her. 'I'm tired. Me and Dolly can just nap together. Sleeping is all I want to do.'

'What's next for you?'

Bella sighed. 'Now The Grange is done, I have no excuse not to move my business up to London. I've already got meetings with clients. Rufus has been amazing . . .' Her voice trailed off. 'I'm just so tired.'

Caroline looked concerned. 'Well I can't pretend I wasn't looking forward to going to the party myself, a little bit,' she admitted. 'And your husband – no, don't look at me like that, he's still your husband – is playing some silly joke

about there being someone there he wants to "fit me up"
with, is that right?'

'"Fix you up with"?'

'Yes, that might have been it.'

CHAPTER TWENTY-FIVE

Charlie, with grey man in tow, had returned to the hospitality tent where Chris and Zach were waiting anxiously. Chris, having dug in his heels like a dog being dragged to have a bath, was sitting with *The Observer* journalist in the corner. Zach was drinking black coffee, which was not improving his stress levels or his mood and Charlie was pacing and phoning anyone he could think of.

'I'm just not getting hold of anyone,' he said to Zach in despair.

'Is it any surprise at' – he looked at his watch – 'nearly eight o'clock in the evening on the Saturday of a bank holiday weekend? Are you sure Maddy didn't do it?'

'How can I tell? Maddy isn't picking up her phone and Ben is refusing to ask her. It's as good as not having it with Mr "Elf and Safety" out here threatening to shut us down – it's not about having it, it's about being able to prove it. And I can't.'

Charlie slumped down on the sofa in despair and put his

head in his hands. Sensing someone new coming into the tent and suspecting grey man with clipboard had returned to gloat and definitely pull the plug, he looked up slowly.

'Rufus,' he said, in surprise.

Rufus nodded curtly as he prowled in, scowling. He was wearing the narrowest of tailored charcoal suits with an open-necked white shirt, cut to emphasise his broad shoulders and impeccably toned torso. His hair was slicked back, his face tanned and the gunmetal grey watch on his wrist, glinted with expensive restraint. Bryony the journalist, had looked up and was flicking her hair self-consciously, sliding one leg slightly forward to show off its length a little better before turning back to her victim, Chris, with reluctance.

Charlie gathered himself up and stood, all thoughts of his own desperate position forgotten. He had something to say and it was long overdue.

'Rufus,' he said again, holding out his hand. 'Mate. I hope you'll let me have a chat with you. There's something—'

'I was wondering when you'd realise,' said Rufus, watchful and dangerous, a pulse going in his clenched jaw.

'Sit down, mate, please,' said Charlie, putting his hand on Rufus's shoulder. 'What can I get you? Coffee? Beer? Whatever you want . . .'

'Give the man a chance to answer,' said Zach, stepping forward. 'Rufus, mate, me too with the realising who you were – ridiculous, isn't it? Mind you, I'm hopeless with faces. And you – well – you don't look the same.'

Rufus allowed himself to be sat down and the two other men sat at angles to him.

'It's nice to hear you call me by my proper name too,' he said.

'Yeah,' said Charlie, hanging his head. 'Fair point.'

'We were a bit crap, weren't we?' said Zach. 'I'm thinking back and . . .' he swallowed. 'I'm ashamed, mate. I'm sorry.'

'Me too,' said Charlie, leaning forward. 'We were little shites, basically. Didn't know how to behave – no excuse – but it was dog-eat-dog at that school wasn't it? Talk about bullying victims becoming bullies, the whole "fag" thing . . . No excuse, though. It shouldn't have been so hard for you and that's totally on me.'

'And me,' interjected Zach.

'You know,' Charlie paused, 'I feel like I've kind of got more – I dunno – evolved? Bella . . . she . . .' He swallowed hard and clenched his fists before consciously releasing them again. 'Bella, she's a great girl – as you know' – he waved a hand at Rufus – 'and she taught me how to function like a normal human being. And it's made me realise . . .' He stopped, overwhelmed.

Rufus sighed. It was a long, deep sigh and at the end of it his face had softened. He slumped slightly into the sofa.

'It's funny,' he said. 'I've thought, over the years, about what it would be like to hear you both say that to me. Something like that. "Sorry" or whatever. And now . . . it feels . . . a bit irrelevant. I won't lie, when The Grange came up I was aware I would likely be coming back into contact with you both again. I wondered if you would twig who I was. I'll be honest, if you did, I wanted you to see me as very different to that little ginger boy who was weedy, who cried a lot . . . I honestly can't say that if I had been like you were – strong, sporty, popular – if I wouldn't have behaved like you did. I owe you thanks, if anything. You've lit the fire in my belly and it's served me well. I've achieved. I've become successful. Who knows if I would have done that if I didn't feel I had something to prove.'

Charlie and Zach nodded.

'And you're right about Bella,' Rufus added.

Charlie's jaw clenched, and Zach put a staying, calming hand on his arm.

'She *is* a great girl,' Rufus went on. 'She's a real star – she's beautiful, kind, clever . . . to be honest, I was vengeful when I offered you that loan. I wanted to have power over you. I wanted to – to hurt you but now . . .'

Charlie's eyes had filled with tears and he dashed them angrily away.

'Now I should be apologising to you. I'm sorry,' said Rufus quietly.

Charlie nodded, then kept his head bowed while he composed himself.

'She loved you,' Rufus went on, ignoring a sharp warning look from Zach. 'She – loves you, actually. And I can't compete with that.'

In the silence that followed, the men heard the gathering noise from outside, the musicians tuning up after the previous set, the backstage team shouting to each other on their walkie-talkies, the thrumming chatter of the crowd, sounding from this distance, like the humming of bees. No one out there knew the entire event was just about to be halted and torn apart.

'I nearly forgot,' said Rufus, brightening, his smooth demeanour returning. 'That annoying bloke who's here about the public liability insurance?'

'Yeah, he's out there somewhere,' said Charlie. 'Just about to shut everything down.'

'Get someone to send him in. I've got something to show him.'

Charlie looked confused, but Zach stood up and went out of the tent, returning in seconds with the little grey man who was looking increasingly smug and superior.

'I am sorry to say,' he said, looking officiously at his watch, 'I really can't allow—'

'Scrap that,' interrupted Rufus. 'I believe this is what you want to see.' He tapped his phone a couple of times and held it up to the man's face.

'What's this?' he said, peering myopically.

'That, my pedantic little friend,' he said, 'is a public liability insurance certificate for ten million pounds, covering this event, its participants and all who sail in her.'

'Where did it come from?'

'Never mind. I think you'll find it's all in order.'

'Yes, well,' the man said bossily, 'it's supposed to be printed out, you know. It's supposed to be up on display in public . . .'

'Yeah, yeah,' said Rufus, taking him by the elbow and guiding him protesting out of the tent, before coming back to the other two men, rubbing his hands together.

'Right,' he said. 'That's that dealt with, let's get on, shall we?'

Zach and Charlie looked at him in disbelief.

'How did you . . . ?', 'What did you . . . ?' They both said at once.

Zach held his hands out wide. 'What just happened?' he added, a broad grin spreading across his face.

'Friends in low places,' said Rufus. 'My people know people, which is useful.'

'Useful?' said Charlie, wonderingly. 'Also, why would you?'

'Because Bella told me,' said Rufus, bluntly. 'My money's riding on this, remember. I don't want it to fail. Plus,' he paused, 'she asked me. I'd do anything for her.'

'Yeah, yeah,' growled Charlie. 'Don't push your luck.'

Rufus was unfazed. 'I know, mate,' he said easily. 'I know. What I mean is I've got to know you both a bit over the last few months. I've been sort of invisible to you but, seeing you, hearing people talk about you, I'm not stupid, I can tell you are decent blokes. I don't deny, there was a bit of a motivation initially, a hope you'd cock up, but now' – he said, visibly considering – 'yeah . . . I wanted to help.'

'How do I look?' asked Caroline, handing Bella a cup of tea and then giving her a twirl, in the limited space.

'Gorgeous! No one could resist,' said Bella, truthfully.

Caroline was wearing a scarlet silk shirt dress with a wide, self-tie belt that showed off her still-slim waist. Her hair, recently cut to jaw length, was blow-dried to flippy, wavy perfection and her skin glowed with health.

'You know, you really do scrub up rather well. You might just pull yourself a toy-boy rock star if you play your cards right.'

'Not sure I've got the energy for that,' said Caroline, pleased. 'I'll settle for a gentle old soul who wants to potter in the garden and go to the odd choral concert with me,' she said with a wistful smile. 'But what about you? Are you sure you'll be all right?'

'There is nowhere I'd rather be tonight,' said Bella. 'I've got thinking to do. And being with Dolly helps me get my head straight. Now, off you go, Cinderella. You can tell me all about this blind date lover-boy you're meeting up with when you get back. Unless you're too busy to talk.'

Caroline gave a shout of laughter, blew her a kiss and left.

Other than calling Rufus about the insurance, Bella had been focusing entirely on Dolly for hours. Despite Caroline's earlier concern, the dog seemed fine, no longer pacing anxiously but in her bed, content with her pups who, at five weeks, now rarely fed from her but clambered all over her before flumping down to sleep, warm against her flank, exhausted as only babies can be.

Hunkered up in the corner of Caroline's porch, her hair tied up in a rubber band, wearing her scruffiest sweat pants and a hoodie, she watched entranced as Dolly cared for the six squirming creatures, only giving them a warning motherly growl when they nipped too hard.

'You're such a good mum,' Bella said softly, later, fondling the dog's ear as she dozed. 'I've missed you . . .'

Dolly groaned, opening one eye, and licked Bella's hand lazily before drifting back off to sleep.

The air smelt warm, with an intoxicating mix of puppy and a peppery lemony scent from the geraniums lined up on the window sill. There was a leavening odour of wellington boot alongside, which was less appealing, but Bella was content, dozing intermittently too, and only briefly thinking how horrified Rufus would be to see her looking so scruffy and unkempt, sitting on the dirty floor.

Charlie watched Chris with interest in the lead up to going onstage. His old school pal's eyes were sparkling, his body starting to twitch with adrenaline and he had been pacing the tent like a caged tiger, swigging from a can of Coke.

Outside, onstage, the support band – more of Chris's mates – were doing a brilliant job whipping the audience up into a euphoric frenzy of excitement, even segueing into a cover of one of Inspire's greatest hits to roars of approval.

'Good, aren't they?' asked Chris, coming over to Charlie and draping a hand on his shoulder.

'They are,' he said, 'that lead guitar . . . amazing.'

'I know. He's one of my session musicians,' said Chris. 'I encouraged him to leave me, which he did in a heartbeat – the bastard – just so he could set up his own band.'

'In competition?'

'Nah,' said Chris, comfortably. 'You can't look at it like that. He's a mint guitarist, bloody talented. If he'd stayed he'd have been constantly under my shadow.'

'If you say so yourself.'

'Yeah,' Chris grinned. 'So I made a few calls for him. Smoothed the way, if you like. Plus, of course, I got you lot to take him on as supporting act so, yeah, things are going well for these guys.'

'Because of you.'

'Not entirely, obviously, they've gotta have the talent, but, yeah, it feels good to give people a leg up. After all, I'm the old man of rock, practically, now.'

'You can't say that,' protested Charlie. 'We're only in our thirties, for heaven's sake. What about all the bearded greying rockers around us, they're going on for bleeding decades, some of them.'

'That's not me, though,' said Chris. 'Like I said, I'm ready to step down. I've made my money, pretty much. I've got a life to lead well away from all this crap.'

'You're a decent bloke, aren't you?'

'You're not so bad yourself.'

'I'm touched that Rufus – of all people – has said so,' admitted Charlie.

'Don't be too grateful,' said Chris. 'He stole your girl, remember. Two wrongs don't make a right. You've got stuff to forgive too.'

'Ah, but it was all my fault, you see,' said Charlie, shaking his head. 'Pretty much, all my fault, anyhow. I allowed things to get as bad as they did. Forced her hand, really, so . . . my fault and only myself to blame,' he added softly, staring into the distance.

He reeled away, with Chris looking after him in concern, but the supporting act's set was coming to an end and what Charlie had started was going to continue, with or without him.

The set from the warm-up band was electric. The festival-goers were in a benign, happy mood, buoyed by the fantastic weather, the universally good-natured crowd and the amazing music.

Zach had gathered Charlie up and both were watching from the side in the backstage area as Chris's band began the set. Chris, out of sight of the crowd, had been still and solitary, amidst all the activity around him, but – when he was announced – he raised his head, broke into a run and burst onto the stage in a huge leap. The crowd roared their approval as he, with no hesitation, took his guitar as it was handed to him and broke immediately into their first song.

Hits and new material alike, the crowd loved it. For most of the old favourites Chris worked the audience, getting them to sing along, repeatedly cutting the music so the crowd could carry the tune, which they did with gusto. Interspersed with the hits was some new material from the next album, which the band – Chris explained in between the songs – had chosen to premier at the festival. From midnight, it would also be available to download. Immediately heads bowed right across the crowd as they tapped on their phones in response. Zach was pretty sure a couple of the tracks would be topping the charts by morning.

One new song, written solely by Chris, was a ballad, sung with heartfelt simplicity by him on the acoustic guitar, finishing to a moment of silence followed by thunderous applause. There was even more cheering and whistling when he announced that the proceeds from that one were all for his favourite charity, an organisation that supported terminally ill children and their families. Because it was also local – the Havenbury May Ball was its major annual fundraiser – the section of the crowd that lived in and around Havenbury roared their approval, on and on.

All in all, thought Charlie from the wings, the skinny little squirt from school had done pretty good. He grinned with almost parental pride.

Chris had finally bounded off the stage, dripping in sweat but just as explosively energetic as he had been at the start. The crowd had insisted on three encores and had groaned and hissed with good-natured disappointment when Zach had gone on and taken the mic, explaining that future Rainbow Festival plans would be dead in the water if they allowed Chris—sorry, 'Zane'– here he gave Chris a little ironic bow – to go a minute past the reluctantly granted eleven o'clock deadline of their live music licence from the local council's licensing committee.

'Bloody good job, mate,' said Charlie clapping Chris on the shoulder as he went past.

'Right, where's the party?' he replied.

'Christ, you really don't give up do you?' said Charlie, who had started to yawn. 'Exactly which illicit substances are you taking for these energy levels of yours? You're making me feel old.'

'You *are* old,' said Chris. 'I'm not, though, obviously . . . Also, it's less about the hard-arse illegal substances stuff – that would have killed me by now – I swear by my personal trainer, turmeric and nine hours' sleep a night. Preferably in the company of a beautiful blonde with big tits,' he added, thoughtfully.

'Come on,' said Zach, grabbing Charlie's arm as he went past. 'We've got a party to get to. Anything to distract from thoughts of how we're going to get through the next two days plus the breakdown and clean-up after all this.'

'Yeah, mate, I dunno,' said Charlie. 'I wouldn't mind an early night, plus Bella's at the cottage looking after the pups for Ma so, I thought I'd – you know – casually drop by and see her . . . casual, like,' he added. 'Subtle. Because I'm just passing . . .'

'Mm,' said Zach, 'you don't really do "subtle", do you? Listen, I think, given the revelations we had from and about Rufus earlier, it might be taken the wrong way if we don't show up and support his big moment. Especially given his extremely useful intervention ensuring your big moment. Talking of which, it's been amazing, hasn't it? Aren't you a little bit pleased, relieved, thrilled . . . delete as required?'

Charlie shrugged. 'I guess so.' Then he took a deep breath. 'I think we're probably going to do okay. I've not done all the number crunching . . . but, yeah . . .'

'So, that's all right, then. Come and celebrate.'

Bella and Dolly were having a lovely evening together with the pups. Bella had propped herself into the corner by Dolly's bed, close enough to rest her hand on Dolly's head, which Dolly seemed to be grateful for, turning occasionally to lick Bella's hand. The little dog was sleepy, nicely full after the poached chicken and rice Caroline had given her for supper, and now she had her darling mistress with her to admire her beautiful new family, all was right with the world.

Bella felt the same. She could see the spotlights from the main stage, tracking backwards and forwards across the night sky, which had now darkened from indigo to black velvet, studded with stars so bright they competed and won

295

against the unaccustomed glow of hundreds of little lights from the camping fields, bordering the vineyard. She could hear the *thump, thump, thump* of the amplified music and every now and then a strain of a melody would blow her way on the breeze. She hugged her knees and gazed delightedly at the little family. Rufus had been tight-lipped when she told him she would be missing the Grange's launch party, preferring nursery assistant duty at Dove Cottage. She had been relieved to have an excuse. She felt like an alien at his smart parties, full of smart friends who weren't really friends – he didn't seem to have proper friends – just people he wanted to do business with. Despite her new wardrobe and her tanned, toned, glossily manicured self, she felt awkward, never knowing quite what to say or do. It was a million miles away, she mused, from those nights at the Havenbury Arms when she first admired Charlie from afar, watching him larking about with his friend Ben, playing practical jokes and making a tit of himself, but with such boundless charm and grace, his dark wavy hair and deep blue eyes, always laughing. He had entranced her, making her tongue-tied and red-faced whenever he turned his jokey, good-natured attention to her. And then, later, when they were living together here at Dove Cottage, ramshackle and rundown as it was at the time, they had always been laughing – Bella laughing in spite of herself often, as she begged him to be serious. She gazed at a tear-shaped mark on the terracotta floor tiles, remembering how it had got there. One sunny Saturday morning she had got up out of bed, despite Charlie's attempts to stop her. Dressed only in his old rugby shirt and a pair of pants, she had been painting the wooden window frames in the porch while Charlie, drinking coffee, watched admiringly and made unhelpful comments. Dove grey, the colour was, and for its name alone she had loved it, using it throughout the little cottage for continuity. Too impatient to get a ladder, she had been reaching for the top of a frame when he had tickled her under the arm, making a big splodge of paint fall onto the floor. Even though she had waited for it to dry and scraped it off with a knife, the mark still showed.

As she rubbed her finger over it, feeling the roughness of the terracotta, smoothed a little by the layers of wax polish Caroline had applied, a tear trickled down the side of Bella's nose, running off her chin and dripping onto Dolly's head. She wiped it away apologetically, but Dolly didn't stir. Gosh, she was deeply asleep.

Bella wondered if it was moving from the cottage that had ruined their relationship. They had been so happy here, hadn't they? People did say that a marriage can break a relationship, but they had both wanted it, not needing to convince each other of their commitment but keen to show the world. Plus, Charlie had had some funny ideas about children being better for having a mummy and daddy with the same surname. Bella had teased him for it but secretly she had agreed. She had wanted that solidity, that sense of continuity, imagining a horde of scruffy, happy, suntanned children scrapping and running around on the farm. Even plans to move from the cottage into the farmhouse had seemed exciting at first, with Bella keen to take on a larger interior project and thrilled at the potential of the building. And then, with her father-in-law's death, it was like the sun went behind the clouds and never came out again. Charlie didn't laugh and joke any more. And their relationship – the one thing they were both so sure of – began to crack and fall away.

CHAPTER TWENTY-SIX

When they drew up outside The Grange, Charlie doubted his decision to come all over again. The front of the graceful Georgian building had been spot-lit, the light washing the facade with tints of pink, blue and green. Box balls in square pots flanked the front entrance, which was open, although there was a beautifully severe young woman in black with a stony face, ticking off names on her list. Even getting as far as her meant guests had successfully navigated the first line of security. It amused Charlie to see the pumped-up, muscular security men with their headsets and shaven heads, checking out Zach's knackered and filthy old estate car with its bale of hay in the boot. He mentally dared them to turn Zach away, but then felt bad that such an underling would end up being responsible for turning away Lord Havenbury himself. Impressively, though, the staff all seemed to have lists with mugshots for the most important guests. Charlie wasn't on it, but Zach was. Zach threw him a comedy grin and said, 'Oh, Charlie's my stylist, I have to have him with me at all times.'

The security officer nodded as if this was the most normal thing in the world, which made Charlie laugh even harder.

Inside, the whole building was throbbing with some deeply cool and massively loud mood music, which seemed to somehow be linked with the lighting. It changed gradually from pink, through to blue, green, violet and back to pink again, throbbing and pulsing in time to the beat. There were waitresses, all of model proportions, either drifting around with frozen bottles of vodka, offering shots, or with slabs of black slate covered in minute and delicate canapés. To each guest, the waitress was offering complex explanations of what they were: Charlie heard something about 'salsify foam' and 'sea urchin' but mostly people were waving them away, concentrating instead on the important matter of drinking and taking in the decor, which – despite being partly obscured by the crowds and the lighting – was spectacular.

Charlie wandered around, his chest bursting with pride at finally seeing Bella's work. The chandeliers in the main lounge were utterly spectacular. A woman that even Charlie recognised as one of the Sunday newspaper interiors journalists was snapping pictures of them and tapping notes into her phone. Actually, she was probably posting on Instagram, he thought. That Bryony woman, who had been interviewing Chris earlier, was sitting on one of the low, chestnut sofas, the leather gleaming with wax, nose to nose with a woman whose fake tan glowed orange in the low light, and whose teeth were so preternaturally white they looked fluorescent. The long, silk curtains gleamed with a soft light of their own, like moonlight; dropping straight and pooling on the polished floor, they provided the perfect framing for the high-arched Georgian windows and the floodlit lawns outside.

Chris was sprawled on one of the sofas flanking the windows. He was swigging a glass of red wine and, in his lap, was his acoustic guitar. He was fiddling idly with it and Charlie was sure, before long, he would play, and then the room would fall silent to listen, such was his talent and charisma.

And there was Ma. She hadn't seen him because she was nose-to-nose with Geoffrey, still in his patched tweed jacket, Charlie smiled to see. Ma was in the red dress she wore on the evening of his and Bella's wedding day. The day she was widowed. Plenty of women would take that reason to never wear a dress again, but his ma was always pragmatic. 'It was damned expensive,' she would say. 'I'm going to get the wear out of it.' Talking to Geoffrey, she glowed like a young woman. Geoffrey leant forward to say something in her ear and she threw back her head to laugh, making him look quietly and sweetly pleased with himself. Charlie was glad. They would be all right, Geoffrey and Ma.

At the far end of the room, near the bar, a group of people were starting to dance. They were cool, of course, not flinging their arms around and doing the type of Dad-dancing he and Ben would do whenever the stereo went up a notch at parties. Abba was a favourite – purely ironically, they always added, to justify it to each other. This music he didn't know at all. He felt old. Rufus, his jacket gone, and a blindingly white shirt unbuttoned another notch, was swaying liquidly opposite Flora, who seemed to be dressed entirely in chiffon scarves, with a daisy chain around her neck. She was persuading Rufus to wear another daisy chain on his head, and he smilingly allowed her to place it on his slicked-back, auburn hair, pulling her hips towards him in payment and holding her against his undulating torso as she moved in synchronicity with him.

Charlie wondered about punching him for dancing with a woman who wasn't Bella, but then realised how ridiculous he would look if he picked a fight with a guy for not seducing his wife.

Instead, he wandered around, glass in hand, feeling invisible and alone amongst the crowds. By dint of apologies and turning sideways through narrow gaps he managed to navigate his way into the conservatory, which doubled as the dining room. This, too, was packed, pulsating with the music, which was getting ever louder. Pinpoint LED lighting studded the Victorian conservatory frame, creating constellations of internal stars against the backdrop of the navy sky. The tables and chairs, a mismatched array of metal garden furniture, beautifully aged, with peeling layers of paint, all in several shades of white and green, were a perfect foil for the earthy, plant house atmosphere. The brick floor, the raised beds, planted with scented stocks, nicotiana and lilies, their strong, architectural shapes, all in white, meant no flower arrangements were needed elsewhere. In the corners of each of the raised beds, climbers were planted. Jasmine and bougainvillea twined around their frames, climbing the walls and up across the ceiling. How on earth had Bella got them to look so established? Charlie had an image of her reaching up, on tiptoes, patiently twining the stems around the wires herself. That's what she would do. He could see her in his mind's eye. And then he could see her, vividly, in his memory, painting the porch in Dove Cottage, dressed only in her pants and one of his shirts. It was early on Saturday morning. They had just made love. He had tried to persuade her to stay in bed with him but – as always – she was up, doing something. Making something. Creating beautiful spaces that people wanted to live in.

Suddenly, strongly, he wanted to be with her. Just to be in the same room as her would be enough, if that was all he could have. As if by telepathy, his phone buzzed against his hip. He pulled it out to look at the screen. It was her.

Bella must have slept because she opened her eyes blearily to see Dolly had gone, leaving her six little pups in a mound of limbs and fur, fast asleep on top of each other. Sitting upright so quickly her head spun, she saw Dolly had pressed herself up against the door, hunched miserably, head down.

'Sorry darling, do you need to go out?' said Bella, getting stiffly to her feet. Dolly looked back at her anxiously.

'What?' said Bella. There was something . . . she opened the door and watched as Dolly went out, tripping on the lintel and nearly falling on her nose. Then, she collected herself, took a few steps and crouched gratefully to do a wee.

Bella shook her head, as if to shake away her doubts and fears. Dolly was fine. She looked back at the little pups who were now squirming, feeling their mother's absence as they each tried sleepily to get themselves at the warm, cosy bottom of the heap.

She turned back to Dolly and her heart plummeted. She was lying on her side on the grass, her legs stuck rigidly out in front of her. Her eyes rolled in her head, showing the whites. Bella ran to her, sinking down on the lawn, not feeling the dew soaking her trousers.

'Dolly?' she sobbed.

In response, the little dog – who was panting in short, sharp huffs – met her gaze, her eyes filled with alarm.

'Don't move,' said Bella, scrambling to her feet. Within seconds she was back at the dog's side, this time with her phone.

'Charlie?' she yelled, as soon as she heard his voice, shouting against the music and crowds of people in the background. 'It's me. There's something wrong with Dolly . . .'

CHAPTER TWENTY-SEVEN

Years passed, or so it felt. Dolly continued to huff strangely, her legs now both rigid and pulsing with the muscle contractions that racked her body. Bella laid down full length on the soaking grass next to her, so they could maintain eye contact. 'You're fine, darling,' Bella kept saying, not bothering to wipe away the tears and snot that ran down her face. 'You're fine.'

She heard a bang, Charlie crashing through the front door.

'Here,' she shouted, but it came out as a tiny croak. 'Here,' she yelled again, sitting up but keeping her hand reassuringly on Dolly's head.

Her relief at seeing Charlie was huge, made even bigger by seeing that – miraculously – he had brought Aidan McRory, the local vet, a great lumbering ex-rugby player whose size and strength belied his gentle attitude and abiding love for animals.

Aidan got to her first.

'Shit,' he said under his breath, his eyes raking over

the little dog appraisingly. 'Okay, my lovely,' he added to Bella putting his hand firmly under her elbow and propelling her to her feet. 'Up you get, out of my way just for a moment.'

Rising she turned and threw herself into Charlie's arms. He cradled her head against his chest, his arms wrapped tightly around her to stop her falling as her knees buckled in relief.

'Charlie,' she sobbed.

'I know,' he said, not loosening his grip but resting his chin reassuringly on the top of her head. 'I know.'

Aidan stood, and turned to them, grim-faced. 'It's not good.'

'What?' said Bella, tremulously.

'It's eclampsia. Relatively rare, thank God, just bloody awful bad luck.'

'Can you?'

'I'm going to push some calcium into her,' he said, 'straight away.'

'Will that . . . ?'

'Honestly? It might kill her. Stop her heart.'

'Then don't do it! Why?'

'Because if I don't treat her she'll certainly die,' said Aidan, rolling up his sleeves. 'And soon.'

Charlie and Bella watched as he delicately shaved an area of Dolly's front leg, holding it tight to keep it still despite the convulsions that were relentlessly, exhaustingly, racking her body.

'Here, let me,' said Bella, detaching herself from Charlie who let her go reluctantly. She wiped her snotty face unselfconsciously with her sleeve and knelt by Dolly's head, stroking her with one hand and holding her foreleg still with the other.

Aidan nodded his thanks. 'Right,' he said. 'Here's the moment where – if you're churchy – you might want to say a little prayer . . .'

Attaching a large syringe to the tube going into Dolly's leg he slowly depressed the plunger.

At first, nothing happened. Dolly's legs were now paddling furiously in the air, her eyes bulging and ribs heaving in her attempts to catch her breath.

'It's not working,' sobbed Bella. 'Hurry.'

Aidan ignored her, keeping the steady pressure on the syringe, gradually feeding the fluid into Dolly's vein.

Minutes passed.

Gradually, Dolly's limbs relaxed, she slumped under Bella's hand.

'Is she better?' Bella breathed.

Aidan gave a tiny shake of the head. 'Too soon to tell.'

They waited.

Dolly seemed to now be asleep, still and relaxed, breathing deeply. And then – almost imperceptibly – her body gave a little jolt.

Bella looked up at Aidan.

'Shit,' he said, fumbling in his bag for his stethoscope.

Bella held her breath, her hand not moving from Dolly's head.

He held the stethoscope to Dolly's chest and then hung his head.

'I'm so sorry . . .'

Belle dragged air into her chest with a heave. 'No,'

307

she said, shaking her head. 'No, no, no, no . . .'

Charlie crouched down next to her and put his hand over hers on Dolly's head.

'No . . .' said Bella, looking frantically from Aidan to Charlie. 'No, no, no . . . you've got to . . . she can't be . . .'

She looked down, making herself look at the dog's face, at her eyes, the beautiful brown eyes that had so adoringly, pleadingly, mischievously met hers, every day since Charlie had brought her home as a squirming armful of black fur. Dolly looked sightlessly into the distance and would never meet her mistress's gaze again. Even now, her eyes were becoming dull and sunken. Her fur, so soft and black, already felt brittle under Bella's questing hand.

Aidan got heavily to his feet.

'I'm so sorry,' he said to Charlie, over Bella's head. 'It was worth a shot, but sometimes – this thing can be so sudden, so violent, there's nothing to be done I'm afraid. It's just one of those utterly shit things.'

Charlie nodded. 'We need to see to the pups,' he said in a monotone. 'I'll get Ma to come.'

'Stay with Bella. I'll see if I can find Caroline,' said Aidan, resting a hand on Charlie's shoulder. 'And would you like me to . . . ?' He gestured at the body, slumped on the lawn, in the frozen, unmistakeable stillness of death.

'No,' said Bella, vehemently, her eyes flashing. She gathered up Dolly's body, dragging as much of it as she could into her lap as she knelt on the grass. 'No,' she said again, more quietly, into the top of the dog's head.

'I'll sort it out later,' Charlie told Aidan. 'When Bella's asleep or something.'

Aidan shook his head. 'Don't do that. You need to do it with her. It's important.' He gave Charlie a direct look, impressing it on him. 'Call me . . .' he added, 'If there's anything else I can do.'

When Caroline arrived with Geoffrey, Bella was still clutching Dolly's body in her arms. She was no longer sobbing but was still and staring. She barely blinked as Caroline called out to her.

'I'll see to the pups,' she told her son. 'You need to see to your wife.'

At first Charlie just positioned himself behind her, legs either side, cradling her in his arms as she held Dolly. They stayed that way for a while, watching the sun rise fully over the brow of the hill, warming the earth beneath the vines, warming them a little too as they sat there, stiff with cold and fatigue. It wouldn't warm Dolly's body into life, though. Instead, imperceptibly, and for no describable reason, Dolly's body became less and less like her. More like a 'thing' than a 'person'.

Eventually, gently, Charlie reached around and put his hands over the top of Bella's. 'We can bury her in the orchard,' he murmured in her ear. 'She can go under the old crab apple in the corner. It's peaceful there. She'll be safe.'

There was a pause. Charlie wondered if she was listening. Then, he felt her give a tiny nod.

He waited a little longer, gauging his moment.

'Shall we let her go now? We can go and find a blanket to wrap her in, we can see her pups, and then later you can come and hold her again. For as long as you like.'

Bella gave another tiny nod so Charlie, pressing his advantage, prised her hands away and lifted her to her feet, laying Dolly's stiffening body gently, reverently, down on the ground.

Charlie brought Bella inside and sat her at the kitchen table, bringing a blanket from the sitting room to wrap her in so she could sit and watch Caroline work. Geoffrey was there too, making the tea, quietly, unobtrusively reading what people needed and dealing with it.

'Are they okay?' Bella asked through stiff lips, looking at the basket of pups. Her voice came out creaky and her throat was sore, like she was a hermit who had not spoken for years.

'They're very small to lose their mum,' said Caroline. 'It's going to be hard work,' she went on, smiling reassuring. 'We'll cope. You'll see.'

'She needs to see a doctor,' Caroline told Charlie when Bella was distracted by Geoffrey who was trying, gently, to engage her in conversation.

'She's not ill.'

'Can you not see?' said Caroline. 'I don't know what she's been doing to herself over the last few months, but look . . . She's exhausted. Spent.'

Charlie looked over at her. His mother was right. How had he not noticed? Her arms protruding from the rolled-up sleeves of the thin top she was wearing were stripped of fat, showing clearly the sinewy muscle. Her expensively cut and highlighted hair was thinning and the prominent cheekbones were only partly due to expert shading. Most striking of all, though, her eyes were dull, unseeing, as she stared into the middle distance.

'Yeah,' said Charlie. 'I see it. I'll call Simon. He'll come.'

CHAPTER TWENTY-EIGHT

He persuaded Bella to come back to the farmhouse with him, but only by reassuring her that Dolly's body would come too. 'You've not slept,' he said. 'Do you think you could? Get some sleep and then, I promise, you can go back to the cottage and help Ma with the pups.'

Bella seemed to like that idea. She wasn't talking much, but she allowed Charlie to lead her up the stairs. She was swaying so he clutched her arm, shocked at its sinewy leanness and her prominent collar bones, which were framed by the scooped neckline of her flowing, cotton top.

'You need some warmer clothes too,' he said. 'Autumn's coming.'

And it was true. They could feel it in the air that morning; a decided shift; the autumn chill had come overnight.

'In our bed?'

'Clean sheets yesterday,' he reassured her. 'I'll sleep in my study,' he added hastily. 'Stay a few days. Please?'

Bella gave him a sad look but didn't refuse.

'I need a wee,' she said. 'Before I sleep.'

'Ah,' said Charlie. 'I hoped you might.'

He stood back nervously as she pushed open the bathroom door.

'What?' she said, swaying in the doorway, not able to process what she was seeing.

'Big improvement, eh?'

The brown shag pile and avocado bath suite were nowhere to be seen. The free-standing bath was on a plinth in the centre of the room, positioned for the occupant to see out of the window and over the vineyard. The window dressing was simple, just long white muslin curtains framing the view. The entire room, floorboards, wooden panelling, walls and ceiling were painted in soft shades of grey.

'Is that . . . ?' said Bella, running her finger over the wooden cladding behind the basin.

'Dove grey,' confirmed Charlie.

'It's all . . .' she said, going to stand in front of the pair of basins, his and hers, each a white porcelain trough with a matching arched mirror above, cunning storage below, with clutter entirely absent, just a few carefully positioned bottles of bath stuff and a basket of natural sponges.

'You left your mood board,' said Charlie. 'With your plans for it. I just thought . . . I mean . . . it bloody needed doing and I thought your ideas were pretty reasonable on the whole.'

'I think my ideas were better than "reasonable",' said Bella with a tiny hint of spirit. 'It looks flipping amazing,' she said, checking out the walk-in glass shower space, which was set into a dramatically dark, slate-clad alcove.

It had exactly the impact she had been aiming for.

'Obviously there's an awful lot more to be done,' admitted Charlie. 'The rest of the house is largely a tip. I did the bathroom cos I thought we'd need to sell. Thought it would add value.'

'And now?'

'No,' said Charlie. 'We're all right. The festival . . . it saved the day. The Wellbeloved family will live on at the Dovecot Estate. For now, at least – God knows there'll always be some drama or another.'

Bella nodded.

By the time she settled into bed, with Charlie tucking her in, she was yawning. Tears trickled slowly down her cheeks as she relaxed but, despite her grief, she slept.

CHAPTER TWENTY-NINE

'So sorry to wake you,' came a gentle male voice, cutting through a nightmare.

Bella opened her eyes to see GP Simon by her bedside, bag in hand.

'May I?' he said, indicating the bed and then sitting beside her.

She sat up, rubbing her eyes to hide the tears that sprang anew when she woke up enough to remember.

'I'm not ill,' she said, when she had composed herself.

'That's good, I can't bear ill people.'

There was a brief silence.

'So . . . ?' said Bella. Really, the effort of having to sit upright in the bed was enormous. She wished Simon would go, so she could slide back down and go back to sleep.

'Charlie's a bit worried about you,' he continued, conversationally, crossing his legs and lacing his hands over his knee. 'You've had a tough few months, both of you. He seems to feel you're a bit run-down. Not yourself . . .'

'No? Well,' Bella stiffened defensively. 'I think I'm fine.'

'So, just wondering . . .' Simon went on, his sharp eyes noting the chiselled planes of her face, the extreme slenderness of her arms, which were, at the same time, lined with muscle, quite different to the luscious plumpness of just a few months before. 'Have you lost any weight recently, for example? Charlie says you've been running? Doing a lot of exercise, maybe not eating enough, possibly?'

'Aha! No! You see, I haven't,' said Bella with hollow triumph, her lip trembling. 'Actually, I've put it on, and I know what you're thinking . . .'

'What am I thinking?'

'With all the exercise, it must be muscle because it weighs more than fat, blah, blah, but that's because you haven't seen my tummy, because – you see – my waist is really big and I've been reading up about it and the tiredness, the hair thinning, the – the – the . . .' Bella was waving her hand around in the air, searching for words, '. . . the brain-softening thingy and everything . . . I know what it is!' she finished triumphantly.

'Go on,' said Simon, clamping down on a smile that was trying to turn up the corners of his mouth. 'What's the diagnosis, Dr Wellbeloved?'

'I'm in the menopause.'

Now he didn't bother to hide his amusement. 'How old are you, Bella?'

'Nearly thirty, and I know that's young, obviously, but it can happen because I read about it on the Internet. I've got no eggs. I'll never have babies.' Her chin wobbled but she continued, holding up her hand to stop Simon interrupting,

'You can't tell me it's not true because I know it is. I haven't even had a period for months. Not a proper one, anyway. So, there you go,' she went on, taking a deep breath and wiping fresh tears away from her eyes. 'I'm barren. I'm a dried-up old prune and better off with a man like Rufus, who's too damaged to know what to do with kids, than I am allowing myself to be shackled to Charlie, who deserves to be married to a woman he can have children with.'

Simon manfully wiped the amusement from his face and said, seriously, 'Bella, you are exhausted, you are borderline underweight, I suspect you may even be a little jaundiced, although I am prepared to accept it may be the effect of the fake tan. The fact remains, I'm here now and I would beg you to consider that my seven years of medical training might – just might – be superior to Dr Google . . .' He raised his eyebrows. 'Would you mind if I examined you?'

'You might as well,' said Bella, dead behind the eyes now she had voiced her fears, slumping back against the pillow in renewed lassitude.

Simon carried out his tests with gentle thoroughness; her pulse, her blood pressure . . . his expression was impenetrable as he checked her over, leaving the abdominal examination until last. When he had got Bella to shuffle down in the bed until she was lying flat and she had lifted her top, shock flitted across his face before he adopted a mask of professional detachment.

'See? Middle-age spread,' said Bella, looking down at her tummy with disgust as he palpated her abdomen. It had failed to respond to a million sit-ups and looked even worse in the context of her newly slim thighs and arms.

Simon helped her to rearrange her clothes and sit up in the bed. Once she was settled he sat himself back down on the edge of the bed and looked at his hands for a moment.

'Bella . . .' he said.

'I know, it's fine . . . I accept it.'

'Shut up.'

She blinked.

Simon smiled and took her hand, gently. 'Has it occurred to you, at any point over the last few months, with the missed periods, the fatigue and the swollen abdomen, that you might be – well – pregnant?'

'Yeah . . . no . . . definitely . . .' Bella began on autopilot, and then she stopped. She stared into space for several long moments.

'No,' she said at last.

'Well, I'm pretty sure you are,' he said. 'In fact, with all the weight you've lost there's no difficulty at all in feeling the exact state of your uterus. By its size and position in your abdomen I would say you are definitely very pregnant. Obviously, we can do a little test right now . . .'

Bella nodded dumbly.

'. . . but really, I think the most urgent thing we need to do next is to get you a dating scan and a full examination. You've got some serious antenatal care to catch up on.'

'But . . .' Bella was shaking her head, 'I was so sure . . . I've even been having hot flushes.'

'It has been quite a hot summer this year, to be fair.' He sat for a moment in silence. Letting things sink in. Patients needed that sometimes.

'Oh my God,' said Bella, in horror, as a new alarm struck

her, 'I've not done the right things. Maddy was – like – doing all this different stuff and I've been doing everything all wrong, I've been drinking, eating soft cheese, not taking the right vitamins, it'll be . . .'

'It'll be fine,' Simon reassured her. 'An unborn baby is the most extraordinarily efficient parasite known to man, it takes everything it needs, even if it leaves the mother with nothing. I'm not surprised you've got run-down, with all the exercising and the extreme diets. There's no reason to believe the baby is anything other than completely healthy.'

CHAPTER THIRTY

'It's not yours,' said Bella.

She was lying on her side, staring at the wall.

Charlie, sat on the chair opposite the bed. He held his head in his hands and sighed with infinite, weary sadness. 'Are you sure?'

Bella nodded.

'What are you going to do?'

'Tell Rufus.'

'Are you going to stay with him? Play happy families with him?'

'I don't know. I don't think so.'

For long minutes, she didn't move, but then, slowly she heaved herself out of the bed. On standing, she swayed, but gently pushed Charlie away when he went to support her.

Caroline was using a wet wipe to clean the face of the pup she was holding with a mixture of impatience and infinite care as it wriggled and protested. 'I suppose you imagine being a father means being there at the conception,' she said.

'I think it's a start,' said Charlie. 'It's sort of considered the norm, even nowadays . . .'

'It's the most staggeringly irrelevant bit of the whole damned mess. Tell him, Geoffrey,' she snapped before sighing with irritation and fatigue.

They were all in the big kitchen at the farmhouse. Caroline had brought the puppies up from Dove Cottage. Geoffrey had also turned up and taken up quiet, useful residence in the corner. His job appeared to be mainly making the tea and agreeing with her.

At Caroline's command Geoffrey had come forward to sit opposite Charlie.

'Your mother's right,' he said, giving Charlie an apologetic look.

'Of course, I'm right.'

'And precisely what is it she's right about this time?' Charlie asked Geoffrey.

'I think she may well be referring to my role as stepfather. When I met my wife, she was – inconveniently – married to someone else, which wasn't ideal. However, he was violent towards her – which also wasn't ideal, so – when I had managed to extricate her from that situation and made her my wife I found myself with the delightful privilege of bringing up her two daughters. This was,' he paused with sad modesty 'by far the thing of which I am most proud in my life to date.'

Charlie blinked. 'And where are they now?' he asked, bluntly.

Caroline made as if to remonstrate, but Geoffrey held up his hand. 'The boy asks a fair question. I regret to say I have not been in the same room as my stepdaughters or their children, for nearly fifteen months now.'

'Why?' It came out blunter than Charlie intended.

'To keep them safe.'

'Congratulations,' replied Charlie. 'You got me there. Totally not what I was expecting you to say.'

'It's an – unusual – situation,' Geoffrey agreed.

'So?'

'I rather thought you might be able to tell me,' said Geoffrey, 'given that you have been keeping me under surveillance, I gather . . .'

'Ah, sorry about that.'

'Not at all. I'm touched that you would be so protective of your mother. I wouldn't dream of replacing you, naturally, but I feel the same way.'

'We didn't manage to work anything out,' Charlie admitted. 'Except that we probably shouldn't be keeping the two of you apart.'

'I'm grateful for that,' said Geoffrey inclining his head.

'So am I,' piped up Caroline, checking one of the pups from head to tail before popping it back down on the floor. 'Whilst I am touched and all that, you really must let me make my own mistakes. God knows I've made a few in my time but I'm pretty certain Geoffrey isn't one of them.'

Charlie looked up to see the two of them exchange a secret smile.

'Well go on, then,' said Charlie, 'seeing as I'm such an idiot . . .'

'Not at all,' said Geoffrey. 'As I said, these are extremely unusual circumstances. The truth is, for the safety of my family – and,' he added as an afterthought, 'myself . . . I've been put into the witness protection scheme.'

CHAPTER THIRTY-ONE

Charlie's jaw dropped. 'What did you do?' he said at last.

'Me? Nothing criminal. Not myself, you have to believe me . . . What I did is testify against my employers, who were not good people. My being a witness in court meant long prison sentences for them but exposure to some considerable risk from their associates. It was proposed that the witness protection scheme was the best and most practical way to keep my family safe.'

'So, you're married?' said Charlie, bristling.

'My wife and I divorced amicably a few years before, but the men I sold down the river were entirely aware that I adore my daughters and their families. I have four grandchildren,' he said, smiling in pride. 'Step grandchildren I suppose, technically, but they are astonishing and amazing. So . . .' he shook himself, returning to his story, 'after years of becoming slowly aware of certain financial irregularities, which as the firm's accountant I had a responsibility to point out – actually that's partly the reason for the divorce,' he broke off to explain, 'my wife quite reasonably got fed up with my always working and fretting about the situation without ending it. Anyway . . .' he sighed. 'When I finally woke up and realised it was down to me, my life as I knew it came to an abrupt halt.'

'Where were you working?' said Charlie.

'The men ran a firm called "Environt".'

'That was you?' said Charlie, astonished. 'No shit?'

Geoffrey nodded.

'I know, me too,' said Caroline. 'When he told me, I could hardly believe he had been wrapped up in that. He was the brave witness the papers were talking about. The one who brought down the whole edifice, the people trafficking, the drugs, the prostitution, all hidden behind a company supposedly investing in saving the planet . . .'

'That was amazing,' said Charlie. 'I remember reading about it. Like Al Capone, the justice system got them on accounting irregularities, but the police knew they were involved in all this other stuff . . .' Charlie shook his head in admiration.

'That's why I had to do it,' admitted Geoffrey. 'Looking at my grandchildren, wondering if my employers were going to smuggle in the MDMA that they might be offered at a pop concert, that might take them away from me. Knowing that other families were losing their children to this filthy poison they were peddling.'

'How could you not have known?'

'I was just doing my job. I was an accountant. I didn't lie about that when we met. I really was an accountant. It took a while. And a lot of digging.'

'So that woman we saw, coming to visit you. With the letters?'

'My handler. She brings letters from my family. It's all I have at the moment, but I hope that will gradually change. Realistically, though, that life is over for me now, but . . .' He held out his hand and Caroline came to stand behind his chair, taking it in her own. 'I do feel I might have something to live for here. With your mother, if you have no objection?'

'None,' said Charlie faintly. 'It's too much to take in. I'm so sorry I thought you might have stolen the jewels, though.'

'No matter. Nature abhors a vacuum. It is to your credit that you were so concerned about your mother's welfare and – well – with no evidence to the contrary, and with what you saw, along with your quite natural interpretation of it . . .'

'He forgives you,' said Caroline. 'Now, back to discussions of my grandchild in all but actual genetics.'

CHAPTER THIRTY-TWO

Rufus's house had a closed, unoccupied air but Bella wasn't perturbed. In her mind she called it the 'stealth' house, because on the approach from the road it hunkered so low in the landscape, shuttered and blank on the roadside, only opening up to the views once you got beyond the front.

She pressed her thumb against the biometrics pad. No joy. She pressed again and then tried the other hand. Still nothing. It was new technology, it could be flaky sometimes. She rang the bell and then hammered hard on the door. Nothing. She knocked again and waited a bit longer.

Ears tuned, she could hear someone coming up the stairs from the bedrooms below, a light, scampering tread quite different to Rufus's.

The door opened a crack and then was flung wide.

'Bella!' exclaimed Flora delightedly. She was standing barefoot with her blonde ringleted hair tousled, wearing nothing but one of Rufus's shirts and a broad smile. 'You missed the most amazing party, where were you? There was a magician, there was vodka jelly and we had a sing-song with Zane Stringfellow and . . .' The young girl's face fell. 'Oh my God,' she exclaimed, her hands clutching either side of her face. 'I'm here and I've had sex with your boyfriend. Yikes, that's really, really, really bad . . .' She froze, staring at Bella in horror. 'I'm so, so sorry Bells,' she exclaimed, exploding into action and throwing her arms around Bella's neck.

Bella disentangled herself gently. 'It's fine, actually,' she said, as much to herself as Flora. 'These things happen.'

Rufus, hearing voices had also now come upstairs wearing just his boxers. With his hair rumpled and with sleepy eyes he looked boy-like and vulnerable.

'Bella,' he said, his face returning to its usual state. Watchful. Calculating. 'Where were you last night? You should have been there.'

'Never mind,' said Bella. She couldn't tell Rufus about Dolly. Not yet. Not until she could do it with a modicum of dignity. 'I've got something I need to say.'

Before he allowed her to speak, he sat her at the breakfast bar, overlooking the hills and made coffee. Bella could see the vineyard. She yearned to be there, walking up and down the rows, seeing the grapes growing heavy and full. Like her. In the adjacent fields, the ones where the festival-goers had camped, teams of litter pickers were working their way across in lines, like a police scene of crime officers searching for clues. They were mainly the workers Charlie got in for grape picking, turning up early, for the extra work. They would be harvesting soon. This year, Bella realised with sadness, she would not be there.

Rufus had put on his tracksuit and now sat opposite her, shoulders tense. 'You'll be wanting an explanation,' he said, chin jutting.

Bella could hear Flora in the shower. She was singing.

'No, actually,' said Bella. 'I don't think I do. It's not what I came for. Although, now you raise it, you're an unlikely combination,' she said, 'but I think it could work really well. Just don't . . .' she paused. 'Don't break her, Rufus. She's an innocent soul. Fragile.'

'It's just sex.'

'Oh,' said Bella, wryly, pulling a face. 'I'd rather hoped you had thrown away our relationship for something a little more profound.'

'No, sorry, I didn't mean that . . . Things happened yesterday, with me and Charlie,' Rufus went on. 'And Zach and Ben. They've made me think, that's all . . . I feel . . .' He thought, staring into the space above Bella's head. 'I feel lighter,' he said at last, spreading his palms wide. 'You've been crying,' he said, looking at her properly at last. 'Are you going to tell me something bad?'

'Something very, very sad has happened,' said Bella, her chin wobbling again as she remembered the floppy weight of Dolly's body in her lap, 'and it's too sad for me to talk about today, but,' she took a breath, 'I also have something . . .' She paused, searching for the word. 'I also have something "happy" to tell you.'

'Bloody hell,' he said, a minute later. 'That definitely wasn't the plan. How did it happen? No, never mind, that doesn't matter now.' He looked dazed, like he had just been

329

punched. 'I'll provide financial support, obviously.'

'Obviously,' she echoed dryly.

'I can't be a father, Bella.'

'I know.'

'I'm too messed up. Too busy . . . I said I never wanted . . .'

'I know.'

'I'm sorry.'

'For what?'

'For not being able to deal with this. For . . . getting you into this whole thing. For damaging you and Charlie. Especially that. It was unforgivable.'

'What do you mean? Was it some big tactical thing of yours?'

'Not the baby bit but, yeah,' he admitted with a sigh. 'I suppose it was. I think I imagined Charlie would recognise me. That we'd have a big showdown. Turns out he didn't even know who I was, so that was the end of that little plan.' Rufus couldn't keep the bitterness out of his voice. 'I could never have forgotten him, though. I've kept an eye on him – and Ben and Zach – over the years . . . from a distance . . . measuring my success against theirs. Proving myself. And then I come back to show them all and they don't even recognise me, because I'm totally insignificant all over again, just that red-headed runt from school. A distant, unimportant memory.' He sank into a reverie and then roused himself. 'Anyhow, back I came, and I saw him with this life, with his mates and the farm and the vineyard, and you . . . so effortlessly owning all the things, the life I wanted for myself.' He stopped. Looking at her for understanding he continued. 'And I wanted you.'

Bella blinked. 'Did you?'

'You're beautiful, funny, clever . . . of course I did.'

'But now?'

'Now,' he said, carefully, 'I realise I wanted you at least partly because Charlie had you. And that's not right. I'm really, really sorry . . . So, are you and Charlie . . . ?' he asked, hopefully.

Bella looked at him. His face had changed. The tough, ruthless businessman was still there, but there was something else increasingly often now. A glimpse of the boy. Someone softer and kinder.

She shook her head. 'I don't see how,' she said sadly. She rested her hand on her belly. It seemed to have swollen just in the hours since she knew, expanding in relief, she supposed, at finally being recognised, her abdominal muscles giving up the fight to help her deny the reality.

'When's it due?' asked Rufus, looking at her tummy as if it was an unexploded bomb.

'Working back, I'm pretty sure we're talking early next year. Beginning of February, most likely.'

'Blimey, that's only six months away. How could you have not noticed?' said Rufus in disbelief.

Flora came scampering up the stairs. 'Will you stay for breakfast?' she asked Bella excitedly. 'We're going to make pancakes. You should stay. Rufus says he's got maple syrup and everything.'

Bella hugged her and then she dropped a chaste kiss on Rufus's cheek. 'Be nice to each other,' she said.

CHAPTER THIRTY-THREE

Driving off, with no plan, she found herself parked outside The Grange, just like she had when she left Charlie months before. She stared sightlessly through the windscreen, her hands tense on the wheel and her shoulders aching and burning with the effort.

She didn't know how long she had been sitting there when Charlie found her, but she was stiff and cold, her head pounding.

'For God's sake,' said Charlie, slipping into the passenger seat. 'I didn't know where you were. I even called Rufus. He said you left hours ago.'

She turned her head towards him, feeling her neck creak almost audibly. 'Sorry,' she said. 'Thinking.'

'Come home.'

After he had insisted on getting into her car and driving her back to the farmhouse, Charlie led Bella into the orchard. Dolly's body was wrapped tightly and tidily in the blanket from her bed. It lay, looking tiny, by a freshly dug hole at the far end.

'We need to do this,' said Charlie gently. 'Then we'll talk.'

There was a mound when he had finished. A scar on the ground. It seemed inconceivable that the earth would heal, that the rain would gradually flatten the little hillock, that the grass would grow back over it. That the meadow flowers would appear again. But Bella knew it would.

'I won't be here,' she sobbed. 'I want to be here, with her, so I can come and remember her.' She laid her hands on the earth above the dog's body, feeling the last warmth of the summer sun in the soil, contrasting with the dank, damp air of the autumn day.

'Stay, then,' said Charlie, anguished. 'Why would you not stay? We've got each other, we've got the pups, Dolly is here and now we've got the baby too. Is this not what you want?'

'Of course, it is,' Bella wailed, her composure of the last few hours finally broken again. 'Everything is what I want and I don't want to leave you, and Dolly, and everyone, everything . . . but this baby isn't yours.' She hung her head and sobbed.

'Being a father isn't about being there at the conception.'

Bella just shook her head sadly and sobbed some more.

Eventually, when she had composed herself, she tried to explain: 'You say it'll be okay now, but the knowledge that you are not the genetic father, it'll always be there, admit it. If the child has problems, if it gets into trouble, when it wakes you up at night for the millionth time. You'll feel resentful.'

'I won't,' Charlie insisted. 'It's your baby. You're mine so the baby's mine. I want to look after you both.'

'Okay, so . . .' said Bella wiping her eyes and sitting up straighter. 'How about this. I have this baby and then we go on to have another one together. Can you honestly say you won't favour the second child? The one who is genetically yours?'

'I won't,' he said, helplessly.

'You can't say that. You don't know. It's human nature . . .'

'Simon called,' said Charlie at last. 'He's booked you an ultrasound scan at the hospital for tomorrow. Something about anomalies and dating.'

'I don't need a dating scan,' said Bella. 'I know when it's due.'

'But what about the other thing?'

'The anomaly scan,' said Bella. 'It's to find out if there's anything the matter with it.'

'That's important, isn't it?'

'Not really,' said Bella listlessly. 'I wouldn't abort it. I couldn't now anyhow, I imagine. Not with it being so far along. Can you imagine . . . ? By three months a baby is fully formed. Fingers, toes, the whole thing . . . I couldn't.'

'You will go though, won't you?'

'Will you come?'

'Of course.'

'As a friend?'

'Of course.'

'I'd ask Maddy, but . . .'

'You said you were sad that you and Maddy wouldn't be

going through this "mother" stuff together,' said Charlie, cheering up slightly. 'And now you will.'

'Except I won't be here.'

'Yeah, except that . . .'

'When's yours due?' a cheerful woman asked Bella in the waiting room. She had a pronounced bump and a double buggy with two children in it. One was a baby under one, Bella reckoned, although she wasn't too good at that sort of thing, and the other looked older, maybe three or so.

'February, I think,' she said, listlessly, cracking a lopsided smile out of politeness.

'Goodness,' said the woman, checking out Bella's bump. 'You're blooming rather early, aren't you? Sure it's not twins?'

They were spared from answering by a cheerful, athletic-looking young woman who ushered them into the darkened room.

'Is it your first?' she asked Charlie in a broad Australian accent.

'Actually, it's not mine.'

'Oops, sorry, done it again . . . I'm from a bit of an Australian backwater. Haven't been here long . . . can't get used to these cosmopolitan ways.'

'First time I've heard Havenbury described as "cosmopolitan",' joked Bella, clambering awkwardly onto the narrow couch.

'Oh, you'd be amazed. You're the third woman this month who's brought in her gay best friend rather than her partner, and then there's all the ones who bring their mum, and then,' she reminisced, waving the ultrasound wand, with a large blob of goo on it alarmingly close to Charlie's nose, 'there was the couple where the woman was in the process of becoming a man, the man was dressed as a woman but telling me how he'd just come from having his facial hair lasered . . .'

'Which of them was having the baby?' asked Bella, intrigued.

'The woman, darlin', obviously . . .' she said. 'I may be out of my depth with the LGBTQ stuff but I know my flippin' biology.'

'Actually,' said Charlie, keen to return to the earlier point. 'I'm not gay.'

'He's my husband,' explained Bella.

'Oh, sorry, I thought you said you weren't the father.'

'He's not.'

'Crikey! So, it says here this is your first scan. Hmm, you don't seem to have any antenatal notes, that can't be right . . .'

'It is,' said Bella, briefly explaining.

'So, you're about four months gone and you didn't know you were up the duff?'

'Yeah.'

'Oookay,' she said raising her eyebrows. She turned the monitor towards herself and positioned the wand on Bella's tummy. For a few minutes, the room was quiet, the silence interspersed only by mouse clicks as she worked on the screen, moving the wand and taking notes as she went.

'February you said?'

Bella nodded.

'I don't think so . . .' she said, shaking her head.

'Okay, could be later,' Bella admitted. 'I've not had periods since May, so I assumed it was from then but – well – things have been weird . . . so . . .'

'You're telling me, girl. This ain't no Valentine baby. You've got amazing muscle tone by the way. And that's a neat little bump, tucked away down low like that . . .'

'So, how long have I got?' asked Bella, relieved that it looked like she might have a little longer before the baby came. Good. A few more weeks would come in handy, what with relocating and getting herself settled.

'You'd better get painting that nursery,' said the woman, interrupting her thoughts. 'According to this I reckon you've got about six weeks until she comes.'

'Six months,' corrected Bella. 'You said six weeks . . .'

'Yeah, I meant six weeks.'

'But that can't be right,' whispered Bella. 'I was still having periods . . . I was still having periods,' she said louder. 'The thing,' she turned to Charlie now. 'The thing I did. With Rufus.' She looked intently at Charlie while they both remembered. The loan, the conditions, the decision to agree to Rufus's appalling terms. 'I did it in May, and I remember, I was . . . I'd just finished my period,' she blushed.

'Yeah, that can happen,' interjected the woman, trying hard to grasp the subtexts that were flying around the room. 'That's common. Especially in the first three months. Little breakthrough bleeds. That's how a lot of women don't realise they're pregnant. Although they do tend to cotton on before you,' she went on tactlessly.

'When was this child conceived?' asked Charlie,

barely breathing in anticipation of the answer.

'End of February? Early March at the latest I'd say so we're looking at early November, fair enough that's a bit longer than six weeks. It's not an exact science.'

Charlie gave a shout of laughter. 'This baby was conceived in the Tavistock Hotel on the twentieth of February this year,' he said triumphantly. 'I know this,' he said. 'I know because I was there.'

'Eeuw,' said the woman. 'Why were *you* there? I know you're her friend but . . .'

'"Husband", remember?' he reprised. 'Also, not gay . . . hang on,' he added, as something occurred to him. 'Did you say it was a girl?'

'No.'

'Yeah, you did, you said "you have six weeks until *she* comes"!'

'Oops again, I'm not supposed to say unless they ask,' she said, looking stricken. 'I'm no good at this. Did you want to know?' she added, hopefully.

'We want to know,' said Bella, her heart hammering in her chest, her hand reaching for Charlie's.

'We're having a girl,' said Charlie, his smiling face blurring as Bella beamed back, her eyes filling with tears of relief and joy.

There was no specific discussion over getting back together – Bella simply came home with Charlie and that is where she stayed. Over the following weeks she was constantly relieved that she and Charlie had discovered the pregnancy so late. Charlie had turned into a Dadzilla, staying up late into the night researching what Bella should and shouldn't be doing. He would shake her awake at three in the morning to announce that they needed to buy some Brazil nuts. But not too many. And maybe apricots. Also, she needed to rest with her feet higher than her head to prevent ankle oedema.

When Morag the midwife had got over her indignation at Bella having avoided her ministrations for the entire first seven or so months of her pregnancy she was reassuring and supportive. Bella had developed mild gestational diabetes, which set Charlie into a flat spin of panic. She loathed checking her blood sugar, which involved having to prick her finger three times a day, but Charlie was insistent.

The days were growing shorter, but they were blessed with a mild autumn. Misty mornings gave way to warm, humid days with a low, yellow sun and beautiful sunsets. With The Grange all finished and open and the many other offers of work on hold, Bella submitted often to afternoon naps. The rest of the time she was working on the house and allowing Charlie to wrap her in a blanket and sit her on their bench overlooking the vineyard while he tended his grapes. He was checking the weather and the grape sugar levels daily, poised to harvest when the grapes were at their pinnacle of sweetness. She felt the loss of Dolly acutely, often glimpsing a shadow and stepping sideways to avoid treading on a dog that was not at her heels and would not trip her up ever again.

Caroline had kept the puppies at Dove Cottage, where they were all thriving, thanks to her care, and running riot as they became more mobile and more mischievous. In his turn, Geoffrey was looking after Caroline, coming to see her daily, always with a bunch of flowers, some wine or a cheese she particularly liked from Pandora's Pantry, which was conveniently just a couple of doors away from his bookshop.

'Have you done your sugar test?' Charlie asked as Bella came downstairs in her pyjamas.

'Have you?' she countered, seeing his grape testing kit on the kitchen table.

'I have,' he said, unable to suppress a smile. 'It's looking good. As a matter of fact, I've called in the picking team just this morning. They're coming tomorrow.'

'And booked the winery?'

'Yep. They've promised me all the capacity I need. No hanging around. I don't want oxidisation. Two days should do it.'

Bella nodded, slowly. 'This is the latest you've ever left it,' she said, looking at the calendar on the wall.

'Yep, living on the edge,' Charlie agreed. 'The sugar levels have never been better. I'm going to get the Meunier in first. The Pinot would benefit from an extra day so it can go last . . . I'm feeling good, Bells, I'm thinking this could be a vintage year.'

'Shall we go out to celebrate? We could have lunch?'

'Ah,' said Charlie with regret. 'Meeting with the bank manager.'

'The loan for the winery?'

'Yep.'

'Problem?'

'Absolutely not.'

'You'd tell me?'

Charlie grasped her by the upper arms. 'I absolutely would. I promise. No secrets . . . no, it's just a boring 't' crossing and 'i' dotting exercise. They're matching the festival profits – which gives us just enough, by a narrow squeak.'

'And the terms?'

'Solid and fair. Fixed term, fixed interest. No penalty for early payment, yada, yada . . .' Charlie waved his arm expansively.

'Shame we couldn't have done that the first time.'

'Banks don't lend unless you can prove you don't need the money. That's the irony.'

'Fair enough . . . and the main thing is, I know what you're doing.'

Charlie nodded, apologetically.

Bella smiled at him. 'I've got stuff I need to sort out for the nursery. It's looking lovely, have you seen the wallpaper?'

'I'm sure it's great,' said Charlie, wrapping his arms around her now huge waist. 'Now, don't go up any bloody stepladders or anything. The last thing we need is you going into labour while we're harvesting. If you're bored, go and see the puppies. I'm sure Ma would love to have a catch up. You can tell her all about your wallpaper.'

It was a tradition, at the end of the harvest, that the grape-picking team had a barbecue and a few beers. The Dovecot Estate contribution to celebrations was a keg of ale from the Blackdown Brewery just down the road.

Charlie hadn't had a drink since his conversation with Ben several weeks before but – as he watched the final truck, piled high with grapes, negotiating the narrow gateway on

341

the way to the winery – he accepted the pint glass that was pressed into his hand, and took a long, welcome swig.

'Not now,' said Bella, appearing behind him and taking the glass from his hand. She had made herself scarce in the farmhouse all day. Little did Charlie know, she had secretly taken the tin of floor paint she planned for the nursery floorboards, which were in good nick but not looking great, and painted the entire nursery floor, working backwards towards the door and painting herself out of the room. Kneeling down was exactly the position she wanted to be in. She just stopped for a minute whenever a contraction hit her. Now she was finished with the floor, she was ready to go.

'I need you sober,' she added before placing her hands on the gatepost and leaning forward to pant through another contraction.

'Bloody hell,' said Charlie. 'She's early. We thought the picking would be done before she came.'

'Nature has its own ideas,' said Bella. 'Just one more thing to harvest before we call it a year.'

EPILOGUE

It was a double christening with Erica and Freya together because – as Maddy and Bella pointed out – they would all be inviting the same people and, age-wise, the girls were practically twins, especially with Freya having come a bit early too. It was also the first time all the puppies had been together since they left home. Now nearly ten months old, the reunion of the entire surviving litter of six was an absolute riot.

Thankfully, it was a bright and sunny May day, which at least allowed everyone to be outside on the lawn. The Labrador teenagers swarmed through the crowd, creating turbulence in their wake as they raced, tumbled and yipped with excitement. Occasionally a melee was too violent or a playful nip too hard and there would be a sudden, high-pitched yelp.

'They're fine,' said Zach as his own little dog emerged dishevelled from a collapsed scrum of black and fox-red fur. His choice had been the smallest female because he was keen on the fox-red colour, of which there were only two pups in the litter. He had called her Poppy in acknowledgement of her russet fur. Simon and Genny had chosen a black boy who they had called Trigger because he wasn't too bright. Maddy had managed, after much wheedling and persuasion, to get Ben to agree to taking one and he now adored Adam, saying he was relieved to have another male in the house for moral support. Bella and Charlie had kept the little black girl, with Bella desperate to – not replace Dolly, obviously – but to have a reminder of her. Little Betsy was fabulous with Freya already, regarding her as a litter mate, and she constantly provided bittersweet reminders of Dolly with her comic mannerisms and happy-go-lucky nature. Caroline kept one too, of course. Having practically raised them single-handed from about four weeks she could hardly bear to let any of them go. The one she felt she had to keep most strongly, though, was a feisty little dog she and Geoffrey called Nelson because whenever the puppies were marauding anywhere he was always leading from the front. Geoffrey took his responsibility for raising Nelson to be a credit to them both very seriously. He and Caroline attended puppy training classes with him from very early on and, by the christening, he was not only the leader of the bunch but arguably the most able to follow human instructions. When he chose to. The final pup, a boy called Rory, also fox-red, had gone to Rufus. They matched perfectly and looked very handsome together when they went out for a run. Although he was the official owner, Flora did most of the day-to-day stuff because Rufus was always working so hard. He spent much of his week in London, working on his other projects but Flora insisted he spend at least three nights a week with her and Rory in the country and – with The Grange as his excuse – he was happy to do so. Although Flora was completely different to the hard, glossy women surrounding him in the city, he enjoyed the chaos she and her Bespoke Consortium mates at Home Farm always seemed to create. It was a very different life to his London world and, increasingly, he preferred it. The Grange was being positively reviewed by all the cool crowd, and Havenbury residents had become quite used to seeing actors and pop stars trudging up the high street or popping into Pandora's Pantry before going back there to hang out. Zane Stringfellow, who was also at the christening, was practically using The Grange as his second home and the rumour was he was looking to buy in the area. There was much speculation as to whether he might end up living at Havenbury Manor, being as he was great mates with Zach Havenbury from way back.

'I do like to see a man who is confident enough in his masculinity to be seen with a glass of pink sparkling wine,' joked Bella who was holding a very awake and alert Freya in her arms.

Ben and Charlie were standing on the edge of the terrace, each had a champagne flute and they were admiring the view of the vineyard. The bright green vine rows, stretching across the sun-washed slopes with their tiny, tiny white flowers, barely visible, were the perfect backdrop to the tall, elegant glasses filled with a prettily blush-coloured wine that matched Bella's dress. She had found, to her relief, that her tummy pinged back quickly after Freya was born. The sit-ups that had seemed hopeless before, finally paid off. It had been a ridiculous rush, of course, but Freya had even arrived to a beautifully decorated nursery, although Bella was pleased to have been able to take her time with the rest of the house. This – funded with the leftover profit from the festival which, in the final reckoning, was even better than they had first thought – was going well, thanks to her impeccable project management. The Grange had won design awards for its decor, she had a satisfyingly long waiting list for her as she slowly returned to work in her old office at Home Farm. Back at the farmhouse, though, the hand-built kitchen, with the old Rayburn in pride of place, was looking amazing, which was just as well, with the crowds they were feeding today.

Luckily, Maddy's mum Helen had agreed to help out, taking time away from doing the catering at the Havenbury Arms to put on lunch for everyone. She was making things look easy with salads, quiche, baked potatoes and cold meat all ready to go and there was an entire shelf of the larder devoted to puddings and cheese for later too.

'You both look well,' said Ben. 'How are you not looking tired and prematurely aged like the rest of us?'

'Formula, mate,' said Charlie, knowledgeably. 'Bella's still feeding Freya herself, but she also gets a bloody great big bottle of formula milk last thing and – I can't tell you – sleep happens, sanity is restored, we hardly know ourselves.' He spoke with immense relief. Freya had been a hungry baby and appeared to consider that sleep was for losers.

'I wish I could persuade Maddy,' said Ben. 'She's all

about the whole "breast is best" thing. She's adamant to the most ridiculous degree, in my opinion.'

'But if Maddy's insisting on doing the feeding herself, how come *you're* so tired?'

'I dunno,' said Ben, scratching his head. 'She gets up a couple of times a night at least. Usually three. You'd think I'd be sleeping through it but she always seems to accidentally knee me or shove me with her elbow. I think we need a bigger bed.'

'A bigger bed sounds great,' laughed Bella, 'but I think you'll find it still happens.'

'I've been sent with this,' said Maddy, arriving at the little group with a pint glass in each hand. 'Patrick says you'll be needing it.'

'He's not wrong,' said Charlie who, perversely for a winemaker, preferred beer. He swapped glasses with relief.

'It's good stuff, though,' said Ben, also apologetically relinquishing the pink fizz.

'The girls can't get enough of it,' agreed Maddy, taking a swig from his rejected glass. 'It's definitely the next big thing.'

'I hope so,' said Charlie, picking up the bottle, with its distinctive rose-gold cap of foil, to show Ben. 'Dovecot Estate Rosé' proclaimed the label. The simple logo showed the stripes of the vineyard curving up the slope and there was a dovecot tucked away in the corner. 'It's in the Havenbury Arms and The Grange this year. I don't have enough to supply it to anyone else but, if anything, the rarity seems to be helping with the marketing.'

'How are the plans for the winery?' asked Ben.

347

'Funded, more or less, as you know. Just waiting for planning. Shouldn't be a problem. The planners are keen for new uses to be found for farm buildings. Stops them falling down.'

He slipped his arm around Bella's slim waist, encompassing Freya in his hug and dropping a kiss on her cheek.

'Looks like we managed to snatch victory from the jaws of defeat, doesn't it, my darling? Who would have guessed we would come so close to losing it all and then suddenly wake up one morning to discover we have everything we ever wanted?'

ACKNOWLEDGEMENTS

Living in Sussex I am surrounded by some of the very best and innovative wine producers in the country. Being a great lover of wine – but not in a particularly discerning way – it was inevitable I would want to write a book set in an English vineyard, so many thanks to the team at Allison & Busby for agreeing with me that it 'had to be done' and for realising the dream with all their skill and expertise. My thanks is extended wholeheartedly to my editor Lesley, to Daniel, Susie, Kelly, Ailsa and the rest of the team. Huge thanks also to the delightful Emma Finnigan, without whose impeccable PR skills the Havenbury series would struggle to see the light of day and to my inimitable agent, Julia Silk, at MBA Literary Agency without whose insistence Havenbury would not even exist.

I've adored writing this second story in the Havenbury series, having the chance to develop new characters and reintroduce some of the people readers met in *The*

Homecoming. Havenbury is my world, and I couldn't be happier here.

For the accurate information on vineyards and winemaking I credit the ever-patient and enthusiastic Art and Jody at the Tinwood Estate. For the inaccurate information on the same I blame myself and myself alone.

Thanks to friends for insisting on breaks from writing, thanks to family for providing the necessary ballast and bringing me back down to earth. Your contribution is noted and valued, even if I fail to specifically mention it here.

Thank you.

Oh, and a special mention to my beautiful dog, Rosie, who I wholeheartedly credit for inspiring the character Dolly and who, heartbreakingly, 'did a Dolly' in dying on me far too young shortly after this book was completed.

This book is dedicated to her.

After obtaining a degree in music, ROSIE HOWARD pursued a career in PR, campaigning and freelance journalism but realised her preference for making things up and switched to writing novels instead. She lives in a West Sussex village with her husband and two children in a cottage with roses around the door.

rosiehoward.com